Published by
www.inkubatorbooks.com

Copyright © 2022 by Cole Baxter

Cole Baxter has asserted his right to be identified as the author of this work.

ISBN (eBook): 978-1-915275-20-2
ISBN (Paperback): 978-1-915275-21-9
ISBN (Hardback): 978-1-915275-22-6

THE PERFECT SUITOR is a work of fiction. People, places, events, and situations are the product of the author's imagination. Any resemblance to actual persons, living or dead is entirely coincidental.

No part of this book may be reproduced, stored in any retrieval system, or transmitted by any means without the prior written permission of the publisher.

THE PERFECT SUITOR

COLE BAXTER

PROLOGUE

CAIRO, EGYPT

I couldn't believe we were here. Cairo was an amazing city, and Egypt was just mind-blowing. Standing at the apex of the Pyramid of Giza had been incredible, and the next day, we planned to see the Sphinx, but presently, I wanted to do something romantic.

"Christopher, please? I heard it was one of the most romantic restaurants in all of Cairo. Can't we go there for dinner?"

"Baby, it's in the off-limits area, not the best place for Americans right now." Christopher frowned. "It's dangerous. Why don't we find a nice restaurant near the hotel?"

I pouted. I'd been reading about this place with its outside dining and mood lighting that had a sweeping view of the Nile River. It was part of another hotel in the inner part of Cairo. How dangerous could it be?

"Please?" I batted my eyelashes at him and kissed his chin.

Christopher sighed and shook his head, but he smiled and kissed my nose. "All right, peanut. We'll go, but stay close to me."

I threw my arms around him and kissed him fully. I loved this man more than anything on the planet. He was my love, my life, and I couldn't believe how lucky I was to have him, especially considering how unlucky I'd been growing up. I never knew my father, and my mother treated me like I'd ruined her life. My stepdad was okay, but if Mom and I were fighting, he always took her side. I'd pretty much cut myself out of their lives, rarely speaking to them at all.

My life revolved around my husband of three years, Christopher Bell. I even worked for him as his research assistant as he was writing a book on Egypt. Christopher was a brilliant anthropologist and a professor at the local college. Ever since we'd gotten together, I had felt like the luckiest girl on the planet.

"Charlene, if we're going to go to this restaurant, we'll need to leave now," Christopher called from the bedroom of our hotel room.

"I'm coming!" I touched up my lipstick in the bathroom mirror and stepped back into the bedroom. "Don't you look handsome!" I eyed him up and down in his tweed jacket and jeans. He was definitely a sexy professor.

"And you, my darling peanut, are gorgeous, as usual." He kissed me. "Come on, we'll get a taxi."

The drive to the inner part of the city wasn't very long, about thirty minutes with traffic. Once we arrived, the driver explained that we shouldn't leave the hotel lounge to get a taxi and to call for one to pick us up when we finished, as it was a dangerous area after dark. It didn't really bother me. There were people everywhere, and I figured he just wanted us to call him for a ride so he could make some more money off us.

That was one thing about Cairo I didn't like. There were all kinds of people looking to scam and hassle you here to buy stuff that wasn't worth the price. But the town was gorgeous, and there were some very lovely people here as well, and that outweighed the bad.

Christopher led me into the restaurant and to the hostess. They chatted for a moment in Egyptian Arabic, a language I still hadn't mastered, and then she led us to a table near the pool. Christopher pulled out my chair, and I sat down facing the Nile and the gorgeous skyline as the sun set, leaving the sky awash in pinks and purples. It was absolutely beautiful.

"Oh, Christopher, this is so stunning. Thank you for bringing me here," I said, feeling my heart swell at the look of love in his eyes.

"I can never tell you no, peanut. And you're right, this place is beautiful. I'm glad we came too." He squeezed my fingers.

I wished he could lean across the table and kiss me, but public displays of affection here were not welcome. After ordering, we chatted about some of the notes I'd taken on the city, and we talked about his plans for the book he was writing. And then the conversation turned to us.

"I do think we should start trying for real to have a baby again when we get back. Start filling up those rooms in the house. What do you think?"

I blushed. "We could start trying again tonight," I murmured, grinning back at him.

"That's my girl," he replied, chuckling.

The waiter brought out the food, and we ate, exclaiming over each delicious bite. It was truly a magical evening. I couldn't wait to be alone with him again to show him how much I loved him and appreciated his bringing me here.

After dinner, we headed out and began walking a bit, looking for a taxi, but the streets were devoid of them. Sure, there were cars passing, but not one was a cab. "Maybe we should go down a block?" I suggested.

"Or maybe our driver was right. Let's head back to the restaurant and call—"

"*Atni malek! Alaan!*" a man dressed in black with a head scarf that wrapped around his nose and mouth said as he shoved Christopher. He held a large knife toward us.

"Christopher!" I cried, my heart pounding in my chest.

"*Alaan! Alaan!*" the man screamed.

"What does he want?" I asked, terrified.

"He wants our money," he said softly and then looked at the man. "*Tehdia wassouf tahsal mahfadhti*," Christopher said calmly as he reached toward his back pocket. He held his other hand out in a defensive manner.

I watched as Christopher began to pull the wallet from his pocket.

"*Mahfada walmjohrat asada!*" he shouted, moving the knife toward me.

"Peanut, he wants your purse and jewelry," Christopher explained.

"But my wedding ring! I can't give him that!" I exclaimed.

"*Alaan! Alaan!*" the man cried. His eyes were bugged out, and he looked down the street past us, and then before we could do as he asked, he raised the knife and slammed it into Christopher's chest, pulled it out, grabbed my purse, ripping it from my arm, and then seeing Christopher's wallet fall from his hand as he fell, grabbed that and took off down the street.

"Oh my God! Christopher!" I screamed, falling to the ground beside him as he gasped.

Blood poured from his chest, and his eyes fluttered. "I . . . I love you . . ." he murmured, his fingers wrapping around mine for a moment, and then the pressure was gone. He was gone.

"No!" I screamed, collapsing over his chest. "No! Come back! Please! Please don't leave me, Christopher!"

1

THREE YEARS LATER

I wish to fall asleep and never wake up . . .

"Come on, peanut, you can do it," he said encouragingly with a smile.

"It's easy for you to say, with those long legs of yours."

He chuckled. "I'm not that tall."

"But I am that short," I pointed out in high spirits.

"Do you want me to carry you?"

"No." If I truly wanted to do this, then I wanted to do it on my own.

"Give me your hand, then."

That somewhat helped, so we continued with our climb.

"Remind me why we're doing this?" Climbing to the top of the Great Pyramid of Giza.

"Because it's fun," Christopher countered with a grin, which made me smile in return, although at this point, I really couldn't feel my legs.

"Yeah, I'm having loads of fun while trying to prevent myself from having heatstroke."

My grumbling only made him laugh that much harder.

"Let me just carry you, peanut," he offered again.

"No, I'm fine. I'm just whining," I reassured him.

He stopped so abruptly I actually ran into him. Christopher turned toward me and then kissed me. It was a bit salty from the sweat, yet neither of us minded.

Just like that, all my problems went away. I was no longer overheated, at least not because of the sun. And I wasn't tired at all. More to the point, I could have proven my stamina to him if we weren't in such a public place and in a foreign country.

"I love you," he told me gently, as he had many times in the past.

"I love you too," I mumbled against his lips, not ready to break the kiss. I just needed him so much. "With all my heart."

The sound of my own voice woke me up.

It was just a dream. Of course it was. *Christopher is gone.*

I buried my face in the pillow. *Please let me sleep some more.*

I didn't want it to be a new day. I didn't want to be conscious, wandering about in this kind of reality. In a reality where he didn't exist anymore.

Please come back to me, I prayed, sobbing.

The pain that hit me was unbearable. It spread through my heart, throughout my body, shredding everything in its wake.

Will it ever stop?

When the pillow became completely soaked by my tears, I pushed it away from the bed and then pulled the comforter over my head. Perhaps if I recreated nighttime, I would be allowed to see his face again in another dream.

Although these days, I had nothing to do, nowhere to go. I felt pretty bone-tired, exhausted, and most days, I didn't feel like getting out of bed at all.

Why should I, anyway?

I shouldn't.

Besides, I wanted to sleep some more, dream some more. I got to touch his face and lips this time. It was a good dream, which only made reality that much worse.

Although the dreams in which I was so happy with him caused me immense pain afterward, I still didn't want to lose this connection with him. Perhaps I'd gone completely insane, yet I considered it a fair trade.

It was precious to me to see his face, hear his voice as he called me his love one more time. Even if it was only in a dream. I was losing that in real life. I couldn't recall the exact tone of his voice or how his forehead looked while he was deep in some thought, reading a book. So I needed this like a junkie needed his next fix.

Seeing Christopher in dreams was all I lived for these days, although this one was different. Us being in Cairo, going to see the pyramids, wasn't only a dream. It was a memory since it had happened in real life.

I thought it would be such a great adventure, so we indeed ended up climbing Khufu's Pyramid. The view from the top of the Great Pyramid was spectacular, breathtaking, so worth the sunburn I got. The view from the top was even more majestic than I could have imagined.

And then it was a race against time to climb down before our tour group bus headed back to the hotel, although those big blocks of limestone were even trickier to climb down than to climb up. It took us twice as much time to get down than it did to climb up.

The trip had started out amazing from day one. I recalled that on our first day there, we'd taken a day trip to Alexandria and seen where Alexander the Great had founded that legendary city. Christopher had been thrilled to see where the massive ancient library had once stood. That night, back at the hotel, we'd made love the whole night, celebrating. *"I hope we will have a baby girl," he whispered into my ear afterward as we tried to cool down, still wrapped in each other's arms.*

Nope. I had to stop that train of thought right now. Otherwise, I would completely lose my shit. More than I already had.

The pain was so great that I had to wrap my hands around my chest to prevent that beating thing from shattering into pieces. That was what it felt like, that only skin and bones were holding it in place.

Reluctantly, I forced myself to stop thinking about that dream, that day in Egypt.

Thinking about Christopher and those days, which were the happiest of my life before turning into the most painful in a blink of an eye, was a forbidden topic.

Although Christopher was always on my mind, his being still present inside this house in all his things, I couldn't allow myself to think about Cairo. I got carried away this morning. And I would now pay a heavy price.

It was pretty masochistic of me. I was still glad I got the chance to see him so happy. The way he'd smiled back then at me, all red in the face, joyful, victorious as we reached that last plateau, was one of my favorite memories of him.

Stop that, I snapped at myself. Thinking about that would drive me insane. *Even more insane.*

There was a reason Cairo was forbidden.

A ringing at the front door made me groan. I'd told them many times not to use the doorbell. *Are they blind? Don't they know how to read? I left a note, for crying out loud.*

The ringing persisted.

Son of a bitch. A person couldn't even cry these days without someone bothering her, in her own home, I might add.

"Leave me alone," I said in a muffled voice, still hiding under the comforter.

That's all I want, to be left alone.

Unfortunately, no one listened to what I wanted.

I decided to simply play dead in hopes that whoever made this cardinal mistake of disturbing me would simply go away. No such luck.

"Fine!" I yelled. "I'm coming."

The abruptness of my movement, standing up, made my head dizzy.

Ignoring it, I threw a bathrobe on and shuffled down the stairs. I wasn't drunk, but I still felt like I was. *Maybe I got up too fast.*

Wait, when was the last time I ate? I couldn't tell for sure.

Reaching the door, I yanked it opened simply to stop that damn noise already.

"Yes?" I snapped.

"Mrs. Bell?" a courier inquired.

I nodded. "You should have left it on the porch." I glared.

"I need your signature, ma'am. Besides, there's a note here saying to ring as long as it takes," he explained.

To his credit, he didn't flinch or anything at the overall disheveled appearance of me. *That's what I call a professional.*

He actually showed me the note in his log. Did I write that note? I honestly couldn't remember. My mind operated in a state of a daze most days.

"Give me that." I reached for the pen and scribbled something against the screen. In return, he handed me the box. It was heavy.

I mumbled my thanks before shutting the door on him.

I started opening the damn thing that was wrapped so tightly, so thoroughly as to withstand being dropped in a volcano. It took me a while. As I walked toward the kitchen, I left a trail of discarded pieces of the packaging.

Eventually, I reached the original box and saw what it was. My new laptop. The guy at the door was right. I did write instructions for the courier to ring until getting me up because this was important. It was just that I had completely forgotten about it.

That happened to me a lot.

I placed the new machine on the kitchen counter. Although it looked new and shiny, I still hated it. I preferred the old one. Unfortunately, the one I had been using up until a month ago died on me. It was Christopher's, and it was always a piece of crap, but he had adored it.

I cried for a week straight when a repairman told me it was beyond help. The old piece of junk would never work again.

So I had to buy a new one.

That did not mean I got rid of Christopher's old laptop. Not a chance. It was standing on the nightstand, where it always stood, on his side of the bed. As it appeared, I had serious trouble letting go of any of Christopher's things. Even after all this time, all his belongings were right where they were supposed to be, where he last left them.

I was working on that with my therapist.

I was working with her on a lot of things, yet I was not very good at it. Probably because I didn't believe in therapy in the first place. Not that I believed she was a quack. It was simply that talking about my feelings wasn't for me.

All the same, Dr. Neal once told me I was dependent on my sadness, and perhaps she was right. I was. That was all that I had left, anyway.

Yet at the same time, I didn't know how to stop that. I missed Christopher too much, and although it hurt, this way, I knew what we had was real. That what we shared was a true love that could have lasted for decades.

With a heavy heart, I fired the new laptop up. I decided to call it *The Thing* and started to set everything up.

Thank God for online shopping. I would be completely lost without it. Thanks to the internet, wonder of modern technology, I'd managed to build a small world inside this house for myself without having to leave it.

Ever since Christopher . . . ever since I lost Christopher, I preferred not to interact with other people apart from my therapist and one friend. I didn't need anyone else, anyway. *People can only hurt you, disappoint you.* So everything that could be done online was preferable.

Seeing the date, I groaned. The fact that I would be receiving this laptop wasn't the only thing I'd completely forgotten.

Sitting on the kitchen counter, sighing heavily, I yanked the rubber band and tried to retie my messy hair as I called my therapist over Skype.

She was old-school like that, no Zoom for her. I didn't have to wait long for the other woman to answer.

Unfortunately.

"I got my new laptop," I stated the obvious, greeting Dr. Neal.

"Good, I was worried."

Truth be told, I had kind of avoided speaking to her in the last couple of days since I didn't see the point in doing this anyway.

I'd agreed on therapy partly because of my attorney. He'd advised me to start going since it looked like my family, meaning my mum and stepdad, would try to pull some shit, try to take my money from me if they sensed I was mentally unstable in any way. It certainly wouldn't be the first time she'd tried that. That person who called herself my mother had even sued me once, trying to get her hands on my inheritance.

Due to all that had happened to me, here I was, being a

good girl, chatting with a therapist, although I would much rather go to bed and forget about the world.

Even my best friend, Selina, thought that talking to a complete stranger would be good for me. I was still waiting for that miracle to occur, though. Not that I still believed in miracles, only in curses.

"How are you feeling today?" Dr. Neal asked, diving right in, snapping me from my reverie.

I really hated that question. *How can I be?* "The same."

"I think you can do better than that."

I sighed loudly. I was so tired. "I dreamed about Christopher."

"What were you doing?"

"We were climbing Khufu's Pyramid."

"Like you did in real life?"

Exactly the same. "Yes."

"On the day he got killed?"

It was hard not to get all teary-eyed, even though three years had passed since that day.

"Yes," I choked out.

"Is this the first time you had it?"

I nodded and could see her writing something in her notebook.

"How did that dream make you feel?"

Was this woman for real? Instead of being difficult, I answered the question. "Great, until I realized it was only a dream."

"You were happy?"

"I felt like I was right where I was supposed to be."

"And afterward?"

"As though someone had ripped my heart out and used it as a shooting target."

Christopher was my whole world.

Having similar backgrounds and personal stories, without true family members around guarding our backs, we'd instantly bonded. And when we fell in love, we simply decided that from that day forward, we would be each other's family. Unfortunately, our story did not last.

Being with him was like a dream, right up until the moment it turned into a nightmare.

"Did you get a chance to think about what we discussed last time?" she asked me at some point.

Dr. Neal was sure I was too focused on my pain and that all this free time I had on my hands was just keeping me from moving on. She was not aware that everything was precisely as I wanted it to be.

I didn't want to move on. I wanted to remain in this house, where my memories of Christopher were most vibrant. And if it hurt in the process, then so be it. That was a trade I was willing to make because these memories, these feelings, good and bad, were the only things I had left from the love of my life.

"Charlene?" she called out to me.

Clearly, I'd spaced out again. *What was the question again? Did it really matter?*

"Yes," I replied, simply to say something. It was expected of me.

"And?"

"And what?"

"Will you do it?"

I was starting to remember what she was talking about. "Honestly, I don't see a point in doing something like that."

Dr. Neal pursed her lips, the gesture she made when believing I was being unreasonably difficult. "The point is to change your scenery."

Why would I want to do that?

"The point is to leave your comfort zone."

No, thank you. Besides, she'd already tried that once. When my laptop refused to fire up again, I called and told her our sessions were postponed indefinitely, but Dr. Neal refused to let me go, seeing that as a perfect opportunity for me to start coming to her office, hence my immediately buying the new laptop.

"The point is to allow yourself to experience something new, something that doesn't involve Christopher."

I made a face. "I have been to plenty of coffee shops in my life. That experience certainly would not be new and would not rock my world," I pointed out.

Because that was her master plan, to make me go and have a cup of coffee outside my house. *Idiotic.*

"It doesn't have to be a coffee shop. Go to the movies, visit a local bookstore, sit in a park for a couple of hours."

I cringed at all of it. "Maybe I can give a coffee shop a try," I said just to shut her up. Besides, that sounded like a lesser evil.

"So you finally agree?"

"Maybe."

"When?"

I shrugged. "Sometime later in the week."

"You are stalling why?" she demanded.

"Because I don't want to go anywhere," I said.

"Why?"

I really did my best to answer that. And to her credit, she gave me all the time I needed without pressing.

I tried to picture myself doing something like that, going out. I would get dressed, maybe even shower beforehand, and then leave this house, walk to the coffee shop. As all those images passed through my head, my heart started to beat a little bit faster, and then a great deal faster. It felt like I was running for my life although I was perfectly still.

"I can't do it."

"Why, Charlene? Talk to me."

"I'm dreading it," I said honestly.

"That is completely understandable," she said, taking me by surprise.

I was expecting that she would say I was acting ridiculous, childish. My mother would certainly use even worse descriptions.

"You created these safe places inside your house, and although you are hurting, you feel at ease."

She really nailed it. However, something in her tone suggested she didn't consider that to be a good thing like I did. "Why is that bad? Shouldn't I want to be at ease?"

"It's bad because it is preventing you from moving on."

Here we go again. I rolled my eyes.

"The house you confine yourself in is nothing more than a shrine to Christopher, and it's not good for you physically or mentally."

Her words hurt, and I started crying. "I don't want to forget him." *How can't she understand that? Hasn't she ever loved someone?*

"No one is asking you to do that," she countered. "But don't forget about yourself in the process either."

I frowned. I didn't understand.

"Charlene, you were always more than simply Christopher's wife. You *are* more, and you need to remind yourself of that."

I shook my head. "It's too hard."

"What scares you the most?"

I shrugged. "I don't know, everything."

"You are clearly imagining worst-case scenarios, needlessly scaring yourself. That's understandable, considering your past experiences."

It's my fault Christopher died.

"However, try to change the narrative for once. Nothing bad is going to happen if you for once let your guard down and go outside, get some fresh air, and order some delicious espresso."

That had always been my guilty pleasure. And although I'd bought myself an espresso maker, it wasn't the same.

"I'll give it a try," I replied. There was a coffee shop a few blocks from my house.

I could walk myself there. But then I remembered Christopher and I went there together. Could I go there? To a place that reminded me of him? Perhaps that was why I could. There was a connection there, no matter how painful.

"Good." Dr. Neal sounded pleased.

At least one of us was. We talked some more before our hour ended.

For some reason, I regretted saying yes to going outside the instant I ended the conversation. It was a stupid idea anyway. I didn't have to go outside. All that I needed was right here.

"What would that accomplish, anyway?" I asked no one in particular. *I won't stop missing Christopher less just because I went and grabbed an espresso outside the house.* I couldn't understand what she was thinking about suggesting something like that to me.

As I pondered the absurdity of my situation, I started picking up the box remnants I had discarded around the house. And I didn't stop there. I picked up all the take-out leftovers and all the other trash from the living room, then vacuumed. Truth be told, I was surprised how good it felt doing something like this for a change.

There were a few seconds while I was cleaning our lovely two-story house where I didn't think about him, about how he died. Naturally, realizing that instantly made me feel guilty. Christopher deserved all my attention.

I am so messed up.

Remembering I hadn't eaten the whole day, I decided to make myself a sandwich. Waiting for delivery to bring me something else to eat would take too long, so I settled for a turkey sandwich, which I ate standing up.

Christopher would be horrified seeing me eat like this. He was a true hedonist when it came to food and believed each bite should be savored.

Banishing all those thoughts, I went to the basement. It was time for a workout session. At times, when I wasn't feeling too depressed, it felt nice to punch things and scream.

I found a trainer online who taught self-defense, and I downloaded all his videos, trying to mimic his movements as he explained them. It was important for me to know how to take care of myself.

A normal person would simply hire him. I was not a normal person. The less contact I had with other people, the better.

The only person I could honestly stomach these days was my best friend, Selina. I'd met her online two years ago in a chat room where people were having a heated discussion about one of Goya's paintings.

Being an art major, I always liked to talk about the works of great artists. That was one of my greatest passions in life, apart from Christopher. Nowadays, I didn't participate much, but I loved to read what others had to say. Even if they were revealing their complete idiocy. Especially then.

Selina was different. She was smart and witty, and her comments were always spot on. The fact that we'd had similar experiences regarding our significant others only made us bond on a deeper level. She was my confidante, my friend who was always there for me, as I was for her.

Speaking of Selina, I noticed she'd left me a couple of messages while I worked out. Not bothering with showering,

I simply discarded my sweaty clothes and wrapped myself in my bathrobe before looking at my phone.

It didn't take her long to hit me with another message once I replied.

When she asked me how I was doing, I paused.

How am I doing?

The loss was something we were both very familiar with, although her husband hadn't died, merely left her, but I knew she would understand me because she felt her loss just as badly as I did for Christopher.

The same. And no matter what, I don't see that changing.

If I said something like that to Dr. Neal, she would chastise me, yet not Selina.

I know. It's a cliché, but it will get better.

I rolled my eyes. Selina wasn't like me. Despite everything, she'd retained some of her hope. *With time, right?* I wrote back, hoping she would sense my sarcasm.

Wrong. Not with time alone, but with how you spend it.

Since that got all too real for me too fast, I decided to log out for the day. I'd already agreed to go to the coffee shop. I wasn't ready for any more wisdom on how to properly grieve for your husband. There was no proper way as far as I was concerned. It was all wrong. Especially since he should not have died in the first place.

As I was about to turn everything off and just go to bed, I noticed how I had a new friend request.

Is this my mom again? I thought, clicking on it. *Samuel Northman,* I read. It was definitely someone I didn't know. Usually, I would ignore something like this without sparing it another thought, but something made me linger. Instead of a normal profile picture, Mr. Samuel Northman had a reproduction of a rather famous painting. It was one of Degas's dancers, one of my favorites, actually. I hadn't seen it in a while.

I hovered over the *Accept* button but reconsidered at the last second. *What am I doing?* I scoffed at myself, turning the phone off and putting it on the table with greater force than was necessary.

It was time to sleep, to dream . . .

2

In the next couple of days, I felt like a complete psycho with a split personality. On one hand, I promised I would go outside, have a coffee, and give this whole new experience, something I hadn't done in a while, a chance. On the other, I really didn't want to.

And that was pissing me off. I wasn't a person who would go back on her word, and at any rate, this wasn't such a big deal. I was capable of leaving this house, going outside if I wanted to. It was only that I had no desire to interact with the outside world. There was nothing there for me.

Besides, Christopher's death wasn't the only reason I'd decided to shut myself inside this house. He was the biggest reason, but definitely not the only one. My family, if I could even call them that, was the other.

My world collapsed once Christopher died, but when my father passed away as well a year and a half later, I lost all hope in humanity.

When my father died, a man I didn't really know, the shit in my life really started. I was already a mess from Christopher's death, and that finished me off. And why? Because I inherited a shitload of money. Mind you, it was only a small fraction of his wealth. And I knew I only got it because he felt like he should appease his guilty conscience, but none of that mattered. My circumstances had changed overnight. And suddenly, everybody wanted a piece of it.

Being so completely, terribly abused by my family, especially my mother, made me retreat to my little world completely. At the time, it was simply easier that way. As it turned out, what was once done as a conscious decision became my compulsion. That was why my heart started to beat erratically every time I only thought about leaving this place.

I didn't feel safe outside of my home.

However, Dr. Neal made me realize none of this was making me feel any better. If anything, I felt worse.

People were not to be trusted. And family members should be trusted even less. At least the family I was born into. From a mother who hated me to a stepfather who tolerated me, at best, to a sister who tormented me. Not one of them could be trusted.

It was a miracle I had been capable of trusting Christopher and surrendering to this love we felt in the first place after everything I'd been through.

Yet I did, and it was magical.

Unfortunately, it wasn't enough that I'd had a shitty childhood. The universe, God, whoever, decided I hadn't been hurt enough. I had to lose my love and then be tormented by that same family anew.

No wonder I need to go to therapy.

And Christopher wasn't better than any of them in the end. He was like the rest of them because he hurt me beyond measure. He'd promised he would always be there for me, love me, raise children with me, grow old with me, but he'd lied. He'd died, leaving me all alone in this world, surrounded by vultures and bloodsuckers.

And it was all my fault. *I killed him.*

I banished all those thoughts as I wiped the tears off my face.

That was enough mental aerobics for today. I had to leave something for tomorrow.

I will go to that stupid coffee place just so I can say to Dr. Neal that I did it. Afterward, when that accomplished absolutely nothing because I was beyond help, beyond repair, things could return to normal. My normal.

That's the spirit.

That last thought almost made me laugh as I tried to fall asleep. As always, I cried a little first. Being in bed always made me miss Christopher more. This was our sacred place where we talked, laughed, shared plans for the future, made love. And now, it was just me in a place that was too big for me alone.

Wasn't that a perfect metaphor for my whole life? Eventually, I managed to fall asleep.

The next day when I woke, I felt like weeping, but this time for a different reason. I didn't want to get up, especially since I didn't get to see my love's face last night. The dreams eluded me as I tossed and turned. And I knew why. It was because of that stupid deal I'd made with my therapist. It was making me stressed.

After some internal coaxing and swearing about the unfairness of life, I forced myself to get up. Very slowly, like my feet were shackled with chains, I walked toward the closet. I needed something to wear on this excursion today. I spent so much time in my PJs matched with a robe that my regular clothes felt completely foreign to me.

After staring at all my clothes for a while, I decided to abandon that endeavor and return to it later. I went to shower first so people in the coffee shop would not look at me oddly or smell me. I drew the line on my hair. There was no way in hell I would wash it now, especially since it would take me forever to dry it. For today's task, a messy ponytail or a messy bun would suit me just fine.

Check me out, functioning like a normal human being, I joked as I washed. Sadly, my cheerfulness was short-lived. I used to have showers with Christopher all the time. And he'd adored washing my hair.

I miss you so much. At times, it was hard to breathe. In this case, the scorching water producing so much heat and steam could be the culprit. I turned the water off, practically running out of the shower. At this point, I didn't even care if I slipped on wet tiles and broke a leg. I needed to get away. I sat on the bed, still naked, dripping and all, putting my head between my palms. *I can't do this.*

And I wasn't necessarily thinking about this outing. Living without him was too damn hard.

Why don't you simply end it all, then? Kill yourself.

That stopped me from spiraling.

I couldn't do that either.

With a heavy heart, I picked out some clothes, then dressed. I looked at myself in the mirror. I looked like crap. My skin was beyond dull, I had dark circles around my eyes, and my hair was beyond help. All the same, no matter what, I had to go.

Why am I bothering, anyway? Getting coffee in some random place wouldn't change the fact that I was all alone in this world. That I'd lost my husband and that I missed him like crazy. Nothing could ever change the fact that he'd died in my arms a couple of days after his thirty-second birthday during a robbery gone wrong. We barely had a chance to be together, spend any time together, and enjoy our love before he died.

Trying to escape all the painful memories—Christopher's smiling face, kneeling down before me as he proposed—I practically ran out of my house.

Stop it, Charlene, stop it.

Before I knew it, before I came to my senses, I was already there, arrived at my destination. I started looking about as if expecting someone to jump in front of me and kill me.

Calm down. No one will hurt you. I forced my raging heart to calm the fuck down. The thing would not listen.

It took me a second to decipher if I was at the right place. The coffee shop looked completely different from what I remembered. *Did they remodel? Did the owner change?*

The world around me tended to change no matter how long I remained standing still.

Not that I cared. For some reason, I suddenly started feeling extremely nervous about actually going inside, and forcing my legs to start working anew was a challenge.

I bet they would return me home in a flash. Sadly, I couldn't go home. Not yet. I had to do this stupid thing first. Despite my bravado, I realized how maybe this was not that stupid, because if it was, then why were my palms sweating? Why was I so nervous?

Nothing bad is going to happen to you inside the coffee shop.

The place looked packed.

Maybe if I'm lucky, there'll be no empty seats available and I'll have to go home.

That would only mean you would have to come back again, stupid.

As I argued with myself, I looked at all the people inside. There was so much commotion, so much life going on inside that I almost felt overwhelmed. Groups of people, friends smiling, lovers holding hands, older couples sharing papers, all those images assaulted me. Everywhere around me was life. Only I was shrouded in death.

Some teenagers left the coffee shop in haste, and I looked at that front door with dread as though it were some kind of monster that would swallow me whole if I went near it.

You can do this. Don't be such a coward.

Dr. Neal told me to go inside, order a coffee, and enjoy it, and that was precisely what I would do . . . or die trying.

Putting my earbuds in, I took a deep breath as Billie Holiday started to sing, and forced my legs to start moving. They obeyed. I managed to get inside, all the while ignoring all the happy people around me as though they were extremely contagious.

I loved the dark clouds around me, thank you very much. I saw an empty seat at the bar, right in the corner, and practically ran toward it in fear someone else would steal it from me. That place was perfect because the alternative would be to sit at some table, and I wanted to avoid that at all costs. No one tried to take my place, and I sat down with obvious relief. *I made it.*

A barista approached me, and I could see his lips were moving while wearing a professional smile. I couldn't hear a word since my music was blasting, which was by design, but I figured he probably asked me what I would like.

"One espresso, please," I countered. Was I too loud? Not that I cared.

To that, he started speaking again, and once he finished, he looked at me expectantly.

Okay, that definitely wasn't a 'coming right up', I realized. Reluctantly, I removed my earbuds to learn what was going on, what the holdup with my drink was. "Could you repeat that?" I asked politely.

"I said our espresso maker has been acting up all morning."

"What's that mean?"

"It means I would advise you to order something else. Or if you know how to fix the machine, that would be great too," he tried to joke.

"Don't you have a repairman for that?"

"He's running late."

"Great."

Just my luck. The only thing I was actually somewhat looking forward to when accepting to do this was that I could get a chance to drink a decent cup of coffee. *I guess that's out of the question* since I wasn't a jack-of-all-trades.

Today of all days, their machine was not working.

That would teach me a lesson. To not expect anything in this life, not even a cup of coffee.

On the other hand, I could leave now, go to some other coffee place and enjoy my drink, but I nixed that idea immediately. It sounded like too much of a hassle. And I already had my seat here and everything.

"Can I get you anything else?" he prompted.

Apparently, I was taking too much time figuring out what to do next. "Like what?"

He smiled. "Well, this is a coffee shop. I can make you some other type of coffee."

A sassy barista. Precisely what I need this morning.

"Yeah, but I bet you need a coffee machine for most of them," I countered.

"True. Would you like a shake? Or a smoothie?"

Yuck.

I sighed, looking at a gigantic menu behind his back. *What to get?*

"I make a mean strong-brewed hot coffee," he offered,

because he was sick of me or to end my suffering, I couldn't be sure.

"Sure," I replied halfheartedly. This day already sucked. Why not add something like that into the mix?

He went to make it.

With this tiresome exchange finally over, I returned my earbuds to my ears and concentrated solely on music, trying to forget where I was in the first place. 'I'll be Seeing You' started playing, which almost brought tears to my eyes. I always had this fantasy of dancing to this song, yet Christopher had had two left feet when it came to dancing. He had been really self-conscious about it, so we never danced. Nevertheless, the song made me miss him even more, two left feet and all.

One lonely tear escaped my eye, and I brushed it away immediately.

Pull yourself together, woman, I snapped at myself. There was no chance in hell I would allow myself to fall apart inside this place. *Once I get home, I can go to bed and cry my eyes out for hours if I so please, just not here.* Despite everything, I had a shred of dignity left, which I wanted to preserve.

My drink arrived, and the barista said something. To that, I simply nodded because it really didn't matter either way.

I took a tentative sip from my mug. The drink in question was not my thing. It was definitely too strong and bitter, so I worked on it quickly. I had an ulterior motive for drinking it fast. I wanted to return home as soon as possible. This was all wrong. I didn't belong here.

About halfway through, I decided this drink wasn't worth the effort, so I abandoned it completely and simply rose to leave. This outing was disappointing on so many accounts it was ridiculous. Then again, I knew it would be like that.

Leaving enough cash on the counter for the drink, plus a

generous tip, I practically ran out of that place as though in fear someone would try to prevent me from leaving.

I'd made a mistake agreeing to this. It was a complete disaster, and it didn't make me feel any better.

Nevertheless, I did it. And I could share that with Dr. Neal. She should be proud I did exactly as she asked.

Did you really? a small voice in my head challenged me.

There was a strong possibility that Dr. Neal would have issues with how I handled this. She would definitely frown upon the fact that I wore earbuds the entire time and pretty much ignored everything that was going on around me.

On the other hand, she never told me I couldn't listen to music, so it was her fault, really. I did as asked, mission accomplished. Or not, as it turned out, because this achieved nothing.

This was supposed to be some kind of learning experience, a way for me to reconnect, in baby steps, with the rest of humanity. Yet the only thing I learned was that I never wished to leave my house ever again since the universe clearly hated my guts.

As I pondered all that, I slowly walked home. They all told me this would make me feel better, being out and about, but it didn't. It only made me feel worse.

I was such a fuckup. I couldn't even do this one small thing the right way.

What was the big deal, anyway? Why was this so important to Dr. Neal? Why did I feel like this now, like I'd failed miserably? In what, exactly?

Nevertheless, all this was making me very angry. I realized I couldn't stand being around other people and looking at their faces as they interacted with one another, laughed, and enjoyed life while my world was in ruins.

It wasn't fair that other people got a chance to grow old with persons they loved when my Christopher died, and so young. All I ever wanted was to start a family with him, grow old next to the person I loved most in this world. Why was I not allowed to do that? What was my crime? What great sin did I commit in my life to be punished in such a manner? And I didn't simply lose my other half, my soul mate. I also lost all the children we never got a chance to have.

Children I could walk to the park with, teach how to swim, shop with for prom attire, watch them graduate and get married. Suddenly, I couldn't breathe. There was no air.

Why did you do this to me? I accused the heavens. Was there even anyone out there listening to me?

I couldn't say what would be worse, that there was no God or that there was.

Hyperventilating and in tears, I barely managed to reach my house. I felt like I was dying.

"Oh, come on." I dropped the keys because I was in a panic.

Once I managed to get the door open, I rushed inside and grabbed my bottle of medications. Dr. Neal had prescribed me something to calm down. I slumped on the floor, waiting for the storm to pass. This was the worst experience ever. I was never returning to that place. I was never again leaving this house.

But for some inexplicable reason, among all else, I felt guilty. I was so useless I couldn't even go and sit in a coffee shop without completely falling apart. And it didn't matter whether it was that specific place. I was sure the same would occur anywhere. I was beyond help.

Feeling all over the place, I picked myself up from the floor and went to the bedroom to grab my laptop. I wanted to send a message to Selina and tell her what had happened to me today. Instead of doing that, I stopped to look at the friend request I'd received from one Samuel Northman, a stranger to me.

Who was he? I was sure I didn't know him. *Does he know me?* From where? What did he want from me?

On impulse, as though needing something to show for how this day wasn't a complete fiasco, I clicked *Accept*. There. Now, not only had I had a drink at the coffee place, but I'd also accepted a new friend. Dr. Neal would be super impressed with that, I was sure.

What if she asks me about him? came the sudden thought. There was a slim chance of that, but to be on the safe side, I decided to check out his profile page and see who this man really was.

As his photographs uploaded, my eyes practically bulged. It couldn't be helped. I definitely didn't know this man because a person like him was memorable. I was still very much a woman in love. With that said, this Samuel person was gorgeous.

His info stated he was a forty-two-year-old businessman who worked as an antiques importer, which could explain his profile picture. He was in the art world.

It was pretty ridiculous of me to notice, but he looked perfect in all of his pictures, not that there were many of them. He preferred to capture and post other things, antiques, which made sense.

Samuel Northman was a well-dressed man. As far as I could see, he was tall and looked like he worked out. His hair was jaw length, and I presumed he had blue eyes. In most pictures, he had sunglasses on, so it was hard to tell.

Even in my state, I could acknowledge the man had an impressive appearance coupled with a dazzling smile. He was not merely handsome. He was a category all to himself.

Which raised a question. Did he confuse me with someone else?

A distinct *ping* indicated I received a message. Both my

eyebrows went up upon seeing it was actually from Mr. Samuel Northman.

Speak of the devil . . . There was a slight hesitation on my part.

I didn't like this feeling as though I was caught doing something wrong. Banishing the silly feeling, I opened the message and started reading.

Hello, Charlene, I just wanted to say thank you for accepting my friend request. Best regards, Samuel.

3

I reread the message. *Huh?*

What was that about?

I never expected that he would write to me, and so formally. *It's just a courtesy message, so get over yourself.* That was why I replied with *You're welcome*.

There. It's done.

With that weird occurrence settled, I closed my laptop and decided to go to sleep. It was still late afternoon, but I felt bone-tired. This was a tiring day on so many levels, and the sad reality was that I preferred dreams to real life anyway since once in a while, I got a chance to see my love.

Only when I stretched on top of the comforter, preparing to fully wrap myself in it, did I realize I was still fully dressed. And had sneakers on.

Well, that hadn't happened to me in a while.

Still lying down because I didn't feel like getting back up again, I stripped off all my clothes before crawling under the blanket. I forced myself to fall asleep. I always tried to fall asleep the natural way since when I took sleeping pills, they prevented me from having dreams, and that was not acceptable. Luckily, I quickly drifted into nothingness.

No dreams of Christopher was my first conscious thought.

Waking up later in the day after realizing I didn't get a chance to see my husband put me in a seriously depressed mood, and I had trouble getting up. That wasn't so different from most days, and since I had nothing better to do, I decided to simply stay in bed and wallow in my sorrow. It was my favorite thing to do, anyway.

I could just picture Dr. Neal's disappointed face looking at me in those moments. And that seriously pissed me off.

If I wanted to stay in bed all day and cry over my dead husband, then I freaking should. And I should not be made to feel guilty about it. *This is my life, after all.* And Dr. Neal could shove it.

I jerked in bed, sitting up. *Oh, crap.* I had a session with that woman today. If I didn't sleep through it. I groaned. If that were the case, I would never hear the end of it. But then I realized something. *I could simply cancel my session.* I didn't feel like talking, or anything else, for that matter. I wanted to sleep and think of Christopher. That was all.

Picking up my phone from the nightstand, I fully intended to send my therapist a message yet got sidetracked by something else. I had a notification. Apparently, I'd received another message from Samuel Northman.

I grabbed my laptop next.

I read your take on Monet's Impression, Sunrise. It blew my mind away. I'll certainly be more appreciative of him in the future.

It was a short message, and I still had to read it a couple of times.

My take on Monet? What the hell is he talking about?

And then I remembered. Over a decade ago, while I was in college, I'd written for the papers. The editor recruited me personally since he wanted an arts major to write short articles about the most famous paintings in the world, but from a slightly different perspective. He didn't want mere facts printed on the piece of paper but something a little bit more personal and fun. I had done my best to achieve that.

People seemed to like it. I knew Christopher had. He'd told me years later, when we reconnected and started dating, how he'd enjoyed reading my descriptions and seeing great works of art through my eyes.

I honestly couldn't even remember what I'd written about that specific painting. All the same, if this man liked it, that was good with me. However, I started to get curious.

Where on Earth did he uncover something like that to read? They had only been published in university papers. Not even I had copies of them. Correction, I probably had them, but it had all gotten lost somewhere, thrown away during the move. I was never that sentimental. Or at least I wasn't before Christopher.

I did a quick Google search in hopes I could perhaps find some of my works, and fortunately, a couple of minutes later, I found the whole database. Someone at the university had really put in the effort to get all the newspaper issues online. I was excited.

I found a bunch of my work in the archives. That writing job was how I met Christopher in the first place. He was the young anthropology professor all my friends and I were in love with. I hadn't taken his class, but I'd seen him around the campus all the time. And one day, I decided to seek him out and ask about a painting I was doing for my next article.

At first, my request had confused him, and he'd tried to turn me down, saying he wasn't an artist. But I had been persistent. I'd wanted to pick his brain about that specific era, hear how people had lived back then, what their biggest fears, joys, and things like that had been, hoping that would give me an insight into the artist's mind. I'd wanted to know what he felt like, what he'd experienced while creating the image.

And that was no lie. I'd honestly wanted his help on all of that. At the same time, I could probably have found all that information online or read it in a book in the library, but this had felt like hitting two birds with one stone. I'd gotten what I needed and flirted with the sexy teacher as well.

Being the kind-hearted man he was, Christopher had helped me. On several occasions, as it turned out.

Nothing had happened between us back then. We didn't start dating until many years later, well after I finished college.

I stopped myself there as tears blurred my eyes, wiping them vigorously as I tried to focus on the article I'd written about Monet's painting. *Sunrise* wasn't the only one I'd written about, but this piece was what enticed a message from Samuel Northman, so naturally, I was the most curious about it.

As it turned out, the article wasn't half bad. It was obvious I had been young, perhaps slightly idealistic and naive, but I'd forgotten I was good at writing and enjoyed it immensely.

Why did I stop?

Oh, right, I finished college and got a job at the art gallery.

Glad you liked it, I replied to Samuel Northman because it felt like the polite thing to do.

Liked it? It made me want to visit La Havre, came his instant reply that pretty much surprised me.

He was online now.

Although his reply did make me smile. Port of La Havre was Monet's hometown, and I was impressed that he clearly knew that.

Impressed he knew that. See what I did there? Monet was an impressionist. Inspired the name of the whole movement. Oh, never mind . . .

It's a lovely city, although there are better places to visit in Normandy.

You've been there?

Yes.

Christopher and I had gone to Europe on our honeymoon. We started in Portugal, then visited Spain, France, Italy, Belgium, and circled back to England. I was only saddened that we didn't have more time to visit Scotland as well. Nevertheless, to this day, it was the best month of my life.

Samuel's message snapped me from my thoughts. *Did you go to Alsace, by chance?*

Of course. A lovely woman named Corentin was the best guide I'd had a privilege to meet.

I had also been pretty blown away by their unique cuisine and was astonished to learn how that part of France had been producing wine since the second century.

Christopher and I had gotten thoroughly drunk in Alsace, but Corentin and our other hosts hadn't taken offense. They had been pleased we were enjoying ourselves, although as Americans, we still had a long way to go toward learning how to enjoy wine more, as well as food and life in general.

I got extremely drunk there, Samuel confessed, and despite myself, I laughed.

Me too.

Great. I am not the only one who made a fool of myself there.

Glad to help.

He replied nothing to that, so I added, *I love your profile picture.*

It was Degas's *Dancer in Green*.

It's Dancer in Green *by Degas,* he explained.

I know.

Right. Your bio says you are an art history major.

That's one of my favorite paintings, actually, I shared.

Mine too.

Why?

I like the duality of it.

Degas had been obsessed with painting dancers and had been very good at portraying them in motion. They always looked so full of life in his paintings, and the observer could almost see them dancing.

What do you mean? I asked.

She looks so real, and while doing that movement, you can almost see all the hard work, commitment, and resolution that went into it. You can see the sacrifices of a professional dancer. It is serious and majestic, graceful and beautiful in its simplicity. And at the same time, there's almost a childish playfulness to the pose. Like when children are playing, running around, pretending to fly. Degas managed to convey all those things simply by observing a dancer doing what she loved.

Wow, I thought while looking at that painting. His words were beautiful, as though while trying to describe an art piece, they became art.

This was one of my favorite paintings, maybe even *the* favorite, except I had never looked at it that way. That was very insightful of him.

That probably sounds silly to you, he added as though in a moment of self-consciousness.

Not at all, I was quick to reassure him. *That is the beauty of art, to entice, to make us react, to think. What you wrote about it resonated with me.*

Really?

Before I knew it, we had been texting for hours about Monet, our favorite places in the world, and art in general.

I care not for his paintings. He's too dark for me.

At the moment, we were discussing Goya. For some reason, I was very fond of that artist from an early age. I'd seen his painting *Saturn Devouring his Son* while I was in elementary school and had become completely fascinated by it.

Perhaps because I could relate to that poor child. I constantly had a feeling that my mother was eating me alive.

I don't know. There is beauty in the darkness too, I countered.

In passing, I learned that he had been doing this import business for quite some time, over fifteen years, and that he lived in Manhattan, which meant we were in the same city.

Samuel was single, not that I asked, was never married and had no children. By his account, it was not because he never wanted them. It simply wasn't written in the stars. Yet.

It took me by surprise quite a bit to look at the time and see how much of it had flown by as we texted. It was the best conversation I'd had in months. Probably more. I used to have such engaging conversations with Christopher. My heart squeezed painfully inside my chest, and I placed a hand over it as though that would stop it from tormenting me.

Samuel turned out to be quite a surprise. Who knew my new online friend would be such a great conversationalist? Although I talked about these same things with Selina as well, this felt different. Samuel had a fresh perspective that I welcomed. I appreciated that I had a chance to experience something like this and be reminded of some things about my past that I had forgotten.

This day, which had started bleak like so many others before it, had an unexpected turn. Truth be told, my bars were very low these days since the only people I talked with were my therapist, sometimes my lawyer, and various couriers who came to drop off my food and all the rest that I needed to survive while never leaving my home.

It was a pleasure meeting you. I had a lovely time chatting with you. And I appreciate exchanging thoughts with a fellow Degas enthusiast.

Likewise, I replied without a thought, because I meant it. Even before he wrote that, I was thinking about that very same thing.

Maybe we could continue our conversation in person sometime, over coffee? I've recently moved back to New York, and it would be nice to speak with you in person, he offered.

My whole face fell. I instantly felt like I needed to shut my laptop and run away from this room as my heart started to race. Which was ridiculous. I was safe inside my house. No one could hurt me while chatting online. It was okay to say no and move on.

Besides, I was sure he didn't mean anything by it. He was probably glad to have someone to speak with about such things. Not everyone liked that. My own family frowned upon my studying art. My mother particularly considered it a waste of time. When I got a scholarship, there was nothing she could do to stop me. Perhaps Samuel had similar difficulties in finding a willing ear, I rationalized.

Maybe, I replied, ending the conversation.

Perhaps that was a bit deceitful of me. I had no intentions of meeting him in person or going to coffee with him, yet I still hesitated to say that because I was hoping we would get a chance to chat sometime in the future like we did today. I just hoped I was not giving him false hope. This was all he could ever get from me, a few lines every once in a while, and that was all. I had nothing more to give.

What if he did mean something by it? A thought I couldn't stop penetrated my mind. *What if he's interested in me?* I stopped myself there. I couldn't bear such thoughts. I couldn't imagine something like that, being interested in another man, let alone dating anyone ever again.

I instantly felt sick to my stomach. My whole being rebelled against such a horrible idea. I'd already met the love of my life. That was the beginning and the end of every discussion.

And still, I caught myself thinking about Samuel a couple of times during the night, remembering some of the words he'd said that put a smile on my face. It was a rather insightful take on Monet's work.

Samuel was an interesting man.

However, I was painfully aware that he was nothing more than a fleeting distraction in a world of agony and sorrow.

Sighing deeply, I took out my phone to do something I should have done hours ago. I wrote Dr. Neal a heartfelt message, expressing my deepest apologies for missing our session, asking to reschedule it at a time of her convenience. Was I going overboard? I definitely was, but a little sucking up was necessary when I was in the wrong. I even offered to pay for the hour she lost because of me.

I didn't care about the money, never had. Besides, I would pay an even greater price to not have my session with her, because as it turned out, I'd found someone else with whom I actually enjoyed having a conversation.

4

In the days that followed, Samuel and I texted regularly, daily. At times, I had a feeling like I was texting him more than Selina, which was unheard of. It couldn't be helped. I simply found him fascinating. He had a very unique mind in how he looked at things, and besides, we had so many things in common it was insane.

And while I was in such a strange state, Dr. Neal managed to convince me to try going out again, since my first time was such a fiasco. And I did. Two more times. I returned to that coffee shop and had my espresso. It was delicious. And the second time, I took a stroll in the park. That made me cry uncontrollably, so I returned home.

A picture that Samuel sent me pulled me back from the chasm of despair. I was surprised by how much I actually missed talking about art in general. It was true. I did that with Selina too, but we shared all the same views and liked the same things, so this felt different. It felt as though Samuel and I were constantly challenging one another, and that felt nice. Except that was not all we discussed. There was a range of topics we brushed over since we'd started chatting.

He never once asked me to go get coffee again, as though sensing that would make me feel uncomfortable, and I appreciated that greatly. This was all that could be, and luckily, that was enough for him as well.

Honestly, I couldn't handle a love interest at the moment, or in the future, for that matter.

At the same time, I saw no harm in having another online friend in my life. Naturally, I told Samuel all about Christopher. Well, not all, but enough for him to understand me and my situation.

Selina found it fascinating that I'd opened up so much to this man, but I didn't see it that way. It was something that needed to be done, plain and simple. I wished to set firm boundaries for our friendship, and this was the only way to go about it. I had to share the story about the love of my life for him to understand.

Just because he was gone didn't mean he was erased from my heart. Nothing could change how I felt about Christopher. He would always be my one and only, and luckily, Samuel understood that.

Or at least I believed he did. His comments certainly indicated that to be the case.

I wish that someday, I'll be fortunate enough to love another person as deeply as you love him.

What surprised me the most was that Samuel didn't mind if the subject we were discussing at times got depressing or sensitive, as it did when we were speaking about my Christopher.

Loving a person who loves you back with whom you can share all your dreams, hopes, and fears is the best feeling in the world. Something worth living and fighting for too. But let me tell you, losing all of it, and so suddenly, without a warning, is no picnic, I said. And that was the understatement of the century.

Was it worth it, though? he asked in return.

I really gave it some thought, not wanting to rush with my reply.

The coward in me wanted to say no, except I couldn't do that, no matter what, because it wasn't true. It was all worth it, despite everything, and if I had an opportunity to be with Christopher again, I would. Even if it was just for one day, no matter the cost. No matter the pain. Because that was what true love was all about. Putting everything on the line, giving all of yourself without trying to guard your heart against any potential pain. That was what made love so all-consuming. That was what made it so terrifying.

Eventually, that was exactly what I wrote to Samuel.

It wasn't all that blue, though, and we weren't so extreme to speak only of art or death. Samuel had a keen, curious mind and loved to ask me questions about everything. And surprisingly, I found myself answering all of them.

At times, his questions appeared completely random, asking me about my childhood before moving on to my favorite subject, traveling places, only to ask something about my marriage. I didn't mind. His directness was refreshing, and as I'd realized before, it was also distracting. He always found some way to get me engaged, even on a really bad day. And speaking about Christopher wasn't as hard as I envisioned.

I spoke about Christopher with Dr. Neal all the time, but those soul-searching, gut-wrenching confessions always left me feeling raw and exposed. Speaking with Samuel made me remember the good times as well, not only the loss and the pain.

I only went through one box of tissues while sharing my story of Christopher to Samuel, which was progress. Naturally, I couldn't bring myself to go into details about what had happened on the day he died, and he didn't press. I was too ashamed to tell him the whole truth, and perhaps slightly selfish as well.

I was lonely in this house, surrounded by my memories alone and in pain, and texting with Samuel each day felt nice. I didn't want him changing his opinion of me once he discovered how I was the one who actually killed my husband. Dr. Neal tried to convince me that was not the case, that it was an accident and this was only my guilt speaking. The guilt of surviving that night, but I disagreed.

I wasn't the one who plunged the knife into my husband's chest. Some evil man did that, but his getting killed was still my fault. I had wanted to go out that night and insisted that we should go to that one very specific restaurant. We were warned many times to avoid certain parts of the city, especially at night, but I wouldn't listen.

I had been overconfident and dismissive. I had acted like an idiot, and Christopher went along with it because he loved me and wanted to make me happy. That action cost him his life.

A ping on my phone saved me from completely drowning in sorrow. It was a text from Samuel, of course, that had me chuckling. He was a delight and a blessing. He was a small relief in my world of pain.

It wasn't like I was using him or anything. This was not some kind of one-sided friendship. I didn't use him as an emotional crutch, nor would I ever. I didn't cry on his shoulder, expecting him to comfort me. We spoke about everything, and as much as he asked questions about me and was interested in my life, he also offered a great deal in return.

I loved to hear him speak about France, Italy, and England because those were the places I had visited as well, and his words made me feel as though I were there once again, seeing those things, experiencing those delights.

At the same time, it was even more interesting when he

spoke about the places that I never got a chance to visit. At times, he was making me feel I should pack my bags right this instant and just go, leave, start traveling the world, see all the wonders that were hidden someplace.

I would never do that, but it was a nice sentiment in passing.

As I mentioned, it was refreshing hearing his stories about his time in Brazil, Russia, and Dubai.

What do you remember the most about Dubai? I asked with enthusiasm.

Sand, he deadpanned, and that made me spit my tea with laughter. He was a goof at times.

Is it really that cold in Russia, as it's said?

People always joked about Russian winters, but I wondered how true those stories were and how much was exaggerated.

Even worse.

You are playing me.

Not at all. After a year there, I can now go around NY in a denim jacket in January.

You must be joking. I got chilled just picturing something like that. I couldn't imagine anything colder than New York's winter air.

I am not.

I was about to reply, but he beat me to the punch.

Hey, can I call you on the phone so we can talk? I don't feel like ending this, but I am driving in the car, and I don't think what I'm currently doing is completely safe. There was a goofy emoji at the end of that sentence.

I was horrified that he was texting and driving, and I sent him my number without a thought. And then I actually had a second to process what I'd done, and the panic started to rise. In the blink of an eye, the moment passed, and my phone was ringing.

What to do? I panicked. There was only one thing I could do.

"Hello?"

Why did I sound like that? Like I was answering from the bottom of a well. Did my voice have an echo, or was I just stressing?

"Hello, Charlene. It is nice to finally hear your voice," he greeted.

His too. He had a nice British accent. Now I knew where he was originally from.

"You too," I replied politely, then paused. My mind went completely blank. I had no idea what I was supposed to say next. I couldn't even remember what we were discussing before this call.

A navigation app telling him to take the next turn snapped me from my strange state, and I was able to be a normal person again. Or at least pretend to be one.

"So where are you going?" I asked conversationally, hoping that wasn't too personal a question.

"Just visiting one of my wheelhouses. A very important shipment is arriving today, and I want to make sure everything is on the up-and-up."

He had such a lovely accent I could listen to him speak all day. He could probably read me an instruction manual for a Honeywell thermostat and I would be completely okay with that. Was that shallow of me? *Probably.* However, I only felt slightly guilty about it.

"It's tiring work, but someone has to do it," he joked.

"Do you like it? What you do, I mean."

"It pays the bills." He chuckled.

"Do you like it?" I insisted.

"I do, and I'm grateful I'm good at it."

That went without saying. He would not be able to travel so much around the world if he sucked at it.

"Something that started as a humble enterprise turned into a multimillion-dollar company, which gave me the freedom to explore other aspects of life. I get to meet some truly incredible, talented people, all while traveling the world." He sounded truly passionate saying all that.

That's how life is supposed to be, a part of me pointed out.

My life was like that once, but not anymore. My spark was gone. However, I was glad Samuel was still keeping his going.

"That sounds amazing."

That was precisely how I'd envisioned my life once upon a time. Sadly, someone else had other plans in store for me. Call it a God, a higher power, a sadistic bastard, or Fate, the result regarding my life was pretty much the same. I was completely alone in a house Christopher bought for us, for our family.

The day we moved into it was still fresh in my mind. I was so happy, and then he died. So now, I was like a lightkeeper wandering about a broken lighthouse, unable to do my job but unable to move on.

I had no children, and I had no husband, yet here I was, still holding on to that house, to that dream . . .

"Hey, Charlene, you there?" Samuel inquired.

"Yeah."

"I thought I lost you for a moment there."

I lost myself a long time ago. "Still here," I tried to reply cheerfully.

"Anyway, I found out something I think you will find interesting."

"Oh?"

"Yes, it's about Jusuf."

Jusuf was one of those contemporary artists. People couldn't seem to agree whether he was completely despicable for showing such rawness of this world or if he should be applauded for his bravery and candor. There was no middle ground with Jusuf, and I suspected that was by design.

I, too, couldn't decide how I felt about him, yet one thing was certain. Jusuf was always entertaining even when what he was showing us was borderline terrifying or heartbreaking.

"What?" I asked, genuinely curious. Jusuf was such a reclusive person that it would be something special if Samuel managed to learn any kind of gossip about him.

All of a sudden, I could hear some kind of commotion on the other side.

"Samuel?"

"Hey, could you give me a moment? Please do not hang up," he said abruptly.

"Okay," I replied, although I had a feeling he'd already left the conversation.

In muffled voices, I could definitely hear a conversation between several people, and one of them was Samuel.

"What?" he snapped. "Explain what happened."

I couldn't hear the reply. Part of me felt bad for eavesdropping, but then again, he did tell me to stay put, so it wasn't like he had anything to hide from me.

"What do you mean there was a problem?"

I guessed this shipment was extremely important to him. His next words confirmed as much.

"If something happened to it, you are both fired," Samuel snapped.

I wouldn't like being at the receiving end of that. I could just picture his face glaring at other men.

The other men were saying how sorry they were.

I was somewhat curious to know what was going on. This was the first time I'd gotten a chance to witness this business side of Samuel. Then again, this was the first time I'd heard his voice.

We had known each other for only the briefest of times, a couple of weeks. *You can't really know a person after only a couple of weeks*. Sometimes, you can't know a person after a whole lifetime.

"Charlene? Are you still there?"

"Yes. Is everything all right? We can talk later if you're busy."

"No, all is resolved. All is well," he reassured me.

I was glad, so I said as much. "I hope those poor men haven't gotten themselves fired," I said.

"Almost." Some of the darkness crept back into his voice. "That is the import business for you, never a dull moment."

"So what is it? This new item of yours," I inquired.

After all that tension buildup, I would really like to know what became of his possession.

A couple of seconds later, I received an image.

"See for yourself."

I put him on speakerphone before opening what he sent me.

On top of a massive crate stood a set of pottery he'd so clearly arranged in haste, for my eyes only. It was some kind of handmade teapot with six small cups.

"It's lovely."

"It's a ceremonial tea set from the fourteenth century. It's made of clay."

I figured as much.

"I didn't know you dealt with that kind of stuff."

"I deal in all kinds of stuff," he replied, mimicking my phrasing.

"So is this for a client?"

"Actually, I got this for myself. I've been looking for it for a long time, so this is a very special day for me."

In that case, no wonder he was on edge before. "Well, I'm glad you managed to achieve your goal."

"I always do." And then he added after a pause, "And all that I need now is a wife to share this with. Know someone available?"

Before I got a chance to reply, he started laughing.

"Samuel," I chastised. He was such a fool at times. He really had me going there for a moment.

Although he turned everything into this big joke, I could still hear genuine longing as he spoke about having someone to share his life with. He couldn't mask such deep feelings that almost rivaled mine.

What a lovely pair we make.

He longed for some unknown ideal, true love, while I longed for my lost love. Perhaps that was why we were so drawn to one another in the first place. Misery loved company.

"Talk to you later?" I asked as though needing to end this on a high note.

"Always."

5

Chatting over the phone with Samuel every day became the new normal. Between speaking with Dr. Neal, Selina, Samuel, and hearing occasional rants my mother left on my voice mail, I almost felt like I actually had a life. *Almost.*

There were still days I didn't like getting out of bed after crying myself to sleep, but I wasn't about to dwell on that. Some things couldn't be changed, so there was no point in dwelling on them.

And my talks with Samuel were great. He was cheerful, funny, and so full of life, which was in complete contrast to me. Perhaps that was where the attraction lay.

There was only one awkward silence between us during those talks. And it occurred when he asked me what I did for a living.

Well, after Christopher died, I didn't do much for a living. And thanks to my father's money, I didn't have to work now, either.

Before I married Christopher, I had worked in an art

gallery. I loved my job, but I hated the gallery owner. She was a world-class bitch who was beyond shallow and was disinterested in true art. She only cared about making money.

Christopher had seen how miserable I was, so he'd offered me a job as his assistant.

"You do know men offer this position first so they can sleep with their assistants. Not the other way around," I'd teased.

"I'm serious, Charlene. Quit your job and work with me."

I had.

He'd planned on writing a book about the Egyptian modern age, so I did a lot of initial research for him while he taught at the university. Although it wasn't strictly speaking my area of expertise, it was engaging work, and I liked doing it. Of course, getting to spend some extra time with Christopher while discussing my findings was precious as well.

After he passed away, all that research went to waste. The university took everything, although I was sure they didn't plan to do anything with it.

Anyway, I told Samuel how I was currently unemployed but had enough savings to live on. I didn't feel comfortable enough to go into my situation or explain my screwed-up family dynamic in which my mother slept with a wealthy man to move forward in life. It backfired when he in turn didn't want to have anything to do with her or me. The fact that he had a little case of a guilty conscience at the end of his life made no difference. Although it certainly complicated my already screwed-up relationship with my mother.

"I understand. You're still trying to find yourself." Samuel was full of empathy.

Honestly, I was constantly floored by his reactions. No matter what I said, he never seemed to be bothered by it. It felt liberating, interacting with a person who didn't judge in the slightest. I felt like I could speak with him about anything, and usually, we did.

At one point, he had me laughing so hard my face hurt. Although that could be due to the fact that my muscles had forgotten their basic functions.

"I laughed so hard some of the pastry got stuck into my nose," Samuel confessed.

I simply lost it, trying to picture that whole scene.

"No," I managed to say through the cackles.

"Yes," he insisted.

"You must be exaggerating."

"I assure you, I'm not. And I'll prove it to you."

"How?" I challenged, finally settling down.

"Let me take you to dinner, and you can meet Pietro for yourself," he said without missing a beat.

Although he couldn't see me, I started shaking my head vigorously even before he stopped speaking.

"I . . . I . . ." I started to stumble, not sure what to say or how to say it.

"I understand you don't like to go out, and I know you're not prepared to date anyone, but please listen to me. You already like talking with me, correct?"

"Correct," I replied hesitantly.

"And you do need to eat, right?"

"Occasionally." My attempt at a joke failed miserably.

"Then why not share a meal with me? It wouldn't be much different from what we have been doing for over a month now."

Was it really that long since we'd started speaking over the phone? Time flew by.

"I don't know."

"I want to meet you in person, Charlene. We'll go strictly as friends, and to emphasize how much this is not a date, we can even sit at different tables," he pressed.

Can I sit at home and you at a restaurant?

"We can both have our own separate corner booths."

"Stop goofing around."

"I will when you say yes."

I remained silent. I simply couldn't say it.

"I beg you, Charlene. Let's give it a go. Besides, don't you want to meet me too?" There was that genuine vulnerability in his voice again. "I promise I'm quite dashing in person. Besides, I have a few things I would like to show you," he added as though in afterthought.

"Of the painting variety?"

"Perhaps."

"So basically, you're bribing me?" I teased.

"Of course," he replied without a thought. "So what do you say?"

I sighed, getting serious again. "Could you let me think about it?"

"Certainly. However, bear in mind that I like to eat around eight, which gives you exactly three more hours to say yes," he deadpanned.

"Samuel."

"I'm kidding. Take all the time you need. There's no pressure."

His words really took me by surprise, although it was exactly what I wanted and needed to hear. Part of me expected he would get offended and stop speaking with me, so this was a surprise.

"Samuel, can I ask you something?"

"Of course, anything."

"Why are you in such a good mood? I didn't say yes."

I wasn't trying to be cruel or anything, I was genuinely curious.

"Honestly? Because *maybe* is not a *no*."

And before I could reply to that and point out that it

wasn't a yes either, he ended the conversation, saying he needed to deal with some paperwork regarding the precious tea set.

I looked at my phone, completely baffled. *What just happened?*

Naturally, by the time my scheduled therapy with Dr. Neal started, I'd already had three mini-mental breakdowns and cried for an hour straight without stopping. That conversation with Samuel where he expressed a desire to meet me in person shook me to the core. And the real problem was that I couldn't even say why it affected me in such a way.

It was true that at times I felt extremely guilty for cultivating this friendship with Samuel because it looked like I was cheating on Christopher or something. It was ridiculous on so many levels, not to mention crazy, but knowing that didn't change how I felt.

It didn't help that I was the only one seeing all this as a bad thing. Selina thought Samuel sounded amazing and encouraged me to say yes to having dinner with him. Dr. Neal too.

"Your fear is irrational, so you should ignore it and go to dinner with that man," was my friend's reply. But that was easy for her to say. She didn't fully understand what it was like to lose the person you loved the most. Her partner left her, and for his secretary, no less. Talk about clichés.

I instantly regretted those thoughts. A broken heart was a broken heart, and it was totally moronic of me to try to make some kind of measuring scale of who'd suffered the most in life. Selina was a good friend, and I was truly blessed to have her in my life, especially during this time.

However, the same could be said for Samuel. It shouldn't matter that he was a man. A true friend was a true friend regardless of gender.

Nonetheless, did that mean I should go out with him? If

Selina lived in NY, would I want to see her? And the answer was a definite yes. We would not go out clubbing, but perhaps I would like her to come and visit me. *Should I tell Samuel to come to my house instead of going out to dinner?* I instantly banished that idea. I didn't want him inside this house, nor did I want to go out. What did that leave me with? *A headache.*

Should I say no to him?

Would Samuel stop speaking with me if I said no to dinner? That thought made me uneasy.

Since there was no way I could solve this puzzle on my own, I shared all this and more with my therapist. She listened intently while I spoke, while I tried to list all the reasons I'd accepted Samuel in my life but was still reluctant to move past the digital and telephone world.

Eventually, I realized she was not focused on my words. Her image was frozen. Our connection broke.

Son of a bitch. I felt like hitting the damn thing with a brick. We had to re-establish the connection, and by that time, I didn't feel like speaking anymore. The momentum I'd felt before had definitely passed.

At the same time, I tried not to be too bitchy about it. These things happened. Eventually, Dr. Neal managed to guide me back into the same mind frame as before, and as a result, the second time around, I really managed to better articulate some of my feelings and concerns.

"I think it's commendable that you formed a new friendship."

"But?" I prompted.

"No buts, quite the contrary. I see no faults in your behavior, and I think you should most definitely say yes to this dinner thing," she said.

I cringed inwardly.

This was not what I wanted to hear, but then again, it

wasn't as if Dr. Neal would ever tell me how it was okay to hide inside my house for the rest of my days. That woman had been trying to kick me out of it, to engage me in some kind of hobby for years now.

No wonder I was dreading this session so much. Deep down, I knew this was precisely what she would say to me.

And I was not ready for this. Not at all. I already felt like things were changing around me too fast, without my control. More of that, and I was bound to lose it.

You have only yourself to blame for all of it. I banished that.

"I'm not ready to date," I said in a panic.

Dr. Neal waved her hand. "Who said anything about dating?" she challenged.

"I'm afraid he'll get the wrong impression."

"Did you make sure to let him know about your feelings?"

"Yes."

"And he agreed to your terms?"

"I think so, yes."

"Then there you have it. It will not be a date, so don't think of it as such. It's merely practice," she reassured me.

"For what?"

"Socializing."

At times, that woman made no sense to me. And since I remained quiet, she pressed on.

"You already made the first step, going outside occasionally for coffee."

I made a face. "Highlights of my day," I grumbled.

And if you asked me, those were poor excuses for socializing. Perhaps that was due to the fact that I really didn't want to. I preferred my own company. It was easier that way.

"And this is even better, since you will be in the company of someone you like speaking with."

That was true. I couldn't deny that. And then it hit me.

"What if things are different, awkward when we meet?" I wondered out loud.

"No matter. Either way, it can be used as a great learning experience."

She really had an answer to everything. It was annoying at times.

As she droned on and on about the benefits for my mental state or something like that, I realized there was no way she would leave me alone until I said yes to this.

In a moment of desperation, since I really needed her to shut up, those treacherous words left my mouth. "Yes, I'll do it."

"Excellent. I want you to call him right now and accept his offer for a date."

"It's not a date," I snapped in return. "Just dinner."

"You shouldn't be so exclusionary."

That statement made me build up my defenses anew.

"I'm not interested in dating, or in men in general," I insisted.

"Perhaps lightning will strike twice for you," she countered with a half-smile.

On some level, I knew she meant well and was paid to help me, but her words cut like a knife, and I wanted to scream.

"It won't," I said through gritted teeth. "And if I go to this damn dinner, it will only be as friends." I felt the need to set the record straight. There was no way in hell I would ever be interested in anyone else.

Luckily, Dr. Neal nodded. "If those are the boundaries of your comfort zone, then so be it."

I didn't have the energy to tell her we'd left my comfort zone weeks ago. Besides, all I did was complain. I felt sorry for myself in having to deal with this, with her. I still loved Christopher. That would never change, but one dinner wouldn't kill me. *Right?*

Dr. Neal took pity on me and suggested that I speak with Samuel the following day, but she still insisted that she be included when I made that call. I must seriously be out of my mind since I agreed.

It was almost an out-of-body experience when I called Samuel to let him know about dinner as my therapist watched me like some creepy aunt.

I totally related to convicts who had to pee in a cup in front of an audience since they couldn't be trusted. Truth be told, I couldn't be trusted. I went back on my word so many times, agreed to do this or that but failed. Like when she made me promise to pack all of Christopher's clothes and donate them to charity. I couldn't do it and changed my mind. So I supposed it was completely understandable that Dr. Neal wanted to make sure I would stick to it this time around. I wouldn't trust me, either.

He answered almost instantly.

I gulped. Part of me really wished I could have just left a message on his voice mail.

"Hello, Samuel."

"Hello, Charlene. It's very good to hear your voice. It's been a tiring day."

At times, he said the strangest things, like those were lines from movies or romance novels. Not to imply it wasn't unappealing, because it wasn't. I found it rather nice.

"About dinner," I started, then faltered.

Dr. Neal looked at me intently. Her face was saying *don't you dare chicken out.*

"Yes?"

"I'll go to dinner with you, as friends, of course."

"Of course. Great. I'll pick you up at seven thirty."

"Tonight?" I practically screeched in surprise.

"No better time than the present."

"Okay." I stumbled over that word.

"If you would be so kind as to send me your address?"

"Of course. I'll text it to you."

"Excellent. See you tonight."

And before I knew it, the call ended.

Oh, Mary, mother of God, what did I just push myself into?

6

I *can't believe I said yes to this.*

I was having a panic attack. Dr. Neal tried to calm me down since this was not the end of the world—although it definitely felt like that—and cheer me up by applauding my bravery. None of that shit worked.

And then she was simply gone since our hour ended, and she couldn't continue encouraging me because she had other clients, so I had to deal with all these contradictory feelings on my own.

I found the whole situation hysterical. That was probably due to my nerves. I ended up taking one of my pills to try to calm down, although I had a feeling nothing could help me in this situation.

Selina did her best to be the voice of reason, constantly reminding me that this was not a bad thing. I couldn't say whether it was working or not while hyperventilating into a paper bag.

"This is great news, Charlene. You're finally leaving your shell."

I liked my shell very much. Besides, it was called a shell for a reason. Its purpose was to protect against the world.

"If that's the case, then why do I feel like throwing up?" I stopped with my endeavor to challenge her words.

And I wasn't exaggerating. Everything inside me was rebelling against this outing, including my digestive system.

"You're rusty, that's all."

"What do you mean?"

"You've forgotten what it's like to be around people, so now your body treats that as a threat. It will pass."

"Are you sure?"

"The same thing happened to me, but I'm confident it will pass once you meet him and start up a conversation. Trust me."

At least one of us is confident.

"So in order to stop this, I have to push through it?" I asked, needing to make sure I got that right. I couldn't say if this was my medication speaking, but that made perfect sense to me.

"Yes, you feel nervous now about the hypothetical, but it will all go away when you actually start socializing and dating. It's like riding a bike. You can never forget how to do that, not really. And you can never forget how to date."

I rolled my eyes although she couldn't see me. "Selina?"

"Yes."

"I don't know how to ride a bike. Besides, this is not a date."

"Call it whatever you like. Just don't try to lie to yourself."

"Lie to myself?"

"This gorgeous man is coming to pick you up and take you to dinner. That's a date."

"That's it, I'm calling it off."

"Don't you dare. This is good for you, so suck it up."

"Suck it up? That's your advice? Don't I have a say in this?" I argued.

"No, you don't. Not when you're acting all shades of unreasonable."

"I'm not ready for this, for any of it," I said, on the verge of tears.

"Charlene, if that's truly the case, then you would never have said yes in the first place," she pointed out.

"Dr. Neal pressured me," I defended, yet it was half-hearted at best. I couldn't blame her for everything.

"She what?"

"Yes, she was even online with me when I called him."

"I can't decide whether she's a crazy bitch or a genius."

"Selina, this is serious. It's too soon."

"No, it is not. Three years isn't soon."

"I am not ready," I repeated stubbornly.

"Look, Charlene, I know it's hard, and you can call him and cancel if you like, but I think that would be a mistake."

"Why?"

"Because I truly believe this will be a good thing for you. So try not to sabotage it simply because you're afraid."

I am not afraid. Well, I was, but only partly. I mostly felt guilty, like I was about to cheat on Christopher. It was ripping me apart. All the same, I couldn't ignore the fact that Selina had a point. Fear shouldn't rule me.

"I get what you're saying. I can't go against myself. But I'm not ready to date."

"You are too fixated on that word," Selina almost snapped in return. "There are all kinds of dates, not just romantic ones. So stop stressing about such nonsense and go, enjoy yourself for once."

"You really think I should?" I asked in a small voice.

"*Yes.*" She stressed the word. "Go out, spend some time

with him, have some delicious food, and have fun. You deserve it."

I sighed. "I know you're right."

"Hallelujah."

"But part of me still feels like I would be doing something wrong."

"That's all in your head. Try not to think too much."

I made a face. "Easier said than done," I deadpanned.

"I know. But for one night, put all your worries on pause."

Selina really did know me all too well. Nevertheless, despite all my craziness, her words worked.

I can do this.

"Okay. I will give this socializing a try," I tried to joke. "I will share a meal with him and try to have some fun."

Can you force someone into having fun?

"And after dinner, if you decide to bring him home, that's okay too," she added.

"Selina," I chastised.

"Okay, okay, I'm just saying. Seriously now, no one deserves happiness in life more than you."

That brought new tears to my eyes. "Thank you for saying that." I didn't even realize how much I needed to hear that.

Ironically, Dr. Neal had told me the very same thing, but it was different hearing all this from her. Or maybe I was simply weird that way.

Glancing at the clock, I jumped up to my feet. "Oh, crap," I exclaimed as my panic started to rise again, but from totally different reasons this time around.

"What is it?" Selina asked, matching my level of anxiety.

"Look how late it is, and I have no clue what to wear."

"Thank you, Lord. That was the reaction I was waiting for this entire day."

"Stop heckling me and help me."

Just because I was a basket case did not mean I wanted to

look like one. For some reason, I wanted to make a good impression on Samuel, and I couldn't do that while wearing my favorite bathrobe.

"Sure, let's switch to video call first."

Selina grinned at me as we did. "Now carry me to your closet so I can see what we're dealing with."

Without wasting any more time, I showed her some of my top choices.

"Oh, hell no. I put a veto on that shit," she said dramatically at some point as I showed her one of my favorite black dresses. It was an oldie but goodie.

"Why not? It's one of my favorites," I rebelled.

"You are not going to a funeral, that's why."

"Okay," I said slowly, putting the dress away.

"I'm sorry for saying that. It was stupid of me."

"Let's move on," I said in haste, not wanting to dwell on this.

"That, however, reminds me that we should definitely go shopping in the future."

"You don't live in New York, remember?"

"I will figure something out. You clearly need help."

"Ouch." I pretended to be hurt, and we both laughed.

"What do you think about this one?" I offered next.

"Let me see it on you."

Half an hour and dozens of combinations later, we settled on a choice we were both pretty happy with. In the end, I wore a pair of black slacks and a cream silk shirt.

"That looks great," Selina applauded. "It really complements your skin."

I had to agree. I was middle toned, which basically meant my skin always looked sun-kissed, which I loved. Although when I was younger, I avoided the sun like the plague, not wanting my skin to get any darker. I hated the idea that I would look any more like my father than I already did.

It took me years to stop hating the man I'd never met. Eventually, I got over it. I got over him. Perhaps that sounded hypocritical considering I'd accepted the inheritance he left me. It was the least he could have done for me, as far as I was concerned. I couldn't even say he was a shitty father since he was no father at all.

David was the only father I had ever known, and he was okay, although my mother had done her best to poison that relationship. He was a good guy but was easily swayed, so I never truly blamed him for always taking my mother's side.

"The only good thing I got from my dad," I joked, patting my arms. "That and the hair."

"Not to mention eight million dollars," Selina deadpanned.

At times, I regretted telling her that. She constantly made fun of me because of it.

"There's that too," I replied with a grin.

Selina returned us to the main topic, getting me ready.

"Wear those black shoes, let your hair down, and put some earrings on."

I complied without complaints.

"How's this?" I did a little twirl for the camera.

"For a non-date, you look amazing."

"Is it too much?"

"No," she replied immediately. "You look stunning."

I sat at my vanity, putting the phone against the mirror so I didn't have to hold it anymore. Selina could see me just fine.

"I'm scared," I confessed. *Is it too late to cancel?*

"Don't be. I mean, I know I was giving you a hard time earlier, but Samuel sounds like a great guy, and I honestly think he simply wants to get to know you a little bit better without any ulterior motives."

"Yeah, I think so too."

"And there's nothing wrong with that," she insisted.

I looked at the floor before saying, "I don't trust myself where he's concerned," in a small voice.

"What do you mean?"

"I feel like he's constantly pushing me outside my comfort zone."

"And?"

"And I specifically told myself I would never, ever go out with him, yet here I am."

Even before that, I didn't want to accept his friend request or chat with him, and then I ended up speaking over the phone with him. Despite my best efforts to keep everyone at arm's length, he found his way into my life. And that was terrifying.

Selina laughed at that.

"What are you laughing about?" I asked, a bit irked.

"I am laughing because everything you described is a good thing."

Now she sounded like Dr. Neal, and I really didn't need two of them in my life.

"Perhaps," I hedged. "It's just that I don't feel completely in control when with him."

If history served as any indication, I tended to act on impulse rather than think things over regarding Samuel. So far, nothing bad had happened, yet what if that changed?

"What if he manages to persuade me to do something reckless?" I asked. There was a possibility I was doing precisely what Selina advised me not to do, think too much, yet it couldn't be helped.

"Here you are, blowing things out of proportion again," she said, calling me out on my bullshit. "You really think too much."

"I'm serious," I insisted, mostly to save face since she was spot on and I didn't like it.

"So am I. Listen to yourself. That idea is ridiculous.

Samuel is not some criminal mastermind ready to get you, trying to manipulate you into doing nefarious things." She actually laughed saying all that, and then she grew serious again, probably because she saw the expression on my face.

I was not amused.

"You are the most cautious person I know, so you got this. Relax. Breathe."

I nodded, trying to do that. Something was pressing me in the chest area, and I ignored it. She was right. I was spiraling out of control without reason.

I offered a sheepish smile. "Thank you for putting up with me."

"Only because I love you." She blew me a kiss, and I did the same in return.

"Although this counseling shit will cost you a million dollars," she commented dryly, and we both laughed.

After she wished me luck, we ended the call. Both Dr. Neal and Selina were right. I was acting silly, to put it mildly. And over what? Over a single meal. However, talking about it really helped make me feel better.

Although some of the uneasiness crept back in as I was left to my own devices. Nevertheless, I was handling it like a pro.

Checking the time, my stomach did a little twirl. *He will be here soon.* And since my mouth felt a bit dry, I went to the kitchen to get a glass of water.

Everything will be all right. You've got this.

As I gave myself a little pep talk, my phone started ringing. Since it was my house phone, I made no gesture to get it. There was only one person who called me on my house phone, anyway. The answering machine took care of it.

Hello, Charlene, it's your mother.

Bingo. I couldn't suppress the urge to roll my eyes. *What does she want this time?*

Pick up the phone, Charlene. I know you're there.

Hearing her speak like that did wonders to my blood pressure. She'd used that tone frequently while I was growing up. It showed her deepest displeasure. Not that I gave a fuck these days.

I know you never leave that wretched place.

Wrong, Mother. I am about to leave right now.

So pick up this phone. She paused there, and I continued drinking my water.

Hell will freeze over before I do anything she wants of me.

Laura Corbett-Samson, also known as my mother, sighed deeply. *Very well, have it your way. I just called to inform you that David* (her husband and my stepdad) *needs hip replacement surgery. You know we don't have that kind of money, so I want you to pay for it.*

Of course you do, Mother.

You owe me that much.

That made me put the glass down on the counter with greater force than necessary. Owe her? *I owe her?*

Also, Lana (my half-sister) *told me you've been avoiding her calls as well. She needs your help, so try to behave like an older sister for once and be supportive.*

I gritted my teeth. Right then and there, I realized I'd heard enough. I would wait for Samuel outside.

My mother always did that, acted like she was the victim when all my life, she'd treated me like I ruined her life simply by being born out of wedlock. *Well, sorry, Mom. You were stupid enough to get pregnant by a married man.* How was that my fault?

And the fact that I got money from my father when she

got jack shit only deepened this animosity she nurtured toward me.

Without hearing any more of her nonsense, I left the house. I would much rather spend my evening with a nice man than listen to my mother's angry antics. I was sure David was fine. This was yet another ruse my mother had come up with to get money from me. It wouldn't be the first time. So I'd learned not to trust anything that came out of that woman's mouth.

Oh, he's here. I was taken aback for a second, noticing a car in my driveway.

All thoughts were banished from my head as I saw Samuel waiting for me, leaning against his car.

And then he smiled.

Oh, crap . . .

7

Approaching Samuel very slowly, I realized how all my previous worries were ridiculous. Selina would probably slap me for that since she had been trying to point that out the whole day. What could I say? I was a slow learner.

It would be an understatement to say Samuel looked better in person than in his photographs, although I couldn't believe something like that was possible.

A cynical person would probably say he looked heavily photoshopped in those images, but now I knew better. The images did not do him justice. He was sporting a slight tan as though he'd just returned from some tropical destination, and the highlights in his hair supported that theory. His eyes were so sky blue one could get lost in their vastness.

Naturally, I got irked by my own thoughts. So what if he was pretty? That was not why I agreed to meet him. I liked to talk to him, and I hoped that would not change now that we were face-to-face.

I came to stand in front of him. I was glad I'd decided to

wear heels since he was really tall and muscular, broad shouldered. That was obvious through his sport jacket.

"Charlene, finally," he greeted as his smile grew bigger. And instead of offering me his hand, he kissed me on the cheek.

It all happened so fast I was stunned for a second.

"You look lovely," he complimented.

"So do you," I said in return, recovering.

"These are for you." He offered me a big bouquet of flowers. *Wow,* I was so focused on his face I hadn't even realized he was holding those.

"Thank you. That's very kind of you."

I put my nose to them and was not disappointed. The flowers were an exotic mix of colors and fragrances. The main colors consisted of big violet, purple, blue, and pink flowers, which were all of unknown origin to me, coupled with a hint of orange and white blooms. The end result was beyond beautiful. And I was sure it cost a fortune. The only flowers I did manage to recognize in all that splendor were small violet orchids.

Christopher had bought me potted orchids once, and I'd managed to kill them in a matter of weeks. Taking care of plants was definitely not my thing.

"Are you ready to go?"

I nodded, and he opened the door for me.

For a moment, I worried it would be a tight fit inside the car, but as it turned out, there was plenty of room inside the luxury vehicle.

He entered the address in the GPS app.

I looked at him questioningly. Didn't he know where we were going?

"I usually don't like driving around town in the evenings, but I figured you would appreciate some privacy," he explained.

That was very thoughtful of him. "It is better this way," I agreed. I was already nervous about this dinner thing; adding another stranger into the mix would definitely be too much for me.

"I knew that would be the case, and that is why I expect you to take full responsibility if we get lost." Although he managed to remain straight-faced, I knew he was joking.

"Noted," I countered with a smile.

"While I try to appear all manly and in control, check this out," he said, offering me his phone. "Go to the gallery."

I did as he asked.

"Open the last image."

I did and then had to smile again.

"It came in this morning," he explained.

It was a lovely painting of a dancer. Although I tried to zoom it in, I still couldn't see all the details, and that was a misfortune. I would really like to see it in person because it was something else. And that made me realize that although the style looked rather familiar, I couldn't recognize the painter.

"Who's the artist?" I asked, genuinely curious.

Samuel half-shrugged. "Your guess is as good as mine."

"You don't know? How's that possible?"

"The owner died, and the bank liquidated all his assets, including this painting. My associate saw it at an auction in London last month and bought it for me."

"Wasn't there a certificate of authenticity?"

"Apparently not."

"And you still bought it?" My meaning was obvious. This painting, no matter how beautiful, could be pretty worthless or, worse, stolen, which could bring all kinds of hassle to Samuel.

"I liked it; I wanted it. End of story."

I could only stare at him. To him, it was as simple as that.

I would have to remember that and apply it in my life every once in a while.

"Do you think it could be one of Degas's missing paintings?" I asked, feeling silly for even saying something like that out loud.

"Not really. However, it would be a funny story if we could authenticate it in some way."

Funny wouldn't be the word I would use to describe such a situation. It would be monumental, groundbreaking.

"Do you like it?" he asked me in return.

"Yes, very much."

I enlarged it one more time, really trying to picture all the details.

Inside a delicate-looking frame was a painting of a young woman doing a grand jeté. She was in a blue dress, and there was an expression of such tranquility on her face, as though in that precise place, while in midair, she felt the most at ease.

I would like to get a chance to see this painting in person yet did not voice my desire. I did not want to presume too much. Besides, this was Samuel's job, and it would be rude of me to butt in, in any way.

Quite suddenly, I realized I couldn't fully concentrate on the painting because I was very much aware of the gorgeous smell inside the car. And I wasn't talking about the flowers. It was all Samuel. He smelled good. That was definitely one of the things his online pictures didn't provide.

"Are you feeling all right?" he inquired in concern.

"Yes," I said, forcing a smile.

"I think you made a sound investment with this painting," I said simply to say something.

"You do?"

I nodded.

"How much money would you offer for it?" he asked, taking me by surprise.

"To buy it?" I asked for clarification.

"No, hypothetically, but I wouldn't say no if you made me a real offer," he added with a wink.

Always working, I see.

"How much did you pay for it?" I asked instead.

He shook his head. "That would be cheating."

"I don't know. I'm not an appraisal specialist," I answered.

"Give me your best shot," he insisted.

There were so many different variables in play here that I shouldn't have said anything, but I wanted to indulge him.

"Well, if it's from a well-established painter, which we already ruled out . . ." I added, looking at him.

"If we didn't," he interjected.

"Then millions would be at play."

"And if it isn't?"

Unlike my former boss, I truly believed there was no such thing as a worthless piece of art. There was a right audience for everything. "It could still sell for a lot of money with the right crowd, at the right auction. You probably know better than me how unpredictable those things can get."

"Right. I thought so too." And then he added, "So are you interested in purchasing this lovely painting?" he teased.

"Perhaps," I replied in the same manner.

"Excellent. However, I do have to warn you the price is going to be pretty steep."

"How steep?"

"It might cost you another dinner with me."

I laughed. "Let's see how this night goes first."

I handed the phone back to him. We chatted for a bit more as we pulled in front of a restaurant. A man in a blue and gold uniform opened the door for me and offered a hand to get out of the car, which took me by surprise. As Samuel got out as well, he handed the car keys to him, and the helpful man drove the car away, probably to some back-alley parking garage.

Fancy.

Samuel offered me his arm, and together, we walked inside. The restaurant was called Lacy's, and I felt like we'd just stepped into some twenties speakeasy kind of establishment. Everything looked so glamorous. A hostess in a stunning black dress greeted us.

"Good evening, Mr. Northman. Your usual table is ready," she told him.

"Thank you," he countered before she escorted us to our table.

I noted how she mentioned he was a regular here. I liked the idea that he brought me to his favorite place.

There was a big bar at the far right and a small stage right in the middle of the room with a piano on it. The pianist was playing a tune I didn't quite recognize, yet it fit perfectly with the theme.

"Allow me," Samuel offered, pulling a chair for me.

"This place looks amazing," I told him as I settled.

"I'm glad it's up to your standards," Samuel said as he took his seat, flashing a smile at me. "I was worried you wouldn't like it."

"Are you kidding me? I love the theme. It's like nothing I've ever seen."

It felt like we'd time traveled. If the food was half as good as the ambience, then I would leave this place a happy person.

"I'm sure that's not true," Samuel countered.

Was he thinking I was placating him? I didn't have the chance to reply since he continued, "You must be used to a rather posh life."

What? "What gave you that impression?" I asked with a smile.

He looked at me as though confused, which confused me in return. There was a lot of confusion flying around the table.

"Well, aren't you?" He gestured at me with both his hands as though that alone was explanation enough.

"No." I emphasized with a shake of my head. "That's the furthest from the truth, actually."

"Really?"

"Yeah. I was raised by a single mother who barely finished high school, and when I was eight, she married a healthcare lawyer. We did all right, but I would not call us posh."

Samuel frowned at my words. "I distinctly remember you saying something about being a trust fund brat."

I chuckled. "No, that must have been someone else you were chatting with. I did come into some money two years ago, an inheritance if you will, but that didn't change my lifestyle."

"Oh? That's interesting. I must say you have a lovely home. You live alone?"

"Yes. My late husband and I bought it years ago."

"I see. I'm sorry for your loss."

"Thank you." I pushed the thought of Christopher out of my head. I couldn't think about him while I was out with another man. It didn't seem right. I could think about him later, after I returned home. I turned my thoughts back to the house and the money I'd inherited from my father's death two years ago. That money had allowed me to pay off the mortgage in full and had given me one less thing to worry about.

"You know, I've always wondered about houses like yours. Do they come with big gardens and pools?" he inquired.

I giggled at the thought. "Not really. I have a small garden, and I don't use it."

"Shame," he said, making a face. "Gardening is my favorite hobby."

"On the other hand, I could kill a rock," I joked.

Samuel leaned backward in his chair, looking at me, assessing, as though I were a puzzle he didn't know how to solve. Yet before I could become uncomfortable, he said, "So no green thumb for you?" He chuckled. "Do you have a gardener, then?"

I shook my head and grinned. "Nope, just me."

"No?" He looked at me curiously. "You have no staff or cook or even a chauffeur? Just you in that house and that's all?" He seemed incredulous at that thought.

His tone was light, but I started to suspect something else was going on and began to get uncomfortable. Then again, this wasn't something I liked talking about, so it might be my nerves making me crazy.

"I don't like being surrounded by strangers. Besides, I like doing things on my own. I love to drive, and cleaning helps me clear my head."

"I'm going to guess that you are an amazing cook." He smiled, his eyes twinkling at me.

I shook my head. "Nope, not at all. That's why God invented takeout and delivery." I grinned.

He chuckled. "You are one peculiar woman, Charlene Bell."

"Thank you?" I didn't know why it came out like a question. Probably because I had no idea why he was giving me this compliment. If it was a compliment in the first place.

"It's just that you are not what I expected at all," he explained.

"What did you expect?" I asked curiously.

"I suppose I assumed you would be a bit wild, not that I'm

not pleased with how you actually are," he quickly assured me.

I shrugged. "I was never the wild type."

"I can see that." He smiled. "So tell me more about you. Are there places you want to visit? I mean, you've got the money now, right? You should take advantage of it."

I didn't look at things that way, so I shook my head. "I've done some, but right now there's no place I want to go and nothing I want or need."

"Oh, I don't believe that for a second. Everybody wants something."

"Not me."

He sighed. "That makes me so sad to hear. Let's move on to some other topic," he announced.

Was it my imagination, or did he look slightly disappointed by what he'd discovered? It was probably just me, my nerves getting the better of me, since talking about my past or money was making me uncomfortable. Then again, it was for the best that he heard all that. How I was nothing more than a shell of a woman. My spark was gone, so I was simply biding time on this earth now and nothing more.

"I bet you regard money differently from me," I said simply to keep the ball rolling. "I bet you surround yourself with all kinds of staff members," I joked, putting him in the spotlight for a change.

He flashed me a smile. "Of course. I could not imagine my life without my food taster."

"Food taster?" I repeated, shocked. "Are you afraid of being poisoned?" That notion frightened me. Why would he feel like that? Was someone threatening him? I didn't know being an importer was such a risky business.

"That was a joke, Charlene."

"Oh." I smiled, feeling embarrassed that I didn't immediately catch that. "That was funny."

He chuckled. "I can see that. But all joking aside, I too had to climb my way from humble roots."

That was far more impressive than my story. I had been handed the money. He'd earned his.

I said as much. "And you made it," I added.

"Yes, I did. And let me tell you one thing."

I leaned slightly forward as though he was about to share some big secret with me or impart some timeless wisdom.

"After experiencing all that, pawing my way from nothing to everything, I will do absolutely all in my power to always remain at the top. The view is much nicer up here," he said with a wink.

8

I was about to reply to Samuel's heartfelt revelation when a waiter approached us. "Are you ready to order?"

I made a guilty face, only then realizing I hadn't even looked at the menu since sitting down.

"Could you give us five more minutes?" Samuel asked.

The waiter nodded, moving away.

"We're being rude," I commented, picking up the big book of a menu, trying to see what I wanted to eat.

"Don't worry about it," he countered in reassurance.

"So what do you recommend?" Since I figured he'd dined here many times, he probably went through most of the dishes, if not all of them.

"What do you like? Poultry, fish, red meat?" he asked in return.

"Well, I'm not a meat person, but I love fish."

"In that case, try the smoked salmon. It's a life-changer."

Since I liked his description, I decided to go with his recommendation.

When the waiter returned, I ordered salmon with some

side vegetables, and Samuel stuck to the basics and got himself a steak.

That was probably what Christopher would have ordered too. I always thought that man was allergic to any kinds of vegetables, most of the fruits too. He was a carnivore through and through.

Samuel ordered us wine as well. I knew nothing about it, but he swore it would complement my meal, so I went with it. It had been a while since I drank alcohol, and I figured one glass wouldn't kill me.

Wait, should I mix alcohol with those pills Dr. Neal gave me? I was betting the answer was a resounding no, so I stopped myself altogether. The last thing I wanted was to make a fool of myself.

During dinner, I was further reassured that my worries regarding Samuel were completely unfounded. Samuel and I chatted pretty much in the same manner we had earlier over the phone. Nothing changed, but this was slightly better since I could now see all his facial expressions and the emotions behind each sentence very clearly.

As always, he entertained me with some funny anecdotes.

"So there I was, starting a meeting without my translator, who lay in bed from food poisoning, trying to close a deal with this very important Chinese businessman who didn't understand a word of English."

"What did you do?" I urged, overly invested in this story that was already nerve-racking up to that point, with lots of unexpected hiccups, to not use harsher words.

Samuel rubbed his forehead as though in embarrassment before replying, "I did what I felt I had to do. I started gesticulating with my hands, trying to mimic words while talking really slowly, all the while praying with all my might that the other man understood something, anything of it."

I could picture that scene in my head perfectly, and it was hard not to laugh.

"Did he?"

Samuel nodded. "Mr. Liang asked me in perfect English if I was having some kind of seizure and would I require medical assistance."

I started laughing so hard my stomach hurt. "How is that possible?" I managed to say through the cackles.

"As it turned out, the businessman I was supposed to meet sent his oldest son instead, who finished Oxford. Unfortunately for me, nobody bothered to tell me that before I completely made a fool out of myself."

I felt sorry for Samuel, but I still couldn't stop laughing. It was simply too funny. "I'm sorry for laughing."

"Don't be. I looked like a complete ass."

"Did you get the contract?" I asked, hoping there was a happy ending to this story.

"Yes. I don't know how, but I managed to save face after that unfortunate incident."

Samuel was full of stories, and I was surprised by how much I liked to listen to them.

Our dinner came to an end in no time.

"Would you care for some dessert?" Samuel asked me at some point.

"No, thank you. I'm full."

He was right. The smoked fish was to die for. I wondered if this place did deliveries.

"Right. Let us go, then."

After he took care of the bill, which he insisted on paying because he asked me to dinner, we stepped outside.

It was still pretty early, and although I didn't want to admit it, not even to myself, I didn't want this night to end so soon. Despite myself, I was having fun, and it felt nice. As we waited for the car to be brought to us, Samuel turned to look at me.

"After dinner, I was planning on taking you dancing," he shared.

"Dancing?"

"Yes. There's a great club I stumbled upon by chance. It's nearby, and Cuban bands are playing live music."

I instantly put two and two together. "Oh, you mean salsa dancing?"

He nodded. "Do you dance salsa?"

"No," I replied, wearing a nervous smile, "and before you say anything else, let me confess that I would be too embarrassed to even try." Especially in a club full of dancers.

Samuel simply nodded. "Say no more. We'll go to the theater, then."

That honestly surprised me. I was sure he would insist, then be disappointed when I continued to say no and simply take me back home. I was sure he would pout that I ruined his plans for the evening, yet instead of that, he completely turned around and went with it, adapted.

He actually listened to me and came up with an alternative, which I appreciated. I didn't know a lot of men who were capable of something like that. And that was not the cynic in me speaking or anything like that. That was an opinion based on personal dating experience and the experiences of a lot of my friends.

I was really touched that he was prepared for something like that. *I guess he really wants this night to keep going.*

To be absolutely honest, I couldn't say how that made me feel. Obviously, I was touched, pleasantly surprised, and I was flattered too for sure that he saw me worthy of putting forth any effort. Especially since I was having fun with him. At the same time, I was additionally having all these negative emotions as well. I felt extremely guilty, sporadically sad, and afraid of what all this meant.

Stop it, Charlene. Stay in the moment. Enjoy this, I snapped at myself, realizing I was doing precisely what Selina told me not to do, overthinking things. Besides, this was no time for analyzing anything. I would have plenty of time for that during my scheduled therapy session. For tonight, my only task was to socialize. *Plain and simple.*

Once again, we were riding in the car. Samuel continued to be very attentive, asking me if I was warm enough, would I like to listen to some music, and things like that.

"Pick any radio station you'd like."

"I don't listen to the radio much," I confessed. "However, I have my playlist with me."

"Play whatever you like."

After connecting my phone with the car's sound system, I put some Billie Holiday on.

"Really?" he asked while raising an eyebrow.

"You don't like it?"

"No, no, it's not that. I just didn't peg you as a jazz fan."

"Why not?"

"I didn't mean anything bad by it. You are a woman of many wonders."

"That I am."

"So I am starting to gather. And for the record, I love Billie too."

I grinned. For some reason, that made me pleased.

After I realized we were going in circles, I said, "Are we lost?"

"Oh, buggers," he snapped. "I was sure the theater was right here. But for some reason, I can't seem to find it," he confessed.

"For a person living in Manhattan, you are tragically bad at orientation."

"I know. Even perfect people are allowed some flaws."

"True," I agreed before continuing, "Turn on that street, then make a left."

He glanced at me really quickly. "Did you know where it was the whole time?"

I nodded.

"And you remained quiet trying to protect my masculinity?"

"I didn't know that was our destination," I hedged.

He knew I was being kind. "Well, thank you for that," he said while smiling.

I smiled as well.

Shortly after that, we managed to reach the movie theater without further delays.

We both looked at the list of movies available at the moment and spent a couple of minutes going through it.

"Do you have any preferences?" Samuel asked, breaking the silence.

I wasn't familiar with any of the titles, so it was pretty much all the same to me. But I did feel the need to put a veto on certain genres.

"I don't like romance movies."

Those types of movies, especially of the romantic comedy variety, simply rubbed me the wrong way every time. They always ended after the boy and a girl got together. That wasn't how real life worked. That wasn't the end but a beginning.

Sadly, they never wanted to show what happened afterward. What happened when the boy died, robbing the girl of her happily ever after? Was I reading too much into it? Absolutely. But it couldn't be helped.

"Noted," Samuel replied, unaware of my small mental rant. "How about that one?" he offered after a small pause. "It's a comedy."

I read the short description. Two grandfathers were trying to save their grandchild from some mischief. Apparently, big names in Hollywood decided to star in it, so that piqued my interest.

"Okay," I replied, but apparently, Samuel wasn't too convinced about it.

"We can go and see something else if you prefer it," he offered.

"No, this one looks interesting."

"Then it's settled. Oh, shoot, it starts in five minutes. We'd better hurry," he said in haste before grabbing my arm. We started running toward the box office so we could get the tickets. After paying for them, Samuel ushered us toward the right hall.

The lights were already off.

"Let's be rebellious," he whispered to me as we sat in some random seats. As it turned out, we could sit wherever we pleased because the room was completely empty. We were the only two people inside.

Where were all the people? Did people still go to the movies, or was it all Netflix and chill these days?

Samuel figured out we were alone at the same time I did.

"What do you say to this?" he said louder than he would have if there were other spectators present.

"It's pretty cool that you managed to arrange a private screening for us," I teased, playing along.

"I am rather resourceful."

After a fifteen-minute-long commercial intro, the movie finally started. During the movie, I was able to discover yet another trait of Samuel's. He was a chatterer. He liked to speak during the movie, but I didn't mind.

It wasn't anything overwhelming or tiring. It was simply that every once in a while, he would lean closer to say something funny into my ear. It was true we were alone, but I still appreciated that he didn't yell against the movie. Those small tidbits about him made the experience even more enjoyable and the movie funnier.

Afterward, we went to have some coffee.

Once again, I ordered myself some espresso. I had no idea why it tasted so much better when someone else made it for me as opposed to my preparing it at home. *Maybe I'm doing something wrong?* Although I couldn't see how something like that was possible. Those things were pretty user-friendly, with no room for major mistakes. *Yet here I am.*

"That was rather an enjoyable movie," Samuel commented, snapping me from my thoughts.

"It was good, funny."

"I loved the bit about the cat," he provided.

And I chuckled. "That was some good comedy, pure."

I hated when things turned too banal. There was something to be said about subtlety.

"I agree. The screenwriters and the rest did a fine job."

"Thank you for taking me to see it. I can't remember when the last time I went to the movies was."

Or watched a movie in general. These days, my TV simply stood in the living room, collecting dust.

It was probably used last when Christopher was around. He was probably the person I saw the last movie with as well.

And all that was changing now. I was starting to do things without him. And part of me really hated that.

"Well, I am pleased you enjoyed yourself."

I nodded and yawned at the same time. "Sorry."

"That is my cue to take you home."

"Please don't read too much into it," I was quick to reassure him. "It's not that I'm bored or anything like that."

He offered a reassuring smile in return, patting my hand. I wanted to move it out of his reach, but I didn't.

"I understand completely, but you do look a bit tired, so please allow me to escort you back home."

What could I possibly say to that? "Okay."

I teased him ever so slightly for not entering my address into the GPS app as we sat in the car.

"If you are doing that for my benefit, don't. I would much rather have us get there than have you struggle to recollect the way." *And get lost in the process* was heavily implied.

He gave me a look. "I got this."

And I laughed. He joined in.

A very short ride later, we arrived in front of my house. I expected that we would say our goodbyes there, but he exited the car to help me get out, then carried the flowers for me up the steps.

And then I started to panic.

Did he want to be invited inside? Did he expect that? Did I give the wrong impression that sex was on the table?

And then I ran out of time because we reached my front door. Luckily, he solved this conundrum for me.

"I had a lovely time with you tonight."

"Me too," I replied and honestly meant it.

I was close to tears only once while thinking of Christopher, which was huge progress.

"I hope you will consider doing this again with me sometime."

"Sure," I blurted out before I even realized what I'd just agreed to.

Samuel kissed me on the cheek again, handing me the flowers.

"Good night, Charlene." And with that, he turned away and walked back toward his car.

"Night," I mumbled after him.

The smell of his cologne lingered in the air as I watched him drive away.

This was some strange night. This day was full of events, actually, but this was the one that caused the biggest impact on me.

In a dazed state, I walked inside my house. As I took care of the flowers, putting them in a nice vase and placing them in the living room in the most visible place, I tried to sum up my feelings.

Despite all my craziness, I honestly had a great time with Samuel. For a while, I was happy, which in turn made me sad.

I am so fucked up.

Before going to bed, I sent a text to Selina, simply to inform her how it all went.

"Dinner and a movie non-date just ended. He was a perfect gentleman. I survived." I added a few smiley faces before hitting *Send*.

And then I washed my face, brushed my teeth, and prayed to the heavens I didn't really believe in anymore that I would get a chance to dream about my love.

Things took an unexpected turn when I dreamed about Samuel instead.

9

"I am very proud of you," Dr. Neal said to me at some point during our session once I told her about my evening with Samuel. "You demonstrated immense progress, and not only that, but you're also finally showing willingness and motivation to do the work in these last couple of weeks," she observed.

That was all thanks to Samuel. I was aware of that. Without him in my life, I wouldn't be able to do anything.

I had a strange, almost out-of-body experience listening to my therapist praise me in such a manner. First time in history, I might add.

One could imagine I was a pro athlete or something who just won a gold medal, hearing Dr. Neal go on and on about my accomplishments. And not a regular person who went on a damn dinner with a friend. All the same, I didn't interrupt her because it still felt nice to hear. I did something out of character, and my leap was monumental since those were the depths of my issues, making this an impressive achievement.

Perhaps to someone looking from the outside in, that would look like nothing special, but it was to me.

I was a woman who completely stopped going outside, stopped interacting with other people because the pain of loss was too great, something I couldn't bear. And by some miracle, here I was, starting to get out of my shell again.

A miracle named Samuel.

I rolled my eyes at that last thought. I wasn't about to mystify my relationship with Samuel. He was a good man who simply reminded me that there were two sides to the coin, and nothing more. Yes, there was pain and suffering in this world. And there was joy and happiness as well. *You just have to dig a little deeper to find it.*

All the same, despite what Dr. Neal was saying, despite the fact that she was beyond pleased, secretly patting herself on the back for my admirable progress, I had mixed feelings about the whole thing.

I was no idiot. On one hand, I recognized that things were starting to change in my life. On the other, I wasn't one hundred percent sure that was a good thing.

Then why did you start therapy in the first place? Because at the time, I felt like I had no other choice. My mother was trying her hardest to take all my money, and despite my grief, I wasn't about to let her do that. Yet almost a year later, the therapy finally started to make some sense to me, and that was terrifying.

I could, on a more rational level, acknowledge that all was well, except I had deep concerns about what this would all mean in the long run.

Would I in the future manage to leave the house every day, go to work, maybe even have a family with someone else? No matter how all that sounded, normal, perfect, it made me want to throw up.

Part of me wanted to move on with my life and be happy again, but at what cost was that achievable? If letting go of Christopher was that price, I was not ready to pay it. I couldn't lose him twice. That would kill me, I was sure of that.

And I could say with utmost certainty that I would never be able to fully let go of my husband or forget him.

I just hoped Dr. Neal was aware of that. I didn't want her to get her hopes up. No matter what was happening at the moment, I was permanently broken. Part of me was missing, and although I was sure I could achieve some level of normalcy, it would never be the same as before.

"How do you feel about it?" she asked me, snapping me from my musings. I tried my best to articulate all my feelings. That was exactly what I had been thinking, analyzing since I returned home from that dinner last night.

"I feel torn, conflicted."

Dr. Neal nodded as though she expected to hear something like that from me. That gave me the confidence to continue.

"I had a lovely time with him. It was comfortable, easy."

It was a shock how good it felt to be in his company.

"Did you think about Christopher?"

I nodded.

She probed for details. "How did that make you feel? Did you feel pain?"

"It did make me feel sad, but I didn't feel the unbearable pain," I replied honestly.

"Why did you feel sad?"

I half-shrugged. "I was doing something without him. I was unable to share my happiness with him. And that made me feel guilty." No matter how crazy it sounded.

"Guilty for experiencing life? Having fun?"

"Yes."

"We talked about this before," Dr. Neal reminded me, but there was no reprimand in her voice.

I nodded. I knew this was called survivor's guilt. Dr. Neal

told me all about it, but that alone never stopped me from experiencing it.

"I don't know how to stop feeling like this." I didn't know if I wanted to. This was my last thread connecting me to Christopher. Did I really want to sever that? Could I?

That would make me feel all alone.

You are already alone.

"You loved Christopher very much."

"I still do," I corrected.

"I apologize. And he loved you."

"Of course," I replied, not even having to think about it. That was obvious in everything he did. In that way, we were always well-matched. That was probably the reason living without him was so damn hard.

"Do you think he would want you to be happy, even if it meant living without him?" she challenged.

I remained silent. Why was she asking me that all of a sudden?

"Let me ask you this. If he were still alive and you were having a bad day, would Christopher do everything in his power to help you try to solve your problem, cheer you up?" she questioned.

"Yes, of course."

"And if he was not around, would he still want you to receive help from others? Would he be happy knowing you were left alone to your own devices?"

Now I could see where all this was going. That was why I said, "Christopher loved me enough to want me to be happy no matter what. Of course he would prefer I was surrounded by friends and family."

Unfortunately, in my case, family was a synonym for enemies, so I couldn't really expect any kind of help from them.

You can create your own family. I could almost hear Christopher's voice saying that.

"What do you think he would say upon seeing you like this?"

I took a deep breath before replying, "It would break his heart seeing me this sad about him, unable to move on." He wouldn't want that for me.

"And if roles were reversed, would you want him to be caged inside your house for years, alone?"

Just thinking about it caused me immense pain.

"No, of course not. But it's not the same."

"How come?"

"I deserve to be punished for what I did. I'm the reason he died."

"No, you are not. And you have to stop blaming yourself. Charlene, you are not this omnipotent being. You had no control over that night. What happened was a tragedy and nothing more."

I started to cry. "I just miss him so much."

"I know."

I really needed that cry. It felt different from all the previous times. It was as though this cry was purifying. I was not letting go of Christopher, I would never allow that, but I was trying to wash away all the guilt I had felt for so long.

Christopher died because a man tried to rob us. He had been impatient that we were taking too long giving him our money, and then something spooked him, and he reacted. It was a tragedy. And I spent so many hours thinking about it, coming up with all the ways that scene could have been prevented. Yet the truth was, nobody knew the future. Nobody could say he wouldn't still have died even if we didn't go out to dinner that night. And that was the hardest thing to accept.

Some things were inevitable, out of our control. And

although it was heartbreaking, that was something I would have to live with for the rest of my life.

Dr. Neal really gave me something to think about. And that I did.

I'd always believed I was expressing my love toward Christopher by keeping his memory alive, mourning him to this day, but I was wrong. I was only punishing myself because of all the guilt I was feeling. And instead of doing all of this, mourning him, shrouding myself in darkness, sorrow, and pain, I should have been celebrating him and our life together.

I knew this was all easier said than done, but I vowed to myself that from now on, I would try to honor him by doing all the things we didn't get to do together. I alone would be trying to lead a happy life for both of us. Thinking about all that brought fresh tears to my eyes. But I wasn't sad, not completely at least.

I love you, Christopher, I sent to the heavens. *I always will.*

Simply because I had this little breakthrough, I wasn't magically cured. I wasn't all that much better. This would take a while to sink in. I wanted to be better, for Christopher, for myself, but I didn't know if I could.

Despite the monumental aha moment, I felt conflicted. And I was aware that was something I would have to work on in the days to come. Luckily, I had a rock star of a therapist to help me on my journey.

Selina was also of great help to me on my journey to overcome this deep sadness that coated my heart and soul. She tried to help me sort through the maze of my emotions to get to the truth.

Before we started analyzing all my feelings, she wanted to know every single detail about the dinner, and I was more than happy to oblige.

She demanded a video chat the instant I sent her that

text, but I'd already gone to bed, so we did that the very next day over breakfast.

She did not look happy when I called her. Irritated would be a better description. "You cannot send me something like that, girl, then ignore my texts," she accused.

"Sorry, I fell asleep."

"*I survived*?" She continued as though I'd said nothing. "What the hell does that mean?"

"I thought that in a positive way," I replied, making a guilty face, only now realizing how stupid my message was. "I survived. You know. Nothing bad happened."

She shook her head. "It's a good thing you are not a writer or something because you would needlessly emotionally scar a lot of people," she commented.

And I completely deserved that.

"I'm sorry. I didn't mean to freak you out."

"You're forgiven, but only if you tell me everything that happened last night."

She didn't have to tell me twice. I'd wanted to speak about it with someone from the moment I opened my eyes. Someone other than Dr. Neal. I would much rather speak with my friend than with my therapist. Selina wouldn't make me dissect each emotion.

First of all, I showed her the flowers, and she acted accordingly.

"They must have cost him a fortune," she commented.

"My thoughts exactly," I replied, grinning. "And they smell divine."

"I can imagine."

Then I proceeded to tell her everything about what we did. I even mentioned the part that confused me the most—where Samuel had all those misconceptions about me.

"You know, I told him about my inheritance, and he saw

the house, but I guess he assumed I was a bit of a snob or something."

"What? You?" Selina shook her head.

"I don't know, he seemed shocked that I didn't live like some kind of royalty with a chauffeur, gardener, and cook."

Selina waved it off. "Maybe that's what he thinks all rich people do. We all have prejudices, Charlene, but it's good you set him straight and showed him you aren't like that."

That is a good point. I said as much. "Still, I wonder what made him think that I was like that, you know?"

"Rich guys like him are all the same. He assumed you have the money and live in a certain way because he does," Selina provided.

"Maybe," I muttered in return. That was as good an explanation as any. *Am I doing now to him what he did to me, assuming things?* That was a good point as well, but I decided this wasn't something I should bang my head about. I did tell him I preferred to do things for myself and that I don't buy what I don't want or need. If he couldn't understand that, then that was on him.

We moved on, and eventually, I came to the end of the date. "He was a perfect gentleman," I said, wearing a small smile. "He kissed me on the cheek before wishing me a good night."

"Did he call you afterward?"

"He sent me a text an hour ago saying how he had a lovely time with me last night."

"That's great, Charlene."

It was great because I felt the same way. We did have a lovely time, and part of me wished we could repeat that experience. Although I didn't want to push for another date. No matter what, I still didn't want to give him false hope. And if I acted too eager, then he would definitely assume I was interested in him as a man.

Are you? I banished that immediately. I was not ready for that deep dive.

Some kind of strange optimism continued to hold me even after I finished my conversation with Selina.

A couple of days later, after my session with Dr. Neal ended, I noticed I had a missed call from Samuel. Wiping the remaining tears from my face, I immediately dialed him back.

"Hello, Charlene," he greeted in his usual manner.

"Hi, Samuel. My phone was off, so I didn't hear your call," I explained, not wanting him to think I was blowing him off.

"I see. Is everything all right? You sound a bit off."

My voice did sound a bit off, and that was due to all the crying. Since I didn't want to tell the truth, I opted for something else. "Busted. I just woke up." I lied like a pro.

He chuckled. "The carefree life of an heiress," he teased.

"That's true."

And we both laughed.

"Did you need anything?" I asked once we settled.

"Well, I was wondering, since we had such a lovely time together the other day, when I can see you again?" he asked, all hopeful.

"I'm free this weekend," I replied too quickly, too eagerly.

Truth be told, I was free every day, the weekend included, but I didn't want to appear too desperate. I guess that ship sailed with my reply.

He didn't seem to mind. More to the point, he sounded happy. "Excellent." And there was a smile in his voice.

I smiled too.

"I will let you know about the details."

"I can't wait," I murmured, and that was no lie.

10

On Saturday, Samuel took me horseback riding. When he first suggested something like that to me, my whole body rebelled, and I wanted to say no to him. I loved animals, but the notion of riding a horse left me in a state of panic. Even when I was in Egypt with Christopher, I refused to ride a camel.

I shouldn't live in the past and let past experiences govern me. I'd already done that plenty, and what did it bring me? Nothing good.

Based on our previous experiences, I knew Samuel wouldn't take offense no matter what I said. Even if I declined, he would simply change plans. However, I didn't want to be that person who always says no to him, to everything he was suggesting, and why? Because of fear. So instead, I decided to get over myself and said yes.

Samuel looked excited for our outing when he came to pick me up, which made me feel excited in return.

Today is going to be a happy day.

He took me to a ranch, a riding school owned by one of his friends. It was an hour's ride outside the city, and the time flew by on our way there as Samuel and I chatted about everything and nothing in particular.

The place was amazing. There were a lot of horses milling around the land as others were trained by professional trainers and riders.

"Do they compete as well?" I asked.

"I believe so."

Samuel introduced me to Tom. He was something like a foreman on that ranch. He was pretty much in charge of everything.

After they gave me an outfit to change into, complete with a pair of riding boots that fit me like a glove, I spent the next hour and a half, maybe more, getting to know a couple of horses. I was encouraged to pet them, take care of them, and basically get used to them while they did the same with me.

One of the horses, a silverish-gray thoroughbred named Dimple, lightened up when he spotted Samuel. They were clearly buddies.

After enough time passed, Tom deemed me ready to try to ride one of the horses. I tried not to be too freaked out by that since horses could sense fear, anxiety, and so on.

So I used all the techniques Dr. Neal taught me to try to remain calm. This was supposed to be fun, after all, and I didn't want to blow it by having a panic attack or something.

Tom decided the most docile mare on the ranch should be my partner for the day. Her name was Bella, and she really was that. She was black and white, with her head completely black, and her tail as well. Everything else was snow white.

"You are doing splendidly," Samuel complimented as Tom led Bella out of the barn while I was riding her.

"Thanks," I replied sheepishly.

Naturally, I was riding her in name only since Tom was actually walking her around, but I was not complaining. For the first time, this was precisely what I needed. Anything more and I would definitely get overwhelmed. Although I felt like a toddler being led around the tracks, we did a couple of rounds. Bella was a true sport, walked at a steady, slow pace, and after a while, I found myself relaxing completely.

"How do you fancy it?" Samuel wanted to know.

In truth, I was a little jealous of his skills. Next to me, he was a freaking professional, and he looked so natural, so relaxed on horseback. Not to mention, he looked so damn regal.

I definitely fancied what I saw in front of me.

Focus.

"It's great," I replied simply. "I can totally see myself doing those obstacles next," I joked.

"That's all I wanted to hear," Tom joined in. "That means you are ready for a solo ride."

"Are you sure?"

"Are you?" he challenged.

"I believe I am." I grinned, excited.

I reined it all in, all the emotions. This was not a joke, and this beautiful animal was not a toy. I always had to keep that in mind to not become overconfident and remain mindful, respectful.

"Now remember what I told you. Be decisive and firm," Tom said, handing the reins to me.

I simply nodded in return.

Tom jumped on a horse as well, coming next to me. I liked that, that both of them were making sure I was safe.

I gave a command for Bella to start walking. Nothing happened.

Um, did the batteries die on me or something? This was so embarrassing. Yet no one judged me.

"Don't falter. Remember, you are in charge."

"Right."

I tried again, and miraculously, Bella started walking at her previous slow pace. I grinned as the men cheered.

"That's it, keep going," Tom encouraged.

He continued to give me tips, guidelines on how to navigate around those tracks, and I felt so happy I wanted to cry. But I held off, not wanting my company to know what a basket case I truly was. Bella was a great companion. No matter my internal turmoil, she never ratted me out, simply continued carrying me around the ranch, for which I was immensely grateful. After a couple of hours of that, I was ready for a long break. But first, I had to take care of Bella, groom her, feed her, and show her my appreciation for today.

Despite the fun I was having, I would have to say being in a saddle was highly uncomfortable. I didn't care for that position one bit, and I was sure I would be feeling it even worse tomorrow. There wasn't a doubt in my mind that I was walking all kinds of funny afterward.

"Are you hungry?" Samuel asked me as we left the stable.

"I could eat."

"Good, because I prepared us a little snack."

That piqued my interest. "You prepared us a snack?" I asked for more details, and Samuel grinned.

"I ordered us some food," he said.

I cheered. Nothing could make me happier than that.

We walked for a bit, while my legs protested, and reached a small clearing that was surrounded by trees.

Underneath one of them was a spread blanket and a basket waiting for us.

"A picnic," I exclaimed, picking up my pace. I desperately needed to sit down with my legs closed.

From there, we could see the entire ranch in front of us. It was very lively, and all that commotion, the animals and people coming together, put a smile on my face. I didn't know such a gem with nature untouched could exist so close to the city.

"I selected all your favorites," he announced, opening the basket, and true enough, take-out containers from all my favorite places were inside.

"Wow, you know me so well."

"I'm doing my best."

He helped me to sit down.

"I didn't know what we would be in the mood for, so I simply ordered a little bit of everything," he explained.

"Smart," I replied.

Suddenly, I realized just how hungry I was, and as though to make sure I got the message right, my stomach started growling.

Without wasting any more time, we started eating. I jumped on some Chinese food as Samuel ate Thai. The fried chicken was next for the both of us. We laughed as we fought for the last piece. I was quicker, although I had a sinking feeling he'd let me win. That was why I let him have the last spring roll.

"Thank you for bringing me here." I remembered my manners after we pretty much ate everything he'd packed for us. I didn't care. I was full and content.

"It was my pleasure. And let me just say, you're a natural. Tom was really impressed by your talent."

"Really?"

"Indeed."

I grinned at that. I felt like the teacher's pet for some reason, and it was nice.

"And for that, you deserve a treat," he announced, getting a cupcake from the basket.

I accepted it as though it were a trophy or something, with pride.

"You are a pretty good rider yourself," I complimented in

return as I munched on my cupcake. "How long have you been riding?"

He looked away as though trying to remember. "For years. One of my clients brought me to a place similar to this, and I never stopped."

"That's great."

"Luckily, Joshua allows me to come as often as I please."

"He sounds like a good friend."

"He is. And now that invitation extends to you."

I was surprised by that, touched as well. "Wow." I didn't know what to say. "Thank you."

I believed there was a chance I wanted this to become something I did regularly. Dr. Neal pestered me for a long time to find myself a hobby, since crying over Christopher didn't really count. Maybe horseback riding could be that hobby for me.

"Although I have to warn you, this is an expensive pastime," he warned in a light tone.

"It's good, then, that my father left me some money," I joked, and he laughed.

The wind blew, and a strand of my hair fell over my face and mouth just when I was about to have another bite.

"Allow me," Samuel said and brushed it away, tucking the loose strand behind my ear. His fingers were soft, warm.

"Thank you," I muttered in return as my heart started to beat a little bit faster.

"My pleasure," he said with a smile.

I took a sip of my drink, needing something to do. We chatted about his work and finished our dessert, but I couldn't fully concentrate on any of it. My mind kept returning to that moment when his fingertips brushed my face.

Nothing like that happened again. He remained at a

respectable distance. And I was relieved. Except . . . there was a part of me that wasn't.

I felt like I was suffering from a split personality disorder with all these conflicted emotions.

It scared me that I felt like that.

We spent the entire day together, being on the ranch among animals, and he returned me home after we watched the sun go down.

"Won't your boss be furious you took the entire day off?" I teased.

"I know how to handle him," he said with a wink. "Besides, how does that saying go, 'all work and no play makes me cranky'?"

I laughed.

Once again, he left me in front of my door after kissing me on the cheek and wishing me pleasant dreams. Samuel remained the perfect gentleman, and although there was a certain comfort in that, I did wonder why he hadn't tried to kiss me properly yet. Especially since at times, I could feel how much he wanted to.

Do you? Perhaps his reluctance had more to do with my hesitation than his lack of desire. Which brought us back to why he was still such a gentleman.

The real question here was did I want to be kissed by him?

I didn't know the answer to that question. Was I avoiding the answer out of fear, guilt? Perhaps.

Regardless, I knew I liked spending time with him. Samuel was an amazing guy, but all my former issues were still alive and kicking. I wasn't ready.

Will I ever be ready? I asked myself. And although it was on the melodramatic side, it still had merit.

I didn't know the answer to that question either.

So was it wrong of me to go on dates with him and spend

so much time with him while being this uncertain? Was I just stringing him along? That made me feel guilty too.

Since I was this conflicted about everything, I turned to my best friend. I called her. We did that a lot as of late.

"You shouldn't feel guilty about anything." Selina was adamant.

"How can you say that?"

"Because you've been perfectly honest with him."

"I guess."

"And he is an adult, capable of making his own decisions, mistakes too, so don't try to take that away from him."

I nodded. That made sense to me. "I'm so happy I have you."

"I know. Now stop overanalyzing things and just enjoy."

"Yes, ma'am," I joked.

"Where is he taking you tomorrow?" Selina wanted to know since I'd told her we would be going on yet another date.

I smiled before answering, "I have no idea. He said he wanted it to be a surprise."

"Doesn't he know you hate surprises?"

I shrugged, although she couldn't see me. "He said I would love this one."

"Confident, isn't he?"

"Extremely," I said through a laugh.

"I like him," Selina complimented.

"Me too."

We both froze after I said that, and Selina was the first who recovered. "*Like him*, like him?" she asked for clarification.

"I don't know," I replied honestly, "but I want to find out."

"That's good. You should," she encouraged.

Although I wasn't sure how I felt about him, I knew one

thing. I did find him attractive. That little moment at the ranch had showed me that.

Afterward, each time I saw him, it would hit me, this desire, like a tidal wave. At first, I was stunned by the intensity of it. Apparently, I wasn't dead yet, although I had tried to follow in Christopher's footsteps for years. However, I wasn't going to act on it. My body had no say in this. I wasn't going to do anything until I was one hundred percent sure I was ready, mentally and physically, because I wasn't some hormonal teenager who couldn't resist.

I needed to be sure I was ready before taking any kind of steps because I owed that much to myself. I owed that much to Christopher.

At the same time, I was maybe jumping to conclusions. Samuel had never tried to kiss me, and at times, I couldn't decipher whether that was due to the fact that he was trying to be patient, tender, and understanding with me or simply because he was not interested.

The logic dictated the simplest solution was the truest.

But then he would look at me, and there would be so much longing and desire in his eyes I would have to look away so the intensity wouldn't overwhelm me. Which brought me back to the beginning of this complex problem.

When we ended up on a private yacht, enjoying a romantic dinner, I realized he was most definitely interested in me because no one went to such lengths for a friend. Samuel was doing his best to charm me, and it was working.

All the same, each time he escorted me back home, kissed my cheek, then lingered there a few seconds too long, I would start to feel apprehensive about inviting him inside. I wasn't ready to invite him into my bed. But I could feel my resolve was lessening, and despite everything, that notion was freaking me out.

11

"Do you like this?" he asked, whispering against my ear, grazing my earlobe with his teeth before lowering his lips down my neck, placing small kisses on my skin as he went slowly downward, following my collarbone and reaching my breasts.

My back stretched, giving him better access. "Mmmhmm," I murmured, too far gone for any concrete words.

In those moments, only the feel of him existed, and no matter how intoxicated by the sheer presence of him I was, I wanted, needed him even more. I craved him like no man before. I needed his lips on mine and his hands on my skin forever. He smiled, slowly, predatory, as though it thrilled him, turned him on that he could elicit this kind of response from me.

"How about this?" he wondered in a husky voice that sent shivers down my spine, curling my toes. His hands were pretty skillful. I moaned when he found a particularly tender spot.

"Lower," I ordered, although in those moments, it sounded more like a plea.

"Someone is getting impatient," he teased as his fingers did the same. He was driving me crazy.

"You have no idea," I practically growled, locking our lips in a passionate kiss. I climbed on top of him, still refusing to break the kiss. Apparently, he was more than happy to let me lead for a while.

I wanted him so damn much. The taste of his skin made me feel heady. No matter how close we got, I still wanted him closer. When he entered me, we both shouted, and then he started to move.

I felt like something deep inside me broke down, as though he'd managed to demolish that last defensive wall inside my soul, leaving me completely bare. All my holdups, fears, and inhibitions disappeared, and there was only this moment that mattered, only this man.

We moved together, trying to reach our climaxes, and it felt so good, so right, I never wanted him to stop.

"Faster," I encouraged.

He obliged.

"Don't stop," I pleaded.

"I won't," he promised. "Never."

And then we were both beyond words, beyond reality.

All too soon, the pleasure became almost unbearable, and I reached my end. "Oh, Samuel," I cried out in ecstasy as he followed me closely behind, professing his undying love to me.

I OPENED MY EYES, feeling freaked out beyond measure. *Oh, my God.* I was sweaty, hyperventilating as though I'd just had sex for real.

I pushed the comforter off my body. I felt too hot.

This was the most bizarre sex dream I'd had in my entire life. It felt so real I still had trouble accepting that it wasn't. Yet I was glad it wasn't.

I'd dreamed of having sex with Samuel. I could still feel

his body pressed against mine, his body heat communicating how much he wanted me as we kissed.

Stop it. I was starting to overheat anew. But I couldn't stop. This rattled me to the core. I'd just had an extremely erotic dream about Samuel. *Holy shit.*

I jumped out of bed as though needing to leave the scene of the crime and ran into the bathroom. I was desperately in need of a shower. And a cold one at that.

Sadly, no amount of cold water prevented me from reliving the entire dream over and over.

And then I started to scream, balling up in the corner as the water continued to fall on top of me. I didn't move even when it started to hurt. Tears started streaming down my face, mixing with the cold water. It hurt so much that not only had I stopped dreaming of Christopher, but as it turned out, another man had replaced him in those dreams.

Unbearable pain filled me, and I cried even harder. *I'm sorry, my love.* I sobbed, feeling like I'd cheated on Christopher with Samuel. I forced myself to pull my shit together. *Stop crying,* I commanded. *This is wrong.* I was spiraling without reason.

Nothing happened, I reminded myself. Not really. It was only a dream. Once I calmed down, I managed to rationalize everything, remembering what Dr. Neal had told me. My moving on didn't mean betraying Christopher in any way. My dreaming about Samuel didn't mean I was replacing my late husband or forgetting him in any way.

My heart had room for both of them.

If I wanted it to, I hedged.

Getting out of the shower squeaky clean, I felt pretty proud of myself for how I'd managed to pull myself back from the precipice. This was the first time I'd done something like that.

I guess therapy is working, not that I would ever admit that out loud, I joked.

Throughout the entire day, I tried not to think about that dream, and not simply because I continued to have some remnants of guilt inside me. It was disturbing me on so many levels it was downright frightening. I couldn't banish how free I was, how willingly and completely I gave myself over to him. But I tried, keeping myself busy.

The problem with that was that I literally had nothing to do. I tried working out and almost broke my ankle while running on the treadmill because I spaced out, thinking about the kiss Samuel gave me.

The kiss that never happened, I reminded myself. This entire dream was a figment of my imagination and nothing more. At the same time, I wanted to applaud my creativity. That dream was beyond hot. No wonder I mistook it for reality.

However, all that musing did make me wonder what that dream meant in the first place, apart from the obvious.

Was this my subconscious telling me—more like screaming at me—that I was ready for that next step?

I wasn't so sure about that despite the feelings that dream elicited. Although there was no denying I wanted to, I still didn't know if I should, if that made any sense.

Samuel deserved better from me than to be treated like some kind of training wheels. He was a good man. Then something Selina said resonated inside my head. He was a grown man. I shouldn't decide for him.

Samuel was so full of understanding, so considerate, so mindful for us to go at my own pace that he showed me how committed he was. And in a way, it made me want him even more.

All the same, every time I tried to envision asking him if

he wanted to come inside for a drink, it filled me with dread, among other things.

This house belonged to Christopher and me and always would. How was I to invite some other man to such a sacred space? How was I to invite Samuel to a bed I had only shared with my husband?

I couldn't do that to either of them. It wouldn't be fair.

"Charlene? Earth to Charlene?" Selina called out for me, irked, while we video chatted. "Are you listening to me?"

"Yeah," I lied. "Could you repeat that last part?"

"I said, he wanted us to go Dutch at dinner, although he clearly asked me on a date, the cheap bastard," Salina ranted.

"I'm sorry you had such a crappy night," I replied dutifully, like a good friend.

"It's okay. I wasn't that into him, anyway. Now tell me about you. What's new?"

"Nothing," I replied, not wanting to get into the whole issue of how I'd had a sex dream with Samuel that was so good.

"Stop lying." She instantly called me out on my bullshit. "You've been moody and distracted. Now spill," she ordered.

I saw no other way than to confess everything.

"I had a dream about Samuel last night." For some reason, I kept my eyes closed while saying that.

"What kind of dream?"

"Sex dream," I replied, making a face.

"Really?" she exclaimed, getting all excited as though I just told her we were going on a paid cruise around the world. I was slightly exaggerating, yet the sentiment was spot on. "Was it any good? Well, of course it was since you're acting like this."

"I can't stop thinking about it."

"Good."

"Good?"

"Think you're ready to give him a try in real life?" she asked instead. Selina was not known for her subtlety, yet I still loved her.

"I don't know," I replied honestly. I was trying to figure that out this whole day and came up with nothing. I was conflicted no matter the intensity of the dream. It certainly made me think about having sex with him. Yet would I, in real life, was an entirely different matter.

"I'm conflicted."

"I think you should definitely go for it," she countered.

"You do?" I asked, full of doubt.

Selina nodded. "It's obvious he has a thing for you, and you definitely have a thing for him. And I'm saying that with all due respect to Christopher."

I looked away. "He's the reason I'm conflicted."

"I know, but look, I'm going to be super blunt here."

"Okay."

"Christopher is dead, and I know he loved you and you loved him, but that doesn't change the fact that he's gone, for good."

"I know," I said, closing my eyes.

"On the other hand, Samuel is very much alive and into you, and you're into him, so start living. Take that race car for a spin, girl."

Her last words made me smile. This was so typical for Selina, to try to make me laugh in the midst of a serious conversation.

Then I sobered up, sighing. "I want to," I finally admitted out loud, "except . . ." I looked around myself, and Selina caught that.

"What's the matter, Charlene?" she prompted.

"Everything around here reminds me of Christopher," I admitted.

"I see," she said, deep in thought. "If you can't move past

it, then go to a hotel and problem solved," she offered after a short pause.

"I think I like that idea," I replied honestly.

Selina grinned. "I know. I'm a genius."

"Thank you, my personal genius."

"You're very welcome."

"Expect a very generous birthday present."

"Now you're talking my language," she said, blowing me a kiss.

Once we wrapped up our conversation, I decided to be a bit proactive. Before I chickened out was implied. I went to the drugstore to get some condoms. I couldn't be having sex without them. *It was better to be prepared than to ruin an evening* was my motto.

Unfortunately, standing in front of the rack with all the prophylactics made me realize I was way out of my depth here. I had no clue what I was doing.

This is a mistake, I thought glumly. There were so many different brands, different shapes and sizes, and I was completely dumbstruck.

And then I started to be self-conscious standing in front of the display for so long.

Just pick something. However, that was easier said than done. What to get? I didn't know Samuel's preferences or even his size.

Thinking about that made me blush. I was no prude. It was just that I was way out of practice. I'd forgotten all about this hassle, especially once I married Christopher. We hadn't needed any of this since we were trying to start a family.

Focus, Charlene. What to buy? I reached for one box, then faltered. What if I inadvertently insulted him by making the wrong buy? I had a serious case of second-guessing. I didn't want to assume he was well-endowed, yet at the same time, I couldn't rule that out.

This is impossible!

Should I get extra-thin? For my pleasure only, or some with flavors? Why do they have flavors in the first place? I wondered.

And do not get me started on lubricants. That was a different headache altogether. I never had that kind of problem with Christopher, but years had passed, and I had no idea if things had changed with me. I had no idea what my current state was considering I hadn't had sex with anyone since my husband died.

And then it hit me. I was doing all this because I wanted to have sex with Samuel. Actual sex with another human being. Did I even know how to do that anymore? I started to panic.

What if I forgot everything? What if I was bad at it?

Christopher never complained, but he was a man in love, so that didn't count.

I stopped that train of thought before my heart decided to leave my rib cage.

Likewise, I decided to abandon this endeavor since I clearly had no clue what I was doing. I left the store. That was the only thing I could do. I needed too many products, since I had no idea about the specifics, so I figured it would be better to cover all my bases.

However, I would feel too embarrassed to go to the register carrying a dozen boxes of condoms, not to mention other products that promised extra pleasure, causing Mrs. Grant, a woman who worked at the drugstore since forever, a coronary.

I was an idiot for leaving my house in the first place. I already had the perfect method to get all that I wanted and needed without leaving my house. It was called shopping online. I would order everything, and the best part was that the couriers delivering all that would not be giving me a judgy look and wouldn't be privy to the fact that I would finally be having sex after three years.

It was a win-win situation.

I felt much better settling all that. Nevertheless, there was another thing on my to-do list.

What kind of bikini wax do I need?

12

"Are you all right?" Samuel asked me for the fourth time since we met that night. He took me to dinner, as he had every other day this week.

I wasn't all right. Not by a long shot. I couldn't decide whether I wanted to invite him to a hotel this evening, or how to do it in the first place. Should I be blunt and say something like, 'Hey, want to see me naked?' or be more civil and ask him if he wanted to go and have a drink at the hotel with me.

What if he actually wants a drink? My mind was in shambles.

"Charlene?"

"I'm fine," I replied as I had before, forcing a smile.

Stop stalling, I snapped at myself. This should be the night. I'd strung him along for far too long, and besides, I wanted him. All the same, knowing that didn't mean I stopped being a nervous wreck. I had no idea what I was doing, and it wasn't like there was a handbook about such things. The last thing I wanted was to ask my therapist how to get laid without making a complete fool of myself.

I'll play it cool and just have him take me home. Then I can ask him if he wants to come inside, then see where that will take us.

After a moment of thought, I decided my house was the only place I wanted to have sex with Samuel. No matter how crazy it sounded, considering every part of that house reminded me of Christopher, there was no other place I wanted to be.

I wouldn't feel comfortable in some sterile hotel room. I needed all my things around me to reach the levels of confidence I needed to pull this off. It had been three years since I'd allowed a man to seduce me, and to play the seductress in return. I needed all the help I could get. And that was where I felt the most comfortable. That was my sanctuary.

And then if he said yes to me, I would just have to pray like hell that no thoughts of my late husband invaded my mind while I was with Samuel. *Piece of cake.*

Besides, this had nothing to do with Christopher. This was between me and Samuel, and I was sure when the moment came, I would be solely focused on him. Like I had been in that dream that still wouldn't stop tormenting me.

Over the last week or so, I realized that as long as I kept things simple, I could function just fine. So I wouldn't freak out focusing on tonight, on the sex I hoped would take place. However, if I started thinking about the future with Samuel, where all this could lead—another marriage, another death—then I got in serious trouble. Hence, I wouldn't allow myself to let my mind wander.

Keep it simple.

"Charlene?"

"I'm fine."

He looked at me oddly. "That was not my question, but hearing you say that makes me think you're not fine."

Busted.

Maybe I should just come clean, tell him I am extremely attracted to him and be done with it? I instantly banished that.

"Could we go for a little walk? It's a bit stuffy in here," I said with a small smile.

"Certainly," he replied like I knew he would. He was a gentleman to his core.

After he took care of the bill, we left the restaurant, and instead of getting into the car, we crossed the street and started walking toward the park. After a while, my legs started to protest. These high heels were not meant for walking, but the fresh air did me good.

I was aware I was blowing things out of proportion, yet it couldn't be helped. This was a big deal, and I needed to make sure I was making the right choice. Sadly, that wasn't how life worked. No matter the preparations, no matter the plans, things didn't always go as I wished. Christopher's death was the best example of that.

What was the alternative, let go and go with the flow? I wasn't sure I was capable of that. All the same, I was determined to try.

"Did you like your dinner?" Samuel asked as though needing to break this silence between us.

I was aware I was creating this awkward situation, but I had so much on my mind. I couldn't focus on anything else.

"It was delicious," I replied with a small smile.

"You barely touched your meal," he countered, and there was slight concern in his voice.

I hated that I was doing this to him.

Just make up your damn mind and stick to it. "I wasn't that hungry."

Samuel pushed his hand through his hair, as though in frustration. "Charlene?"

"Yes?"

"I hope you know that if something's the matter, you can confide in me," he offered.

I was genuinely touched that after everything I'd put him through, he would still think of me first. His concern warmed my heart.

I can't keep doing this to him. To us.

Gathering all my courage and steadying my nerves, I turned so I could stand in front of him.

He looked at me questioningly.

It's now or never.

I leaned forward, closed my eyes, and kissed him.

The instant our lips came together, all my worries went away, and I couldn't believe I'd made such a fuss about this. While we kissed, it felt like the most natural thing in the world.

After a lifetime, or so it seemed to me, Samuel decided to break the kiss first.

"Are you sure?" he asked, and there was truly no reason for him to clarify what he was referring to as he cradled my face between his palms.

I simply nodded in return. "Yes, I am." I couldn't believe how short of breath I sounded. And after just one kiss.

Apparently, that was all he needed to hear before kissing me anew. And it was no chaste kiss. I felt it with my entire body, setting it ablaze. Samuel really knew what he was doing. This was far better than I could have imagined, better than that dream, which started all this for me in the first place. And now I was glad I'd had the dream because it pushed me into action. I wouldn't know exactly what I was missing without it.

Yay for my subconscious. I could only imagine what other skills he possessed apart from being a phenomenal kisser, yet I was determined to find out. *Tonight.*

The wind started to blow around us, and Samuel wrapped his arms tightly around me, but I wasn't cold, I was on fire.

"It's getting cold," he murmured at some point against my lips.

Now that I'd discovered this delight, I didn't want to let go.

"I'm fine."

"You're shivering," he pointed out. That definitely wasn't from the cold. "Let me take you home." He pleaded with his eyes.

"All right," I replied, instantly realizing that the faster we got to my house, the sooner I would have him all to myself.

He kissed me on the forehead before letting me go.

As we started walking back to the restaurant, toward the parking lot, he wrapped his jacket around my shoulders.

"We don't want you catching a cold."

"Thank you," I said with a smile. All of a sudden, I was feeling so giddy I felt like skipping. I did no such thing.

That kiss was phenomenal, and it only made me crave him more. I was surprised by my reactions but in a good way. It was a relief to know I was still capable of such strong emotions.

He entwined our fingers, and I looked at our hands, grinning. I couldn't believe this was happening.

Holding hands, we reached his car, and he opened the door for me, but before I entered, he couldn't resist kissing me one more time.

He continued to hold my hand, kissing it every once in a while as he drove.

"You've made me so happy, Charlene," he confessed at some point.

"You make me happy too," I said, and I actually meant it.

And then, in the blink of an eye, we were in front of my

house again. This time, I didn't want us saying good night to one another.

He leaned in for the kiss, and once we parted again, I knew that was my chance.

"Good night, Charlene," he murmured.

At the same time, I said, "Would you like to come inside?"

So this didn't go as smoothly as I'd envisioned.

Samuel patted my cheek. "I would love to, but you don't have to feel pressured. We have all the time in the world," he said.

"I'm not feeling pressured," I insisted. "I want this." *I want you.*

"All right, then," he replied with a nod.

I gulped. Now that this was actually happening, my nervousness returned, but I ignored it. I wanted Samuel, and he wanted me. Our spending the night together was the most natural thing in the world.

With that said, I still had trouble unlocking the door. My hands shook.

"Allow me," Samuel offered, and I flashed him a grateful smile in return.

We stood in the doorway as he brushed his lips against mine. "We don't have to do anything you aren't comfortable with."

"I know."

"I would be happy simply kissing you the entire night and holding you in my arms."

"Please come in," I breathed.

Once I managed to peel myself off him, I showed him the way to the living room, and I went to the kitchen to get us something to drink. I wanted to stick my head in the freezer because this was too much. He was too much.

Stop stalling.

Once I returned with two glasses of red wine, I caught him snooping around. He looked adorable looking about.

I offered him a glass, and he nodded his thanks. Apparently, he was fascinated by the decor, and then I discovered why.

"For someone worth multimillion dollars, your house is pretty modest. Almost bare," he observed.

I hadn't disclosed how much money I had, though I supposed it wouldn't take anyone long to discover how much I was worth. It had been in all the papers when Mom tried to take it all from me. Anyway, I didn't take offense at his explanation. This was clearly a professional habit for him. He was an antiques dealer, after all. Besides, he was right. I never cared for material possessions that much. I didn't even want to have famous paintings in my house because I truly believed the works of great masters belonged to the museums for all the people to enjoy their genius.

Nevertheless, I found his comment a bit odd. Why did it matter how my house looked?

Maybe he's nervous too. I shouldn't assume he was taking this lightly, especially since everything in his behavior suggested otherwise.

I was about to reply, tease him how he was apparently always working, when he put the glass on the table before approaching me.

He wrapped his arms around my waist, pulling me close to his body, and said, "Where were we?" And then he kissed me, and this time, he didn't stop.

All thoughts were banished from my head. I felt completely heady, breathless in no time.

"Oh, God, how I love doing that," he murmured against my lips.

I could only grin like an idiot in return. Part of me felt like this was all happening too fast, and the other was outraged this wasn't happening fast enough.

"Would you like a tour of the house?" I asked, trying to sound all sexy and seductive.

"Only if we start this tour in your bedroom," he replied in the same manner.

I didn't know where this sudden courage came from, but I took him by the hand and started leading him upstairs. I put an extra sway in my hips as I climbed the stairs, giving him a little show, and I knew it was working by the way his eyes were ablaze once we reached the bedroom. His smoldering eyes never left mine, and that felt quite empowering.

"You are so beautiful, Charlene," he said as though in awe.

I closed the distance between us, showing him all that I was feeling with a kiss.

Quite spontaneously, we started undressing. He helped me get out of my dress; I helped him get out of his suit. There was something particularly sexy about taking clothes off his body, and then I could only gape like a fish once I discovered he had a six-pack.

I wanted my hands all over his body, and luckily, he was more than happy to oblige.

"I mean it. You are beautiful, Charlene. I can't get enough of you," he breathed against my skin as he urgently, passionately kissed my neck and shoulders, sending shivers down my body.

I couldn't say precisely when we ended up in bed, but the weight of his body pressed against mine as I opened myself completely to him was what I lived for. I couldn't get enough of him, and by the way he was holding me and kissing me, he felt the same way. I reached over to the nightstand and opened the drawer, blushing.

"I wasn't sure what kind to get . . ."

He grinned and grabbed a box. "These will do fine," he murmured and then returned to kissing me.

We ended up making love two times before I fell asleep out of sheer exhaustion, securely snuggled inside his arms.

"Sweet dreams, Charlene," he whispered, kissing the top of my head. "Relax. I got you."

Still smiling because of his sweetness, I managed to do just that. I let go.

13

I woke up with a start. I felt disoriented for a second. Although I lay in my bed, naked, everything around me felt wrong. And then I remembered what I'd done. *What Samuel and I did,* I corrected and smiled. If what we did was wrong, then I never again wanted to be right.

The bed beside me was empty, but his scent lingered all around me. It was embedded in the sheets, pillows, not to mention on my skin. *I did it.* I slept with him, and it was fantastic. It was better than I could have imagined. I patted myself on the back for finally gathering enough courage for such a step. It was so worth it. He was worth it.

The connection between us was simply off the charts. I knew sex was great between people who were in love. It always was between me and Christopher. But now I knew it was pretty amazing when pure lust was at play as well. Because I knew I didn't love Samuel. I honestly thought he was a great guy, and I liked him a lot, liked spending time with him, so who knew? Perhaps in time, it could turn into something else, something more. This connection between us unquestionably showed a lot of potential.

I stretched happily, thinking about last night. Part of me was happy he left before I woke. I wouldn't know how to act around him otherwise. Would it be awkward? Would he think this meant more than it did? And then it hit me—what if it wasn't that good, at least for him? What if that was the reason he left? I stopped myself there because stressing about my sexual skills would cause me a massive aneurysm.

Besides, I was worrying without reason. I knew how much Samuel enjoyed being with me last night, and it was definitely mutual.

I tried really hard not to think about Christopher in these moments while I still enjoyed this postcoital bliss. Not only because it would be too weird but because I knew something like that still had the power to break me. It was hard to abandon old patterns of behavior, to not feel guilty for being alive, to experience joy, happiness, but that was exactly what I needed to do if I wanted any kind of future with Samuel.

Christopher had died because of me. I still believed that. It was something I would have to carry with me and live with for as long as I breathed, but Dr. Neal was right. He would hate seeing me all torn up because of him. He would want me to be happy. So that was precisely what I intended to be from now on. And at the moment, that happiness included Samuel. He truly made me happy.

With that in mind, the question was, if I was truly ready to leave Christopher in the past, did I want Samuel to become my future? While lying there alone, I wasn't so sure of that, but at the same time, when he was around me, something like that felt like the most natural thing in the world. Samuel had this strange ability to make all my fears and worries go away.

And in retrospect, that wasn't such a bad thing.

A strange sound coming from downstairs put me on high alert. I rose, tensing. What was that? *Is someone inside the house?* I started to panic. On impulse, I turned the bedside lamp on as I concentrated. I practically stopped breathing in anticipation of other sounds. There weren't any. Was that all in my head? That was when I noticed how all of Samuel's things were scattered around the bedroom.

He's still here. He didn't leave, I realized as my heart skipped a beat. I was sure he'd snuck out while I was asleep, and as it turned out, I was wrong. He'd made that noise, and I hoped he hadn't hurt himself.

Slowly rising from the bed, although why I was creeping about my own house, I couldn't say for sure, I picked up his discarded shirt and put it on. His scent invaded me, and for a moment I was reminded of what it felt like to make love to him. I really hoped that was something that would occur again, and soon.

I went downstairs and found Samuel snooping around my kitchen. Since he was operating in semidarkness, the only light coming from the backyard window, I couldn't say for sure what he was looking for. Although I still pretty much enjoyed the view. He was only wearing his boxers, and if he were not already a successful businessman, I was sure he would make a fortune being a model.

Take it easy; calm down, I told my raging hormones.

I decided to end his misery and turned on the light. The bright light blinded me for a moment. He turned toward me and looked completely apologetic. "I apologize for waking you up. I needed a glass of water, and then your island decided to attack me," he said all at once, a bit sheepishly.

I opened the right cabinet to get him a glass.

"Thank you. And while you're here, I do crave a power snack."

"A power snack?"

"Well, someone depleted my energy levels, and I require nourishment to recharge."

I couldn't help laughing. "My fridge is pretty bare," I said once I settled.

He made a face. "I noticed. Apparently, that is a recurring theme in this house of yours," he teased.

"I thought you left," I blurted out before I could stop myself.

"You expected that I would simply sneak out in the middle of the night? Not my thing," he said, coming to wrap his arms around me. "I'm not done with you yet," he said before kissing me.

I rose on my tiptoes, giving him better access. "Want me to order us something to eat?" I asked as we parted.

The last thing I wanted was to starve this fine man to death. If nourishment was what he required for such high performance, then that was precisely what he would get. I almost laughed at my own joke.

"That's not a bad idea," he said, still not letting go. And I was fine with that.

"You won't regret it. My ordering skills are legendary," I joked. And luckily, I knew a lot of places that were open twenty-four seven.

"On second thought, I believe I'll stick to dessert."

That confused me. "What dessert?" I asked. I was certain I didn't have anything sweet inside the house.

"You," he replied before kissing me on the mouth so passionately, so fiercely it completely took me by surprise, took my breath away.

I recovered quickly, giving everything I possessed in return.

In the next instant, I was airborne. Samuel scooped me off my feet and started carrying me back toward the bedroom for another round of sex as I laughed with delight, wrapping my arms around his neck. I couldn't resist kissing him every once in a while, although I was mindful that he needed his sight to navigate through the house.

This man was truly something else. And I felt grateful he'd entered my life when he did.

It could be just my impartial opinion, yet I believed the third time around was even better than the first and second. I orgasmed so hard I was sure all the neighbors could hear me. Not that I gave a shit. I was finally liberating myself, learning how to live in a world without pain and sorrow, and it felt amazing.

Afterward, we simply lay next to one another, trying to catch our breaths. Yet even in those moments, our fingers were entwined. I liked that. But I didn't like how light-headed I felt. I was tragically out of practice. I needed to start doing more cardio if I wanted to keep up.

Then again, I hoped Samuel would help me get back in shape with this amazing sex. I smiled at my thoughts. They didn't belong to the woman I knew. They didn't belong to the woman who'd secluded herself inside her house for years. They belonged to someone else, someone I couldn't fully recognize. That woman lived for the moment, unburdened from the past, and I had to admit I liked her better. That woman was trying to be happy.

Regardless of all that, I was definitely hooked now, and I couldn't wait for us to do this again. Although logically, I knew we needed sleep, nourishment, and time to recuperate, I still wanted him with a burning passion that would scare me in normal circumstances. Yet I refused to be intimidated. This was the new me, and the new me would be with Samuel in any way I could, for as long as I could.

"Thank you."

His words snapped me from my reverie. As he uttered those words, he coupled them with kissing my knuckles.

I turned so I could look into his face. "For what?" I asked, genuinely confused.

"For trusting me enough, for letting me be part of your life." He shifted, rising on top of me before continuing, "For trusting me with your heart and your body." He lowered his head so he could kiss me.

Despite the fact that we had just finished making love, my body started to heat up all over again.

What was I to say to that? *You're welcome?* That would be wrong, and besides, he wasn't the only grateful one.

"Thank you for being so trustworthy," I replied eventually.

He lowered himself, nestling his head between my breasts. Absentmindedly, I traced patterns against his back. I couldn't stop touching his skin. It was addicting.

Suddenly, he shifted again so he could look me in the face.

I didn't get a chance to ask what the matter was because he grinned. "I have a present for you," he announced.

I smiled as well. "A present?"

"Yes. It's in my car, don't move," he said, getting out of bed.

"You're going to get it now?" It was in the middle of the night.

"No time like the present," he announced.

"You can give it to me tomorrow," I tried to argue, but he was already leaving the bedroom.

I could only shake my head, grateful he had enough presence of mind to put his boxers back on. Some late dog walker could be scarred for life if he encountered him.

Unable to remain still, I wrapped myself in the sheet, then neared the window, trying to spot him. As it turned out, it wasn't that hard seeing his perfect shape in the moonlight. He looked downright comical creeping toward his car before diving inside.

Oh, Lord, I hope he won't get arrested.

He emerged seconds later carrying something rectangular. I couldn't see what it was because it looked wrapped.

How didn't I spot it earlier tonight? I wondered. He must have hidden it from me. While he returned, I realized my excitement was starting to rise. I couldn't wait to see what he'd gotten me.

The man was always surprising me.

He returned shortly, looking slightly out of breath as he carried the present, which was wrapped in brown paper.

"This is for you," he announced, putting it on the bed.

Holding the sheet that I'd wrapped myself into with one hand, I started walking toward it.

"What is it?" I asked, although by the shape of it, I had a clue to what it might be.

He wouldn't, would he? Knowing him, there was a good chance I was on the right track.

"Open it up and discover for yourself," he urged.

Before I did that, I kissed him on the mouth. "Thank you. You didn't have to do this."

"I know. I wanted to. Now open it. I want to see your reaction." He grinned, and there was boyish playfulness on his face.

"Okay." I grinned in return. With one quick movement, I tore the paper.

"Oh, Samuel," I said, putting a hand over my heart as I unwrapped it. It was the painting of a dancer I liked so much. And I was right. The details were exquisite.

I looked at this man in front of me. "I can't take this." I was beyond touched that he would do something like this for me.

"I want you to have it," he insisted. "It would make me so happy."

What could I say to that? "Thank you." I gave him another kiss.

"And don't worry. I made an appointment with an appraisal specialist to come and see it," he reassured me.

I waved my hand. "You know I don't care about that."

"You deserve to know its origin. Besides, aren't you a bit curious whether we discovered some lost treasure?" he asked with a smile.

We were both looking at the painting as we stood in an embrace.

"A bit," I confessed.

It would be fantastic if this painting turned out to be, as he said, a lost treasure from some master. Maybe even the Master. However, I wouldn't feel robbed or saddened if it wasn't. The painting itself was beautiful in its own right and spoke to me.

"Then it's settled."

"I think I will hang it in the bedroom," I thought out loud. That way, I could see it each time I woke up, and smile.

"Excellent choice."

I kissed him. "Thank you again. I love it."

Samuel simply nodded as though my gratitude was making him embarrassed or something. He was British, after all.

We moved the painting to my vanity table so we could return to bed.

"So what happened with your plan to convince me to buy it?" I teased.

Samuel chuckled.

"Oh, I will find some other way to extract money from you," he deadpanned.

And we both laughed.

"So where did you plan to hang it, here or there?" He

pointed, and he looked pretty excited, like a little boy who just got the best present imaginable.

Isn't that how I'm supposed to act?

"Probably there," I replied.

He made a gesture as though wanting to take care of it immediately, but I held him back.

"Let's take care of that tomorrow," I said, licking my lips. I wanted to show my appreciation first.

He caught my meaning immediately. "Tomorrow," he agreed.

14

When I woke up the next day, the bed next to me was empty. *He must have an early start,* I rationalized.

However, the evidence of what we'd done last night lingered in the air. And also, I had the painting. Looking at it put a smile on my face. That was very thoughtful of him. Despite all the teasing while trying to portray himself as a tough businessman, Samuel had a big heart. And he was very kind to me. Not to mention how patient he was, giving me time to become ready to be with him.

That rascal. It was obvious he knew we would be together even before I did. Selina knew that too, I was sure of that.

Only I was an idiot. Well, not so much an idiot, simply a person blinded by my own grief, my own pain. It was preventing me from seeing the truth and, subsequently, from living.

Turning, I realized the painting wasn't the only thing he left me. There was a single red rose on the pillow. I took it to smell it. Where on Earth did he find it? If he broke into Mrs. Jerningham's garden to take it, then I would be in a world of trouble. That woman was overly protective when it came to her flowers.

Relax, Charlene. She will never know, I assured myself, wearing a small smile.

Samuel was a bad boy as well. I believed I liked that. As I mused about him and what we did last night, I started brushing the delicate flower against my lips and neck. I closed my eyes, picturing him beside me as I began to touch myself.

Samuel was an amazing lover. That was probably one of the best nights of my life. I orgasmed so many times I lost count. Remembering some of his more advanced moves put a blush on my cheeks. I couldn't believe what I let him do to me. What was happening to me?

I was finally living again, and it felt good.

Reaching my climax, I kissed the rose and left it on my chest as I lay still, trying to catch my breath.

I had to stop thinking about him or I would never leave this bed. That thought almost made me giggle.

I really was out of my mind.

The problem was, I had been out of the dating scene for too long. I wasn't even sure what we were doing was dating in the first place. Perhaps it was just casual sex.

Could it be even called that, after just one night?

Was this a one-night stand?

I was sure I would get all my answers in time. I just had to relax and let it happen.

Although I did find it strange that he'd stayed but then left before I woke. Wasn't it either, or? Either stay the entire night or leave right after sex? At the same time, I'd never specified that I wanted him gone after we finished.

Did I want that? What would I prefer? For him to leave right after, or for him to spend the night with me and sleep next to me? I wasn't one hundred percent sure. There was something to be said about waking up next to that gorgeous man. Besides, I always liked a quickie in the morning.

Perhaps I had my answer.

Not that it really mattered. It wasn't all up to me. Perhaps Samuel had his opinions about the subject. Realizing I'd gone too far with analyzing this specific occurrence, I stopped. I was definitely reading too much into it.

There was a great chance that he'd wanted to stay but had to leave because of work and didn't want to wake me, plain and simple. *Case closed.*

All the same, I wished he'd left a note or something.

He left you a rose, which was far better and more romantic. It showed how appreciative he was of last night.

I couldn't help grinning at that.

I finally rose from the bed, feeling giddy all of a sudden, and picked up my new painting, searching for the perfect spot to hang it. I wanted to place it on the opposite side of the room from the bed so I could see it upon waking, and eventually, I found the perfect spot. One quick trip to the pantry, and I returned with a hammer and some nails.

Once I was satisfied with my handiwork, I went downstairs to the kitchen to make myself some pancakes. I craved them, although I never cooked. I was beyond starving, which was no wonder considering how many calories I'd burned last night thanks to Samuel.

As I enjoyed my breakfast, my phone started ringing. I hoped it was Samuel, but it was Selina.

I made a face. I swear, that girl has a sixth sense or something.

"Hello?" I answered with a smile as I shoved the last piece of pancake into my mouth. It was dripping in syrup just the way I liked it.

"You had sex last night," she announced.

I practically choked on my food. I swallowed it quickly. "How did you know?" I wondered.

"Oh, please. That I-got-laid swagger can be heard in your voice."

That was not a thing, was it?

"So how was it?" she added after a short pause.

I couldn't help grinning. "Amazing." Better than amazing. It was life-changing. "I forgot how much fun it is." How much I liked it. I really missed it.

"I knew it," Selina said confidently.

That was so like her.

"I want details."

"No way, there's this thing called oversharing, and I'm not a fan."

Selina sighed. "You are such a buzzkill."

"Okay, I'll tell you this."

"I'm all ears."

"He gave me a painting."

"A what?"

"He gave me a beautiful painting of a dancer."

"When? Before?"

"Well, more like during."

"What?" she exclaimed.

"Not like a kink, more like in between, during intermission," I corrected, hoping she would understand my meaning.

"Wow," was Selina's comment, which by her standards was pretty mellow.

I must have really shocked her. For some reason, that cheered me to no end.

"Let me see it."

I ran upstairs really quickly to snap a picture of it, then sent it to her.

"It's beautiful. It reminds me of Degas," she observed.

"Me too."

"Who is it?"

"I don't know." Then I proceeded to tell her the history of the painting.

"That's a cool story."

"I think so too." And like I said to Samuel, it didn't matter to me whether we could prove it was an original Degas. I liked the painting no matter what.

"Amazing, Charlene. If you got this after one night with him, I can't imagine what you'll get after you officially start dating," she joked.

"Selina," I chastised.

"I'm kidding."

"He took me by surprise."

"I'm happy for you."

Truth be told, I was happy for me too.

Just as I finished my talk with Selina, my phone started ringing again.

Wasn't I Miss Popular that morning?

Thinking how this time around it must be Samuel, I wasn't paying attention to the number and simply answered it.

Big mistake.

"Hello, Charlene."

I groaned inwardly.

"Hello, Lana," I greeted in return.

Was I a bad person if I didn't want to speak with my sister? *Half-sister,* I instantly corrected, since she always did. Lana was ten years younger than me, and we were never that close. The fact that my mother never hid the fact that she loved her more and wished she was her one and only daughter created this tense dynamic between us, where she felt entitled to torment me.

Obviously, things changed once I got money. At first, she

sided with Mother, tried to take everything away from me, but since they lost, she changed her tune. I wouldn't say she was sucking up to me, except she was definitely sucking up to me, and I felt sorry for her. The way my mother raised her, privileged and protected, did her no favors in real life.

"So how have you been?" she asked conversationally.

I wasn't buying it.

"What do you want?"

"I can see someone woke up on the wrong side of the bed." She dared to sound hurt. "Can't I call my sister and ask her how she's doing?"

"Half-sister. And I know you better than that."

"You're not being fair."

"I'm simply saying you only call when you need money."

"Well, it's not my fault I need money to get a decent job in this city," she defended in a meek voice.

"What do you mean?"

"I want to be an actress," she announced.

I rolled my eyes. "And you need money for?"

"Well, my friend Sally's hairdresser has a brother-in-law who is an assistant manager to this big producer guy, John MacCabe."

I seriously had no idea what she just said.

"And he said to her, the brother-in-law, not the producer, that he would totally give me a part in his next movie if I give him ten thousand dollars."

"What?" I exclaimed as my eyes bulged. "Ten grand for a part? I hope it's a lead."

"Actually, I would be an extra, but you can't put a price on such an opportunity," she argued in return.

Apparently, someone could and did. It was ten thousand dollars.

Lana was always pulling stunts like this, trying to get something for nothing. Before acting, she swore she wanted to be a singer and begged me to give her money to make an album. The fact that she didn't know how to sing or know anything about songwriting didn't stop her from throwing a fit when I refused.

And before that, she wanted to be a dancer. That wore off quickly, though, because she realized being a dancer was hard work.

She even auditioned for reality shows and managed to get into one, but the viewers kicked her out after one week. They found her too spoiled, whiny, and useless. Couldn't say I disagreed.

I blamed our mother for the way Lana turned out. She expected to get everything in life without putting in any work because Mother always made sure all her wishes were fulfilled. There was one problem with that. Her wishes got bigger and bigger with time, and Mother couldn't keep up because David's salary didn't really scream Rockefeller.

That was why she started coming to me. And at first, I was enraged. How dare she come to me asking for money after everything she'd put me through, after tormenting me my whole life? But then I decided to let it go. Anger would bring me nothing good.

I couldn't change who she was. I couldn't change our screwed-up relationship. And although that was sad, I could live with it.

"So, Charlene, what do you say?" she prompted since I'd remained silent for too long. "Will you give me the money?"

"Absolutely not."

"Why not?" she started to whine. "You clearly have more than you need, and I want this part. It's my dream."

Yeah, for about five minutes.

"That's a lot of money. I just don't see any gain for you here."

"Please, Charlene. I want this. Besides, if you give me

money for this, I will never ask anything from you ever again," she announced.

That was tempting. And she would definitely be the first member of my family to act in such a way. Although I wasn't being completely fair. David never asked anything of me. Only when my mother made him, and that didn't count.

Once again, I was saddened by the state of our relationship. We were worse than strangers since once upon a time, we had been forced to live together, yet there was never true affection between us.

I had been ecstatic when I first got a sister, but my mother never let me be around her. She didn't want my bad karma to rub off on Lana. My mother was one cruel woman, and I could never forgive her for everything she did to me. She was the force that divided us, but she wasn't the only one to blame. Lana liked the hierarchy in our family since she always got what she wanted, and David was too weak to confront either one of them on my behalf.

Nevertheless, I was at times lenient toward David and Lana. Most of what had happened to me in childhood wasn't Lana's fault. She didn't know better. Our mother did and still didn't care that she was tormenting me for her mistakes.

That was why I said, "I'll think about it." Perhaps I was an idiot, but she was still my sister, no matter what.

"Thank you, thank you, thank you."

"I didn't say yes, Lana."

"Oh, I know you will."

"I'm hanging up now."

"I need the money by Friday," were her parting words.

Shaking my head while muttering I was the biggest idiot on the planet, I went to the living room to my escritoire since that was where I kept all my receipts, checkbooks, and things like that.

I frowned, reaching it.

That's odd.

It was unlocked, and I always made a point of locking it. It was simply the way I was. Although I was all alone in this house, I kept certain things in a secured place. That was how I needed to be while growing up if I wanted to keep something hidden from my mother. Unfortunately, even during adulthood, the habit stuck.

I looked about, but nothing was amiss. I must have forgotten to lock it the last time I used it, I realized, since there was no one else in this house besides me. That was the only logical explanation.

Forgetfulness is the first sign of getting old, I joked.

Besides, all the really important things were not in there, so it wasn't such a big deal. I kept all the real sensitive things, like my financial information, net worth, and some emergency cash, hidden in the safe that was located on the floor of my bedroom closet.

The house came with it already installed, and it had proven quite useful over the years.

While I debated whether I should write that check for Lana or not, because ten thousand dollars was a lot of money despite the fact that I'd inherited millions, something hit me.

Samuel had been in the house last night. More to the point, he had been downstairs alone. However, I banished that thought immediately.

He would never go and snoop around my house while I was asleep. It wasn't in him. He was a gentleman who had always respected my privacy.

I must be suffering from temporary insanity for having such thoughts in the first place. What reason would Samuel have for going over my receipts, anyway? I shook my head, putting all thoughts of Samuel doing something like this out of my head.

15

A brand-new pattern developed between me and Samuel. We went on dates, and he was always trying to outdo himself, each time taking me on some unique, creative outing that included dinner as well, and afterward, we would return to my home and have sex. Lots of it.

I felt like a teenager around him. I couldn't get enough. And not all could be explained by the dry spell I'd had before him. It was because it was with him. Plain and simple.

I would feel overwhelmed by his sheer perfection, but I was having too much fun, so I decided I didn't care to overanalyze things. And Dr. Neal agreed with me one hundred percent.

Two weeks after the first time we slept together, Samuel came to my house, which wasn't that unusual, and I started kissing him from the moment he stepped inside. I hoped we could squeeze in a quickie before dinner or anything else he'd planned for us.

Samuel chuckled in return, breaking the kiss. I pouted, which was ridiculous since I had never pouted in my life.

"I have a big surprise for you," he announced.

I got all excited instantaneously, since his surprises were the best. I knew that by now.

"What is it?" I inquired, looking over him to see if he was by chance hiding something behind his back.

He wasn't.

"Did you get me a pony?" I joked, making a show of looking outside through a window.

"Nice try, but no."

"Tell me," I urged.

He shook his head, kissing the tip of my nose. "I can't tell you, not yet."

"Why not?" I argued in return. I wasn't truly irked, it was more for show, and he was aware of that.

"Because that would be cheating."

I started booing, and he laughed. At times, I thought he enjoyed tormenting me just a little bit too much. All the same, I couldn't complain. He was doing all of this for me. And it was super fun, despite my complaints.

"If you want to discover what I have in store for you . . ."

"I really do," I interjected.

"Then be a good girl and put on a nice dress, darling, so we can be on our way."

"So we're going on a trip?" I fished.

"Everything will be revealed in due time."

I rolled my eyes at him, which amused him to no end, but I did what I was told.

What to wear? I mused, opening my closet. Since I had no idea where we were going, I didn't know if I should wear something formal or casual.

In the end, I opted for a dress that could, with the right accessories, pass for both. I had a strange feeling as I started to change. Was this really my life now? I wondered while looking at myself in the mirror. *Here I am, still me, yet I definitely look different.*

All dolled up in a black dress with silver high heels on and my hair blow-dried, I could hardly recognize myself. And that wasn't simply because of the outfit. There was color in my cheeks. There were sparkles in my eyes. In other words, I looked happy. I'd forgotten how that felt, but Samuel was certainly making me remember it.

My eyes landed on the framed photograph of me and Christopher, and my heart squeezed painfully inside my chest. *I was happy with you too, my love.*

"Five more minutes, and then I am coming to get you," Samuel yelled from downstairs, breaking my spell.

"You promise?" I teased, laughing.

"Behave and hurry up," he chastised in good nature.

I grinned, zipping my dress, and after grabbing my purse, I went to join him.

"I'm finished," I announced, getting downstairs.

Samuel's eyes told me everything I needed to know about how good I looked.

I felt amazing.

"You look lovely, as always," he complimented, kissing me on the cheek. He knew better than to ruin my lipstick.

Actually, he'd learned that the hard way when he kissed me while I was wearing red lipstick. He'd tried to get it off for the rest of the night while I'd laughed so hard my stomach hurt.

"You're not too shabby yourself," I countered, giving him a hungry once-over. I was still a bit peeved that we didn't get a chance to hook up before this outing.

Later, I promised my raging libido.

"You are so kind," he countered, and we both laughed.

We left my house.

"New car?" I asked. It was not his usual black Mercedes in the driveway but a red Porsche.

"Just giving it a test drive," he explained. "You like it?"

I shrugged.

"You hate it."

"It's a nice car, but isn't it a bit of a cliché? A red sports car?" I wondered.

It simply felt like every man during their midlife crisis had to buy one. Surprisingly, I'd never pictured Samuel as that type of man.

"You're right," he replied with a sheepish smile. "I guess I was trying to impress you. However, I did promise my friend that I would give it a go. He's trying to get rid of it."

"Why?"

"His wife thinks it's a cliché."

I couldn't help but laugh.

And then we were on our way.

Naturally, I still had no idea where we were going, and no matter how many times I asked, pestered, begged, and blackmailed, Samuel remained adamant.

He refused to spoil the fun. His fun was implied.

When we ended up on Fifth Avenue, my eyebrows went up. I had no idea what we were doing there. And then he turned again and stopped in front of a jewelry shop.

I think all the blood drained from my face as my heart started skipping beats.

He wouldn't . . . I started to panic, unable to even finish that thought.

We'd barely started dating, so there was no chance in hell he would do something so reckless as to bring me to a jewelry store.

Although I was having a full-blown panic attack on the inside, on the outside, I was as cool as a cucumber, smiling, chatting, teasing.

Oh, please, God, no.

"What are we doing here?" I forced myself to ask, wearing a big smile as he helped me to get out of the car.

"You shall see," he replied cryptically, wearing a strange expression.

We entered, and I was surprised the place was larger than I imagined. And we weren't the only people inside. The store, with all those protected glass cases, was transformed into some kind of receiving area.

People in formal wear were milling about. Some looked at the displays of expensive jewelry while others stood in small clusters, conversing and drinking champagne. Models in attractive dresses mingled with the crowd while wearing diamonds. And then I understood what this was. This was some kind of invite-only event for the rich and famous. I instantly got fascinated by all the splendor.

"Oh, my God," I breathed as one of the models passed by me. She was wearing an amazing set of diamonds: necklace, bracelets, and earrings. It sparkled so brightly that I wanted to avert my eyes.

The inner crow in me really appreciated all the sparkling things, although I still couldn't understand why Samuel had decided to bring me here.

Maybe he thought I would like it? It wasn't that I didn't, it was simply that I felt out of place, especially when all the people looked at me, at us, as we walked inside. Being judged by rich snobs wasn't my idea of a fun evening. I pretended not to see it.

Pretty quickly, I didn't have to pretend. It was hard to think about anything else apart from all the jewelry around us. These were not simply decorative objects, symbols of someone's wealth and stature. These were true masterpieces. And all of a sudden, I understood why Samuel wanted me to see this. There was art presented in everything.

With that my panic finally started to subside. He was not about to propose. *Thank God.*

"This kind of show happens only two times a year, when they present new lines to their most valued clients," Samuel explained to me in a hushed voice as he grabbed two glasses of champagne from the server. He offered me one, and I accepted it with a nod.

"It's impressive," I replied simply to say something. I knew nothing about such things, so it was hard not to feel out of place. Truth be told, although I could appreciate the beauty, I couldn't care less for such things. Apart from my wedding ring, I never wore any other type of jewelry.

Samuel started walking me around, eager to show me everything, and I let him.

A few models approached us, posed for us so we could inspect the displays on them, and I always thanked them and quickly sent them away.

"Did you see something that you fancy?" Samuel asked, taking a sip of his drink.

"Everything is lovely," I replied diplomatically. I had no idea who the owner of the store was or who the designers were and didn't want to offend anyone.

"Did something captivate you?" he insisted.

"Not really."

"We shall have to keep going, then."

His comment surprised me.

I was about to ask why on Earth he'd brought me to an event like this when he exclaimed, "Look at that. It is simply marvelous," startling a couple of people around us.

I had no idea what he was talking about. He took me by the arm and started leading me toward one of the models. The model in question was wearing a subtle beige dress, yet the jewelry on her was anything but.

She was wearing a pair of lovely earrings, a bracelet that

was as wide as my forearm, a necklace that stretched almost to her navel, and a tiara. Why anyone needed a tiara in this day and age, apart from a couple of European royals, was beyond me.

"These would look lovely on you," Samuel announced, looking at the earrings.

The model smiled. "Would you like to try them?" she asked me.

I shook my head, hating to be put on the spot like that.

"Of course she would," Samuel insisted, and the model instantly obliged.

"Samuel," I complained.

"I insist," he replied with a smile.

A mirror was instantly provided for me, so I accepted the offerings and put them on. The earrings were in the shape of teardrops, adorned with small diamonds and an emerald stone in the middle. Seeing them on me, I had to admit they were not half bad. They complemented me.

"Beautiful," Samuel praised with reverence.

"Thank you," I replied politely as I tried to take them off. I didn't want to appear rude or anything, keeping them on for too long. I had no idea of protocol at these events since this was my first time.

"No, no." Samuel prevented me from taking them off.

I looked at him questioningly.

"I'm buying them for you," he informed me.

I was shocked. "You can't. It's too much." Although I was not privy to their price, I could bet it was a mind-blowing one considering where we were.

He shushed me with a kiss. "I'm doing it, and never again do I want to hear you say something is too much for you. There's no such thing."

"Samuel," I tried to argue, but he wouldn't have it.

"It would make me happy seeing them on you."

I was very much aware that we were not alone, and I didn't want to argue and cause a scene, so I relented.

Without wasting any time, Samuel took out his checkbook and bought the earrings for me on the spot. I tried not to react to the amount of money he'd just spent on me.

Some of the people clapped, complimenting my good taste, and I smiled in return.

Samuel kissed my cheek before admiring the earrings one more time. "You are a vision."

"Thank you, Samuel. I really love them."

"That is all that matters, then."

He grabbed us two more glasses of champagne and proposed a toast. "Happy two-week anniversary."

I drank to that, realizing he really cared for me. Not because he'd bought me something but because he treated a two-week anniversary as an anniversary. He was a romantic like that, and clearly generous to the point of madness. These earrings cost tens of thousands of dollars, yet he didn't hesitate at all when buying them for me. He was going to spoil me rotten.

I was still in a state of shock as we continued to look around. Part of me felt insecure with those things on. They were too expensive. And although I knew that no one would try to rob me while in here, I was uneasy.

I wondered if I would get used to wearing them.

"Excuse me, miss." Samuel called out for another model, and she came to us.

He put a free hand over his chest. "This is fate," he commented, pointing at the necklace she was wearing. It was very delicate, adorned with green gems and with a teardrop-shaped emerald dangling from a long chain. "That is utterly beautiful, and it looks like it could be a set with your earrings," he commented.

I had to agree. The necklace was exquisite. I said as much.

"You should buy it for yourself," Samuel surprised me by saying, getting excited all over again.

"What?"

"Look how good and naturally it goes with your earrings. It's pure perfection, and it would look magical on you."

"I couldn't," I rebelled.

"Why not?" he insisted. "When was the last time you truly treated yourself with something nice?" he asked while placing the necklace around my neck. "You only live once, remember?"

I looked at it in the mirror. I was surprised by how mesmerized I was by it. It looked really good on me.

"It does look nice," I allowed. I started touching the delicate masterpiece. Should I really spend all this money on it? *Where am I going to wear it? Around the house?*

"If you don't buy it, then I certainly will."

"That's all right. I will take it," I heard myself say.

Samuel was right. It was time I did something nice for myself. I had all this money, but I never did anything with it. I'd paid my mortgage and that was that. If my father couldn't take it to his grave, then why did I act as though I could? It made no sense.

I only had one tiny heart attack as I signed the check. I'd never, in my entire life, spent so much money on something this frivolous. Yet part of me was excited, so I decided not to regret it.

Samuel insisted that I should keep wearing them, but I still got a bag with all the boxes, not to mention a complementary tennis bracelet. Once we saw everything, Samuel declared it was time for us to return home, mine, of course, and I was grateful. I was starting to feel a bit heady from all the champagne I drank.

He was in particularly high spirits as he drove us toward

my house and chatted the entire time. I had to admit his good mood was pretty contagious.

Once we arrived, he turned to look at me. "I need to go to the little boys' room, but when I return, I want to kiss you for hours." He finished that with a searing kiss.

"Just kiss?" I teased.

He chuckled. "Don't be cheeky."

I laughed. It couldn't be helped. I loved teasing him. And I loved when he teased me in return.

As he went to the bathroom, I climbed the stairs to put all the jewelry in the bedroom safe. I felt much better once they were in a secured place. However, I couldn't wait to show them to Selina. She would lose her mind. Like I clearly had when I spent all that money. *I can't believe I let Samuel convince me that was a good idea*. Nevertheless, as I'd decided before, I wasn't about to dwell on that, especially since I looked damn good with them on.

I returned downstairs to put the receipts on my secretary's desk, and that was where Samuel found me.

"You took them off," he commented somewhat glumly.

I made sure I locked the desk before replying, "They're too beautiful to be worn casually at home."

"Point well taken," he allowed, embracing me. "However, I would like to inform you my birthday is approaching, and my birthday wish is to see you wearing your beautiful jewelry and nothing else." He whispered the last part into my ear.

I grinned. "Noted. However, I don't know how the other guests in the restaurant would react to something like that when we go out for dinner," I said straight-faced.

"Oh, you naughty girl," he commented before kissing me, ending our discussion.

Eventually, we managed to stumble into the bedroom to make love.

I woke up in the middle of the night. Still, with my eyes closed, I patted the bed next to me, and it was empty.

Where is Samuel? Did he leave?

Usually, he would spend the night, and we would have breakfast together in the morning.

"Blast." I could hear him cursing from somewhere in the house.

"Samuel? Is everything all right?" I asked, getting alarmed.

I started to rise when he stormed into the room, startling me a little.

"What's the matter?" I asked since he didn't return to bed and started dressing.

"I received a text. Someone broke into my warehouse."

"Oh, my God. Has something been stolen?"

"I don't know. My secretary just called to inform me. I have to go."

I wanted to help but didn't know in what way. "Call me when you know what happened."

"Sure." He went toward the door.

"Samuel?"

"Right," he muttered, barely brushing his lips against mine before hurrying away.

Minutes later, I could hear his car driving away through the night.

I was left stunned, crouching in the middle of the bed.

What just happened?

16

"I don't understand what is going on," I complained to Selina during one of our talks.

It had been three days since Samuel had stormed out of my house in the middle of the night, and he still hadn't called me back.

I'd called him the very next day, the instant I woke, but he didn't answer. So I texted, asking if everything was all right and what happened with the break-in, and he never replied.

"Is he still MIA?" Selina asked.

"Yes."

I tried reaching him a couple more times, but I was not successful at getting him on the phone. And I didn't have his office numbers, so I was solely relying on social media and his cell number in my endeavors to reach him.

Eventually, I stopped trying.

Each time he failed to answer me or text me back, my levels of anxiety increased to the point that I started worrying something bad had happened to him. He'd run away from here in the middle of the night. What if he had been in a car accident and was now lying in some hospital unconscious?

What if he surprised the burglars and they hurt him? My mind was going wild.

"Did you try calling him today?"

I shook my head, although she couldn't see me. "I don't want to appear too needy."

She sighed. "I don't know what to tell you, Charlene. This is beyond strange. And I don't know what to think."

"Me neither."

"Maybe you should try calling him again."

I didn't want to.

There was another reason I became hesitant in calling his number again. I started to worry I'd done something to make him storm out of my house in the middle of the night and disappear without a trace. What if a break-in was just an excuse he used to get away from me? Unfortunately, for the love of me, I couldn't figure out what I'd done wrong.

"He can see all my calls, all my texts. He already knows I'm worried," I replied eventually.

"What if he lost his phone?"

"I tried reaching him through his social media as well."

"I can't believe he just disappeared like that," Selina said, sounding baffled.

That made two of us.

What if he really did all that to get away from me? I continued to stress.

Was I too needy? I didn't think so.

Was I too cold? That didn't ring true either.

Was he starting to feel used because I wanted to have sex all the time?

That is just ridiculous.

Besides, he'd bought me a pair of earrings that very same night. A man who wanted to bolt didn't do such things.

Which made this entire situation maddening. And as my

crazy mind provided, the possibilities were endless as to why this was happening.

"I'm worried something happened to him."

"You can't think like that," she was quick to reassure me.

All the same, how could I not?

"I'm sure he'll reach out to you when he gets a chance," Selina said. Unfortunately, it was obvious she was equally as dumbfounded by this situation as I was.

"I hope."

"Try not to worry too much."

"That ship's sailed."

"Look, I know I just told you everything would be all right, but how were things between you two?" she surprised me by asking.

"What do you mean?"

"Well, I was under the impression that your relationship was blooming."

"I was under the same impression." And it worried me when Selina came to the same conclusion, that all of this was my fault. What if Samuel had decided to cut all ties and move on? If he was indeed ghosting me, then I would still like to know. There was no point in worrying if he wanted to break up.

I would rather hear him say that he'd changed his mind than spend my days needlessly troubled about him. It was agony, constantly worrying whether anything had happened to him while my mind came up with all kinds of gruesome scenarios to explain why he wasn't able to pick up the stupid phone.

Perhaps like all men, he avoided confrontations. I really hoped that was not the case.

"I'm sure all will be resolved quickly."

"We shall see," I replied glumly.

I simply couldn't understand. He'd looked so happy that

night, bought me a very expensive present, and then in the middle of the night, everything changed.

I was so rattled I forgot to even tell Selina about the earrings, and now I didn't feel like it.

After I finished my conversation with her, since we were simply going in circles without finding a solution, I tried to work out, do one of my self-defense classes, yet I didn't feel like it. I wanted to watch some sappy movie and eat ice cream. And I refused to do that. It was pissing me off that I felt like that in the first place. *I will not pine over a man I met only recently.*

I didn't pull myself from the bottom of a well that was filled with despair and sorrow, only to jump headfirst into another.

And I definitely didn't want to call my therapist and whine to her because my boyfriend wasn't calling me back.

After all this time, I should be able to do certain things, surpass certain emotions on my own without running to my therapist each time I felt bad. Wasn't that the point, anyway? To learn to deal on my own?

I'm sure Samuel has his reasons for acting in that way, and perhaps I will learn them someday. Regardless, I refused to feel bad over him anymore.

On impulse, feeling like this house was caging me, I went outside.

I ended up in the local park. Naturally, it made me think of Samuel and the kiss we'd shared. Our first kiss had happened in a park similar to this one because I'd decided to make the first move. No matter what, I still didn't regret that.

Perhaps that would change, but I didn't think so.

You can't hide from life fearing that bad things will happen, because then you miss all the good things. I knew that now.

I realized that although I thought about all those things and about Samuel during my walk, I was all right. Perhaps it sounded weird, but it was strange that I wasn't falling apart because of this whole situation with him.

Was I strong enough now, or was the reason I was able to behave in such a manner because I didn't care too much about him?

That was also an option.

To be perfectly fair, I did care about him. I loved spending time with him and definitely lusted after him, but I was sure I wasn't in love with him. Perhaps that was what saved me from having an overly emotional reaction to his absence.

Despite all of this, I still wanted, maybe even needed, to know what had happened to him. Selfishly, I needed to know this wasn't my fault. Then again, I prayed with all my heart that he was well. I prayed that he hadn't been hurt in any way.

I felt like I stayed in that park for hours, simply walking in circles, which was appropriate since my mind went in circles as well. I was shifting from worry to anger to sadness.

I worried something had happened to him, I was angry he wasn't answering his phone, and I was saddened because I had a feeling this was how our story would end. Which wasn't a true ending at all since there was no closure. He'd simply disappeared without a trace, without an explanation.

However, as I'd already learned, personally, closures weren't something that were God-given. Only a few lucky ones got to experience it. The rest of us had to make do, learn how to live with unanswered questions.

And then my phone started ringing, snapping me from my thoughts.

"Oh, my God," I exclaimed, seeing it was Samuel calling me. Then relief washed over me. He was all right. I rushed to answer, but my fingers fumbled.

I let out a sound of frustration as I finally managed to answer it.

"Hello, Samuel?" There was no way I could play this coolly. I was worried, plain and simple.

"Hello, Charlene." He, on the other hand, sounded normal.

That was good. Right?

"I've been calling you for days. Where were you?"

"I know. I've been busy," he replied.

I made a face. Nobody was so busy they were unable to respond to a single text. *You need ten seconds maximum for writing one that said,* I'm all right.

"I see," I said through gritted teeth.

Although part of me was grateful he was apparently unharmed, well, the rest was furious. *How dare he do something like this to me? Didn't he know how worried I was?* How I was unable to sleep, imagining all kinds of terrible things happening to him?

Now that I knew all was well with him, I didn't want to speak with him anymore.

"I called because I wanted to ask you if you would like to accompany me to Cowentheart's art show this Sunday."

What?

He disappeared in the middle of the night, freaked out over a break-in, then failed to return any of my calls for days, leaving me wondering if he was alive or dead, and now, when he eventually honored me with a phone call, he was asking me on a date as though nothing had happened. *Seriously?*

"Samuel, is everything all right?" I had to ask because although this person sounded like Samuel, it couldn't possibly be Samuel. The man I knew would not act so callously.

How well do you know him, anyway? came a fleeting thought.

"Of course. Why? Has something happened? Are you okay?"

Are you kidding me? And then I simply snapped. "Samuel! You left my room three nights ago, saying something about a robbery, and that was the last time I heard anything from you. I called and called, and you never answered."

"Oh, damn, did you not get my text? I swear I sent you one. I've been so busy that I haven't had a chance to call you till now."

"No, I didn't get your text, and I was worried."

"All is well, darling; no need to be worried. It was just a false alarm."

Was I just supposed to accept that?

I was stunned.

"Well, I'm glad to hear that." Although it was now three days later.

Better late than never, I suppose. There was comfort in the knowledge that he wasn't lying in a ditch somewhere. Although where one would find a ditch in Manhattan was beyond me.

Although I was relieved that he'd finally called back, I was now more confused than ever.

Why was he acting so nonchalantly? I couldn't move past the fact that he had been gone for three days. I couldn't reach him. I couldn't verify whether he was all right or not.

And I was aware we'd only started dating. I didn't have the right to demand all kinds of answers, but this was a matter of basic human decency.

"I apologize if I caused you any kind of inconvenience."

"It wasn't an inconvenience. I was worried about you."

"You don't have to worry about me, I promise."

The way he said that made me pause. Did something bad happen and he didn't want me to worry? Or was I reaching? Was he staying away because he was in a world of trouble, and he didn't want to involve me?

Or was something else entirely at play here?

My mind was spinning.

"Charlene?"

Apparently, my mind had wandered off again. "Yes?"

"Would you like to go to the art show with me or not?" he insisted.

To be perfectly honest, I didn't. I wanted him to come to my house so we could have an open and long conversation during which he would explain the three-day-long absence and the missing text message. I wanted to know what had prevented him from answering my calls.

The only explanation was that something terrible had happened, which probably involved his warehouse, and he needed time to settle it all out. Perhaps there was a reason he couldn't speak about it and he was only lying to me about it being a false alarm.

He did sound a bit cagey.

Besides, after the time he'd had, the last thing he needed or wanted was to talk some more about it, I realized. He did sound stressed. Despite everything, the last thing I wanted was to add stress to him.

This relationship was supposed to be fun, not a burden.

There would be plenty of time to talk about what had happened in the future when the dust settled, when he calmed down, I rationalized.

That was why I said, "What kind of art show?"

"Cowentheart's."

I'd heard something about it.

"It's on Sunday."

"All right, I'll go with you," I agreed.

"Good. I will send you the details. I have to go now."

And before I had a chance to reply, he hung up.

"Weird," I said, looking at my phone.

Despite my previous rationalization, some of my uneasiness reappeared. I knew nothing about what was going on.

All the theories I had were purely conjectures, theories I came up with to ease my restless mind.

The fact was that Samuel was acting all kinds of weird, yet no matter what, I was determined to find out why.

With my mind settled, I decided it was time to return home.

I was going to a very important art show, as it turned out, and there was a big chance I would need something new, something special to wear. And time was running out.

Perhaps I will even put my new jewelry on, I mused, picking up my pace.

17

I couldn't let go of what had happened with Samuel, I just couldn't. Although he'd called and acted as though everything was in order, something deep inside me was telling me I wasn't privy to the whole truth.

He was definitely holding something back. And at this point, it didn't even matter why he felt the need to act in such a manner or what his motives were for wanting to be MIA.

I needed to know the truth, regardless. And if he wouldn't tell me exactly what was going on or where he had been for the past three days, then I would have to find out on my own. And after some thought, I realized I knew precisely what I needed to do. Part of me felt foolish that something like that hadn't occurred to me from the start.

In my opinion, that was the true testament of my current emotional state, all the stress, that I couldn't think of the simplest solution to the problem at hand immediately. To find out what had happened, I simply had to check the news. It was as easy as that.

Luckily, I subscribed to all the local papers. That was one

of my quirks. I liked to be informed, and I couldn't believe I hadn't touched the newspapers in the last couple of days.

Taking the stack of papers and putting them on the bed, I swiftly started going through them, always paying attention to the sections with the crime reports. I hoped that I would read something about a break-in at an import warehouse somewhere in the area.

In the grander scheme of things, perhaps that wasn't such a big deal, but I couldn't assume anything. Perhaps it had been a simple burglary, or perhaps it had turned into something else.

Don't think like that.

Ever since Christopher died, I had become obsessed with crime and followed the patterns, frequencies, and types of it religiously. At first, I'd done it on a global scale. That was probably the reason I took self-defense classes, although online, in the first place. I never again wanted to feel like I did that night, powerless and utterly afraid. So I learned all that I could, and I stayed informed.

I guess I wanted to find meaning in the tragedy that happened to me, to my small family of two. I wanted to know what had prompted that man to act in that manner because the truth was, he didn't have to kill Christopher. We were willing to give him everything we had. Unfortunately, some monstrosities couldn't be explained, no matter how hard one tried.

For a long time, that was all that I did, all day, every day. Read about crimes everywhere, watching documentaries about it as I trained, but with Dr. Neal's help, I contained myself to only tracking it locally. And for this mission, that was precisely what I needed.

I read all the papers from the last three days and couldn't find anything about that specific type of robbery. Someone tried to rob a post office, and one jewelry shop did get robbed, yet that was it. There was nothing about a warehouse where antiques were stored. There was no mention of Samuel's name.

I grabbed my laptop and did an internet search just in case. I still came up with nothing.

That's strange, I mused. These local news reporters were always very meticulous.

Did it even happen? Or maybe it was only an attempted robbery, and then there was a huge possibility no one would bother to write about it, I deduced.

If nothing happened, why did Samuel avoid me for three days? Sadly, even after all this time, I wasn't closer to getting any answers to all these questions.

No matter whether I could find anything in the papers or not, the fact remained that Samuel had disappeared for three days. That by itself made me believe that whatever had happened was very serious. However, what kind of crime wouldn't be published?

An unreported one.

Was Samuel involved with the mafia? My mind started to come up with ideas. Perhaps I'd watched too many movies in my youth about mobsters, but to me, that kind of made sense.

An organization like that could launder a lot of money that way, through an import business. Not that I was that well-informed. There was a big chance this was mob related, and then Samuel covered it up, not wanting his reputation to be tarnished or something like that.

If I was right, what would that mean? What should I do? What could I do? Should I try to confront him or ignore everything?

What if you are just crazy, coming up with crazy stories? Part of me rebelled. I was acting like some Nancy Drew, Sherlock

Holmes character, except unlike any of those detectives from the novels, I had zero evidence to support my theory.

The fact that he'd vanished for three days was odd, and all the same, it was only that. He'd sounded strange over the phone, yet although that too was a bit strange, it wasn't evidence of anything sinister.

Perhaps he was embarrassed that it took him so long to call me back, and inviting me on that date was his way of apologizing.

I sighed. I was tired of all the speculating. It was getting me nowhere. So I decided to stop. Stop jumping to conclusions and wait. The truth would reveal itself eventually. I simply had to be patient.

And then I got another idea since, apparently, I wasn't ready to give up yet. I grabbed my phone and texted Selina about how Samuel had finally called. She called me immediately like I knew she would.

"So what did he say?" she asked without preamble.

I made a face, although she couldn't see me. "Well, actually, he didn't say anything."

"What do you mean?" She sounded precisely the way I felt, confused.

"I asked about what happened, but he was pretty vague. He said everything was fine and then asked me on a date," I tried to explain.

"And why didn't he call you sooner?"

"He was busy."

"No one is that busy," she scoffed. "I don't buy that for one second."

Thank you. That was my sentiment exactly, and I was glad I wasn't the only one who thought like that.

"I think something happened, something that he doesn't want to tell me about."

I didn't mention my mobster theory. I would feel too silly.

"Like what?"

"Something bad."

"Did he sound weird over the phone?"

"Not really. Maybe a bit cagey. He pretended all was well. Those were his exact words."

"And you think that means something really bad happened?"

"Yeah."

"Okay, I'll admit that not calling you for three days was a dick move. And his pretending as though nothing happened makes perfect sense because that way, he doesn't have to apologize."

"What? I'm not following you."

"I'm just saying don't go crazy making excuses for him. He was just a man acting like a man."

That made no sense to me. I said as much.

"If something did happen, then you would definitely hear about it in the news," Selina pointed out.

I frowned. That was a good point.

"You're right, but I still feel like something isn't right," I insisted.

"Did he mention the break-in?"

"Not at all. I had to ask, and when I did, he brushed it off."

"See, that means nothing happened."

"How can you be so sure?"

"I'm not, but it's the most logical explanation."

"Then why didn't he call?"

I really thought he liked me. We'd spent all this time together, had amazing sex, and then he disappeared, without a trace.

Selina remained quiet for a bit before saying, "What were his exact words, Charlene?"

I tried to recollect. “He simply said how I shouldn’t worry and that all was well.”

“That’s it, then.”

She lost me again. “What do you mean?”

“He’s embarrassed.”

“What? Why?” I asked, making a face.

“You saw him while he was freaking out, worrying about his business. He ran away.”

“Yeah, to deal with a crisis,” I defended.

“It doesn’t matter. I’m sure he got embarrassed. Men can be like that, weird over nothing.”

“But why?”

“All this time, he was trying to show this perfect side of him. And now you saw the other side of the coin.”

For some strange reason, that made sense. Kind of. “You really think that is what happened?”

“Yeah.”

“You know, I checked the crime reports, and I couldn’t find anything about a warehouse being robbed,” I pointed out.

“You checked the news? Paranoid much?” she jibed, but I ignored that.

“Well, I was worried. However, I couldn’t find anything.”

“So now you think he lied about it?” Selina tried to follow my train of thought.

“I’m sure he wouldn’t. His action was genuine. He stormed out like his business was on fire,” I explained.

“See, I’m telling you. He presented a certain image that got shaken, and then he needed time to get over it,” Selina explained matter-of-factly.

He needed time while I worried?

I sighed. Apparently, I’d reached my plateau. *I am done worrying and trying to find excuses for him.* Whatever happened, happened. I didn’t care anymore. All this stressing was exhausting. I needed a break from the drama. I deserved it.

"So? What am I to do now? Should I speak with him?"

"I say let it go."

"What?"

"Don't do anything. Treat this unfortunate event as one of his less than desirable traits and move on," Selina advised.

"Just like that?"

"Yeah, forget this ever happened and continue having fun."

Should I do that? *Could I?* I was worried that my reaction showed me I was more emotionally invested than I believed.

Then again, that was such a strange situation, anyone would react the same way in my place. That realization calmed me a bit. I wasn't ready to get attached.

"However, if he tries to pull another stunt like that," Selina continued, snapping me from my thoughts, "then dump his ass and move on. Life is too short for unnecessary drama."

"You're absolutely right."

"I know I am. With me around, you don't need that shrink of yours."

"You're more fun too," I agreed.

At that, we started laughing.

I felt much better after my chat with Selina. She was such a good friend. At times, I felt like I was taking advantage of her, monopolizing all the conversations with all my unnecessary drama. So I made a mental note to be more appreciative and as invested in her life as she was with mine in the future.

And speaking of conversations, I was supposed to have my session with Dr. Neal later today. I decided to cancel it. I didn't feel like talking about what had happened with Samuel with her as well. I'd done all that with Selina, and now I just wanted to do something else, something fun.

Besides, I had another reason for wanting to ditch today's session.

Ever since I'd started seeing Samuel, Dr. Neal was pestering me to end these online sessions with her and start coming to her office like all the rest of her clients. She tried to reason that was the next step in my recovery, but I really didn't want to do that. No matter how many times I left this house to go on dates with Samuel, it didn't include going to therapy as well.

For me, those were two very different things. The mere thought of driving to her office building, then sitting in the waiting room for my appointment, and having to speak with her in her office, in her space, filled me with pure dread.

I liked to be in my own house, surrounded by my own things that offered me comfort and support, while I spoke about my innermost thoughts and emotions.

That wasn't to suggest I thought her office was a hell's pit. I was sure it was lovely, that she as a professional managed to create a safe place for all her patients, but even with that in mind, I preferred this arrangement.

Going there would signal that I was truly going to therapy. By staying home, I felt more like I was conducting a conference call with a professional. And I was very much aware of how weird all that sounded.

Nevertheless, I was strongly opposed to changing anything in our relationship. Naturally, I tried telling all this to my therapist, but she still believed I should give her way a chance, and if I didn't like it, we could always return to how things were, which sounded like a perfectly rational offer. The problem was that I wasn't rational, not about this, so I knew even before I tried how her way would fail.

It would simply be a colossal waste of time and nothing else.

I could only speak about Christopher and my inner

demons where I could feel my late husband the most. He was the one giving me strength, although he was my biggest weakness at the same time. Of course, no matter what, I would stay adamant and continue having sessions online. And I really hoped Dr. Neal would not press this issue because I was willing to go so far as to find another therapist.

Maybe I can even find one who will be willing to do house calls. That thought made me pause.

Was I overreacting? How could I be so sure I was right if I never tried her way? It wasn't like I was infallible. I'd made tons of mistakes in my life, and I was bound to make many more.

My mind found ways to torment me. If I wasn't stressing about Samuel, I was mourning Christopher. And now I was agitated by my own therapist. *Welcome to my crazy life.*

I really should have a break. But how to escape when my mind was the problem? I needed a distraction.

I couldn't simply cancel my session with Dr. Neal. I needed to fill that time doing something else because otherwise, I would simply continue to drive myself crazy. And that was definitely something I was trying to avoid all these years.

And then I remembered my date with Samuel. I still had no clue what to wear to that thing, which was a perfect excuse to go shopping. I was never that girl, but I figured trying out a few dresses, maybe even finding matching shoes, was the perfect way to take my mind off things, at least for a few hours.

With my mind pretty set, I dialed Dr. Neal, except I chickened out at the last second. Perhaps it would be better to simply text her.

The last thing I needed was for her to trick me into speaking with her. I didn't have time. As it turned out, I had more pressing issues, like going shopping.

I almost smiled at my stupid joke as I collected all the old newspapers to throw in the trash. No more stressing about what had happened at the warehouse.

After I cleaned up, I went to get dressed. I was almost looking forward to choosing my outfit for my date with Samuel.

What is happening with me?

18

On Sunday, Samuel came to pick me up at six o'clock sharp so we could go on our date. I was wearing a black and white sleeveless dress that I'd bought during my shopping spree, which had super-thin stripes and would be too long if I didn't wear high heels.

Because Samuel was much taller than me, I made a point to always wear heels, which was something I wasn't used to. But it made the kissing more convenient.

"You are a vision," he complimented, kissing me.

"Thank you," I replied.

I noted that he looked pristine. There was not a hair out of place, and there were no scratches, no marks, no bruises. He definitely didn't look like he had been in a car accident or had gone through a beatdown from a mobster's enforcer. Not that I was still obsessing about what had happened to him during those three days. I'd put that firmly behind me.

Without wasting any time, I left the house, and then Samuel helped me get into the car. Soon, we were on our way to the gallery.

Samuel chatted the whole way, telling me how frustrated

he got with a client who wouldn't admit he knew nothing about French-style furniture or how it was supposed to look while demanding it.

"He stormed out of my office once I suggested he do a quick Google search on the subject."

"You didn't!"

"I did. I admit it wasn't my finest moment, but the man was an utter fool."

"Did he come back?"

"No. And I certainly hope he won't," he replied.

Like always, he had me laughing, gasping for air in no time. It was like old times. Like nothing had changed. The conversation between us was easy, our witty banter stimulating, and our crazy chemistry made me want to ask him to turn the car around, which I didn't.

And that was supposed to be a good thing. And it was. It was only that I still had this knowledge in the back of my head that something was wrong. And that notion wouldn't leave me alone. Which meant I couldn't fully enjoy it because that nagging voice in the back of my head kept telling me everything had changed. And just like that, I started to feel like I wouldn't be having fun, not really, as long as I was in the dark. I had to discover what had happened or I would go mad.

You are already mad, a small voice reminded me, but I ignored that. Selina's words came back to me. *Life is too short for unnecessary drama.* That was exactly what I was doing, prolonging drama and overall being paranoid without a cause. *We all have good and bad days. We all say and do things that we aren't proud of.* That moment was one of Samuel's.

So why was I this hard on Samuel?

It wasn't like he was obliged to call me. We'd never really defined our relationship, and it wasn't like we were that serious. It wasn't like we were married, so he was entitled to his secrets, to keeping his problems private. And if Samuel required some alone time, then I should be okay with that.

If he said he was busy, then I should accept that and move on. And if I couldn't, then maybe I should stop canceling on my therapist because I required serious work.

Regardless of what had truly happened, I should respect Samuel's privacy. It was as simple as that. I understood the need for solitude and privacy more than most, so my reaction wasn't completely fair.

Besides, he'd apologized. Why was I ignoring that?

Was I intentionally trying to sabotage this because I wasn't used to being happy? Since that was too deep for me at the moment, considering I was about to socialize with other people, I decided to shelve that for some other time. Preferably, during my hour with Dr. Neal.

With that somewhat settled, I did my best to focus on Samuel and everything he was telling me. I was determined to have a great time tonight. I didn't have to work hard on achieving that since Samuel was an amazing guy. Being in his company always put a smile on my face.

The gallery that hosted this particular event was one I'd never visited before, so I was looking forward to it, and the art show itself turned out to be highly entertaining. Although I liked the art around me, in this case paintings, because they spoke for themselves, I had to admit that the visual aids that accompanied them really added something special to the whole experience.

Overall, I was highly impressed by everything I saw and felt.

Honestly, I was relieved I didn't have to try so hard to have fun, that I wasn't so far gone as to continue obsessing about everything after putting the matter to bed.

I was having immense fun interacting with the 'art' and

was impressed by the artist's vision for this exhibition. It was a bold move that absolutely paid off.

I couldn't imagine Johannes Vermeer or Picasso doing something like this, but perhaps that was understandable since each period brought its new trends, new techniques, and a new understanding of what art was in the first place. That wasn't necessarily a bad thing, although there were always those who tried their best to keep things as they were, as though afraid of any kind of change.

Maybe I'm the same way. Insisting on living in that house without Christopher, unable to admit how things had changed. I banished that. That was different.

"You should definitely buy something for your house," Samuel suggested, snapping me from my thoughts.

I nodded absentmindedly. What I'd just thought shook me a bit.

"Look at those colors, those lines. It would look perfect in your living room," he continued.

The piece in question was called *Flower*. And it was an absolute explosion of colors. That was the only way I could describe it. Abstract art was never really my thing, although I had to admit I liked this exhibition very much. It was obvious the artist had true talent. However, even though the painting was beautiful, it didn't speak to me. Not in the same manner that painting of a dancer that Samuel gave me spoke to me.

"What do you think?" he prompted since I remained silent.

"I don't know," I replied, really looking at it. I saw a lot of beautiful works here, but I didn't like any of them that much. I wasn't in love with any of them, so that urge to own it was absent. I didn't feel like hanging any of them in my living room either.

Buying a painting was a commitment since that was something I would have to look at for a long time. And I didn't spot anything I would enjoy seeing each day. More to the point, to purchase something without meaning definitely wasn't my thing.

"How about this one?" Samuel pointed with equal enthusiasm.

"I don't like the colors." It would go terribly with everything I owned.

Then Samuel would convince me to change all the furniture inside my living room. I almost laughed aloud at the thought.

"There has to be something here that is to your liking." He almost sounded frustrated while saying that. And it made me pause. I could not understand why he was getting so upset about this. What was it to him if I bought something here? It wasn't something he should feel so strongly about. It was my money, my decision.

Unfortunately, his bad mood definitely rubbed off on me. And once again, I was wondering what was up with him. I could not understand him.

And then it hit me. I didn't have to wonder anything. He was standing right in front of me, so I could ask him anything I liked.

"Let's keep on looking, then," he said with a sigh. That irked me even more, and I refused to move.

"Why are you acting like this?" I demanded, letting my irritation be shown.

"Like what?" he asked, looking genuinely surprised by my outburst.

Honestly, so was I. Usually, I avoided confrontations, but I felt like this time, I had to say something.

"Like it bugs you that I don't want to buy any of these paintings."

He recoiled and recovered quickly. "Because it does."

He surprised me by saying that. "Why?" I asked, bewildered.

He shrugged, and all of a sudden, all the heat disappeared from him. In its place was something else. *Sadness?* But I didn't have time to question that because he said, "Because I see you live your life so joylessly, and it's breaking my heart."

His gaze was so sincere that all the fury and irritation I felt simply disappeared. I was also quite taken aback by his observation.

"Joylessly?" I asked, testing the word. His words shook me to the core. I didn't like how that sounded. Probably because it was true.

Samuel took both my hands in his. "I know you have been grieving for a long time, but enough time has passed, and it's time to live again," he said in a soft voice.

"I know," I replied in the same manner.

"And you have the perfect opportunity to do so."

I looked up at him because I didn't fully understand what he meant by that. Luckily, he continued.

"You have all that money to play with, to help you experience the good parts of life, and I simply want you to have more fun. That is all. And I am sorry if you saw my encouragements as pushy. I never meant to cross any lines. I just want to help you get more comfortable in your own skin."

His little speech was a lot to take in. And I couldn't say I wasn't moved by it. He was right that despite inheriting all that money, I continued to live as though I were still struggling. So maybe he was right. Maybe I should do more, experience life more. Although I couldn't quite agree that shopping was the way to go. There were other things I had denied myself for too long, like traveling or taking a real self-defense class.

All the same, his words showed me, once again, that he was an amazing human being who always had the best interests at heart regarding me. He was mindful of my well-being even when I was too stubborn to see it.

And now that my eyes were wide open, I was very grateful and appreciative of him in my life.

I kissed him before replying, "I appreciate your caring enough to do all this for me, but I want you to know I do have fun. A lot."

"That means my devious plans are working," he said, chuckling.

"To an extent," I hedged.

"What do you mean?"

He was honest with me, so I decided to be fully honest with him in return. "After spending all this time with you, I realized that I prefer your company over any kind of possession I could acquire."

Samuel seemed stunned for a moment, but before I got a chance to get embarrassed by my words, he leaned down for a kiss.

"Thank you for saying that," he murmured against my lips.

I simply kissed him in return.

In the end, I was glad I had this semi-argument with him because, as it turned out, a lot of stuff came to the surface. I now understood why he always had this need to take me to certain places, and I, in return, had told him how I felt about it. And in a way, I felt better about us. I could even feel that the wariness I had over that previous incident was starting to lose its strength.

Samuel was a good guy, and he deserved to be fully forgiven for what had happened because right here and now, he'd showed me how much he cared about me.

So nothing else really mattered. Smaller misunderstandings should be put to rest, especially if I wanted to bring more happiness, joy, and fun into my life. And I wanted to.

After we parted, he looked around, and some strange

emotion I didn't get to identify passed over his face before he returned his gaze to me.

"Have you had enough of this place?" he asked, wearing a half-smile.

I could guess what was on his mind at that moment. That was why I didn't even have to think about my reply. "Absolutely."

"Good, I'm taking you home."

"Good," I mimicked, and we both started to laugh as we left the gallery holding hands.

I couldn't believe how this night had turned out. It had started with a lot of doubt and suspicion, albeit on my part, yet things completely turned around, and now I felt better than ever.

And I couldn't wait for us to reach my house so we could have some serious fun.

19

After the art show, during the next month or so, Samuel continued to take me to all kinds of high-ticket events. At this point, I started to see the same type of people, the same faces, same crowd everywhere.

Being with Samuel was always highly entertaining, but since I was never a social butterfly, I found these types of outings extremely tiring as well. I had zero in common with that crowd, and to politely smile and nod while other people talked about boring things was not my thing.

There were times I really didn't want to spend my evenings around people I had no desire to get to know on a personal level. All the same, I persisted. And there were several reasons for that. The first and most important was Samuel. Although he once said this was all for me, to help me get out of my shell, I could feel how truly happy he was while we were out and about, mixing with these kinds of people, visiting auctions and things like that.

The second reason was me. I felt like I needed to do this. Although it wasn't always what I wanted to do, where I wanted to be, I still felt these were learning moments for me, and Dr. Neal agreed.

Naturally, I wanted to go because of the art itself. I loved being surrounded by what other people managed to create. It filled my soul with the purest form of energy like nothing else could.

The last reason I persisted with these kinds of social events was because of Christopher. That was probably the oddest reason, yet it was still equally as important as all the others.

I vowed I would do things and experience life for the both of us. And Christopher had been an anthropologist. I knew he would be fascinated with this crowd, by the way they interacted with one another, by how they thought. Rich people, especially those born into the riches, were definitely a different species from the rest of us. And at times, I entertained myself with the notion that Christopher would want to write a study, or even a book, about this tribal behavior.

So that was why I continued to follow Samuel everywhere. And we went to all kinds of art shows, auctions, even charity balls, and being around exquisite pieces of art was fun. I had to admit that.

As before, Samuel encouraged me wholeheartedly to spend money on portable pieces of art that weren't always cheap, like paintings, jewelry, investment-quality coins, jewels, and so on. I was far from declaring bankruptcy, but I was always mindful of how much I was spending. Especially since I wasn't working.

And this time around, when he was doing that, I didn't mind it that much because I was aware of where all of it was coming from. His heart was in the right place, and there were times that I relented, but only when I was one hundred percent sure I was doing the right thing. I only bought what I really liked and what could be justified as a sound investment. It was true my father gave me the money, but that didn't mean I should mindlessly spend it all.

So I always made sure I did my homework first, and after speaking with my attorney, we came to a decision that it would be a sound decision to utilize some of my inheritance this way as long as I had the pieces insured as well.

The prices for the pieces I decided to add to my freshly established collection would only go up, I was sure of that, so with time, if I ever chose to sell any of it, I would end up making money without actually doing anything. That was a win-win situation.

Also, there was something else I started doing ever since I met Samuel. He made me think about the future, and although I didn't know what the future held for me, I wanted to make sure that I always had enough money so I could take care of any future family I might have.

I found an investment company, and I allowed them to manage one part of my worth to buy and sell stocks and things like that. I wasn't really knowledgeable in those things, but I was starting to learn, and I had to admit I found the whole process rather interesting. I was learning expressions like 'building a portfolio', which made me feel quite proud of myself.

"You should definitely bid on this," Samuel said, snapping me from my thoughts. We were at another auction. It hadn't started yet, which was why we were allowed to see all the items that would be put on sale, up close, so we could decide on what to bid later. It was called a preview, I learned.

I made a face at what he was suggesting. I looked at him before looking at the indicated item again. Samuel was pointing at a rare coin. It was really old and ugly. "Why? It's old and ugly."

He waved his hand. "That doesn't matter," he said dismissively. "It is a sound investment, and you could probably get double for it in just a couple of years."

As I'd decided early on, this was not all about the money for me.

"I don't want to," I countered. There was no way I would ever buy something so ugly. Each piece I had purchased up to this point was something I truly liked. They were things that had stories behind them.

Samuel looked at me, clearly displeased. "Why are you so difficult at times?"

I crossed my arms over my chest. "Why are you?" I countered.

I never pestered him to buy anything. Which, come to think about it now, he never did. He'd bought those emerald earrings for me, and that was it. We went to all these events, and he only nagged me to buy things, but he never bought anything for himself.

Realizing that, I added, "And for the record, if you like it so much, buy it yourself."

It was obvious I'd put him on the spot, and he didn't know what to say.

I turned away from him and went to sit at my place. I was done arguing. Although I knew he was only trying to help, at times, he was just infuriating. I was not a child who needed constant guidance.

Besides, if I didn't want to spend my damn money, then that was my right. I didn't need his permission either way. He was really pissing me off, and it made me feel good to stand up for myself on this. I didn't need to spend money on things I didn't like.

Samuel came and joined me, but he sulked the entire time. *Men are such children at times,* I thought and could only shake my head at his behavior.

I ended up bidding on a small antique jewelry box that I

liked. It was made of gold and precious stones. Samuel looked surprised that I was doing so but said nothing, probably still irked by our small argument. So I continued bidding.

The only problem was I couldn't be sure if I was bidding for it because I truly wanted it or because I wanted Samuel to start speaking with me again. And that was problematic, I was aware of that. At the same time, I didn't dare to dig deeper to learn the answer to that question.

I ended up winning. It was a very peculiar feeling when you won at an auction. Although you nearly always paid a lot of money, you still felt like you'd achieved something monumental.

"You were absolutely right, darling. That lovely jewelry box is a far better investment than a dingy old coin," Samuel said as the auctioneer moved on to the next item.

"You really think so?" I asked.

"Absolutely," he replied. "I just hope you will keep it in a visible place where everyone can admire its beauty, not hide it away like all the rest," he commented.

I understood his meaning perfectly.

There were a couple of times in the past when he'd objected to the fact that I kept everything in my safe. The first time he couldn't spot the jewelry we bought together anywhere, he got pretty upset. He pointed that out, sneaking a peek at my jewelry box, which stood open on the vanity table. He got concerned that I'd lost it or something, and then he was quite startled to learn I had a safe.

Samuel believed art, in all its shapes and forms, should be put on display to be admired. He detested my home decorations because they were pretty basic, utilitarian. His exact words were 'bare and dull'. And I couldn't say he was wrong.

Generally, I would agree with him, but I had to be mindful in this case. My home was not secured. I had no alarm system, no cameras, so it would be pretty foolish of me if I kept all this wealth on display. It would be like inviting someone to rob me. Of course, I wasn't completely helpless. I did have the gun I'd purchased after . . . A shudder went through me as my mind drifted back to Christopher's death. I'd felt so vulnerable afterward that every sound had bothered me, so I'd bought the thing for protection. I did sleep better knowing that I had it, but I didn't advertise the fact.

Anyway, that was why I made sure all the things I'd purchased in the last couple of months were securely locked up inside my bedroom safe along with the gun. And I ignored each time Samuel teased me about it.

The same thing applied to the jewelry box. There was no doubt in my mind that it could end up somewhere else. Part of me would like to have it in some more special place, as he suggested, yet for that to happen, my house needed to be a fortress. And I wasn't prepared for that.

To celebrate my purchase, Samuel took me to dinner. All the while, I was stressing about the jewelry box that I kept beside me in its container. I was sure I looked like a madwoman looking at the empty seat next to me every couple of seconds.

"Let me look at it one more time. It's such a fine design."

"When we get home." I didn't feel comfortable taking it out in the restaurant full of people. I was sure most people were decent, but why tempt the rest?

We were dining at Lacy's because he knew I was fond of the place. The food was something special. I had no idea who their main cook was, but I was hoping the owners were treating him right because he was worth every cent.

After our meal, as was our custom, he drove me home, and when I reached for the door, he stopped me and kissed me goodnight.

"Aren't you coming inside?" I asked, a bit surprised. He always came inside.

"I would love to, but sadly, I cannot. I am off to a business meeting," he explained, making a sad expression.

"This late?" My eyebrows went up.

Samuel sighed. "You know how these wealthy people can be very eccentric."

I saw myself in that sentence as well. "Sure," I muttered in return. "I hope you close the deal." I tried to be supportive.

"Thank you, and sweet dreams, darling."

After we kissed one more time, he was on his way, and I went inside, pouting.

Although he wasn't spending the night every time, I realized I still preferred those nights. It was just better with him around. *More fun, too.*

Things between us were pretty good after that whole incident, but there were still things that puzzled me about him.

While I mused, I went to the bedroom to take care of my latest purchase. After entering the code, which was the date the first time Christopher and I kissed, I discovered it would be a tight squeeze for all of it to fit inside. I'd really let loose, as it turned out. Without my even realizing it, over the last couple of months, I'd bought a lot of things. And as a result, I'd managed to fill the entire safe. That shocked me.

Maybe I should hit a pause button because if I don't, then I will definitely need a bigger safe.

Like a bank's safe. That thought almost made me giggle. Then I sobered up while taking it all out. As I looked at all the things I'd bought, I couldn't help wondering . . . was I overdoing it?

Why was I buying all these things in the first place? Sure, they were pretty. Sure, they were sound investments. But did I really need them? I already had more money than I could spend. *Do I need more?*

Would these things end up owning me?

And then I remembered how happy Samuel looked each time I won an auction or agreed to buy something he suggested.

Son of a bitch.

I was doing all of this to please him, I realized with dread. And everything else was just rationalization, things I told myself to ease my conscience.

I can't believe I am spending all this money to make him happy. It was such a cliché.

At times, he did act strange, and at times, he appeared as though annoyed, frustrated if I refused to buy something he liked. And I, like an idiot, tried to please him, but in such a way that I wouldn't feel guilty for spending money.

That was so fucked up.

I was fucked up.

It got me wondering, though. Why did he act in such a way? The more I thought about it, the less I believed he was doing all that for me. To a degree, maybe. Then again, he would get angry when I refused to buy something.

And then it hit me. Was he an addict? Like a shopaholic or something? Was he trying to get his fix through me? I started to fear that was precisely the case. Even tonight, he had been beyond himself when I won my bidding war for the jewelry box, which was completely opposite on the emotion scale of how he'd acted before that when I'd refused to bid for the rare coin.

Oh, my God. I was horrified. Naturally, I couldn't know for sure whether I was right or not, but based on his behavior, it was a possibility. And that was troubling. I didn't want to feed his addiction.

At the same time, my behavior was equally troubling, if not even more so. That I would go to such lengths simply so he wouldn't be upset with me was disturbing, to say the least.

When did I become such a person to begin with? Regardless of that, I made a simple decision. Since such behavior was moronic, I would stop it immediately.

No matter whether he was an addict or not, I would stop pleasing him. I couldn't allow him to cloud my judgment ever again. That was as much for his benefit as it was for mine.

I quickly packed everything back in the safe, finally determined that this was my last purchase.

No more. As the automatic lock clicked into place, it rang with finality that resonated with my newfound determination.

20

"Describe the situation to me one more time," my therapist urged during our session.

I nodded, taking a deep breath. I was frustrated beyond reason, and because of that, all my words came out in a rush, in a jumble, leaving Dr. Neal scratching her head and not understanding what precisely had happened. So this time around, I wanted to do better and describe what made me feel like this in the first place.

Firstly, ever since I'd concluded that Samuel might have a problem, I became more watchful of him. Also, as I had promised myself, I stopped my shopping spree of expensive antiques, and as expected, Samuel had issues with that.

"Samuel and I were at a gallery downtown," I began, "and as many times before, he started pushing me to buy this extremely expensive painting.

"'You need more colors in your living room,' he had argued. Then he said, 'This would go marvelously over the fireplace.'"

That was where an enlarged framed photograph of me

and Christopher kissing at our wedding hung, and it would be a cold day in hell before I took it down.

"At the moment, I couldn't decide if he was pushing because he was an addict or because he was jealous. Either way, I wasn't having it.

"I told him, 'That spot is occupied.' I tried to make a joke of it, and then I said, 'For this price, I truly hope the colors are infused with golden dust, maybe even some platinum.'

"I wasn't really joking, though," I said to Dr. Neal. "I would never in my life spend that kind of money on a single painting." *All right, maybe for a Degas,* but this artist certainly wasn't him, and I didn't need to share that part with her.

"He chastised me then by saying, 'Don't be so banal.'"

"I see, and what was your reply?" Dr. Neal asked.

"I told him he shouldn't be so pushy." I had snapped at him at the time, completely irked that we were actually arguing about a stupid painting.

"Who was the artist, if you don't mind my asking?"

"Charlie Dalle," I replied. I knew that for the last decade or so, New York City had been obsessed with his paintings. It was a thing of prestige to own one of his art pieces nowadays. He'd started as a street artist but became mainstream after a well-respected gallery, D'Mondo, offered him a solo exhibition. I liked his work, but I believed he was overpriced. Not that I would ever say something like that aloud at a gallery. An angry mob of New Yorkers would chase me down the streets with pitchforks.

"He's very popular, as I understand," Dr. Neal said.

"I know, but though I like his work, I don't like it enough to want to own any of it."

"I see. And did you continue to argue with Samuel?"

I nodded. "I guess you could say that. He said, *'Excuse me for trying to enrich your life a bit.'* I replied with something like I hadn't asked him to do that."

As I described my fight with Samuel, Dr. Neal kept nodding her head, which confused me since I couldn't decide on which side she stood. And for some reason, that felt important to me.

"And then what happened?" she inquired.

"Nothing, really. I said I was done buying random things that I didn't need, and he started sulking." I just really didn't like the fact that I kept buying things to please him, and it was only making me poorer. Granted, some of these things would eventually turn a profit, but not for a while, and again, I didn't want to show off my wealth. I figured that was just inviting trouble.

"Go on."

"Well, at that point, I excused myself and left the gallery because I was embarrassed that we had caused a scene. Samuel, of course, followed me out, and we made up, but I'm still not happy about what happened."

"Did you get the impression that he sulked because you didn't take his advice or because you refused to buy anything at all?" Dr. Neal asked.

I gave it some thought and eventually shrugged. "I don't know. That's not the only time he's behaved in such a manner. This happens nearly every time we go somewhere."

"That is a bit odd," she agreed.

And that was an understatement. It was infuriating. And it was driving me insane because I simply didn't get it. Most of the time, we were having such a great time together, and the sex was amazing. All the same, each time we went to these events, it was like he turned into someone else. Which only solidified my theory about his being an addict.

I debated whether I should say something about that to Dr. Neal. I hesitated because I didn't want to end up looking silly, appearing as though I was trying to do her job, analyzing people. Nevertheless, I decided to go for it. If I couldn't say such things to Dr. Neal, then what was the point of going to therapy anyway?

"I've even started wondering if he has a problem," I stated carefully.

"What kind of problem?" Dr. Neal sounded intrigued.

"Like maybe he's an addict."

"I was just thinking the very same thing," she agreed, to my surprise. "And that he is actually trying to maintain his addiction vicariously through you," she explained.

I nodded. That was what I thought too, if not in those precise technical terms.

"So you think that's a possibility?"

"It would be unprofessional of me to speculate, but if you believe there are reasons for concern, then you are probably right."

"What should I do? Should I confront him?" I asked.

"That would be rash since there is no proof," she cautioned. "At this moment, I see only one solution."

Dump him? Why did my heart sink as I thought that? "What is it?"

"I suggest that you come up with a date or two for the two of you. If he is actually into you, he'll agree," Dr. Neal offered. "Also, there are signs you should look for if he really is an addict. However, it is entirely possible that you are misconstruing his intentions. Perhaps he just enjoys seeing you with pretty things."

"I suppose that is possible." I nodded. And her date idea was actually pretty good advice. I had never been that fond of those types of events, and I was fed up with seeing the same people I had no intentions of socializing with, so this was a win-win situation for me.

Would Samuel look at it the same way? I wasn't sure, yet there was only one way to find out. I would try to persuade him to do other things as soon as possible. And if he rebelled, then I would have my proof that he was an addict.

I sincerely wished that things would be that simple.

"I will definitely try that."

"Good."

I fully intended to speak my mind, although I was apprehensive of Samuel's reaction. I would have to find the right way to break something like that to him. But no matter what, I was going to dig in my heels, stand my ground, and tell him how I didn't want to go to these auctions anymore.

And not only because I would soon be bankrupt, going by the rate I was spending my money, but also because if Samuel really had a problem, I wanted to help. He was a good guy and deserved my support the same way he'd offered his when I needed it the most. Pulling him away from temptation was definitely step one.

"Is there something else you wanted to discuss with me?" Dr. Neal wanted to make sure all our bases were covered.

"I can't think of anything else."

My mind was preoccupied with Samuel anyway.

"All right then, let me just send you a couple of articles I would like you to read."

"Okay."

I couldn't stop thinking about all we'd discussed even after our session ended. I read all the articles she sent me about shopaholics, yet I couldn't be one hundred percent sure Samuel fit the profile.

What do you want? A face tattoo saying, 'I have a problem'? I got irked with myself. At the same time, it would be prudent not to jump to conclusions. I was worried I was yet again assuming things without actual proof.

First, I'd thought he had been kidnapped by mobsters, and now I was declaring him an addict. *Am I the real problem here?*

All this not knowing mixed with self-doubt was causing me a serious migraine.

Maybe he didn't have a problem and all of this was only in my head. However, if that was the case, then that very important question remained unanswered. Why he did he take me to all those places, pushing me to buy all those things? What was it to him? If he wasn't an addict, then what was the point? Was it really for my benefit? Did he tell me the truth and was simply doing what he believed was right?

Unfortunately, his behavior and the moodiness he exuded each time I refused to play along told a different story.

My ringing phone snapped me from my troubled thoughts. Checking the display, I groaned. It was my sister calling. *What does she want now?* I'd already given her the ten thousand dollars despite my better judgment.

I can't deal with her now, I thought and decided to ignore her calls. I had enough shit on my plate as it was.

A couple of days later, I was still troubled, especially since last night, Samuel had wanted to take me to another art show. Remembering my talk with Dr. Neal, I suggested we should do something else instead. "How about we go out to dinner and then come back to my place and just watch a movie?"

"Are you sure that's not too boring?" He had a sulky tone to his voice.

"No, I think it sounds perfect."

"You know, dinner and a movie does sound really nice." It was as though some kind of switch turned inside him, and he acted as though all was well, like dinner and then chilling at my house were his idea all along.

At times, I felt like I was dating two very different people, and I simply didn't know what to make of that.

"That is a bit weird," Selina agreed with me as I spoke to

her about what was happening between me and Samuel. I also shared what I'd learned from Dr. Neal.

"She told me I should offer different kinds of dates."

"That's good advice. If you don't want to be put on the spot like that, then changing where you go on dates is a really good idea," she agreed.

"Yeah." I was ashamed something like that hadn't occurred to me sooner.

"It will also give you a chance to see what he's really like," she pointed out.

"What do you mean?"

"Sorry for what I'm about to say because I know you like him."

"Just say it."

"Maybe he's just a snob who is with you only because you have money like him," she pointed out.

I made a face. I'd never looked at things like that. Perhaps he was simply trying to mold me by his standards all this time.

"I don't think that's the case," I argued. I'd seen a lot of goodness in him. And although I couldn't deny something was up, chucking everything to his being a superficial asshole wasn't the answer. I was sure of that.

"Okay, you do know him better than I do," Selina hedged.

Did I know him? Did I truly know him?

Although he talked nonstop, I couldn't say what I really knew about him or about his personal life. For crying out loud, I didn't even know where he lived. And I realized that had been bugging me for quite some time.

"Now that you mention it, there is something I just realized."

"What is it?"

"He always comes to my house. We never go to his."

"What? Never, never? Or you visited it once?" Selina asked.

"Nope, not even once."

To be perfectly fair, I never asked, but he never offered either. It was always implied that we would go to my house, and I couldn't help wondering why that was the case. *Is his place filled with things he bought?* I wondered, leaning heavily on my theory about his being a shopaholic. Was he hiding something else? What?

"Really?" Selina sounded shocked. "Charlene, that is a serious red flag," she warned.

"Why do you say that?" I asked. I thought his behavior was weird, but hearing my friend describe it as alarming made me feel agitated.

"Because it's not right," she argued, raising her voice ever so slightly. "It shows he is definitely hiding something."

"Like what?"

"I don't know. Something he doesn't want you to see."

Like a shopping addiction.

"Maybe he has a secret vice," Selina continued to speculate. "Or a wife."

That stopped me in my tracks. "You think he's married?" I exclaimed.

"I don't know, maybe."

I was horrified by that because it was possible, and in retrospect, it should have crossed my mind sooner since it fit perfectly.

Once I started thinking about it, I couldn't stop. All kinds of things, our dates, conversations, started passing through my mind as I tried to see if there were any clues that I missed that could suggest he was married.

"Oh, my God," I muttered eventually. How could I be so blind?

All this time, I was making all kinds of excuses for him,

yet the plainest, most logical solution to all was standing in front of my eyes all this time and I couldn't see it.

Although his being married didn't explain all the shopping.

"What are you going to do?"

"I don't know."

"Are you going to ask him?"

"I should," I started carefully. "I think I'm not going to. He could just lie," I pointed out.

"Good point."

"I will definitely try to find out, though." More to the point, I was determined, now more than ever.

All too late, I realized that questions revolving around Samuel were piling up, and I had no answers, only speculations. It was about time I changed that.

I hadn't even stopped to think what kind of relationship this was when I was so suspicious about my boyfriend. I was too invested in finding answers, proving to myself I wasn't simply paranoid or mad, to call it quits and simply dump his ass.

"Good for you. When will you see him again?"

"I was thinking about asking him on a date tonight."

"Eager to get your answers?"

"No time like the present."

I'd let this slide for way too long. And I admit that some of what had happened was definitely my fault, but all that stopped now. *I will learn what Samuel is keeping from me.*

My obsessiveness shocked me a little. Frightened me too. I couldn't remember the last time I'd felt this determined and passionate about anything, and I couldn't be sure if that was a good thing. I would certainly look at it that way.

All these thoughts running through my head almost made me smile. Dr. Neal did tell me to find a hobby, and I guess I'd found one.

This definitely wasn't something she had in mind, but nevertheless, I would be sticking to it.

Samuel was hiding something. I was sure of that now more than ever, and that was something I wasn't capable of leaving alone. No matter what.

21

I felt slightly nervous while opening the door for Samuel that night, and I couldn't really say why. My mind was set, and I was mentally prepared for anything I could uncover, so why was I acting in such a way? What was the worst thing I could learn, anyway? That he had a whole other life apart from me, that I was a side piece he cheated on his wife with?

Would that break me the way Christopher's death had? Not by a long shot. Putting everything into such perspective, I felt much better.

Samuel smiled upon seeing me. "Hello, Charlene," he greeted.

He was also very surprised when I called him, and I understood why. Up to that point, he was always the one initiating all our dates, and this was the first time I'd taken over that initiative. Part of me felt guilty about that. It appeared as though I didn't care whether we saw each other or not, which was furthest from the truth despite my current doubts.

"Hello, Samuel. Come in."

He gave me a quick kiss, getting inside.

I was about to tell him about my plan for tonight, which involved us staying in and watching a movie, except he beat me to the punch.

"We are going someplace special tonight. I had to pull some strings since it was such short notice, but I managed to get us into this really exclusive, VIP-only silent auction. So you'd better bring your checkbook," he said all in one breath while winking, looking all excited.

I suppressed making a face because this was exactly what I'd feared would happen.

"That's nice, but I was thinking we could do something different tonight," I started carefully.

"Like what?" he asked, confused.

"Like stay in for a change, order some food, catch a movie . . ." I trailed off.

"We can do that any day, but this auction is a once-in-a-lifetime opportunity."

"Will you be buying something for your business, for your clients?" I asked.

"No," he replied instantly.

"Then I would prefer not to go."

"Why?" He looked as though he couldn't believe I'd just said that.

"We've been going to all the same places lately, and honestly, I'm getting bored. And I was feeling like we should hang out for a change, spend some time just the two of us." Without all the unnecessary buying and all the expensive dinners was implied.

It was clear I'd caught him off guard because it took him a bit to respond. Eventually, he said, "Are you feeling all right?"

I wanted to roll my eyes since that felt like such a guy's response. However, at the same time, he sounded genuinely worried. And that was the only reason I didn't get upset.

"Are you coming down with something?" He even placed a hand over my forehead as though to check my temperature.

"I'm perfectly fine. It's just that I don't feel like going anywhere today, especially to that kind of event, which I don't even particularly like," I replied, laying all my cards on the table.

And then I waited patiently, without breathing, for his reply. I didn't have to wait long.

"All right, then. We can stay in."

Although it was completely ridiculous, I actually felt relieved hearing him say that. Part of me was expecting a fight, and I was grateful that part was wrong.

"However, I do expect to be pampered," he joked.

"What do you have in mind?"

"Surprise me," he replied, winking.

I chuckled. That was the Samuel I liked, and I was glad he was still here. Naturally, I still worried that he had a wife, but I decided to tackle one problem at a time.

All the same, as we settled on the couch and he put on some British movie for us to watch, I felt like there was more I wanted to say. We snuggled closer to one another, and he put a blanket over us, although it wasn't that cold.

"This is nice," I heard myself say.

"Indeed," he agreed, kissing my forehead. He took a strand of my hair and started playing with it. It felt nice, but I didn't let that distract me from my mission.

"We should do more stuff like this in the future."

He looked at me questioningly, and I shrugged.

"Just the two of us."

He had a small smile while replying, "It's always just the two of us."

"You know what I mean. No formal wear, no fancy meal, no checkbooks."

"Where is all of this coming from? I thought you loved our adventures."

That is the problem. I think you love our adventures too much. All the same, I bit my tongue not to say that.

"That wasn't what I said at all."

"You just said you don't like our outings."

"I loved some of them. I loved going horseback riding, and the boat cruise was amazing. And I love spending time with you wherever we are," I insisted. "I simply think that at times, all the rest is a bit redundant. And dates like this, when it's really only the two of us, have their charm as well."

There, I said it. And I hoped I did it in a way that wouldn't hurt his feelings. I was also very closely paying attention to his reactions. If he truly was an addict, I hoped there would be some tells, frustrations, irritations, anything.

"I see," was his only reply.

I got nothing from that.

From my perspective, I couldn't tell whether he was mad or not. "Are you mad?" I had to ask.

"Of course not," he replied instantly. And the fact that he still played with my hair reassured me that he was telling the truth.

"And simply to change the scenery, maybe we could at times go to your place." I threw that out there as well, waiting to see how he would react.

After my talk with Selina, I started to worry he might be married. I prayed like hell that he wasn't, but I couldn't ignore how strange it was that we'd been seeing each other for months and he'd never even offered for us to hang out at his place. And as Selina said, that was weird and felt like he was keeping some kind of secret from me.

I tried really hard not to start jumping to conclusions, but as it had been proven several times in the past, that wasn't my strongest suit. And then I realized the room was dead silent. He hadn't said a word after my mentioning his place.

That can't be good.

Is he simply trying to come up with an excuse, or did I spring too many things on him and he needs more time to process things? I wondered. Logically, rationally, I knew I should let him have all the time in the world and let him answer me in his due time. I'd had enough time to deal with the fact that he might be entangled with the mafia, he might be an addict, and he might be married. So it would be only fair to treat him with the same consideration.

I couldn't. The silence was killing me. I looked at him and smiled. He responded in kind, although I could see it didn't reach his eyes. Samuel was tense, and that worried me.

Does this mean he is really married?

I wanted to scream in his face, *talk to me,* but didn't, of course. That would be crazy, and my therapist wouldn't like that.

"You know, I am very curious about your place," I started conversationally, as though I didn't notice that he'd failed to respond. "I picture it as a crossover between Indiana Jones's place and Ian McKellen's."

And that was no lie.

To my surprise, he started laughing. "Do you really?"

I nodded.

"Why Sir Ian McKellen?" he wondered.

"Because he is my favorite Brit," I replied instantly.

Samuel made a face. "I thought I was your favorite Brit," he replied, getting into my face. He got as close as possible without touching me or kissing me. It was maddening. I could smell his cologne, and it was completely intoxicating.

What did he say again? "Almost," I hedged, trying to remain straight-faced.

Samuel pulled away, pretending to be hurt. "I see now that I need to step up my game."

"You'd better," I teased, and he chuckled.

"It's good that I enjoy a challenge."

He pulled me over so that I ended up straddling him. I could see where this was going. Or at least I hoped so.

"So tell me, what would I have to do to push the old fart from his throne and become number one?"

"I don't know, surprise me. Tell me something I don't know."

Like whether you have a wife or not. My libido was not happy with that thought. This was a very strange state to be in. On one hand, I was still madly attracted to him, yet on the other, I didn't want to be anyone's mistress. Not now, not ever.

"Like what?"

"Tell me something about your business. I would like to hear about your everyday life."

Samuel sighed. He started moving from under me as though he wanted to get up and move away. But as I started to rise to give him space to do that, he stopped me.

"It's all very boring, darling, and I never want to talk about boring stuff with you."

"Maybe it won't be boring. I would like to know. Try me."

"Perhaps some other time. Let's enjoy this movie first. It is a very good one."

Was it only my imagination, or was that unanswered answer kind of his thing? Looking back, I was dead sure it was not my imagination or paranoia. He did that kind of thing all the time.

He is married, as Selina told me. That was why he never wanted to share anything personal with me. I was only a fun distraction for him, and nothing more.

"Darling?"

"Yes?"

Did he have a change of heart? I started feeling a sliver of hope.

"I lied about the movie. I would like to kiss you now."

A sane person would say no. A sane person would demand to know the truth on all those accounts. Unfortunately, as it turned out, I was far from sane. That was why I said, "I would like to kiss you too."

The instant our lips met stopped my train of thought.

We kissed for a while, and I hoped it would turn into something more when he stopped. "I have to admit, I approve of these kinds of dates," he breathed against my lips, sending shivers down my spine. "They definitely have their advantages."

"Like what?" I replied in the same manner, biting on his lower lip ever so slightly.

I knew he liked that, or more accurately put, I could feel it.

"Like this." In one swift movement, he scooped me up and started carrying me toward the bedroom. I started laughing. It couldn't be helped.

In the back of my head, I was very much aware that my little talk with him didn't actually solve anything, but as it turned out, my hormones had no problems in postponing all the drama for a couple of hours.

He threw me on the bed, and I grinned. "You are absolutely right. We could never do this at the Met."

His face was wicked in those moments. "I believe I would like to take you up on that challenge."

I started laughing again, and he interrupted it with a kiss.

After we had sex and simply lay in bed holding one another, lost in our own separate thoughts, I realized I actually felt good about our little talk. Without any arguments or frictions, I'd managed to convey all that was troubling me, and although he didn't say anything about it, I believed his actions spoke volumes. The fact that we ended up in bed told me he'd heard me.

Now, only time would tell if anything would change. I hoped it would because I liked Samuel and wanted to continue seeing him. Naturally, that wouldn't be possible if he was not one hundred percent honest with me.

What if he's not? I banished that last thought, not wanting to ruin my postcoital bliss. There would be some other time to stress and be consumed by all the negativity. Not now, not today. Today, I wanted to enjoy my time with my boyfriend, and that was all.

Besides, I had to believe change was possible. If I could change, then the possibilities for other people were truly endless.

Absentmindedly, I started playing with his hands. And in a stroke of inspiration, I looked at his ring finger. I couldn't see any visible signs on it, yet that didn't mean anything.

"What are you doing?" he asked curiously.

"I like playing with your hands," I lied.

"I can give you something else to play with," he joked.

I grinned. "Already?"

"What can I say? I can't get enough of you," he said before kissing me anew.

I wasn't complaining.

He's not married. I had to believe that no married man could ever be capable of this level of deceit. I knew how naive of me that sounded, but Samuel didn't look like the type. And as for the rest? All the unnecessary buying and dragging me to extravagant events, I had to have faith that he could change.

He will change.

22

Samuel wasn't capable of change. Not at all. I had such high hopes after my talk with him because he looked like he understood. As it turned out, I was nothing but a fool. To be perfectly fair, we did go on two more modest and normal dates.

The first was a dinner at a restaurant that was located in the penthouse of a skyscraper, which was great because the view was spectacular. And the second was a trip to the Bronx Zoo. That was a really fun day, and I enjoyed it immensely. Sadly, afterward, Samuel returned to his old patterns, and I stayed quiet because I believed that after we did something he wanted, we would once again do something I wanted.

I was wrong. It was as though he'd completely forgotten we'd had that talk about my not particularly liking going to those specific events, especially since I was worried he was compelled to visit them because of his addiction.

Once again, he took me to a jewelry show, and I wasn't happy about it. Part of me was irked, but the rest of me was worried about him. And once he started saying how this was a must-see show, a once-in-a-lifetime opportunity, I got even more upset because I'd heard him say those same lines before.

To say my mood was pretty sour the entire evening would be an understatement. I seriously didn't want to be there, and Samuel's attitude about all of it, like this was the greatest thing ever, only intensified that feeling.

I was sure my true feelings were written all over my face as soon as we stepped out of the car and I could see where he'd taken me, but Samuel pretended he couldn't see it. *Maybe he couldn't. What do I know?*

Except then I started to doubt myself. Maybe I wasn't assertive enough during our talk. Because apparently, it was easier to second-guess myself than to accept that Samuel had completely ignored my wishes.

Was I being fair at the moment? I paused.

I believed I was pretty clear that I wanted to stop with these types of outings, but wasn't that selfish of me? This was a relationship, after all. I wasn't alone in this. Samuel had a say too. And if he wanted to come, if this was his scene, then shouldn't I be more supportive?

What about his addiction?

I had no proof he was a shopaholic. I'd only seen him purchase one pair of earrings, and those were for me. So maybe I was blowing things out of proportion. It wasn't like it would be the first time I'd done something like that.

I decided I should be more supportive if I truly wanted to be in this relationship, and I did. So I had to accept the fact that at times, we would do what I wanted, and at other times, we would do what Samuel wanted because we weren't always on the same page.

I'd never had this problem with Christopher because we shared all the same interests, but this time, it was slightly different. The kicker was I really had a lot of things in common with Samuel. We both loved art, good books, and movies with a strange sense of humor, not to mention clips with baby animals . . . just not this. I didn't equate happiness with spending money.

But having different interests wasn't necessarily a bad thing. *It's bad we stopped doing what I want completely,* part of me pointed out. I sighed, taking a sip of my drink. It was hard having all these conflicting thoughts.

"How are you, darling? Are you having fun? Isn't this piece marvelous?"

"Not really. I'm kind of bored." I decided to say the truth and see how he would react to that. Perhaps if he was reminded that I didn't like this, he would take me home.

"Give it a chance. I know you will feel differently after the main event," he encouraged.

I groaned inwardly. Nevertheless, I did my best to get through this evening, all the while wondering why I didn't turn around and go home on my own.

I didn't want to appear rude.

I didn't want to cause a scene.

I didn't want to hurt his feelings.

All of the above seemed to be my reasons. So I stayed because this was where my boyfriend wanted to be, and my being here beside him was only fair.

"Charlene?"

"Yes?"

"Look at that exquisite piece. It was made in the nineteen hundreds," he added as though that should impress me.

The necklace in question, decorated with black opals, was lovely. As he started to speak to me about it, I made a face. There was something in the knowledge that it had belonged to some other real, dead woman that made my skin crawl.

"The duchess was very infamous in her day, and that necklace was her signature piece," Samuel continued, unaware of my musings.

Perhaps from the business point of view, as an investment, purchasing a necklace like that made sense, but I could never wear it, not in a million years, while knowing some duchess who was known for her debauchery wore it first. I would just find it too creepy. *Besides, don't opals bring bad luck?* I didn't really believe in things like that, but I did find it interesting that those specific gems had such a reputation.

How did that start?

Either way, I knew such gems were not for me. I loved history, and I loved art, just not to put it around my neck.

"How do you like it?" Samuel prompted since I remained quiet.

"It's beautiful," I replied honestly, not wanting to appear a grouch. "I don't want to buy it, though," I added, knowing the next line that would come from his mouth.

He nodded, and I was relieved he didn't press the issue. Unfortunately, that didn't discourage him. "How about that one?"

"Never," I replied instantly. And I wasn't being unnecessarily difficult. Truly, that wasn't my intention. I'd decided that I was done buying things. Nevertheless, in this case, it was a pretty easy decision since the choker he'd pointed out to me was ugly as hell. It didn't matter that it had the most expensive blue diamonds in it. It was done poorly.

Says I, in my humble opinion, I joked, which almost made me laugh.

"Keep an open mind. This is an investment."

I rolled my eyes. I realized that the more he pushed, the more I pulled away. The next time he asked about something, I didn't even bother to speak, simply shook my head. I was done participating, especially since it was like nothing had changed. He'd only dragged me here so I could spend money, and the infuriating thing was that I couldn't understand why.

Why was it so important to him that I buy any of those

stupid necklaces? Was he in some kind of deal with the dealers? I discarded that immediately. Samuel was plenty rich. He didn't need to do that. Then again, what did I know about his business, anyway? It wasn't like we spoke about it at length.

"Is something the matter?" Samuel asked me at some point. "You seem rather distant."

"I'm tired." *Of this whole scene.*

He nodded sympathetically. "Let's go and see that exquisite piece over there," he said while leading me to the back of the room, "and then I will go and get us something to drink. That will revive your spirit."

I seriously doubted it. I was hoping he would agree to go home and call it a night after hearing me say that, but apparently, he wasn't ready to leave this scene.

Still, for whatever reason, I nodded. Actually, I knew the reason. I wanted to see how all of this would play out.

This time, there were no models around. All the jewelry was placed on holders, and if you wanted to try it, all you had to do was call one of the hostesses to help you out. Not that I would.

Once again, I was underwhelmed by the necklace Samuel wanted to persuade me to buy. Perhaps that fact alone made me detest it from the start. On the other hand, taking the pearl and ruby choker in his hands, Samuel's eyes actually sparkled with delight.

And once again, I started to wonder about his potential addiction. He looked like he wanted to own that necklace like nothing else in this world. Why wasn't he buying it, then? Or anything else, for that matter? Because he was trying to resist the temptation or because he couldn't?

Was the reason he was forcing me so hard because he'd already spent all his money and was now broke? I banished that immediately. We couldn't go to all the places and do all the things we did if he'd lost all his money. Besides, if he spent all his money buying things, then all he had to do was sell them again to get his money back. It was as simple as that.

What if his sickness is preventing him from doing just that?

I looked at his smiling face, starting to feel sorry. *Oh, Samuel, what is the matter with you?* I so wanted to know.

He grinned, placing a choker against my neck and admiring it further. "Oh, darling, the way your eyes gleam while wearing this sparkly thing is exquisite. You are exquisite."

I glanced at the description provided and recoiled. This particular item was several hundred years old, so while he praised me, all I could think about was how he'd wrapped some dead woman's jewelry around my neck. It was morbid but true. I felt like it was actually choking me.

Well, it is called a choker. Sadly, I couldn't really appreciate my bad joke.

I took it off in haste and placed it back on the holder.

Samuel tracked the movement with a slight frown, but it disappeared almost immediately. He leaned against the glass casing to look at me. "I'm astounded. The price is a real bargain," he said conversationally.

I could only stare at him because what he said had to be a joke. If I had decided to buy it, which I certainly wouldn't, then it would be the most expensive thing I owned. But again, I would never buy it because it would be madness spending so much money on something I couldn't even wear.

I wanted to go home this instant and take a nice, long shower and scrub my neck meticulously. I felt contaminated after wearing that thing.

I couldn't suppress a shudder.

"Don't you agree?" he prompted.

I shrugged. "If you say so."

Although it was obvious he wasn't fully happy with my

response, he moved on. "And the best part is that you can wear it, and—" He froze, looking past me, behind me.

He looked so strange all of a sudden, I was about to ask what was going on, but he beat me to the punch.

"You know what? Let's move on. I can see you're not that enthused."

What? It was a complete one-eighty, which only confused me more. At the same time, because that was aligned with my wishes to leave this place as soon as possible, he really didn't have to tell me twice.

As he led me from one display of astounding jewelry pieces to the next, he kept looking behind himself, and although he chatted the entire time, he couldn't fully mask the fact that he was nervous.

Which made me nervous in return. What was going on? What did he see that made him act in this manner? A flood of questions rushed through my head.

And the fact that he wasn't paying attention to anything in front of us told me the situation was serious. If he didn't want to be here anymore, then why were we? It wasn't like I would be broken up about that.

Samuel was like a crow to all the shiny objects, so for him to behave like this, it could mean only one thing.

Trouble.

But what kind?

"Let's keep going," he muttered, looking behind himself once again.

Each time he did that, I did the same. I was determined to see what he was searching for or looking at so intently. Yet I couldn't spot anything amiss, just a bunch of rich guys looking at the fine jewelry and nothing else.

And that was when I spotted her. A woman who was definitely trailing after us. How did I know she was the one Samuel was reacting to? Her face, full of fury, said it all.

She was a tall platinum blonde, probably around my age, yet she'd clearly had some work done. She wore a very expensive black dress that accentuated all her attributes, and she looked ready to murder someone as she moved through the crowd. And I had a pretty good idea who her target was.

Wait, is this his wife? I thought with dread.

What if she's angry with me too? Technically, if he was married, that made me a mistress. It didn't matter whether I knew about her or not.

I suspected.

And now I had my proof.

Oh, my God.

I wanted to break free of him, but Samuel wouldn't let me. He was holding my hand tightly, not enough to hurt but as though he needed it for support, as though without it, he would lose himself.

Naturally, there was a big chance I was full of shit and trying to find meaning where there was none because of the situation. Both of us were very tense, but we pretended all was well.

Why was Samuel so freaked out? Why was he running away from this woman while dragging me away with him?

Well, duh, if she was his wife, then it was all very self-explanatory. He wanted to get out of here before the shit hit the fan.

I was horrified.

Selina was right all along. I'd finally uncovered his secret. Samuel had a wife. I felt sick to my stomach.

What to do now?

23

I couldn't take this anymore. This situation was beyond bizarre, and I'd had enough.

"Samuel."

"You know what, darling? It's a bit stuffy in here," he said, interrupting me, "and the display is wretched. I don't know what I was thinking when I suggested you should buy some of these things," he tried to joke, yet the smile was clearly fake, and it didn't reach his eyes. "Let us take our leave."

He recited all that not looking at me at all, and the woman behind us still wasn't giving up her pursuit. I was convinced she was Samuel's wife, and I was mortified. I didn't want to be caught up in this drama.

"Samuel, what is going on?" I asked, but he completely ignored me as he practically dragged me out of the building. And he didn't stop there. We continued walking, with haste, reaching around the corner toward the parking lot. Except I'd had enough of his strange behavior. I jerked away, breaking contact.

"Samuel!" I snapped, stopping in my tracks. "Tell me what is going on right now," I demanded, not even pretending I wasn't pissed, freaked out, irritated, and so much more.

I couldn't believe I had just been manhandled and hauled out of the jewelry shop as some woman stalked behind us. Was this really my life or the plot to some movie?

He turned to look at me with a slight frown, an expression of utter confusion on his face. "What do you mean?" he asked, completely calm all of a sudden. Yet his eyes betrayed him.

And I was having none of it. I deserved to know the truth after that spectacle.

Gritting my teeth, I took a step toward him. "I saw her," I replied calmly, although I felt anything but.

It was obvious he wanted to say something to that, probably ask what woman, and I wouldn't let him. "I saw that woman, the blonde in the black dress who was following us. Why was she doing that, Samuel?"

"Charlene . . ."

I waved my hand. "Do not try to deny it," I warned. I was barely holding on, and if he continued to deny it, I would certainly lose it.

"Charlene, please calm down."

"That is not an answer to my question. I know what I saw."

"You are utterly overreacting."

And then he did something that completely pissed me off. He looked behind me, and a flash of fear passed over his face as though worrying that woman would appear behind the corner any second now. He wanted to bolt, and I was ruining that plan.

"I am not stupid, Samuel, or crazy. I know something is going on. Who is that woman? Is she your wife?" I demanded, raising my voice.

It was obvious he was frustrated by my behavior by the

way he kept pushing his hand through his hair. It went without saying at the moment that I didn't give a damn whether he was frustrated. I was honest to God pissed off, and I deserved answers. He'd been acting all kinds of shades of weird for months, and I simply couldn't take it anymore.

He sighed, taking a step toward me, reaching for me, yet I took an equal step back. "Don't."

"Charlene, that woman is not my wife."

Of course he would say that. "I don't believe you."

"I'm telling the truth, darling."

"Stop calling me that," I snapped. I was so mad it was beyond anything I'd ever experienced. I could barely speak because my jaw was that tight.

"This is nothing you should be upset about."

Really? I looked at him incredulously. "Really. Who is she, then?" I asked again since he'd failed to tell me before. "And why are we running away from her?" I wanted to know, looking all triumphant, knowing I had him there.

There was no way he could lie his way out of this. The truth was undeniable. That woman had appeared, and Samuel had freaked out. Although he'd tried to mask it, he'd dragged me out of the show, and here we were now, having a fight in the middle of the street like a pair of teenagers while wearing our formal wear. It would be kind of comical if it weren't happening to me.

"We are not running away. We are simply going home."

Wrong answer. I made a face. It was saying *Are you shitting me?*

"Really? Then you won't mind if I go back and ask her myself what is going on?" I asked.

He didn't react to those words, obviously thinking I was bluffing. I so wasn't.

I turned around, fully ready to return to the show and track that woman down, when he stopped me.

"Please, Charlene, stop; don't go," he pleaded.

"Then start talking."

"All right," he said, but once again, he stopped as he looked toward the jewelry store. It was obvious he felt uncomfortable that we were still in such close vicinity of it.

It only made me want to know more who that woman was and why he was so afraid of her.

"All right, what?" I prompted since I had no patience left for his empty words.

"Can we please go someplace else to talk normally, calmly?"

I started shaking my head even before he finished. I was definitely not ready to be calm at the moment, nor was I completely normal since none of this was normal to me.

"There's no way in hell I will go home with you now after what just happened," I countered.

And that was the truth. The mere thought of letting him inside my house after this, after the way he'd tried to lie to me, filled me with so much fury and disgust, I could just breathe fire. The man was definitely not who I thought he was. This was some kind of stranger, one I didn't recognize.

Perhaps I never knew the real Samuel at all. But that didn't matter at the moment. Getting to the bottom of this was the only thing I cared about at the moment.

"Fine!" he snapped in return, spreading his arms as though in surrender. "Then we'll go to my place." And with that said, he took my hand and started leading me toward the car once again.

Since none of that was done aggressively, I let it happen. Besides, I was so shocked by what he'd said, I needed a moment to process it. We were going to his place. By that time, I was already inside his car and we were speeding down the street.

I let him take me away because I craved answers, but part

of me was irked, or should I say additionally irked, that he was doing all this, capitulating simply because he was desperate to get us out of there as soon as possible because he was afraid she would appear and not because he really wanted to speak with me.

Then again, maybe I should not get too worked up over the details. It didn't matter what compelled him to talk to me as long as he did.

Coincidentally, we had to pass the jewelry store on our way, and as though some kind of force compelled us, we both looked toward it. Samuel's glance was much shorter than mine because he was driving, yet mine lingered for as long as was possible.

I could not spot that mysterious woman.

My heart still pounded like crazy, and my mind kept bombarding me with all the questions I'd had for months. Hopefully, I was about to get my answers. At least some of them.

It was a quiet ride to his place. It was quiet but not silent. The space between us was buzzing. There was this current of energy filled by my unanswered questions, accusations, as well as his frustrations that he was put in this spot in the first place.

At the moment, I had zero sympathy for him. Whatever was happening, I knew it was because of him. It was his fault all of this had happened, so it was only fair that he resolve it.

"Here we are," he muttered.

I wasn't that surprised when he parked in front of a remodeled warehouse. Over the last decade or so, this part of the city had gone through what was called gentrification. Usually, that meant tearing a community down so shiny new buildings that would make rich people even richer could take their place. However, in this case, they decided to go a slightly different way. Instead of bulldozing everything, some of the old buildings were preserved and repurposed.

All the old factories had been shut down, but the vast spaces remained, changing them to office spaces for tech companies or hipster freelancers.

This particular warehouse was converted into condos. And I couldn't say I disliked the result. It was a mixture of rustic charm with a few modern elements.

We remained silent on our walk toward the building. The elevator was huge, as though it used to carry cargo, and we each had a corner for ourselves to brood. We resembled two fighters before the match.

We went to the last floor, and I did wonder why he had to use a key card to activate it. That was revealed when we stopped climbing. The elevator led us straight to the penthouse. There was no front door. The elevator was the door.

It was an open floor kind of space.

"Please come in," Samuel said, breaking the silence, and I did.

What else could I do, anyway? I'd come all this way, so it would be foolish to walk away now, when I was about to get my answers.

Perhaps it was a bit rude of me, but I could not stop looking around myself. His condo looked exactly how I thought it would. And it somehow didn't at the same time. It blew my mind.

One corner was filled with all kinds of exercise equipment, so much that it looked like a small gym. No surprise there. Fine art was scattered everywhere, and tastefully so, as though an interior designer came and placed everything in its right place, readying the apartment for a photo shoot, also not a surprise since I'd had many opportunities in the past to witness how excited he got when experiencing other people's creations.

The rest of the space was reserved for very expensive toys. There was a huge video game station, some vintage arcades, and of course, a drone. *Boys and their toys.* No matter how old they got, there were some things they never outgrew.

Very modern-looking stairs made of glass led upstairs, probably to the bedroom.

I also noticed something else or, better put, the lack of something. The place did not contain any evidence that a female lived there.

No married person lives here, I corrected. That much was obvious.

This was definitely a bachelor's pad, I deduced while I snooped around. And I suspected Samuel was letting me roam freely so I could get to that conclusion on my own. That did not mean my doubts dispersed.

He could have brought me to his secret love nest while he lives with his wife someplace else, I mused, deciding to keep my guard up.

Overall, it was an amazing place, not that I got a chance to enjoy it. That was not why I was there.

Taking all of it in, I turned to face Samuel. "Well, I'm here."

"Indeed."

"I'm dying to hear your explanation," I prompted since he didn't look like he was ready to offer anything on his own. The way he ran his hands through his hair suggested as much.

"You are absolutely right. You deserve to know the truth."

Finally. Now I had proof, by his own admission, that he was keeping things from me. Not that I said that aloud.

He said no more than that and instead walked over to the bar and poured us a drink. By the color, I suspected it was whiskey. He offered me a glass, and I shook my head. I felt like no matter what he was about to tell me, I needed my head straight, although I wanted to accept it, and badly.

Nodding, he downed my glass of drink in one go, then did the same with his. My eyebrows went up.

Okay.

If he needed that much liquid courage, this was going to be bad, I realized.

"Please sit down," he offered, pointing at a big couch, and I did as I was told.

He sat next to me, at some distance, and that was preferable at the moment. Unfortunately, he said no more than that. He remained silent, staring into space. Naturally, I was getting impatient. All this buildup of tension was making me nervous. Whatever he had to share, I wished he would do it already because the suspense was killing me. But instead of yelling at him anew, I decided to try a different approach.

"Samuel, please just tell me what is going on," I pleaded.

He looked at me, and after taking a deep breath and pushing fingers through his hair, he opened his mouth. "I apologize for my behavior, but what I have to say is very hard on me," he started.

Everything inside me went rigid. *This is going to be bad. Really bad.* I was convinced he was about to tell me he was married and that he was sorry for lying to me for so long while giving me all the usual reasons he was cheating on his wife. I was prepared for that and knew how I would handle that.

"The woman we saw tonight is not my wife, Charlene. She is my stalker."

24

W*ait, what?* "A stalker?" I repeated like a parrot.

I wasn't prepared to hear that. Like, at all.

Samuel stood up to pour himself another drink after springing that on me, which was fine by me since I needed a moment to digest this strange piece of information. He offered me one too, and I refused again.

"So you have a stalker?" I still had trouble wrapping my head around that. Not that I didn't believe things like that occurred, it was simply that it had never occurred to someone from my circle of family and friends. The only stalkers I knew about were those I saw in the movies. And that was a blessing. Apparently, Samuel was not that lucky.

"Yes." He sounded as though admitting he had a terminal disease.

Poor guy.

"That woman you saw this evening has stalked me for years," he confessed.

I could only stare at him for a moment. *For years? This has been happening for years?*

"How? Why?"

I had so many questions, and my brain refused to articulate any of them properly. This was such a huge revelation. And I immediately started to feel guilty. I'd assumed the worst about him when Samuel was the victim.

Luckily, Samuel didn't look like he took offense to my behavior. More to the point, he nodded at my clumsy questions, ready to reply.

"When I was in my thirties, and more foolish," he added with a humorless smile, "I met this woman, Nora Drake, through a mutual friend." He sat next to me again, leaning against the seat. "It was love at first sight. Or so I believed."

"What happened?"

He half-shrugged.

"We started spending a lot of time together. She took me places, helped me rediscover this city in a new way. You have to understand, at the time, she was much wealthier than me, and I looked at her as some kind of mentor. She had the life I was striving to have." He paused there, as though lost in thought.

"We fell madly in love, and I felt ecstatic that this perfect woman was in my life. She was also kind of unbalanced, but that was something I would discover much later."

So far, I couldn't really predict what went wrong between them.

"In the next couple of months, I felt like I was on top of the world, and then it all came crashing down. You see, I wanted to propose, but then I discovered she was already married."

Here we go. "What? She never told you that?"

Samuel shook his head. "No, nobody told me. We spent all this time together, and she'd never bothered to mention she had a husband." Samuel looked hurt at that moment.

"How did you find out?"

"I saw them together at dinner." And he looked down as

he continued speaking. "I'm ashamed to say that even after I discovered the truth, I didn't stop sleeping with her."

I was expecting to hear that. People in love were not known to make the best decisions.

"Luckily or not, her true nature started to show after some time."

"What do you mean?"

"Well, she would get madly jealous for no reason. Each time she saw me speaking with another woman, she would make a scene, which sounds ridiculous considering she had a husband all along. We fought like crazy, which only made sex even better."

I forced myself not to react to that. This definitely felt like entering too-much-information territory, yet I didn't want to interrupt him. He was opening up to me, and the least I could do was listen.

He took a deep breath before continuing. "The last straw was when she tried to convince me to kill her husband so we could always be together."

"What?" I exclaimed, unable to stop myself. "That is insane."

Samuel nodded. "I thought so too. And that was the reason I ended our affair then and there."

I nodded in approval. "So is that why she started to, um, stalk you? Because she didn't want to let you go?" I wondered aloud.

"Partly," he allowed. "You see, somehow, her husband found out about us."

"Really?"

"We were already done by then, but that didn't matter to Zachary. He kicked her out of the house and intended to divorce her."

Logically. I trusted Christopher immensely, always did, but if I'd discovered he'd had an affair, I couldn't say for sure whether I could ever forgive him for that. So I understood why that man wanted to end his marriage. It was hard getting over such a betrayal.

"What happened afterward?"

"I decided to leave the country for a while again, get away from all the drama. Naturally, Nora blamed me for her misfortune."

"That is crazy. She's the one who cheated on her husband, not you," I argued, although he wasn't contradicting me. I was not upset at him, of course. I was upset at this woman I'd never met.

"That didn't matter to her. And now, each time I come back to town, she somehow finds out and stalks me, makes my life miserable. It is so exhausting dealing with all her craziness."

I bet. I really sympathized with Samuel. It was true he'd made a mistake, but he didn't deserve to be treated like this, punished for the rest of his life.

"For the last ten years?" I exclaimed. I'd done the math, considering Nora's divorce was in all the papers. I was scandalized, to put it mildly.

She really was crazy if she couldn't move on, let go, even after all this time. Instead of accepting her part of the blame, accept that her marriage had ended and move on, she'd dedicated her life to ruining Samuel's. That was absolutely incomprehensible for me.

"Sadly, yes. I'm terribly sorry I had to drag you into my drama," he said apologetically. "I did my best to keep my presence in New York a secret, but I failed." He looked despondent.

I wanted to hug him. He was breaking my heart. The last thing I thought about at this moment was my feelings, but not his. He'd always put me first. That showed what kind of man he was.

It must have been hell living like that, to be confronted with her each time he came to New York. With that person constantly showing up, trying to ruin everything, reminding him of something he did wrong; no wonder he spent so much time out of the country. He had no choice. Or did he?

"Samuel, why haven't you reported her or something?" I asked in concern.

Ten years is a long time.

"I have a restraining order against her," he provided with a shrug.

"I'm sure she broke it tonight."

"She has a lot of powerful friends who let her get away with a lot of things."

I made a face. That kind of thing infuriated me. It was maddening how the law didn't apply to everyone equally. Once upon a time, my father too had abused the law so he wouldn't have to pay child support to my mother. I banished that thought since this was not about me.

"I'm sorry that you had to go through all that, and for so long," I said, taking his hands and showing my support. Perhaps it was too little, too late, but it was the best I could do at the moment.

I was also sorry for jumping to conclusions, for managing to convince myself that he was a bad guy, and so much more.

"No, no, I apologize for ruining our date. I've been meaning to tell you for quite some time and couldn't find the right words, the right time . . ." He trailed off.

"That's understandable." If the situation were reversed, I would act the same way.

"And I hope this clears up any misconceptions you had about me. As you can see"—he gestured around himself—"I'm not married."

He also had a small smile dancing on his lips, showing

that even in the midst of all this, he'd found a way to look at things on the bright side and laugh.

On the other hand, I was mortified and had to look away. "I'm very sorry about that."

And that was no lie. This showed me my brain was a weapon that constantly misfired, so I was thinking of having more frequent sessions with Dr. Neal. I clearly needed help since I'd managed to convince myself that Samuel was not only a married man but an addict too.

He moved closer to me. "Why on Earth did you think something like that?" he asked, but there was no reprimand in his voice. He was simply curious.

I couldn't decide whether that made me feel better or worse.

I shrugged. "Well, we always go to my place, and you never asked me to visit," I replied honestly. That was the least I could do after what he'd shared with me.

To my surprise, he started laughing. I had to look at him because I couldn't understand what prompted that.

"I've been having my kitchen remodeled. The place was a mess," he explained.

The kitchen did look pristine. "Oh," was all my brilliant brain had to say to that. Apparently, it was amazing at creating drama and getting me into trouble, but not so much at getting me out of it.

He kissed my forehead before wrapping his arms around me. "You should have asked."

"I know," I replied.

"You are the only woman I want in my life," he confessed.

I buried my head into his chest. He was so good, I didn't deserve him. And I couldn't even explain why I was acting like this. I'd never behaved like that with Christopher. I didn't have doubts or crazy theories while we were dating, and certainly not after we got married.

So why was this different? Was it possible I was trying to sabotage this relationship because of fear? Losing Christopher hurt like nothing else in this world. Perhaps I was trying to prevent myself from experiencing that again. That was fucked up but plausible, and definitely something I would have to speak with Dr. Neal about.

To Samuel I said, "I have one more question."

"Of course."

"Why not try something else? Sue her or something?" I returned us to the subject of Nora the stalker.

"For what?"

That was a good question I had no answer to.

"Besides, she is a nuisance and nothing more."

I was impressed that he could look at things like that despite the fact that the woman had been terrorizing him for a decade.

"I bet John Lennon thought the same thing about Mark Chapman," I grumbled.

He kissed me again. "You are adorable when you're worried."

"And you're not taking this situation seriously."

"Oh, I am, believe me. It is merely that I feel much lighter now that you know. I am grateful you are so understanding."

"That is because I can relate," I replied.

"You have a stalker too?" He sounded shocked, outraged.

"No, I had to get a restraining order against my mother," I explained.

"Really?"

I nodded. I was not particularly proud that at times, in my weak moments, I felt guilty since she was my mother, after all, but at that moment, it had been necessary.

"Why?"

I sighed before starting my story. "When I first inherited the money from my father, my mother didn't take it well."

"How come?"

"She was convinced she was entitled to that inheritance, not me, and that I simply stole it from her, so she demanded it back."

"Preposterous," Samuel commented.

"When I refused her, she sued me."

"What?"

"She tried to convince the court that I was crazy so she could put me into something called conservatorship, which would basically allow her to do what she wanted with my money."

At the time, I was grieving over Christopher, but I definitely wasn't crazy. Not that it mattered to her. She tried to use any excuse to beat me.

"I cannot believe what I'm hearing. You are a grown woman. What kind of monster is she?" Samuel sounded outraged.

It felt really good to have him in my corner. "A bad one," I agreed. "But as you can see, I won."

Although the battle had been long and exhausting, I had prevailed. And to this day, I couldn't forgive my mother for trying to commit me to a mental hospital. I always knew I meant nothing to her. I was a means to an end that backfired, but after that stunt, my opinion about her solidified. She cared more about the money than she ever cared about me, and as such, there was no place for her in my life.

"Good for you."

"Unfortunately, she didn't stop there. She started harassing me, coming to my home every day, demanding that I should give her a monthly allowance, so my lawyer filed a restraining order against her."

And after spending a night in jail after violating it for the first time, she stopped showing up.

"She still calls me every once in a while, but I can ignore that."

"What about the rest of your family?"

"Well, I have a stepdad and a half-sister, and they sided with Mom during the legal case." They probably believed Mom would win, which would allow them a piece of that cake as well.

Samuel frowned. "Bastards, all of them."

I was slightly surprised that he was more upset about what had been happening to me than about what was happening to him, yet I felt the same way about him. That was probably because we'd lived with our problems and had time to get used to them, to a certain order of things. Thus, the injustice of others rattled us deeply.

One more thing we have in common.

"It is good you managed to cut those toxic people out of your life."

Well, almost.

"I say good riddance."

"Now we just have to see how to solve your Nora problem."

"We?"

"Yes, I want to help."

He kissed me properly this time. "Thank you for caring so much about my well-being."

What was I to say to that? You're welcome? I simply smiled and kissed him again.

"Have you thought about talking to her, trying to reason with her?" I asked once we parted. Perhaps if they had a rational conversation, she would see the error of her ways.

"Let's leave that problem for some other time. I would really like to take you home now. It's getting rather late."

"Okay," I replied, not wanting to press. He'd shared a

great deal with me already. Perhaps he deserved a night off. It had been a stressful evening, after all.

I felt much better on our drive back to my house. Somehow, I felt much lighter now that I knew the truth.

Only when he said his goodbye, leaving me in front of my home, did I realize what had just happened. For some reason, he didn't want me to spend the night at his apartment.

You are doing it again, I warned myself.

He didn't want to spend the night at my house either, which probably meant he felt embarrassed or something, sharing all those things, all those emotions with me, and needed some time alone. That was completely understandable, and I couldn't really blame him for that, knowing I would be the same way.

With my mind eased, I went inside.

So Samuel had a stalker by the name Nora Drake. Who would ever predict something like that?

25

"And that is what happened," I said with a sigh, finishing my story to Selina. I figured I wasn't breaking Samuel's trust if I shared his story with my best friend. She was worrying alongside me all this time, so she deserved to know how all of this had been resolved.

I had to admit, I fell asleep with ease after Samuel shared his problems with me, but after waking, I had this urge to speak with Selina. I'd made many mistakes in the past, so it was like I needed her to be privy to what I'd heard from Samuel, to know it was real. Or something like that.

"Wow, we were completely off base with this guy," she commented in return.

"I know," I agreed, relieved she felt the same way I did.

"I mean, I would never in a million years think something like that was happening to him."

"Yeah, me too. I was stunned and felt sorry for him."

"Of course you did. My cousin had a stalker in high school, and it was horrible. Poor guy, I hope he will find a way to deal with that crazy woman."

"He doesn't want to involve the police."

"I get that. There's not much they can do, believe me," Selina replied glumly.

"What did your cousin do?"

"Eventually, she moved to a different city for college, and luckily, he didn't follow her."

I made a face. That wasn't the solution I was looking for. Besides, Samuel had already done that. He spent most of his year abroad, and nothing changed. Nora still harassed him each time he came back to New York.

It was mind-boggling to me that some people could justify such behavior to themselves. *Or are they simply sick?* I stopped to think.

After my mother tried to commit me for no reason, I was more apprehensive when labeling people crazy. Nevertheless, Nora's behavior certainly couldn't be described as normal. She was stalking someone, for crying out loud, and she'd been doing that for years.

"You know, after hearing his story, I started to feel guilty for ever doubting him."

I had even contemplated breaking up with him because I was convinced he had a wife, which would have been a colossal mistake.

"You shouldn't think like that. You had your reasons."

"I was wrong."

"It doesn't matter. You were not privy to all the information. If he had shared everything with you from the start, all that drama could have been completely avoided," Selina pointed out.

I couldn't say I completely agreed with her on that.

"Actually, I understand his hesitation. We're still in the early stages of our relationship, and this isn't something you spring on your partner and be like, by the way, I have a stalker, and she is mildly dangerous."

Most girls hearing that would run for the hills, I'd imagine.

"Perhaps you're right," Selina allowed.

I knew I was. Conceivably, he could have told me a bit sooner, before we encountered her in the jewelry shop, avoiding all that unnecessary drama, but life couldn't be scripted. Shit happened all the time, and besides, all was resolved now, so everything else was simply water under the bridge. Or that was how I was going to look at it. Or try to look at it.

Instead of blaming him for not telling me sooner, I planned on being more understanding. It couldn't have been easy living like that, always looking over his shoulder, worrying that woman would come and try to ruin his new relationship.

"So are the two of you good now?" Selina wanted to know.

"Yeah." I made a face saying that, and Selina noticed.

"What does that mean?" she asked, moving her hand in front of the camera. She was clearly pointing at my face.

I promised myself I wouldn't be making a big deal out of this, yet here I was preparing to do just that. "Well, after he told me the whole story last night, about Nora, he took me home and then left," I explained.

"Oh, you're worried he didn't offer to have you spend the night at his place." Selina understood what I was trying to say instantly.

"Am I being paranoid?" I asked, although I didn't really want to hear the answer because I was sure I was. I was being silly too, nitpicking his behavior, searching for meaning where there was none.

"Do you still believe he's hiding something from you? Or do you think all of it got resolved last night?" Selina came with counter-questions.

And pretty good ones at that.

I gave it some thought before replying, "Honestly, I don't know what to think at this point. I truly believed we resolved everything last night, but then he did that." Which was beyond strange. We spent most nights together, so why didn't he want to stay? Why didn't he want me to stay at his place?

More to the point, he had never wanted me there in the first place. He only took me to his condo to avoid Nora. *He explained that his kitchen was being remodeled*, I reminded myself.

Regardless, there was one more thing that bugged me. The fact that he had a stalker couldn't fully explain his strange behavior. It explained only what had happened last night yet couldn't be applied to his previous moodiness or the fact that he at times pressured me to buy expensive jewelry and whatnot.

"You know what?" Selina said, snapping me from my reverie. "Why don't you do a little research?" she offered.

"What do you mean?"

"Open your browser and start Googling. Check him out; check that woman out; see what you can find. There's nothing wrong in wanting to verify his story. That way, you will know for sure."

That was pretty good advice.

In normal circumstances, I would be a bit squeamish about doing something like that, finding it a violation of privacy. Yet there was nothing normal in this situation, so I would take Selina's suggestion to heart.

"You're right. I will definitely look into her, and into Samuel as well," I added. No matter how much I wanted to believe him, I needed proof, plain and simple.

"Let me know what you find out."

"Sure thing."

With that settled, I decided to change the subject. "Now, tell me what is going on with you. Did you see that guy again, what was his name, Patrick?"

"Yes, I did. But I just don't know what to make of it. He's been acting all hot and cold. We were at a friend's barbecue last week, and he was, like, all over me. Nothing happened, mind you, just some heavy flirting. But afterward, he didn't even call me," she ranted.

I made a face of disgust over his behavior. "I hate when guys play games like that."

"I know. Me too."

"Do you have a picture of him?" I asked, curiosity getting the better of me, wanting to have an image of this idiot in my head while I spoke with my friend.

"I do." She sent me an image. I had to admit he was a really good-looking man.

"He's a barista in some overpriced coffee shop, but he's also the best dancer I know," she provided. "It's mesmerizing to watch him move."

For years now, Selina had been going to dance classes, learning salsa and other Latin dances, and that was where she'd met this guy.

She started doing that after her husband left her.

At times, I was envious of her, how she'd managed to pick herself up quickly after what had happened to her, how she started doing new things, meeting new people. I wished I were more like that.

Perhaps it would be fun taking dance lessons. That way, I could go dancing with Samuel. Apparently, no matter what, my thoughts always bounced back to him.

"You know what? You should call him, ask him on a date. That way, you'll know for sure whether he's into you or not," I advised.

Selina grinned. "I already did that five minutes ago. We're going out Friday night."

"Good for you." I grinned. I was happy she was taking the

initiative and asking him out rather than waiting for him to pursue her. "I want details after your big date."

"You know it." Selina grinned in return.

The instant I finished my conversation with her, I started Googling.

I did some quick research on Nora Drake first, and I was surprised at how many articles popped up about her. One would think she was a movie star or something by the sheer number of newspaper articles done on her, and she wasn't even a NYC socialite, but whatever. This town was strange in that way.

Did Samuel tell me about her knowing I would uncover so much? I banished that thought immediately. My paranoia was getting the best of me again.

There wasn't much about her before she married. All the same, she was everywhere afterward. No surprise there, as her whole marriage was public, and so was her divorce.

As far as I could see, Nora did divorce her husband at the time Samuel spoke of. And it was a messy one at that, with a complete media circus considering her husband was a rather famous businessman.

When Samuel mentioned Zachary, I hadn't realized he meant Zachary P. Michaels. Even I had heard of him. I couldn't believe Nora had been married to that guy and then decided to cheat on him.

However, that was not the most important thing I read about. The more I read, the less I liked this situation I found myself in.

The biggest story revolving around Nora wasn't about her high-profile divorce. The biggest story was about Nora and her lover. Only his initials were ever disclosed, 'S.N.', but I knew they meant Samuel.

As it turned out, Nora's lover was the suspect in a very large burglary. *Samuel was accused of stealing from her?* I was horrified uncovering that. But I kept going. I needed to know everything.

Before the legal dispute, the spouses realized that some of their possessions had disappeared, and the main suspect was Nora's lover. I suspected that was the real reason Zachary Michaels filed for divorce in the first place.

Was that the reason Samuel decided to leave the country? I wondered. *Did he flee because he did it, or because he didn't and feared he was being framed?* That was yet to be determined.

Either way, the guilty party was never found, which meant Samuel was never officially charged with anything. The couple lost millions of dollars during that robbery. The thief took some of her jewelry, some of his, and one very rare Fabergé egg.

I was sure that last item was the most expensive one. Eventually, the insurance kicked in, and the family was compensated, but the damage was done.

To say I was horrified by what I'd just read would be an understatement. *Did Samuel know I would do this when he told me about Nora? Or did he trust that I would automatically side with him?* I stopped myself there. There was no point in stressing about such things. I couldn't know what was inside his head.

Apparently, I didn't even know the most basic things about him. It was true that each tale had two sides. All the same, this was ridiculous. I didn't know what to think of him before all this. Now, I was thoroughly fucked in the head.

I continued browsing.

My theory that Zachary had divorced Nora because of the theft and not because of the infidelity had the most merit because as far as I could see, they both cheated on one another constantly. *How very original of them,* I thought as I pursed my lips and shook my head at their behavior.

Unfortunately, that wasn't where the story ended. After

filing for divorce and starting the huge legal battle, since he really wanted to leave his wife penniless, Zachary died of a heart attack. Since he didn't get a chance to change his will, Nora inherited everything. Some of his family members tried to challenge the will due to the fact that he was divorcing the bitch, but the judge ruled in her favor.

I couldn't believe that after everything, Nora actually won. *Who says it doesn't pay to be a bad guy?* Life was not a Disney movie, and people like Nora got away with a lot of shit, which was not a surprise.

The surprise was her grudge against Samuel. Was she so adamant in making his life miserable simply because she still couldn't get over the fact that he'd left her, or was there something else at play here? Did she too believe he'd robbed her blind?

Does she have proof of that? I thought with dread. Over the last decade, she probably had numerous opportunities to turn him in, but maybe in her deviousness, she liked to torment him in this way instead.

And what if he's innocent? I couldn't assume I knew what the truth was one way or the other. The newspaper articles weren't enough.

All the same, I couldn't help thinking about all the times Samuel had encouraged me to buy all those highly valuable things. Because of his meddling, I'd found myself buying jewelry, valuable coins, gems, and things like that. Things that could easily end up being stolen.

I started shaking. *Oh, my God.* I was beyond alarmed remembering all the times he sulked when I refused to buy anything. I'd also found him, a couple of times, snooping around the house when he believed I was sleeping. *Was he staking out the house? Is all of this just a setup? Did he seduce me the same way he seduced Nora just so he could steal from me?*

My heart started to beat like crazy as I managed to put all

the pieces of the puzzle together. Could it be that I was so blind all this time and unable to see the truth?

Samuel was not an addict. He was nothing more than a common thief, and as it turned out, I was his latest victim.

26

"You have to stop doing this, Charlene. You have to stop coming up with all these new theories so you can justify keeping Samuel at a distance," Dr. Neal warned as I shared with her the new development regarding Samuel.

Hear me out. Samuel is not a thief. He is your boyfriend. I felt the need to remind myself of that because I acted as though I'd forgotten. So maybe Dr. Neal had a point. I was keeping him at arm's length from the start, and for different reasons.

On the other hand . . . "This time, I have proof," I argued.

She gave me *the look*. "A couple of newspaper articles can hardly be considered proof. If there had been any real evidence, Samuel would have ended up in jail," she pointed out. "Don't you agree?"

"I guess." She did have a solid point, but did she have to beat it out of me? *Would you listen to her any other way?* I hated it when even my conscience ganged up with my therapist against me.

"So you think I'm just paranoid without reason?"

"I believe you've been through a lot and that because of

that, you have difficulties opening up to people and trusting them."

That was true. My father never wanted me, my mother hated me, and then Christopher, the only man I loved, died. It was hard to be any other way in such circumstances.

"And although caution is still advised, you shouldn't go to such extremes to protect your heart. Not everyone wants to hurt you."

When she put it that way, it did make sense.

Nevertheless, what to do with the information I'd gathered? I couldn't dismiss all of it as simple gossip. *'Where there's smoke, there's fire,' the saying goes.* And I didn't think it would be prudent to completely ignore what I'd read online.

"What should I do, then? I mean, I did all that research to appease my mind, and I ended up even more alarmed. And although I understand your point of view, I don't believe I should so callously dismiss everything," I said all in one breath.

"I understand," Dr. Neal replied after a short pause. "Answer me this, though. What would make you feel better at this point?"

Is she joking with me? I stated the obvious. "To have absolute proof that he's innocent."

"We do not live in an absolute world, Charlene."

Tell that to the physics department, I felt like saying.

"We always have to rely on faith no matter what, no matter how certain we are of something."

Was that really true? Daily, we accepted certain things as truths so we could function and interact with other people, yet when you really looked at things, those were nothing but beliefs. We believed a taxi driver would take us to our destination without robbing us blind. We trust that our friends will keep our secrets. We trust the police officers who come to our aid when anything bad happens.

"So do I need stronger meds or what?" I only half-joked.

"There are things you can do to ease your mind," she said in return.

"Like what?" I asked. I really hoped she wouldn't suggest I should dump him because despite everything, I wasn't ready for that.

Perhaps I could hire someone to follow him around? Now, that would be too hardcore. Besides, I already felt guilty enough for having doubts about him. If somehow over time I managed to prove all my theories were crap, that he was an honest, loving man all along, then I wouldn't be able to look him in the eyes ever again.

Maybe that right there was an indicator that I wasn't being fair toward him.

At the same time, how to relinquish all this doubt? A very wise Disney princess sang a song, 'Let it go', but I was aware that something like that wasn't possible for me. There were too many inconsistencies.

"Like listing all the times Samuel told you the truth, all the times you were proven wrong."

That was her brilliant idea? I could only shake my head.

Yes, Samuel had been honest with me and told me about this situation with Nora. However, after Googling her, I discovered he'd failed to mention some key elements. Which only made me wonder what else he'd failed to tell me.

When I Googled him, there wasn't much to find. It was like he made sure not to have an online presence, which in this day and age wasn't that easy. Besides, only really powerful and rich people took such care about their privacy.

And criminals, of course.

The question was, which was Samuel?

"All right, I'll do that." I sighed. "In any case, I spoke to my attorney and made sure all of my new purchases are properly insured and documented." When I'd spoken to my attorney about everything, he'd suggested doing that, and it had given me peace of mind that even in case something did go wrong, I would be okay.

"Oh. Well, good. I'm glad to hear that." Dr. Neal nodded.

After we ended our session, I felt beyond exhausted. Talking with Dr. Neal about Samuel didn't make me feel better at all. If only it were because I felt worse that my therapist and I were at odds in this case. Maybe that was a good thing. *She's showing me the perspective I clearly lost.*

I put my head into my palms and groaned. This was so damn hard.

Maybe I should just call it quits. No relationship is worth all this drama. Yet that wasn't completely true since I believed Samuel was worth it. That was why I struggled. That was why I always tried to come up with all these excuses for him, because I believed I was doing the right thing by preserving our relationship.

Unfortunately, I was also very confused. Was I simply deluding myself in believing he was a good guy? Or was my delusion solely revolving around myself? I couldn't know for sure. Dr. Neal believed the latter was the case, and perhaps this was one of those moments I should trust her expertise more than my own judgment. That was why I was paying her, after all.

Doing all that research was supposed to help me achieve some peace of mind, yet it had completely backfired. Now I felt like I'd fallen deeper into the rabbit's hole instead of getting all the answers.

At the same time, that was the story of my life. In my life, things never went according to my plans. It was as if whoever was in charge of my life, guardian angel or some other being, constantly felt like fucking with me and turning all my plans to shit. I should have been used to it by now, but I wasn't. I continued to bang my head against that wall constantly.

The problems only changed over time.

And the flavor of the month was Samuel. No matter how hard I thought, I couldn't see the end of this problem. On paper, he was the perfect boyfriend. However, what was said in the actual papers painted a very different story.

To be fair, he had looked rather sincere when telling me about Nora, but why didn't he tell me the rest of the story? Was he afraid I would start doubting him? I was doing that either way. And it was more difficult to trust him this way, since I'd had to discover all those suspicious things in the papers on my own and not from him. Was he ashamed? That was also possible.

I wanted to believe him, I really did, but my gut feeling was telling me something wasn't right. And it didn't have to be anything nefarious. I tried to calm myself down. I was just feeling he was not telling me everything. And I hoped, prayed even, he would tell me everything in due time, which would release me from this state of suspicion.

With all that in mind, I decided to do what Dr. Neal suggested. I'd already compiled a mental list of what I believed was the truth and what I believed were still unproven assumptions, so I skipped that and moved on to the next part.

I contacted my attorney and spent a couple of hours going over and making sure all the policies were updated and covered theft as well as damage. Then we made sure I had cataloged everything properly. After getting off the phone with him, I locked all the legal documents in my secretary's desk, then went upstairs to reorganize the safe, making sure nothing would get damaged in such a tight space. Then, with a heavy heart, I decided to change the password to it.

I chose four numbers completely at random and then made sure they were etched in my memory before actually utilizing them. I was too paranoid to write the combination on paper. I couldn't allow there to be any traces of it.

That made me pause. This didn't make me feel better. If anything, it made me feel worse, beyond depressed. If I did all this because I truly believed Samuel was a thief, then maybe it would be best to simply break up with him.

That notion caused me physical pain, although I couldn't ignore the optics of it all. His being a thief could explain his strange behavior perfectly. Then again, I had thought that about his being an addict as well, but I was proven wrong, wasn't I? Maybe not . . . he could still be the addict I'd originally thought him, I supposed.

On and on my mind went in circles, to the point that I started contemplating taking one of the sleeping pills Dr. Neal had prescribed me just to get some peace and quiet for a change.

After I finished with my task, I went down to my small gym in the basement to train. I seriously debated whether I should enroll in one of those self-defense classes for real. I was aware I wasn't learning as much as I could this way, and my urge to learn how to protect myself hadn't subsided over time. If anything, it had grown stronger after the whole Nora incident.

If she was stalking Samuel, then it was safe to assume she wouldn't be too happy learning about me. And then, there was no telling how she would react. It wasn't such a huge leap to assume she would start following me around as well. Samuel did say she had been jealous and possessive as hell while they were together. Considering she was still obsessed with him after a decade, I would say nothing had changed.

I started to feel like a caged animal because of all the plates I was forced to juggle as of late. Even in my house, which was decent-sized, I started to feel claustrophobic. I had to get away. I knew I couldn't run away from my thoughts, but some fresh air could do me some good. So I decided to go for a walk in the park.

That wouldn't solve any of my problems, but I still hoped it would help me find some kind of solution. A change of scenery could help me see things from a different perspective. And that wasn't my take on things. That was basic psychology.

It was strange how life could change so quickly. A few months back, there was no power on earth that could kick me out of the house, and now, it was the other way around. I didn't want to stay in. I almost smiled at that. Almost, since I was deeply troubled.

Overall, my dilemma looked easy. I could either trust Samuel or trust myself. Unfortunately, in reality, this was a little bit more complicated than that because life was rarely black and white but all kinds of shades of gray.

As I walked, completely unintentionally, I started to list all the good things that had happened to me since I'd met Samuel. Since he entered my life, a lot of things had changed, including this seemingly mundane thing. Before him, I basically hadn't left my house in three years, aside from those days I had to go to court against my mother. I'd completely shut down because of Christopher's death and my mother's betrayal. Samuel helped me move past that and rediscover the world. I'd forgotten how much I enjoyed simple things like walking through the park, looking at all the greenery, and listening to the wind ruffling the leaves.

Regardless, that wasn't reason enough to be with someone, especially while filled with so much doubt.

That's odd. Something I saw to my right distracted me from my thoughts for a moment. There was someone in the distance, and I had this strange feeling he was looking at me, so I started paying more attention.

Everywhere I went, I saw that same figure. And the only

reason I noticed him in the first place was that he had a flat brown cap on. It was very similar to the one Christopher had worn when we first started dating. He adored that cap and wore it everywhere, and I detested it. I thought it was hiding his face and his beautiful hair, so I made him get rid of it.

At first, I chalked this up to my being paranoid. Of course, being in the park, I was going to see the same people over and over again since it wasn't that big a park, but I remained on high alert.

Ten minutes later, I was convinced I was being followed. I still wanted to test my theory, though. No matter how fast or slow I walked, no matter which route I took, that figure stayed in my vicinity.

Who would want to follow me, and why? There was only one logical explanation that came to mind.

Eventually, I sat on a bench as my heart started to beat like crazy. The individual sat as well. He was far away but could still see me perfectly.

Son of a bitch. What is the deal with this guy? I wondered.

There's no reason to be afraid, I tried to reassure myself. It was broad daylight. Besides, if this person wanted to harm me, then he would have by now. Somehow, that didn't make me feel any better.

So what is the point of this? To learn my whereabouts? To scare me? Well, color me scared.

Then I remembered something. I had trained like crazy for this specific reason. I carried mace around and had the police on speed dial. *I can handle this.*

While I gave myself this pep talk, I even managed to convince myself that I should confront this individual and demand an explanation.

The coward will probably run away upon seeing me approach.

With a lot of determination, as the adrenaline coursed through my veins, I abruptly stood up and started marching toward him. As he realized what I was doing, he stood as well and started walking away from me.

He's running away, I thought victoriously. That filled me with vigor, and I doubled my pace, but so did he.

Whoever this person was, he didn't want me to know who he was. Now I had my proof. He had been following me around, and when he realized he'd been made, he tried to run away.

Scratch that, he did manage to run away. No matter my determination, I couldn't catch up with him. My legs were just too short, as it turned out.

And I had so wanted to know who was following me and why he was following me. *Who sent him? Was it my mother?* She was the most likely candidate. It certainly wouldn't be the first time she came up with some crazy way to extort money from me. That woman would stop at nothing to have her way. At times, I couldn't believe I was related to her. She had no heart, no soul, at least not where I was concerned.

Unfortunately, the unknown person following me around disappeared into a large crowd, and I cursed. Now, I would never get my answers.

The story of my life.

Son of a bitch.

On top of that, despite noticing that ugly hat and black jacket, I didn't get a good look at him either. It could have been a woman. I couldn't rule that out.

I sighed. *Time to go to the doctor's office and get some glasses.* I clearly needed them.

Feeling beyond pissed off, I went home.

27

It seemed then that every time I went out, I was followed. It was really starting to scare the crap out of me. The same man would keep at a distance, and if I turned to go toward him, he'd turn and walk in a different direction, but then he'd show up somewhere else I happened to be. It was pissing me off but also frightening me. There was only one way I could solve this head cluster I had thanks to Samuel. Since I couldn't trust everything that he'd told me since he'd been holding back on me for quite some time, and I couldn't fully rely on my gut feeling since it was known to screw me over in the past, I somehow managed to come up with a solution to this mess.

I needed someone impartial to solve this for me. If I wasn't capable of solving this, it would be most prudent to outsource it. And it couldn't be anyone I knew because I couldn't trust Dr. Neal or Selina to be unbiased. That was why I wanted to hire a private investigator.

A PI could not only find out who was following me and why, but I could also have them do a thorough background check on Samuel. If I had a detailed look into his past, then that would tell me, once and for all, whether he was a good guy or a bad guy. That would also show me whether I was certifiably crazy or not.

That was the only way I could get myself out of this mess. At the same time, it was making me feel guilty as hell.

I was very much aware of the fact that this would be a serious violation of his privacy, not to mention a betrayal of his trust if I went through with that part of it, which was why I hesitated. I couldn't take this lightly. But if I decided to take this action, it would be solely because I saw no other way.

While I wondered about the pros and cons of hiring an investigator, I saw no harm in Googling some professionals to see what my options were. My first instinct was to start looking through classifieds, and then I reconsidered. I didn't want a PI who wasn't completely merged into the twenty-first century, so I looked online. I wanted to see how many detectives I could find who had offices close to my home.

I decided not to tell anything about my latest crazy idea to either Selina or my therapist. But I couldn't say why. Was I worried they would try to convince me against it or tell me I was spiraling out of control? Or be supportive and agree Samuel was acting all kinds of shady? Either way, I found that to be problematic, so it was better to keep all this to myself until I had concrete proof on my side.

I really tried to rationalize it to myself that I was doing the right thing. I needed help. That much was obvious. I had tried believing him. Unfortunately, this nagging voice in the back of my head persisted, and the only way to silence it was to know for sure, one way or the other, what the real truth was, plain and simple.

It would be a relief to know for sure whether Samuel had told the truth. Of course, it could all just be that I was paranoid. Bottom line, I wanted to know if this relationship was real.

I found three PIs who looked promising. *The business is booming.* Apparently, there were a lot of distrustful people in this city. Somehow, it didn't make me feel any better. However, I did like that they were basically within walking distance from me. And then I remembered that guy following me around, so on second thought, I decided to drive no matter where they were.

One was even a former cop. It said so on his home page. Nevertheless, I didn't like how he looked. I tried not to judge, but he had the face of a serious drinker, and when I said *face*, I meant the nose.

As I pondered which one I should pay a visit to, there was a knock on my door, which was odd because I wasn't expecting anyone. I hadn't ordered anything.

Is it possible I forgot? I wondered. It wouldn't be the first time.

Just in case, I closed my browser and crept to the door really slowly. After I discovered that man following me around, I couldn't be too careful. Looking through the spy hole, I recoiled.

I jerked the door open. "Samuel," I exclaimed, taking his appearance in.

He looked absolutely ghastly. His clothes were all torn up, and I was horrified to see there was blood on them as well. And based on the state of his bruised, battered face, it was definitely his.

He practically fell into my arms. I struggled to keep him up.

"Samuel, are you all right?" I wondered, then felt like smacking myself since that was a moronic question. It was obvious that he was far from all right.

"I didn't know where else to go," he said through a busted lip that was still bleeding a little.

"You drove here?" I was horrified. He looked in so much

pain, but instead of calling for help, he came to my house. It was hard not to wonder exactly what had happened to him.

By the state of his car, it was safe to assume he wasn't involved in a car accident.

"You're the only one I trust," he replied, scaring me even more.

"Let's get you inside," I said, helping him walk to the living room. I used my foot to close the front door. Very slowly, we shuffled toward the couch, and then I helped him settle down on the cushions.

"Are you in too much pain?" I was killing it with all these dumb questions, yet what could I say? I was alarmed.

"I'm all right now," he tried to reassure me. Yet it was obvious that was said for my benefit.

"What happened to you?"

"Could I bother you for a glass of water?" he asked instead.

"Of course." I rushed to the kitchen to get him a drink, chastising myself for not thinking of something like that on my own. On my way back, I grabbed the first-aid kit as well.

"Thank you," he said before drinking from it slowly.

I sat beside him, opening the box to see what to use. Honestly, my knowledge was pretty basic, and I had no idea whether he needed stitches for his busted lip. It looked bad.

"Three men jumped me in front of my condo," he answered my previous question, putting an empty glass on the table.

I stopped what I was doing to look at him. "What?" I exclaimed, horrified. "Oh, my God, who would do something like that?" *Why?*

He looked at me with his one good eye, since the other was swelling before my eyes. "I think we both know the answer to that question."

Nora.

"They were only hired to hurt me, nothing more. That much is obvious."

I couldn't help cringing at that. I should feel grateful they weren't hired to kill him. What kind of crap world were we living in?

In one where your husband got killed for a couple of dollars and an empty purse.

"Why? Why would she do that to you?"

He half-shrugged or at least tried to before wincing.

"Do you need to go to the hospital?" I was beyond worried. What if he had internal bleeding? I couldn't put a Band-Aid over that.

"No. I'm fine. It's nothing serious."

I gave him a look, and he tried to smile.

"It looks worse than it is."

"Are you sure?" I insisted.

"Quite sure."

I didn't like that, but I would respect his wishes and do my best to fix him on my own, although I would much rather drive him to the hospital this very instant.

"And you're sure Nora is behind this?"

"I'm a respected businessman. My list of enemies is quite short," he replied instantly.

It wasn't my intention to offend, simply to get to the bottom of things.

"If you know Nora sent those men to beat you up, then why not go to the police?" I asked.

This was serious and went beyond merely being stalked. These beasts could have seriously hurt him, or even worse. I stopped myself there. I couldn't even think about what else could have happened to him. I had already lived through that once. I couldn't go through all that again. So this time around, I would do everything in my power to protect this man. *My man.*

"I cannot trust the police. Nora has a lot of friends."

"Don't you have friends too?"

"Not like her. Thanks to Zachary, she knows all the judges, all the prosecutors. No one would touch her no matter what I say."

I felt like cursing and screaming from the top of my lungs. This was so frustrating, not to mention infuriating. *Who does this woman think she is? Some kind of gangster?* It was maddening. And that was why I decided to be one hundred percent honest with Samuel.

"Samuel, is Nora doing this because she thinks you stole from her?"

He looked at me in utter surprise. "You know about that?"

"Yes, I read an article about it."

"I see."

"I don't believe it, though," I said in reassurance. And that wasn't a lie. At least not completely.

"Thank you. I assure you I had nothing to do with that. There were a lot of people who had access to their home. I was merely the easiest mark since Zachary hated my guts," he explained, getting upset anew, which made his lip start bleeding all over again.

That made sense. Especially if he suspected Samuel was sleeping with Nora.

"And I didn't tell you because I was too ashamed."

"I believe you, Samuel. Please calm down," I said. Putting some hydrogen peroxide on the cotton ball, I pressed it against his wound, and he winced.

"I'm sorry," I said apologetically, realizing I should have warned him that it might sting.

"This isn't your fault. None of it is your fault."

"It's not yours either," I pointed out.

"I'm sorry for dragging you into this."

"It's okay, just please try to calm down and let me take care of you."

He simply looked at me for a moment. His gaze was very intense, but I tried to concentrate on the task at hand. I needed to clean his face, not wanting anything to get infected.

"You are very kind for doing this for me. I know I can never repay you," he surprised me by saying, taking my free hand in his.

I shook my head. "Of course I'm here for you. And together, we will find a way to deal with Nora," I promised. Whom I was trying to reassure, him or me, was unclear at that point. Probably both of us.

"You really think there is a way out of this?" he said glumly.

I frowned. I wasn't used to seeing him like this. He sounded almost defeated, and that scared me as nothing else could.

"Yes," I replied without a thought. "I really believe that," I insisted. I couldn't let him sink into despair. Nothing good would come of that. I should know. I could write a book about that shit.

He sighed. "You know, this is the first time she's done something like this."

"What do you mean?"

"This is the first time she's hired someone to beat me up. And I think that's because of you."

"What?"

"She clearly saw how happy I am with you and got jealous, like before."

I was horrified by his words. I couldn't believe that woman did something like that simply because Samuel was trying to move on and be happy. She was sick. And we definitely needed to find a way to stop her before she took this to an even higher level. Nora was dangerous, and I didn't want to discover exactly how dangerous.

The image of Christopher's bloody, lifeless body came to mind, and I started shaking. *Don't think about it.* I forced myself to banish those dark thoughts. *That will not happen to Samuel*, I thought, but it was more like a vow. No matter what, I wouldn't let that happen.

History will not repeat itself.

After I took care of all his wounds, I rechecked everything. "All done," I announced, packing all the used swabs to throw in the garbage.

"Thank you, my guardian angel," he replied, kissing my hand.

I wanted him out of those awful clothes too but realized he wasn't strong enough at the moment for something like that, so instead, I grabbed one of my pain medications and handed it to him.

"This will help you with the pain so you can get some rest," I explained.

Nodding, he accepted it. Realizing there was no way in hell I could carry him upstairs to the bedroom, I made sure he was comfortable enough on the couch, throwing a blanket over him and tucking him in.

"Are you sure you don't mind my sleeping over?" he asked, looking at me with sad eyes. Even in his state, he was putting me first.

"Of course you are staying over. I'm not letting you out of my sight until you're all better."

He smiled, or at least tried to. "You are my shining light, Charlene. What would I ever do without you?"

His words warmed me up and broke me down at the same time. He was such a good man. He didn't deserve this, especially not from a woman whose list of sins was probably a mile long.

"Luckily, you don't have to find out." I tried to lighten the mood, but he was already dozing off, so I turned all the lights off and nestled beside him so I could watch over him. I grabbed my laptop and placed it in my lap.

While he slept, I decided to do another search on Nora. I needed to know everything I could about that crazy woman so I could find a way to beat her down.

28

"Here you go, Samuel. Be careful, it's hot," I warned as I placed a tray of food in his lap.

"Thank you, darling. And I have to praise you. The tea you made me was simply sublime."

"It was a regular tea bag, so I think you are still high on medications," I teased.

He chuckled and then winced. He was hurting all over.

Almost a week had passed since he'd appeared at my doorstep all beaten up. After I saw him trying to walk to the bathroom, I became convinced that he had at least a couple of cracked ribs, if not a few broken. So I ordered him to stay at my place for as long as he needed to properly heal since the stubborn man refused to go to the hospital to get himself checked out.

Maybe he's afraid of doctors. Or perhaps he simply liked to suffer.

Either way, he remained here, and despite the circumstances, I had to admit it felt nice having him around. We hung out, we watched TV, and we talked until we fell asleep. The only thing I really needed time to get used to was watching him roam about in Christopher's clothes. Samuel's were all torn up, so what else could I do but lend him Christopher's? Surprisingly, it didn't cause me as much pain as I feared.

Maybe I'm finally moving on . . . And I was okay with that.

There was one more reason I preferred him around, not simply to heal, but for the company. I worried about his returning to his place. That was where he'd been attacked in the first place, so he wasn't safe there anymore. There was no telling whether they would return.

Although I hadn't been successful in convincing him to go for a checkup or in reporting the crime, at least he saw reason in searching for another condo, although he wasn't happy about it. He loved that place.

I couldn't really say what was so special about it, since I'd only gotten a chance to see it once. That was petty of me, though. I was aware of that.

It was a small miracle that he agreed to relocate, yet it was better than nothing. At least it would give me peace of mind that something like this wouldn't happen again.

"This was all delicious, my darling. Compliments to the chef."

Which wasn't me. I ordered everything and simply reheated it when needed. I was still glad he liked it.

He groaned as he tried to put the tray away from him once he finished with his meal, and I jumped to my feet to help him out.

"I'm worried, Samuel. You should be better by now," I observed. I constantly worried some of his injuries might have been more serious than he realized and that it could cost him his life.

"I don't need a doctor," he countered, catching my meaning immediately.

He was so infuriating at times I could just scream and

pull out my hair. I settled for the second-best thing, nagging at him. "Why don't we go and see your doctor, and he can prove me wrong?"

"Darling, all I need is you taking care of me, and I'll be in top shape in no time."

I sighed, shaking my head. He was incorrigible. However, through all of this, he retained his sense of humor. And that was good, *right?*

We were so much different, I realized. I would most definitely seek retribution and want revenge, but not Samuel. He wanted to get better, then simply move on with his life. He accepted Nora and her torments as a part of life, yet I couldn't. I wouldn't.

I would be his angel of justice while he drank his tea and ate biscuits. Despite myself, I almost smiled at that.

"Can I ask you something?" I heard myself say.

"Anything."

"Your refusing help, playing the tough guy, is that a *you* thing or a guy thing?"

He started to laugh. "I have never in my life been called a tough guy before. I am a lover, not a fighter," he added, winking. "Besides, I am not refusing help. I have you."

"You know what I mean," I insisted.

He beckoned me to sit beside him, and I moved the tray away so I could. "This tough guy has a confession to make."

"Samuel."

"I like it when you fret about me, but don't worry so much, darling. Everything will be all right."

"You know. It's hard to take you seriously when you have a black eye," I pointed out.

He grinned. "Doesn't it make me look ruggedly handsome?"

I rolled my eyes. "It makes you look like a man who is in danger."

He reached for my hands, and when I offered them, he pulled me even closer until I was sitting in his lap.

"Seeing you this worried about me makes me deliriously happy," he confessed.

"I think that's my clue that we need to go and get your head checked," I commented with a smile.

He chuckled before kissing me. "You know," he started once we parted, "I wasn't sure before, but I am now."

"Sure about what?"

"That you care about me. And knowing the truth makes me happy." And it showed. His whole face was glowing despite the bruises.

I looked downward, feeling shy all of a sudden. "Of course I care about you," I confessed.

He wrapped his arms around me, pulling me in a tight hug. I worried about his ribs, but apparently, he didn't.

"Charlene, I'm completely smitten by you, and it fills me with so much joy that you feel the same way. I don't even care that I had to be beaten up to learn that."

I wanted to reply, but he beat me to the punch.

"And I know it might be too early for you for such declarations of love, but I want you to know I will wait for you to feel comfortable about opening up to me because I know you are worth the wait."

That almost brought tears to my eyes. *He said 'love'.*

"I want to show you the love you blessed me with."

We kissed. And we didn't stop there.

We hadn't made love since he got injured, but now, Samuel deemed himself well enough, since we ended up in the bedroom. Although it had been only a few days since we last made love, my body still craved him as though months and months had passed.

"Oh, Charlene, you make me the happiest man alive," he declared in the throes of passion.

With my body, I showed him everything I felt for him because I still wasn't ready to vocalize all of that. And I couldn't say why.

Was I afraid? Definitely, except it was more than that.

I thought about his words even after we finished and he fell asleep in my arms. Samuel was in love with me. And he was convinced I felt the same way about him. I was shocked he'd managed to see that before me.

Am I in love with him? I believed I was. Based on my behavior, that was the only logical explanation.

However, when it actually happened, when I fell in love, I couldn't say for sure. He became such a vital part of my life that it was only natural that feelings developed between us.

There was this fundamental connection between us, and part of me was grateful it bloomed into love. The rest was freaked out. I was timid to finally come to terms with the fact that I loved another human being.

Loving someone meant completely surrendering to that person, opening up, showing all your flaws, fears, and despite this big revelation, I wasn't sure I was ready for such a big leap.

You already jumped, girl. You just didn't know it. Yet now I did know. So what was I going to do now?

I looked at Samuel, who was sleeping soundly next to me. There was a small smile dancing across his lips as though his dreams were pleasant ones, and I was glad. He reassured me that he would wait for me to reach his level of sentiments. Was there better proof of his love and devotion than that? I didn't think so.

He was doing everything in his power to show me how much he loved and desired me, and what was I doing on my end? I was trying to hire a freaking PI to look into his past, into his former lover's past.

So much for my love and devotion, I chastised myself. I felt extremely guilty for entertaining such an idea for even a second. Now more than ever, I came to terms with how Samuel wasn't the problematic one in this relationship. He was nothing but kind, patient, honest, and loving from the start. I was the problematic one. I was the one who had doubts, who questioned everything instead of letting go and surrendering to the feelings.

I was the one who had a screwed-up brain that was obviously determined to sabotage my relationship with this man. And why was that the case, someone might ask? Because I was batshit crazy.

Scratch that, I wished things were as easy as that. Sadly, they were not.

It was clear that I was afraid to let Samuel into my life to the extent I'd let Christopher in once upon a time.

Samuel was right. It was hard for me to open up like that again, to surrender. All the same, I wasn't going to be afraid anymore. I would live my life to the fullest. I would live and love and be happy beside this wonderful man.

Samuel loved me, and if I loved him in return the way I knew I already did, then it was time to show him. I had wasted enough time on sorrow, fear, and pain. I wasn't planning on wasting a second more.

Enough was enough.

Feeling quite elated and liberated by my decision, I settled next to Samuel, letting him wrap his arms around me in his sleep while I tried to sleep. While I slept, I dreamt about him. We were in a field having a picnic, watching wild horses gallop by us. I laughed as Samuel pretended to be a cowboy.

I woke up with a start, hearing Samuel's voice. It appeared he was speaking with someone. My first instinct was that I had forgotten about yet another courier, so I went downstairs to investigate. I found Samuel in the living room, and he was actually on the phone.

My shopaholic tendencies mixed with amnesia days are over. Somehow, I wasn't too broken up about it.

He blew me a kiss as he saw me approach.

"Move that to next week," he was saying. "And cancel my Singapore trip. I just don't have the time."

After a short pause while listening to the person on the other side, he continued, "Yes, Jen. No, don't forward me that. I'll deal with him some other time."

I wanted to leave him be, let him do his business or whatever, but he reached for me. I went to sit in his lap.

"That will be all, Jen. Thank you."

Once he hung up, he kissed me good morning. I noted the kiss was a bit more passionate than a simple peck on the lips. Not that I was complaining.

"I hope I didn't wake you up," he said a bit apologetically.

I shook my head.

Looking at his phone, he wore a small frown that I didn't like.

"Is something the matter?"

"Not at all." He smoothed his features. "I was merely conducting some business, and after the marvelous week I've had with you, I admit I became a bit lazy."

I could completely relate to that.

"You were planning on going to Singapore?" I asked, curiosity getting the better of me.

"I was, but as it turns out, I am bound to stay in New York for the time being," he said with a wry smile.

"Really?" I countered, smiling as well.

"Yes, unfortunately, I am quite unable to leave a certain woman. Even when I conduct my everyday business, she is constantly on my mind."

"I am glad because I realized I'm quite attached to you too," I said, hugging him.

"Is it wrong of me to want us to stay like this forever?"

"Not at all," I instantly replied because I felt the same way. I felt so happy, my heart swelled with so much joy, and I wondered how it hadn't burst already.

We kissed again. After we parted, hand in hand, we went to the kitchen in search of some food. I wasn't known for my culinary skills, so our options were pretty limited.

"I'm glad you are feeling better," I observed as we ate some toast with cream cheese.

"Indeed. I am feeling better. And I have you to thank for that."

There was something on my mind, and I didn't know how to tackle it. I didn't know how he would react. I figured there was no use in beating around the bush. *Better tackle it head-on.*

"Have you given some thought about what to do about Nora?"

He nodded. "I will definitely get a new place," he said lightly as though trying to make a joke.

I already knew that. We discussed that at length a couple of days ago, so that didn't answer my question. And I wasn't giving up.

"I really think you should report her," I insisted.

"No, that would be fruitless. I'll deal with her on my own."

And get your ass kicked in the process, I grumbled, yet did not say that out loud. Instead, I said, "Do you really think that to be the best course of action? She's proven how dangerous she is."

He kissed the tip of my nose between bites. "I know you're worried, darling, but let me handle this. I know what I'm doing," he tried to reassure me.

"Okay," I replied grudgingly, still deeply troubled. I wished he would see reason about this.

Perhaps he didn't want to cause a scandal and end up in the papers again. I understood his reluctance, being burned before, but I still felt like he was too lenient toward that woman. She seriously hurt him, and he was prepared to turn the other cheek. That felt like folly to me.

While I pondered all that, Samuel started laughing.

"What?" I asked in confusion.

"You had the most adorable expression on your face. I could actually see the wheels turning in that brilliant brain of yours."

Was he teasing me?

"It's adorable how you worry about me."

Yup, he was definitely teasing. "Not from my perspective," I grunted.

"Don't worry too much. I know how to take care of myself."

"You'd better. Or I'll hire you a bodyguard."

"You are my bodyguard since I entrusted you with my heart."

29

I couldn't remember the last time I was this happy.

Actually, I could. When my relationship with Christopher was fresh, when there were a future and endless adventures in front of us. Nevertheless, thinking about my late husband while mooning over my new boyfriend was a terrible idea.

The point still remained that I was happy.

I couldn't say I was glad Samuel had been beaten up, but that unfortunate event really allowed us to bond on a deeper level. And having him around made all my worries disappear. Now I fully understood how silly I was for trying to come up with all those reasons to paint him as a bad guy.

Not to mention how potentially harmful that could have been for both of us. My unreasonable thoughts had almost ruined a perfect relationship, and I was very grateful I came to my senses about that.

Naturally, I now understood the reasons behind it all. Yes, I was afraid to leave my comfort zone, my world inside the bubble I'd created for myself, but I was also trying to find reasons to justify my loneliness.

I didn't want to be alone anymore. That wasn't my natural state. That wasn't a natural state for any human being. We liked to gather, to group. We functioned better in clusters. However, after all the times I got burned, it was reasonable that I withdrew, and I required someone as good, someone as pure-hearted as Samuel to bring me out again.

He would never know how grateful I was for him. He would never know the full extent of what he'd done for me, but I would try to show him in every possible way.

I finally found someone who made me beyond happy, and I would do everything to make him happy in return.

I wondered how my mother would react to my having a serious boyfriend. I instantly banished that thought because in truth, I didn't really care. Although she would definitely see him as a problem. Discovering there was another person helping me spend all the money she believed should be hers would definitely ruin her day.

What a pair we were. He had a crazy ex; I had a crazy mother. We were a match made in heaven.

And speaking of his ex, she was the only thing, the only person, who was raining on my parade. Or so I thought. Yet as it turned out, she was not the only one.

I was speaking with Dr. Neal about Samuel, overjoyed that all my worries had gone away and giddy that I was finally embracing happiness, when she basically tossed cold water all over me.

Dr. Neal appeared lost in thought while I spoke, and she kept looking at me oddly, to the point I started wondering if she had some personal issue she needed to deal with instead of listening to my problems. Or the lack of them, for a change. I considered that to be a great success, but I was the only one, it seemed.

"I am so relieved I don't feel this weight anymore," I confessed.

"You're having no more doubts?" Her eyebrows shot up, and she looked at me with worry.

"None," I replied instantly. Now I knew it was all in my head, so it couldn't hurt me anymore.

"You have no more fear about his strange behavior or that he has a possible shopping addiction?"

I shrugged and shook my head. "I was wrong; you were right. He's the best boyfriend ever."

She pursed her lips. "And he simply showed up unannounced, injured, and stayed with you for a week?"

The way she said it made me pause. Was there something there I should be concerned about? I didn't think so. Besides, she was the one who told me to get out there and date and give him a chance. "It was an emergency, and he was hurt."

"Because his ex-girlfriend attacked him."

"No, it wasn't exactly her. Samuel believes she paid the three men to beat him up."

She drew in a sharp breath. "Did he report her or the incident?"

"Well, no. I did ask him to, but he's . . . well, he's reluctant to do it." I tried to defend him, which wasn't easy considering I wanted him to report her too, but I would respect his wishes no matter what.

"Charlene, how did it make you feel to have him staying with you for a week? Do you like taking care of him?"

It was hard not to frown at the way she'd asked that. I thought she would be happy I was moving on and trusting him, yet here she was, asking me all kinds of unimportant things.

"It feels nice to be needed again," I replied honestly.

Dr. Neal looked very worried with my answer, which made me feel like I should defend myself and my reasoning.

"But I was scared seeing him like that."

"His seeking refuge with you made you feel good?"

I could only stare at her. "It wasn't like I wished something like that to happen to him. He showed up asking for help, so what was I supposed to do, refuse to help him while he was bleeding on my doorstep?" I countered, getting agitated.

"Of course not," she reassured me, "but I do see some things that concern me."

"Like what?" I asked as I crossed my arms over my chest.

"I think you're showing some signs of codependency."

"What?" *She can't be serious.*

"You're changing your life. You're making it revolve around Samuel, just like you did with Christopher," she explained.

My mind shut down for a few seconds, refusing to process what she'd just said to me.

I'm doing what?

"You're repeating the same patterns," she said, sounding very professional and therapist-like. "You are making the same mistakes, and that makes me deeply worried about you."

As she spoke, I could feel my blood pressure rising. I couldn't believe what I was hearing. I was so infuriated all of a sudden, I wanted to slam my laptop closed on her and be done with this therapy shit. I didn't because I felt like I had a bone to pick with her first.

"I was not dependent on Christopher. I loved him," I said through gritted teeth.

"I'm not questioning the fact that you loved him, but all the same, you quit your job to help him with his, you went on a trip although you wished to stay and work on building a family, and you dedicated all your life to fulfilling his wishes, his desires, molding yourself into a perfect wife. Which was why you completely shut down when your world came crashing down with his death."

Tears pooled in my eyes. I would not let her tarnish my memory of Christopher. None of what she said was true. I made all those decisions of my own volition. No one forced me to do anything. I helped him because I wanted to, not because I needed to.

"Why are you telling me all this? Why now?" She'd had months to spring this shit on me and hadn't. What changed?

Maybe she thought I wasn't strong enough to hear the truth before, I thought suddenly. I banished that thought immediately.

"Because I'm worried about you, Charlene. I'm worried you're taking that same path with Samuel now. You're molding yourself to his wishes, his desires, and that will only cause you pain in the long run."

"You're wrong. You're completely wrong," I said defiantly. I couldn't say what had come over her. Was she having a bad day or something? This was not my therapist. The real Dr. Neal would never say these things to me. Not that I was making excuses for her.

"Charlene, I know this is difficult to hear."

"No." I stopped her. "There's nothing difficult here. It's simple, really. This therapy thing is so over. Dr. Neal, you're fired." And with that, I ended the video call.

I couldn't believe that woman. I repeated all her words inside my head, which only made me feel even worse. I was livid, wiping the tears off my face.

I'm codependent? What the hell? She clearly had no idea what she was talking about. I thought she was a trained professional, yet clearly, I was wrong. No professional would do that to a client, say such nonsense. Besides, she was all over the place. She was a quack, and I was finally onto her.

She was the one needing help, acting all kinds of weird, as though she had a split personality or something.

One moment, she was pushing me toward Samuel,

praising him as a force of good in my life, and now that I was finally accepting her advice, she'd decided to switch it up. All of a sudden, he wasn't good for me. *Codependent, my ass.*

I started to stress. "*Ack!*"

"Darling, is everything all right? I heard you yelling," Samuel asked, appearing by the door.

I got so wrapped up inside my head that I had completely forgotten he was in the house too.

"I'm fine," I tried to reassure him, but my voice was too snappish.

He sat on the bed beside me. "What happened?" he asked in a gentle voice. "I thought you were having your therapy session."

"I did," I said, gritting my teeth. "And I just fired my therapist."

His eyebrows went upward. "Do you want to talk about it?"

I shrugged noncommittally.

"Why did you fire her?" He sounded concerned.

Because she thinks we are in a codependent relationship. I bit my tongue not to say that and then realized there was no reason not to tell him. Samuel was one hundred percent honest with me, and it was time to return the favor. The best relationships were built on trust and respect, as well as love. And that was the kind of relationship I wanted to be in.

"She thinks you are a bad influence on me."

That wasn't precisely what she said, but I definitely understood it like that.

"What on earth for?" He seemed genuinely surprised to hear that.

"I don't know. She completely flipped out. At first, she was telling me one thing, and now she's done a complete one-eighty, and I got pissed off," I explained in a rush. I knew I wasn't making much sense, but I was upset.

"I'm outraged and a bit flattered," I heard him say. His words surprised me.

"Flattered?" I repeated.

"I have never in my life been called a bad influence. I think I rather like it."

"Why are you taking this so lightly?"

He shrugged. "She's your therapist, not mine."

"Not anymore."

Samuel hugged me. I buried my head into the crook of his neck. His scent had a soothing effect on me.

"You should not get this upset over nonsense," he tried to comfort me.

"She thinks I'm in a codependent relationship," I countered. Part of me wanted for him to get properly angry, the way I was at the moment. On the other hand, I should have known he would be the voice of reason. He always was.

"I bloody hope so," he said.

I looked up at him. "What?" I was sure he didn't understand what I said because his reply made no sense.

"We should rely on one another in a relationship," he pointed out. "I want you to need me, to let me take care of you, and to spoil you rotten," he said, kissing the tip of my nose.

"That is not what that means," I tried to explain, yet he shushed me.

"I know what it means, and honestly, I don't care. No offense, but I believe your therapist is just finding ways to keep you paying for her advice."

"None taken," I said in return.

"I believe there are some therapists out there who are quacks and who use people's moments of weakness to profit." His tone grew harsh, and he seemed almost angry.

"I suppose there are some like that," I said slowly.

"I don't think I could ever trust one enough to go see one.

I could probably get better advice from a fortune cookie." His remark was snide, and he seemed so much angrier than when we'd started the conversation and I'd told him that I'd fired her. It was almost as if he was angrier at her than I was!

I'd told him about Dr. Neal almost from the start, and he was fully supportive of it. Yet now I discovered he didn't believe in therapy. Not really.

That was so typical of Samuel. He would never impose his opinion on me and respected what I did no matter what. The realization of how Dr. Neal was even more wrong than she knew pissed me off further.

Now I had my proof that I'd made the right decision when firing her.

"Will you seek a different counselor?" he wondered, sounding a bit worried now, which again was a bit odd, but then maybe this was just his true feelings about therapy showing.

I decided to let his tone slide, and I half-shrugged. "I don't know. Maybe. What do you think?"

"I don't believe you will benefit from more therapy. Don't misunderstand me. I'm sure it brought you comfort to speak with someone during your period of grief, but you're not that same person anymore. You're clearly much better now, much happier, stronger, and able to make your own decisions without having someone at your shoulder making you second-guess everything."

Was that what Dr. Neal did?

"I think I agree with you. I have changed a great deal." I had gone through vast personal growth since meeting Samuel. And shame on Dr. Neal for trying to diminish his influence and tag him as something sinister. "I'm just stunned she would do something like that."

"Don't fret about her. I believe I understand her motives perfectly."

"What do you mean?"

"I mean you made the right decision when firing her. She clearly panicked, thinking she was about to lose a valuable client, and tried to convince you of something that isn't true," he explained.

I had never seen things in that manner, but based on recent events, maybe I should have.

Dr. Neal had changed her tune a great deal. At first, she had encouraged me to get out and reconnect with the world, and when I actually did that, she started objecting, tried to make me believe I was in an unhealthy relationship with Samuel.

She even dragged Christopher into the mix. And that was something I could never forgive or forget.

"You really think so?"

He nodded.

If he was right, then that made me extremely sad. If a person couldn't trust their therapist, then the world was a seriously dark and dangerous place.

You can trust Samuel.

"A therapist who is trying to come between me and my love must be rotten to the core," he declared, kissing the top of my head.

She didn't look rotten. She looked worried. I had a moment of doubt. Then again, what did I know? I thought she was helping me, but maybe Samuel was right. Maybe she was doing all that to keep me in therapy for as long as she could so she could profit from me. That was her profession, after all. If all people were balanced and well-adjusted, she would be out of work.

"Charlene?"

"Yes?"

"I know this was a devastating blow for you, but look at it from the bright side," he said.

There is a bright side?

"You learned about her true character in time, before she could do any serious damage."

I nodded. "You're right. It's just hard, you know." This woman was beside me for years, had listened to my problems. It was hard to accept this new normality where I didn't have to speak with her every other day.

Samuel tightened his embrace. "I see it's time for some cheering up," he said as though thinking out loud.

"Cheering up?"

"Yes. I want you to get dressed because we are going out for some lunch. And then I have a surprise for you."

"Going out, are you sure?"

He understood my meaning perfectly.

We were staying put not simply because he needed time to heal but because we were both very concerned about Nora.

"Quite sure. Now chop-chop. It's a marvelous day, and we need to spend it outside."

I jumped on my feet to do as I was told.

"Good girl," he added, and I grinned.

He was absolutely right. I was worrying for no reason. People changed therapists all the time. It was my fault I got so attached to Dr. Neal in the first place. I was a business to her and nothing else.

Despite Samuel's best efforts, I was still slightly troubled by what had happened with my former therapist throughout the day. Despite my best efforts, it still hurt that she would turn on me, turn on Samuel, so when he fell asleep, I decided to text Selina and see what she had to say about all of it.

As expected, she asked to hear all the details.

I am very disappointed, I concluded.

Are you sure you made the right decision? she questioned in return.

Absolutely.

Just be careful, okay?

I rolled my eyes at that, deciding it was time to call it a night. Wishing her good night, I turned my phone off before joining Samuel in bed.

This day had been full of ups and downs, so it was best to end it as fast as possible.

Tomorrow was a new day, and I hoped it would be much better than this one. Then again, with Samuel by my side, that was guaranteed.

30

A couple of days after my firing of Dr. Neal, Samuel decided it was time to return home. To be perfectly honest, I was against that since he had failed to find a new place to live, and I found it foolish to return to the old one, where Nora was lurking about. He reassured me that everything would be all right, and I decided to respect his wishes. What else could I do, anyway? Tie him up to my bed and forbid him from leaving? *Now, that's a thought.*

I tried my best, but the stubborn man refused to check himself into a hotel. I suspected he was too attached to his condo, considering he'd put so much effort and time, not to mention money, to make it the way he wanted, and he was too embarrassed to tell me. And that was something I could relate to. I would never give up this house no matter what. No matter how many Noras came and tried to harass me, I would stand my ground.

I guess Samuel is simply doing the same.

On some level, I knew I should just ask him to move in with me, at least for the time being, but I couldn't. Although I was crazy about him, I didn't want to rush things.

Unfortunately, I feared Nora could try to force my hand. Because if she was prepared to hire three men to beat Samuel up, then there was no telling what she was capable of doing next. I tried my hardest not to think like that, knowing it would drive me insane, not to mention scare me shitless.

Sadly, I was right.

Nora discovered where I lived as well. We found a couple of Samuel's car tires slashed two times during the nights he spent over. He would try to go to work in the morning, only having to change one of his tires first.

"I'm running low on spare tires," he tried to joke one morning, but I was in no mood for laughing. That woman was clearly out of control, and Samuel refused to see reason and call the cops.

"You are sure Nora did this?"

"Yes. She does this to me all the time. That is why I have a vulcanizer on speed dial," he joked.

"Wonderful," I replied sarcastically, making a face.

When he made light of the situation and joked around, I didn't know if I should laugh with him or cry. This situation was beyond serious, and it was frustrating that I was the only one seeing it.

Eventually, he managed to go to work, and I had a couple of things to deal with as well. I still debated whether I should find another therapist, but I couldn't make up my mind. So I put the decision-making on hold, taking a couple of days off.

After I grabbed something to eat, I left the house as well.

Although I wasn't ready for us to start living together, I wondered if I should give Samuel a key. Logistically, it would make sense.

But lady luck wasn't on my side today, since the only locksmith went on holiday and closed his shop for a whole week.

You have to be kidding me, I grumbled. Resigned to coming back in a week, I resumed my shopping. The point of this excursion was to find a proper dress since Samuel was taking me to the theater on Sunday. While being with Samuel, I quickly realized that my former wardrobe couldn't keep up with his specific lifestyle. But I wasn't complaining. As it turned out, I liked dressing up for him.

A couple of hours later, I was on my way home after a successful mission. I managed to find a champagne-colored long dress, and the best part was I already had pumps to go with it. And that was when I spotted him as I left the small pastry shop that was next to the mall. I was sure that he was the same tall figure from before, from the park. And he was definitely following me again.

I picked up my pace, trying to reach my car. When all this had happened the first time around, I was convinced my mother had sent this figure to follow me around and discover what I'd been up to since I was ignoring all her calls. But then I wasn't so sure since Nora could have done it as well.

In a way, Samuel's crazy ex hiring someone to follow me around did make more sense than my mother. Either way, I was determined to avoid confrontation no matter what.

Although I was full of bravado in the park, this time I deduced it would be more prudent to simply run away. After all the slashing of tires and beating up Samuel, I needed to pick my battles more carefully.

I drove away from him, feeling a huge relief since it didn't look like he was going to follow me home. Unlike Samuel, I wouldn't ignore this. If that figure ever followed me again, especially if he popped up near my home, I was definitely going to call the police.

Unfortunately, my good mood was short-lived. As I parked the car in my driveway, I could see smoke coming from my house.

"Oh, my God!" I started to panic. Rushing inside, bewildered, trying to discover what was going on, I saw that the smoke was actually coming from the backyard. I ran outside and found the cause of it. My small shed was on fire.

"Oh, my God." I stood there, looking at it in shock. That made no sense. I had nothing flammable inside. Or so I believed.

Getting a grip on myself, I dialed 911. The fire department came in less than three minutes, which made me wonder if one of the neighbors had already called them before I did. If that was the case, then I was genuinely grateful.

Luckily, the fire was quickly extinguished, and it didn't get a chance to spread. One of the officers took a statement from me, although I was pretty useless, since I had no clue how it had happened or why.

Afterward, a fire marshal told me that the fire was probably arson. That filled me with dread, and my first instinct was to blame Nora for it. Would she do that? Was she capable of that?

Remembering Samuel's bloody face, I knew the answer to that question was a definite yes.

The fire was arson.

Those words swirled inside my head on repeat as I waited for Samuel to arrive. Naturally, I called him to tell him what happened, and he promised he was on his way.

As the firefighters drove away with my deepest gratitude, Samuel pulled in. He rushed from his car to embrace me. "Darling, are you all right?"

"I am." I was pretty shaken up, but not because of the material damage, more because of the fact that some lunatic had set my shed on fire. And I had a pretty good idea who that lunatic was.

The notion of what might have happened if the firefighters hadn't gotten here on time froze the blood inside my veins. This whole neighborhood could have gone up in flames. *Don't think like that.*

"Only the shed burned down," I reassured both of us.

"What happened?" he asked, leading me inside the house.

The place stank of smoke ever so slightly, and then I realized that was me.

"They think the fire was set on purpose."

"Heavens." He looked aghast. "Luckily, you're unharmed, and the fire didn't spread to the main house. You were lucky, indeed."

I started to shake. I could have lost everything. This house, all my memories of Christopher. It could have all disappeared right in front of my eyes in a puff of smoke.

"Do you think Nora did this?" I forced myself to ask.

"Possibly," he replied.

I made a face. I really didn't like that answer. In a time like this, I wished he'd simply lied.

"Try not to stress too much about it. Do you want some tea?"

I nodded absentmindedly. As Samuel roamed through my kitchen, I sat on the chair, trying to wrap my mind around what had happened. Someone started a fire in my backyard, burning down my shed. *Why?* Not that I was really complaining. Better the shed than the house.

Was that the real target? Was someone, Nora or whoever, trying to burn down my house?

I couldn't think about it anymore. It was too horrible. Was that the reason someone was following me around, to make sure I wasn't inside the house? Or to make sure I was? My mind kept on going despite my best efforts.

And then I realized I hadn't told Samuel about that.

"You know, I think someone has been following me around."

"What?" he exclaimed, stopping in his tracks.

"I'm afraid so," I replied before proceeding to tell him about that day in the park, as well as today.

"Why didn't you tell me sooner?" he asked in concern.

I shrugged. "I thought I was imagining things, but today, I had to give it a second thought." *Because this happened* was implied.

"I'm so sorry all of this is happening to you."

"That's okay. It's not your fault," I was quick to reassure him. And that was true. Until we got to the bottom of things, we couldn't know for sure whether Nora hired that man to follow me around or who tried to burn down my property.

"That's it, I'm gluing myself to you. And perhaps we should skip the theater tomorrow," he offered.

"No." I was shocked he even suggested something like that. "I want to go," I pleaded. "Besides, if we retreat and start living in fear, then that means she's won." And I couldn't let that happen.

"Very well, we will go. Now tell me, do you want some cream in your tea?"

The next evening, we got all dressed up and went to the theater.

"I've heard so many good things about this show. I can't wait for it to start," I said excitedly as we walked inside one of the most beautiful buildings in this city. I tried my best not to let what happened yesterday ruin my mood or my date with Samuel.

"You've never seen it before?" Samuel sounded surprised.

Considering I'd lived like a hermit for the past couple of years, I'd missed a lot of good things. I shook my head.

"Then, darling, you are in for a big treat. It has everything you want from a play, a great intrigue, all-consuming passion, and unconditional love. Not to mention a couple of really great tunes."

I smiled at his description.

We were going up the stairs, trying to reach our seats, when all of a sudden, Nora appeared in front of us, and I recoiled.

What is she doing here? Did she follow us here? All kinds of questions rushed through my head.

"Fancy meeting you here," she greeted while smirking.

Samuel took a step in front of me, as though shielding me with his body. "This is not acceptable. You have to leave us alone," he said, raising his voice ever so slightly.

A couple of people passing by looked our way but kept moving.

I really had to applaud Samuel's restraint. If it were up to me, I would yell at the other woman at the top of my lungs. That bitch needed to be publicly shamed for what she was doing. Perhaps that would put some sense into her.

Nora simply smiled, more like showed us her teeth, then walked away.

I could only stare after her.

"Let's go," Samuel urged.

"I cannot believe she followed us here," I said to him incredulously. The nerve of that woman. After everything she'd done, she'd dared to confront us as though we were the ones at fault.

"Do you want us to leave?"

"And give her the satisfaction of knowing she managed to chase us away? Hell no." I stood my ground.

"Very well."

That woman was seriously pissing me off. So if she wanted to play like this, then so be it. *I will find a way to bring her down even without Samuel's help.* I would report her as soon as I had any proof of her wrongdoings, and then I would really like her to try to use her connections to get out of it.

Perhaps she had money and power, but thanks to my

father, I had those things too, and I would shamelessly use them.

"Charlene?"

"Yes?"

"It's time to take our seats."

"Okay."

He kissed me quickly before we proceeded. I really hoped that crazy woman saw that. Samuel was my man now, and I would defend him no matter what.

We were sitting in one of the balconies that were on the left side, so I had a pretty good view of the rest of the hall. Although I looked, I couldn't see Nora anywhere.

Did she even have a ticket, or had she come here simply to mess with us?

Either way, the play was about to start, so the lights went off, and I lost my chance of spotting her. And then I did my best to follow the plot. I couldn't let that woman ruin my date with Samuel. She clearly had issues, but that was not my problem.

What would Dr. Neal say to all of this? I wondered. I banished that thought immediately, reminding myself that I was still angry at that woman.

Was I making a mistake by not seeking out another counselor? *Do I really still need therapy?* I felt great. I was happy and was pretty confident about my relationship despite all the drama revolving around Nora.

So maybe Samuel was right. Maybe I should deal with my problems on my own. Wasn't that the point of therapy in the first place, to empower people so they could deal with all their day-to-day problems? And I felt strong enough to be able to do just that.

During intermission, I excused myself to go to the bathroom. Thank God for breaks or my small bladder would never make it through the entire thing in one sitting.

Once I did my business, I went to the sink to wash my hands and check up on my makeup, and that was when Nora entered.

Unbelievable. I refused to acknowledge her in any way. I also refused to be intimidated by her. There was no one around us whom she could pay off to beat me up or start a small fire, anyway.

As I washed my hands, she retouched her flawless lipstick. Like I didn't know already this was all for show. All the while, I could feel her eyes on me.

Stare all you like, bitch. I don't care.

I was on my way out when she said, "Has he robbed you yet?"

I turned to face her. "Excuse me?"

She was fixing her hair, looking at me through a mirror. "You heard me."

"Of course he hasn't robbed me. Samuel is not that kind of man," I snapped in return, not caring that the room was echoing from the power of my voice.

"Oh, and by the way, thank you for redecorating my yard," I threw in her face, wanting her to know I knew she was behind it.

She didn't even bat an eyelash at that. "A piece of advice. He's dangerous."

I scoffed. "And you're not?" I challenged.

She half-shrugged. "I'm simply protecting myself."

"Sorry if I have trouble believing that. Based on everything I know, I am far more scared of you than I could ever be of him."

To my surprise, she started laughing. Nora turned around so she could approach me.

"Then you are an idiot," she whispered to me before sashaying out.

31

Upon my return to my seat, I didn't tell Samuel about my small altercation with Nora. I couldn't believe she'd actually ambushed me in the bathroom, but then again, I could. After everything I'd heard of her, that was right up her alley.

Why did she say all those things? I started to wonder. *Because she's crazy,* I answered my own question.

Samuel smiled at me before the second act started, and I smiled in return.

I couldn't tell him about Nora's crazy talk. Besides, nothing had happened, and he would needlessly worry. He already had plenty on his plate as it was. I knew he felt guilty for dragging me into all this, from having someone stalking me, to someone trying to burn down my home. If he learned about this too, it would push him over the edge.

And a true testament to how distraught he actually was could be observed on our drive home. He was all moody and quiet.

Luckily, Nora didn't try to approach us again. Nevertheless, I saw how nervous he was while we tried to reach the car, as though he expected that she would jump out in front of us with a gun or something.

Don't go there, Charlene, I warned.

And then he declared he couldn't stay over and simply kissed me goodnight, somewhat awkwardly, I might add, before driving away.

I guess he doesn't have a spare tire to lose, I tried to joke, although I couldn't find anything funny about it.

Entering the house, dumping my heels to fall where they may, I went to the kitchen to grab something to drink before going upstairs to undress and take a shower.

I shuddered as I looked out at the burned-down shed through the small kitchen window.

That woman had tried to burn down my home, and why? Because I was dating Samuel and she couldn't handle it. As though I needed more proof of how unhinged she was. But she played it well. Looking at her tonight, all dressed up, one would never suspect that she was a sociopath.

With all that in mind, I simply could not understand why Samuel was so lenient toward her. Why didn't he want the police involved? She would think twice about pulling any of these stunts if the police had her on their radar. Besides, that was why they were there in the first place, to deal with crazy people.

Feeling beyond troubled, I finished my drink and went upstairs. I would need to call someone to tear the rest of the shed down, and then I would contact another firm to build me a gazebo or something. I wanted her to know she couldn't win. No matter what she did, I would find a way to ruin her plans.

It took me a great deal of time to fall asleep. I tossed and turned with all these thoughts inside my head, plaguing me.

They kept me up. Eventually, I managed to doze off out of sheer exhaustion.

I woke up feeling mentally exhausted, as though my mind had continued to try to solve all my problems even while unconscious.

As I ate some eggs, wondering what Samuel was doing, I decided I couldn't simply wait around and trust Samuel would take care of things for me. He'd had ten years to deal with her and hadn't. Perhaps that was a bit harsh on my part, but it was still true.

It was also true that Nora was Samuel's problem, but it became mine when Nora involved me as well by following me around and setting fires on my property. And I planned on using that. Unlike Samuel, I planned on being proactive.

I returned to my previous idea of hiring a PI. A willing investigator could dig up dirt about that woman, which I could use to make her back the hell down. So after finishing my breakfast, I once again started looking into PI agencies.

I didn't have to look long since I already had my favorite candidates. Eventually, I chose one and decided to keep the other two as spares, just in case.

I had a good feeling about my pick. Her name was Alice Adams. She was only thirty-three years old, a year younger than me, but she already had her own business. As far as I could see, she wasn't as well-established as some of her older colleagues, but I didn't care about that. Truth be told, I wanted a woman to work this case. I felt like she would understand me better.

For some men, I would be nothing more than a jealous girlfriend. And if anyone was jealous here, that was definitely Nora. All the same, I feared that would make them lazy, sloppy. This case revolved around so much more than petty jealousy and was very important to me, so I wanted the best person on the job. And I deemed that to be Miss Adams.

I planned to ask for a full background check on Nora, and on Samuel as well. Although I trusted him completely, I needed that as proof I was on the side of good. Perhaps I could even use it to rub Dr. Neal's nose in it, although that would be a bit petty of me.

I felt slightly guilty for doing this, but I decided that was something I could live with. The way I saw it, I would feel like a two-faced asshole only if it was proven that Samuel was a stand-up guy. And if he was not . . . Well, I would cross that bridge if and when I had to and not sooner.

I couldn't think about such things now. This needed to be done so I could acquire ammunition in my battle against Nora.

What if she's the good guy in this story? I had a moment of doubt. I banished that thought immediately. A good person wouldn't hire thugs to beat Samuel down. A good person would not hire someone to follow me around. And a good person definitely wouldn't pay someone to start a fire in my freaking backyard.

With my mind made up, I copied the address of the PI's office so I could go and meet her.

Obviously, I told no one about my nefarious plan. It wasn't because I was paranoid or something, it was simply because I knew Samuel would not approve.

Then again, who would like knowing their girlfriend was doing a full background check on them? But I couldn't think like that. This was not about him, at least not to that extent.

The point was if he was against involving the police, it was safe to assume he would be against an investigator looking into Nora as well.

I wondered if he was this skittish about the police because he'd had such a bad experience with them in the past when they suspected him to be a thief in Nora's robbery case.

Or maybe he doesn't like them because he's guilty. I didn't believe that, not anymore, but I would learn the truth either way soon enough.

After making sure I had the right address with me, I dressed, then went to meet with Miss Adams. I didn't have an appointment, but I hoped she would agree to see me.

I was surprised when I got to the right location. I'd passed this building many times since living in this neighborhood and had no idea there was a detective's office in it. Probably because up to this point, I didn't need to know.

Entering and going to the right floor, I almost smiled recognizing that the office had a movie vibe to it. Or more simply put, the office looked the same way it always did in the movies, coupled with black letters on the square-patterned textured glass door.

I wondered if that was intentional. *Probably.* Since looking around, no other door looked like that.

So Miss Adams is a movie buff. Not that it was valuable information or anything. Realizing I was stalling for some reason, I approached the door and started knocking.

A very melodic female voice told me to come in.

Behind a massive desk sat a very petite woman, who was clearly shorter than me, with long dreadlocks pulled up into a ponytail and black-rimmed glasses.

She smiled as I approached. "Hello," she greeted. "How may I help you?"

"Miss Adams?" I asked, making sure I was talking to her and not a secretary.

"Yes, it's just me here, no secretary yet." She smiled.

I nodded, twisting my fingers together. "I think I need your help," I said and felt like smacking myself. That was such a stupid thing to say. I had no idea why I was so nervous all of a sudden. *I am doing the right thing,* I reminded myself.

"Please, sit down," she offered, gesturing to the seat across from her. "Miss . . .?"

"Mrs. Charlene Bell," I said, offering my hand, and we shook before I settled in the chair.

I felt like I was in the principal's office, staring at the other woman from across that massive desk. *Does she really need all that space?* Looking at her computer and all the other papers and files scattered on it, the answer to that was a definite yes.

"So how may I be of service?" she asked again, looking at me with curiosity.

I took a deep breath and tried, very concisely, to explain what I needed from her and why.

"My boyfriend refuses to go to the police, but I can't sit around and do nothing as that woman tries her best to ruin our lives."

She wrote down all the necessary information while I spoke. Every once in a while, she would interrupt me to ask a follow-up question. I took that as a good sign.

Overall, she looked very sympathetic and at the same time professional, which I liked and approved of. I did not need another friend in my life. I needed someone who would do a specific job to the best of her ability, period.

"I would like to start with some basic background checks on the two of them before proceeding to surveillance," she said after she gathered everything she needed from me.

"Whatever you think is best," I replied.

"I think I will have something for you in the next couple of days," she added, reassuring me.

And I really was. I was surprised it was all happening this fast.

"Money is not an issue. I need this done thoroughly," I insisted.

She nodded. "I understand, Mrs. Bell. I will do my best."

"Thank you."

I felt much better after speaking with the PI. I had complete faith in her. She looked determined enough to get to the bottom of things for me. She would do a thorough job even without the incentive of extra money, I was sure of that.

Returning home, I saw that Samuel was waiting for me by the door.

"Where have you been?" he asked.

Did he look worried?

"Just for a quick walk," I lied, too late realizing he saw me leaving the car. "I felt like strolling through Central Park," I added as an afterthought.

He frowned hearing me say that. "I beg you, please do not go anywhere without me."

"It's broad daylight."

"I know. However, I worry."

If you're so worried, then why not call the cops? I bit my tongue not to say that.

"I am sorry for worrying you," I said before kissing him.

"I worry all the time, no matter what," he said as though complaining.

It warmed my heart. Once again, I reminded myself that he needed a key so he didn't have to wait for me on the street like some beggar.

We got inside.

I will give him the key as a present, make a spectacle out of it the way he always did for me. That idea got me pretty excited. All the same, I decided to shelve it for the time being since I had more pressing issues at the moment.

"So what big adventure have you prepared for us this evening?" I only half-joked.

I also felt the need to switch the focus from me to him so he wouldn't keep asking me about my day. I wasn't prepared to tell him I'd hired a PI, not until I had some kind of evidence in my hands, and I didn't want to lie to him further, which put me in a tight position. Hence, pretending like all was well, like when we first met and I had no clue about Nora or what she was doing.

Samuel made a face. He looked apologetically at me as he took my hand. I sobered up instantly. "Samuel, what's the matter?" I asked, trying not to get alarmed by his mood change.

"I was thinking, considering our current situation, would you mind us having our dates indoors for the time being?"

I was relieved at hearing him say that.

"Samuel, don't scare me like that again. I thought you were about to tell me something serious," I chastised.

"This is serious. I want to show you the world, and I'm being forced to show you your dull living room."

I ignored the jibe and simply hugged him, which completely took him by surprise.

"You're not mad at me?" he inquired.

"Mad? Are you kidding me? To me, it's like you just told me we would be celebrating a holiday that's Thanksgiving and Christmas all rolled into one," I said all in one breath.

"Really?"

I let him go so I could look into his face. "Don't you get it by now? I don't care where we are as long as we're together. And spending an evening in my dull living room sounds like perfection to me."

He chuckled. "At times, you say the strangest things, but I love you."

We kissed again. "My point is, don't stress about such things since I actually prefer it when we stay in."

Finally, he looked reassured. "Good," he replied. "Although bear in mind, I will find a way to make it up to you."

I looked at him, then toward the bedroom. "I know a way you can make it up to me right now."

He acted instantly, swooping me up into his arms. "Of course, madam. Your wish is my command."

I started laughing at that.

32

Two days later, I woke up to find a text from the PI on my phone. She'd also called, but I'd missed it. She had some preliminary information she would like to share with me and asked if I could come by the office in the afternoon.

I checked the time to see it was almost noon.

I couldn't remember when the last time I slept in was. Samuel and I had stayed up late and had a quickie in the morning before he went to work.

I sprang into action.

While I showered, I thought about her text. Although short, I was pretty certain she had some bad news to share with me. She wouldn't ask to see me in person if it were good news. She would say what she needed in a text if it wasn't case-sensitive.

What did she find? How bad was it? Questions swirled inside my head. Did she discover something about Samuel? Although I'd told her Nora was the priority, I'd still asked her to look into Samuel's past as well.

And now I had some major second thoughts. I didn't

know if I was ready to hear any bad news about him. *Stop that.* I was spiraling out of control without actually knowing what the investigator had uncovered.

First, learn the truth, then panic.

Since that sounded like a good plan at the moment, I managed to finish my shower in peace, then quickly dressed and rushed downstairs.

I was glad Samuel was already gone because I wouldn't be able to face him knowing where I was going. Each time I had to lie to him, I felt beyond awful, not to mention that would cause such an awkward situation since I wasn't that good a liar in the first place.

Deciding to skip breakfast since my fridge was empty anyway, I practically ran out of my house. On my way to Miss Adams's office, I stopped at the coffee shop to get some coffee.

It was almost one o'clock by the time I arrived at her office, and I hoped she was in.

She'd told me afternoon, except I couldn't wait that long. On second thought, I knew my behavior was rash. I should have called first to see if she was in her office. I was sure I wasn't her only client, but I got so wrapped up inside my head that I completely forgot about the logistics.

I knocked, and no one answered. I cursed. She wasn't in.

What do I do now?

Maybe call her on the phone. I reached into my purse only to discover I'd forgotten my phone at home. *Son of a bitch.* I was really on a roll today.

Seeing no other way, I decided to return home, then come back later. As I neared the steps, Miss Adams appeared.

She was obviously returning from some case since she had a huge camera hanging around her neck.

"Perfect timing," she greeted.

"I was in the neighborhood, so I came a little early," I explained.

"Great."

Unlocking the door, she said, "Come in."

I sat on that same chair as she put her equipment away. Afterward, she grabbed a couple of files that had the names *Nora* and *Samuel* written on them, then sat behind the desk.

"So I have some news for you, but I've only scratched the surface, and I'm not stopping yet," she explained.

"Okay," I replied with a nod.

I was glad to be sitting down because as she opened one of the files, I could feel my legs stop working.

I tried to give myself a pep talk. *Calm down; nothing wrong is about to happen. You will simply learn the truth about Nora and about Samuel, like you wished.*

"Nora Drake, maiden Volans, was born in Boston. She is thirty-eight years old and . . ."

As she spoke, I tried really hard to listen, and I did, but I was also too aware of the second file she had, the one about Samuel, and despite my best efforts, that was the information I wanted to hear more urgently.

I'd been through so much while dating Samuel. I had so many doubts about it, and just as I was about to get rid of them, this happened. It was true I'd asked the PI to do a background check on him, but with that, all these old, buried feelings and doubts came rushing out.

Am I making a mistake again? Am I doubting him without cause again? I would discover soon enough.

"The ME declared his death to be of natural causes . . ."

Overall, she didn't tell me anything I didn't already know about Nora. *I guess that is why it's called a preliminary search.*

And then she hesitated while reaching for the other file. As she started opening it up, my heart started to beat a little bit faster.

Here we go.

"Mrs. Bell . . ." she started.

"Just tell me whatever it is," I interjected. The suspense was killing me.

"As I said, my investigation has only started . . ."

"But?"

"I found some concerning things regarding Samuel Northman."

"Like what?"

"First of all, he changed his name ten years ago. He was formerly known as Jonathon Samuel Clarkson, and he is a suspect in several international robberies. Robberies that include major thefts, such as jewels and Fabergé eggs."

"Robberies? As in plural?" I repeated like a parrot.

"I'm afraid so. His marks are all wealthy people, mostly women, divorced or widows, whom he can seduce to gain access."

I thought I would be sick then and there.

Samuel is a thief. Allegedly, but still. The instant she said it, I knew it was the truth. I knew it in my heart.

I knew something was wrong from the start, but I'd made excuses and ignored it. I did everything I could to glaze over the truth with excuses and rationalizations simply so I could keep on seeing him, no matter what.

I was definitely going to be sick.

"Mrs. Bell, are you all right?"

"Can I get a glass of water?"

"Of course."

I knew there was something wrong with him, that his behavior wasn't normal, taking me to all those shows, urging me to buy expensive things that I didn't need or want, and I did nothing. Well, not nothing. I pretended all was well, that we were in love and happy together.

I'd even fired my therapist, for crying out loud, so I wouldn't have to deal with the fact that I was nothing but a fresh mark to this man, to this stranger I'd let into my life.

Okay, not that she'd said he was a thief. She'd merely said I was codependent. She'd told me my fears of his being a thief were unfounded. I closed my eyes as I thought back over things.

Nora's words at the theater made so much sense to me now. She'd clearly gone through the same drill I was going through now and was trying to mess up his game.

Or is she part of the plan? Not that it really mattered, enemies or allies, it made no difference to me. They were both just people who were trying to hurt me.

"What do you want me to do next, Mrs. Bell?" Alice asked.

I didn't even have to think about it. "Keep on digging. I want to know everything about these two, especially about Samuel."

"I understand. An Interpol agent named Blake Aubrey is the one assigned to the international case. He's here in New York, trying to take him down. I will see if I can speak to him, and then I'll have more information for you in the next couple of days."

"Great," I managed to choke out.

"I know this is all very hard to swallow at the moment, but look at it this way. Isn't it better to know the truth one way or the other?"

I'd been trying to tell myself that very same thing. But as it turned out, all I wanted was proof that I was being paranoid and crazy when doubting him. I wanted proof he was a good man, not a criminal. Instead, I learned that my entire relationship with this man was nothing more than a lie. "I know you're right, but I was really hoping I was wrong."

"I one hundred percent understand. I'll keep digging."

I thanked her for all her hard work before leaving the office. I felt like I was in some kind of daze.

As it turned out, I was right all along and chose to ignore everything because I'd fallen in love like some stupid teenager. I could just smack myself since I felt beyond silly for trusting that man.

All he'd ever told me was a lie. And he'd even used Nora to entice sympathy from me.

Samuel was a crook, but he was no ordinary thief. Freaking Interpol was on his ass.

I really wondered what this Blake Aubrey would have to say about Samuel. *Nothing good, I bet.*

Why hasn't he been arrested yet? If he had been on their radar for years, how come he was still free, roaming about, left to continue scamming unprotected widows like myself?

Apparently, he was too good at what he did.

I couldn't believe this was actually happening, yet it was on me. This had become my life. All the signs were right there from the start.

No wonder he took me places and showered me with gifts and attention. He wanted me to fall in love with him so I would do everything he said. And I did. I went to all those boring auctions and paid an insane amount of money for all kinds of things simply to make him happy. And all the while, he was rubbing his hands together, biding his time, waiting for the right moment to steal all of that from me.

And I had actually contemplated giving him the key to my home. I might as well open the safe for him too. More to the point, I'd even fired Dr. Neal because I was so blind with passion and love for this crook.

I was sick to my stomach. I refused to cry. I refused to fall apart. *My boyfriend is a crook. Get over it and then get even,* I thought. I'd told him I was vindictive. Of course, I had been talking about Nora at the time, but the same applied to him since he'd been trying to take advantage of me.

Since I couldn't be mad at myself at the moment for letting such a leech into my life, I got angry at Samuel. He was the guilty party. He was the one who needed to pay for his nefarious behavior.

Oh, how in love he'd looked while he spoke all those sweet words to me. I felt like punching him in the face. Although there were times when his mask would slip.

Come to think of it, no wonder he looked so disappointed when he came to my house the first time around. That was the moment he realized there was nothing for him to steal. *He sure adapted quickly,* I grumbled. That was why we went on all those shopping sprees. It was all connected. I could see that now.

And the weirdest part was that I wouldn't even know any of this if Samuel hadn't told me about Nora. As it turned out, he told me enough of the truth so I could follow the bread-crumbs to the rest, or in this case, my PI did it for me. And since he had me so wrapped around his finger, I wouldn't have even started digging if it weren't for Nora.

So why did he decide to tell me even that much in the first place? He could have lied, but he didn't. Either he'd developed a soft spot for me, which I seriously doubted, or he got overconfident and sloppy, having too much faith in his scam. All the same, I was glad his ego got the better of him, making him reckless, because if that hadn't happened, he might have ended up robbing me blind.

That's so not going to happen now.

Thank God for my safe! I'd probably already have been robbed by him if it weren't for that.

But that made me ask something else. How did he even know I had money in the first place? It wasn't like it was common knowledge that I was Wendell St. Claire's daughter. He definitely had people helping him in this little enterprise.

I wondered if he even had an import business. Maybe that was a lie as well. Not that it would make a difference. It was of no concern to me either way.

The most important issue for me was to decide how to play this next.

I could go home, wait for him to arrive, then cause a big scene and break up with him then and there, gloating that his plan had failed and he would never get my money. That would bring me some satisfaction. And that would definitely be the most logical thing to do, and just like that, I would be done with all this drama. Nobody would keep following me around or burn down my house if I unmasked his lying ass.

However, I knew I wouldn't do that. I needed to see how all of this would play out. Especially if Interpol had been chasing this guy for so long, then I knew I wanted to help them out, see if there was something I could do to finally nail his ass once and for all.

Because if I simply dumped him, he would merely dust himself off, then find another victim to rob, and that was something I couldn't allow.

Besides, I needed more info. Miss Adams promised she would have more for me in the next couple of days, so I would wait until then to make my final decision.

Perhaps part of me was stalling, still believing there was part of him that felt something real for me. I was aware that it was extremely foolish of me, but it couldn't be helped. No matter how many marks he'd had in the past, for some weird reason, I wanted to be different for him. That was why I needed more information to squash that part inside me and do the right thing.

After making sure this world would be a better place with him behind bars, I would call the cops and cooperate in any way possible to bring him down. I would lose him either way, so why not try to do some good in the process?

It was important to take him down, and Nora as well if she was guilty. Although knowing she was his victim somewhere along the line, I had to wonder if she was actually behind his being beaten up or burning down my shed. My thoughts on her were still confused at the moment, so I couldn't be sure what was true of her or not. In any case, I knew that Samuel was not a good man.

Although it was breaking my heart, I knew I would do the right thing, but what would happen to me afterward? *Only time will tell . . .*

33

Samuel was coming over tonight, and as we'd agreed, we would be staying in because of the Nora problem. Or so he told me. I was planning on cooking him dinner. I normally preferred to order my meals in, but I needed tonight to be special. Nevertheless, because of the fact that my abilities were limited, there was a chance this gamble wouldn't pay off.

I was hoping that even if dinner ended up inedible, he would see this as a loving gesture. I planned to have him comfortable, with his guard lowered, and then observe his behavior. I needed to see the real him.

Since I didn't want to sit around and wait on my private investigator to provide me with more info, I decided to do something on my own. And that was the point of tonight.

I had this need to do something on my own, to contribute to this whole thing. Otherwise, I would go completely insane.

During the day, I'd felt like calling Dr. Neal a couple of times to apologize and beg her to take me back, only to reconsider. On one hand, I desperately wanted to speak with her, and on the other, my pride was not letting me dial her number. She'd said some pretty hurtful things to me during our last session, and although that could be construed as some kind of tough-love tactic, it still hurt me deeply.

But what if she's right? I wasn't ready to deal with that, especially not now when I had to solve this Samuel puzzle. Besides, she'd been wrong to tell me that my instincts were off when I'd said he could be a thief. She'd made me doubt myself. She'd encouraged me to put my fears aside and take that leap of faith; then she'd decided I was falling into old patterns? Something just wasn't right with what she'd done.

And then I had to stop worrying about all that because I ran out of time. The dinner for my thieving boyfriend wouldn't cook itself, and I planned on dressing up as well to make an impression, and that required additional time.

Overall, I believed I'd managed to achieve the desired effect. Samuel's eyes bulged when he saw me opening the door for him. I even wore the earrings he'd bought for me and pulled my hair up so they were always on display.

"You look breathtaking, my darling," he complimented.

"Thank you," I countered with a dazzling smile. "Come in."

We kissed. I felt so ambivalent about that small touch. I had serious doubts. I didn't know if I could do this.

You have to. There's no other way, I reminded myself.

"Something smells delicious," he observed.

"I cooked us something," I offered with a small shrug, somewhat embarrassed. And that was no lie. I felt self-conscious about my cooking, always did.

"You cooked?" he asked with both eyebrows raised. The perfect image of a man being caught off guard.

I shrugged again noncommittally. I tried to make a joke. "I know how to work in the kitchen when I want to."

"What's the occasion?"

"You," I replied without missing a beat. I wrapped my

arms around his neck. "I wanted to do something special, show you how much you mean to me."

"Darling, I'm honored and deeply touched," he said with a flourish, which was his usual manner of speaking.

I wondered if that was the secret of his success. Well, that and an amazing body.

"I hope you're hungry too."

"Always, but not necessarily for food," he breathed against my lips.

I shivered, which was my cue to move away from him.

"Dessert will be served after dinner," I played along.

He pretended to pout as we settled in the dining room.

I really went all out, even decorated the table to make it look like we were having the most romantic evening ever . . . and not that I was on a recon mission.

As always, we chatted as we ate. It was easy, effortless, and it was breaking my heart since this time around, I was trying really hard to see past all the charm. He was an amazing actor. And although I was aware he was a con artist, I still couldn't tell the lies from the truth.

The best lies were based on truth, though. That was what made them so believable in the first place. At some point, I felt like I should simply give up because this was getting me nowhere. I learned nothing about the real him. All he was giving me were more lies.

Was it possible that he was truly that good at keeping his mask on, playing the role the whole evening without losing a beat? I wondered.

Why not? He's had a lot of practice. He's been doing it for a decade, scamming women out of their money. And I'm just another stupid woman down that line. I had to stop myself there since my blood pressure was starting to rise, and I couldn't exactly explain to Samuel why I was getting so angry all of a sudden.

"How are you doing, darling?" He surprised me by asking.

"There haven't been any more incidents, have there?" He looked genuinely concerned asking that.

Perhaps he was since Nora could seriously ruin his game.

I wondered what he would do if I told him about my encounter with Nora in the bathroom. I entertained the idea for a split second. How would he try to get himself out of it? Or would he simply run away from me, abandon his efforts, and accept that he lost one?

I seriously doubted that.

"I'm all right, Samuel, and all is quiet around here, boring."

Apart from my learning the whole truth about you by going to a private investigator who did a background check.

He patted my hand. "I'm relieved to hear that." And then he kissed my knuckles. He liked to do that a lot.

Is that a Samuel thing or a con artist thing? I had a fleeting thought.

While we ate, I constantly bounced back and forth between two states.

At times, I was sad that none of this was real, that this was simply a means to an end for Samuel to get ahold of my money. And spitting mad because he was nothing but a heartless, lying snake of a man who was doing all this just to rob me.

In those moments, it was hard not to throw my drink in his face and tell him to leave my house and never return.

But I reined all of those thoughts in and pushed them to the deepest corners of my soul so I could continue playing my part. I needed to remain cool no matter what. If I wanted to see how all of this would play out, then I needed to be part of the game as another player.

"Dinner was absolutely delicious," he said, leaning in his chair, taking a sip of his wine.

"Is that a British way of saying it was edible?" I joked.

I was very proud of myself. The food ended up better than I could have hoped for. What could I say? Proper motivation made me a better cook.

"Before I answer that, I need to sample one more thing," he said, leaning toward me.

"And what is that?" I asked innocently.

"The dessert." And with that, he kissed me passionately and thoroughly.

And I let him.

When he took me by the hand and started leading me toward the bedroom, I let him do that too.

How far was I ready to go for this little experiment?

Samuel was taking my clothes off, kissing me, touching me, and I was kissing and touching him in return.

The sex was still amazing despite the knowledge that he was a piece of shit who was doing all of this for my money. Afterward, I felt horrible too and hated myself for going through all this, but not as much as I hated him.

Why was he doing all this? The answer was obvious—money, but that was the baffling part to me. He didn't look like he needed money. He'd snatched millions from Nora alone, and there was no telling how many others fell for his charms, which could overall provide him a very peaceful retirement.

So was he simply a greedy bastard, or was he doing this for the thrill of the chase? Did he enjoy making fools of women? Did he like toying with their feelings? Was he turned on by the fact that he was leaving them heartbroken? Not that it really mattered. I wasn't his shrink to give a damn about his frame of mind.

On the other hand, I was worried about myself. What was my damage? Apart from the obvious. Why did I sleep with him again despite knowing all the dirt about him, knowing he would rob me blind the first chance he got?

I didn't have a specific answer to that question. Maybe I wanted to see how it would feel. Maybe I wanted one last time to be with him before everything ended.

Either way, it happened. And now it was all over. Although he didn't know it yet, this was the last time for us because I knew I wouldn't be strong enough to repeat this trickery again. I did not have his skills.

All this brought tears to my eyes, and I forced myself not to cry. I couldn't cry. At least not right now. Not while he was still in my bed, in my house. I didn't want him suspecting anything was wrong because I wasn't done with him yet.

The romantic dinner I'd prepared was just the first step in my plan, and now it was time for the second. I'd taken care of everything this afternoon, so now all I had to do was wait patiently to see if he would take the bait.

That was why I pretended to fall asleep when in reality, I watched his every move through my eyelashes. Samuel pretended he was asleep too. I just hoped I was a better actress than him.

Half an hour later, he got up really slowly, carefully, and went straight for my vanity table.

I'd intentionally taken out all the jewelry from the safe and put it all there on display in my jewelry box. And now I watched him going through it like I knew he would, although there was a part of me that still hoped he wouldn't. That part was an idiot.

Samuel picked out one of the necklaces I'd bought to please him since he had been pouting that night because I wasn't spending enough money. It was an elaborate piece, one I actually didn't like at all because I found it rather gaudy. Oh, the fool I was. And he placed it to the side. Next, he took out the necklace I'd bought to go with the earrings he'd bought for me. He put all three items to the side as well. He was definitely choosing only the most valuable pieces.

That son of a bitch wouldn't even let me keep the present from him. Then again, if he took everything else, it wasn't like a pair of earrings would mean he was a good guy and that something real happened between us. The earrings were bait to make me start spending money. I was aware of that now.

I couldn't believe how easily I'd fallen for that trap. Yet I'd fallen for everything else too. He really was good. No wonder the police had nothing on him.

It was hard remaining still and calm, pretending I was in dreamland while he went through my belongings, carefully choosing what to steal. The bastard had a standard, as it turned out.

All of a sudden, he turned to look at me, and I closed my eyes. And then I prayed like hell he didn't realize I was awake.

Should I start snoring? Of course, I didn't actually do that. We were not in a cartoon.

Because I couldn't hear him moving, returning to bed, after a few heartbeats, I dared to open one eye to see what was happening. He was holding the earrings he'd bought for me. Very carefully, he put them back inside the jewelry box.

What the hell?

And then he returned everything else as well.

What was happening? Did he spot me looking? No, he would definitely say something, try to come up with an excuse as to why he was doing this if that were the case.

And then he simply returned to bed as lightly as before. He kissed my brow before lying on his stomach as though preparing to really go to sleep.

My mind was in shambles. *What just happened? Why?* Why did he hesitate and return everything? Why did he return to bed when it was obvious he was going to make his move? Did he have a change of heart? Did he hope he could score even more?

Why did he look at me, look at those earrings in such a

way? That had to mean something. Did he fall for me for real?

Although he was a thief and sought me out only so he could seduce me and steal my money, maybe somewhere along the line, he fell for me for real? And just now, maybe he decided to turn the other cheek and be with me for real.

Should I dare to hope something like that was possible? Stranger things had happened in this world, but something like that was far-fetched all the same. I couldn't let my heart be so easily swayed, but it was too late. There was a sliver of hope inside it, nevertheless.

All the same, even if that were the case, then what did that mean for me? My heart's desires were known, but what was my head telling me? Should I be with him despite knowing all this? Could I and still be happy? And what about the police? They were involved, like it or not, so that couldn't be ignored either.

Plain and simple, could I be with a criminal, even if he loved me for real and I loved him?

I had no answer to that question at the moment. But one thing was undeniable. *Samuel is with me because he loves me.* That was my last conscious thought before falling asleep.

When I woke up the next morning, it was close to nine o'clock, and Samuel had already left for work.

As I got out of bed on my way to the bathroom to do my morning routine, I made a detour to my vanity table as though compelled. I checked the contents of my jewelry box thoroughly, and my heart broke upon realizing one of my necklaces was gone. Not the most expensive one, but that didn't matter at the moment.

Well, I guess that settles that, I thought as I locked everything else back in the safe, then went to the bathroom to take a shower and do some crying.

34

"I'm waiting on some documents, but I'm hoping they will come tomorrow," Alice Adams provided when I called to ask how the investigation was going.

Because Samuel robbed me, took one of the necklaces, I saw no reason not to proceed with my plan.

After I'd cried my eyes out for an hour or so, I wiped the tears away and dialed the PI's number even though I knew she would be calling me when she had something more, but I couldn't wait. I also told Samuel I couldn't see him today and that I was feeling a bit under the weather. I did that so he wouldn't suspect something had changed between us. He texted wishing me to get better soon and to call if I needed anything.

I needed my necklace back, but that wasn't what I wrote in return. I'd merely said thank you and that I would. As if that would happen.

"And what about that agent?" I asked her next.

"I finally managed to get in touch with him, but he couldn't share much with me since he's in the middle of an open investigation. He told me he would be interested in talking to you if you are willing to talk to him."

I knew what that meant even without her spelling it all out for me. This agent wanted to see what I knew, how deeply I was involved with Samuel's little enterprise. And then if I was willing, he would ask me to help him catch the bastard.

Unfortunately for him, I knew jack shit, but all the same, I was inclined to help bring Samuel to justice. At least that was what I wanted most of the time. A small part of me still hoped he would turn around and confess everything to me, then declare his undying love while begging for forgiveness. I was such an idiot.

That was why I said, "I definitely want to speak with him."

"Great. Do you have a pen?"

"Sure."

She told me his number. "Thanks."

After I finished talking with her, I stared at the agent's number as I wondered whether I should call him. Rationally, I knew I should, but all the same, I still stared some more.

Are you waiting for an epiphany or something? I snapped at myself, irked.

Eventually, I went to the store to buy some food. I needed a moment to breathe, to get away from all this madness. I hadn't seen anyone following me around, which was a relief.

As I returned, I dumped all the groceries on the counter, and without unpacking anything, I grabbed the phone number and my cell and started dialing before I could change my mind.

I held my breath as it rang. *This is the right thing to do.*

"Agent Aubrey," a man answered.

His accent wasn't American, but I wasn't sure what it was. He sounded . . . intriguing, though, and it caught my attention and made me slightly nervous.

I gulped before starting. "Hello, Agent Aubrey, my name

is Charlene Bell." I introduced myself, having no idea whether that name meant anything to him. "I got your number from my private investigator, Alice Adams."

"Ah, *oui*, I spoke with Alice. So, what can I do for you, Miss Bell?"

His accent made my name sound exotic, and I realized it was a French accent. I supposed that made sense since Interpol was an international police organization. They would have all sorts of people working for them, wouldn't they?

"Well, actually, Agent Aubrey, I think there is something I can do for you," I replied.

"How so, Miss Bell?"

Again, the sound of my name coming from him, even if it was slightly wrong as I was a Mrs., not a Miss, sent a shiver through me . . . a nice one, though, not one of horror. It made my cheeks pinken at the thought that I'd never met the man yet I found his voice sexy. I pushed those thoughts aside and returned to his question. "Samuel Northman. He's the man you're after, correct?" I asked, my heart beating double time in my chest.

"*Oui*, that is correct. If I may ask, how is it you know him?"

"He's my boyfriend, at least . . . well, it's . . . we never really put a label on what we are . . . just sort of . . . look, I've been dating him," I stuttered out, slightly embarrassed. "And, well, I think I'm his latest victim."

There was a pause on the other side. "*Je vois*. I think it would be best if we meet in person to talk about this matter, Miss Bell," he replied.

"All right," I immediately agreed. "Where?"

"Somewhere you won't be followed, but public."

I bit my lip, thinking. "What about Rockefeller Park? It's public." I went on to suggest a specific spot in the park that I knew would be hard to be followed to without noticing.

"*Oui*, that will be fine. See you tomorrow at four, then, Miss Bell."

"See you then, Agent," I replied before we disconnected.

So, that is set, I thought as I sat down in the living room. I wondered what Agent Aubrey was like. Was he as exotic as his voice sounded? I snickered, thinking it had been a long time since I had even thought something like that about a man. I mean, yeah, I loved Samuel's accent, and he had pulled me back to the land of the living, but prior to him, I hadn't paid any attention to any person, man or woman. Now here I was, listening to this Agent Aubrey and finding pleasure in the sound of his voice. Life was strange. I shook my head to clear my thoughts and realized I was still fully dressed and there was ice cream melting in my kitchen, but I needed a moment to process what I'd actually just done.

I'd agreed to meet an Interpol agent so I can entrap Samuel. My mind was spinning. How was I going to survive until tomorrow without stressing? What was I to do? I was going to jump out of my skin if I stayed put and did nothing but think about everything. Knowing myself, I would mostly stress that Samuel would somehow discover my plan and decide to retaliate.

And I would break down if he asked me anything. I was no spy. I wasn't cut out for this work. I had to lie to him for one night and I nearly had a coronary. And this was far more serious than that.

And then it hit me. If my meeting with that agent went well and I agreed to help out, then that would only mean I would have to keep seeing Samuel for the time being and pretend I was still his girlfriend.

That was how these things worked, after all. The agent needed evidence, and for that he had to have an inside person, which would be me in this case.

And then Samuel would definitely discover something

was wrong since I was a terrible liar. Who knew what he would do to me then? He could decide to take revenge.

You are reaching, I snapped at myself. Samuel wasn't a gangster. He was a jewelry thief, for crying out loud.

And that meant he was somehow better than a regular gangster? I had no idea if there was a difference, nor did I care. All I knew about that world was what I saw in the movies. And movies rarely showed the truth, so my point of reference was terrible.

What if he hurts me? What if he lets Nora hurt me?

I really hoped it wouldn't come to that.

Since I had no idea who the real Samuel was or what he was capable of, I had to be prepared for anything. And that scared me to no end. *Should I cancel my meeting?* I had a moment of doubt.

No. I couldn't do that. This needed to be settled, and this was the only way. I couldn't deal with Samuel and Nora on my own. I needed help, and this agent looked like the best person for the job. He was already chasing Samuel, so it was a win-win situation.

At least for me. For Samuel, not so much. But that was a hazard of his occupation. Whatever happened from now on, it would happen because of his actions, and I was sure he was prepared for that considering he chose a life of crime.

I let a criminal into my life. More to the point, I fell in love with one.

All that brought tears to my eyes. I couldn't believe this was actually my life. And it had all started so innocently, with my accepting one friend request and answering some text messages. *What a mess.*

I was such a naive idiot. I trusted him, believed he was the right man for me, a man who would love me and make me happy again when in reality, he was simply playing the part.

And now I felt worse than ever. *I fell for the oldest trick in the book. Love.* And why? Because I was so lonely and so desperate for some attention and affection. I had ignored the warning signs because my therapist said I was being irrational when I wasn't. Even when I had some evidence that something was wrong and spoke to her about it, she rationalized it and pushed me to keep the relationship going. I should have trusted myself. I should have trusted my own instincts. Instead, I had relied on this woman to make decisions about my life, about whom I should trust. I should never have given her that power.

I was beyond pathetic. Or at least I had been. Firing her was probably the first good decision I'd made in a while. The second was that I'd trusted myself enough to hire a PI. Although I'd told myself I was going for a completely different reason, I still managed to learn the real truth, the truth about Samuel—who he was and what he was doing with women like me.

Unfortunately, all that knowledge about him was breaking my heart. I heard in a movie once a very disturbing line. *Knowledge is pain.* I understood that now.

All the same, no matter my personal feelings, no matter the fury I felt and the heartache that filled my heart, I would meet with that agent and do what I needed to help him catch Samuel in the act. He needed to be locked up for all he'd done.

And that wasn't an act of petty revenge on my part. At least, not completely. I was a vindictive human being, and since he'd hurt me, I wanted to hurt him back. I wanted him to suffer, knowing I helped lock his ass up. I wanted him to suffer the way I was suffering at the moment knowing he was conning me this whole time while we kissed, while we made love, while he told me he loved me. *Stop, Charlene. These feelings aren't good for you.*

However, this went beyond that.

Being vindictive was only part of why I was doing this. Knowing all that I knew, I couldn't simply send him away and pretend he wouldn't continue doing this act for God knew how many years to other women. I couldn't let him hurt any more women simply so he could spend their money.

He'd shown he was a bad guy, a criminal, and criminals belonged in jail, plain and simple. And it was my duty to help out in any way I could to bring this criminal to justice. If I truly was a good person, as I considered myself to be, then there wasn't another path for me. I needed to do everything in my power to help Interpol catch him.

Although I would never admit this, part of me was impressed he'd managed to elude the famed agency for so long. *He's been conning women for a decade, and they've had nothing on him.* That was fascinating to me, in a way. Was it luck, or was it skill? Probably a little bit of both.

Either way, I hoped with my help his luck would finally run out.

With my mind made up and somewhat at ease, I went to the kitchen to deal with the groceries I'd bought. Realizing I'd purchased the ice cream Samuel liked by default brought fresh tears to my eyes as I cleaned up the melted mess it had made all over the counter. How was I going to survive this? How was I to act like all was well between us without breaking apart while working with this agent?

I guess I will find out what I'm made of tomorrow.

Besides, this wouldn't be the first time I had done something I didn't want to. I'd lived with my mother for years while wanting to run away. I'd lived through her abuse, but I'd worked hard and eventually won the opportunity to start fresh in college thanks to the full ride I'd received.

In a way, this would be no different from that. I would do the work and simply bide my time, and eventually, I would prevail.

So I would smile, go on dates, or stay in because of Nora and pretend I was a loving girlfriend like he would pretend he was a loving boyfriend until the day the agent had enough evidence against him to finally arrest him and lock him up for good.

Despite my bravado, when Samuel called, obviously to check up on me, since I'd said I had a cold, I ignored it. I couldn't speak to him, not yet. I needed a bit more time to prepare myself for what was about to come. He sent a text next, asking how I was. I didn't even open it. *Let him think I fell asleep.* And tomorrow, I would deal with him. Tomorrow, I would deal with Interpol as well.

I would be strong enough to take on the world tomorrow and do everything that needed to be done, but not today. Today, I wanted to mourn for what I'd lost, no matter whether it was a lie or not. I wanted to feel sorry for myself and cry myself to sleep because as of tomorrow, I would be on my own again. And that sucked.

35

The dawn arrived with me still wide awake and none the wiser.

For God's sake, Charlene, look at your life. It was like I couldn't catch a break my entire life. Each time I thought it was finally my turn to be happy and experience something good for a change, life would slap me across the face and turn everything to shit.

Enough, I snapped at myself. *This will accomplish nothing.*

Feeling sick and tired of myself, of feeling like this, of having all these thoughts, I got out of bed and went downstairs to make myself some tea.

But reaching the kitchen, I changed my mind since tea reminded me of Samuel too much, so I made coffee instead. I would need that energy boost anyway, especially after the night I'd had.

Today, I would be meeting that agent. I wasn't having any more second thoughts about that. However, that didn't mean I wasn't nervous. There were a lot of things that could go wrong, or at least that was what my paranoid mind was telling me.

Oh, how I longed for the simpler days of my life when my biggest concern was what to order for lunch and whether I should change my number so my mother couldn't harass me anymore. Not interacting with the world had its perks.

Yet here you are now. I'd made my choices, and now I had to live with them.

Around one, someone was at my door, tormenting my ringer. *Who can that be?* I rushed to respond. I looked through the spy hole first and cursed.

Seeing no other way, I opened the door. "Samuel?" I asked in wonder.

He came with a bunch of grocery store bags, smiling like the Cheshire cat.

"Surprise," he announced, giving me a quick peck on the cheek before entering.

I guess he thinks he doesn't need an invitation anymore. "What are you doing here?"

"Well, since you told me you weren't feeling well, I decided to drop by and take care of you. You look well." There was no reprimand in his voice. It was simply an observation.

"I guess it was one of those twenty-four-hour viruses."

"I'm pleased to hear that. Nevertheless, I was so humbled by the dinner you prepared for me the other day that I wanted to cook lunch for you today."

"Really?" I asked, curiosity getting the better of me.

"If you would be so kind as to assist me," he added.

"Okay," I replied. That was the only thing I could say at the moment since I didn't have any excuses prepared to the contrary.

"Excellent." He grinned, taking all of the stuff he'd bought to the kitchen.

I followed behind him, praying like hell that I could do this.

Samuel came fully stocked, prepared for anything, as it turned out. He even bought us those cheesy matching aprons. He'd thought of everything, which only showed how good he was at this game.

All this stuff also showed me he knew I would say yes to him, to the cooking, and that irked me a little. He was completely confident that he had me all wrapped around his finger.

Well, he's in for a big surprise, I thought as I pretended to be wowed by the sheer quantity of food he'd brought with him.

It was true my refrigerator was always on the empty side, but I wasn't starving.

"Would you be so kind as to wash all these vegetables for me?" he asked, clearly getting into his role of a cook.

"Sure."

As I did as I was asked, he started pulling out bowls and cutlery from all the right drawers and cabinets.

Look how domesticated he is, I mused. He knew where everything was stored. Half the stuff, I had no idea where I'd put them, but he was moving around as though he owned the place. That irked me too.

I also remembered there was a time I couldn't get a date like this from him for the life of me. He'd insisted we should always go out and have 'adventures', stating there would be plenty of time for this later. And look at him now.

Was that because he already had what he wanted, had achieved his main goal? He'd already made me buy enough valuables for him to steal. And now he was staking out the house, biding his time.

He is done staking, you fool. He's already stolen one necklace, I reminded myself. So why was he doing this? Was there some kind of long con in play that I wasn't aware of?

He just needs an excuse to get inside your house again to take some more. As I argued with myself, he chatted about some client who was trying to sell some painting, yet I wasn't paying close attention.

I was focused on my meeting with Agent Aubrey. I had to find a way to get to it.

This was my problem. If Samuel came this early to cook me lunch, it was safe to assume he wouldn't be returning to work this afternoon, if he even had legitimate work to begin with. So he would want to spend the entire day here with me, and I couldn't do that.

Oh, the irony, I thought, remembering what I would give for such a turn of events, to spend the entire day with my boyfriend just chilling around the house, cooking together, watching TV, and making love.

Focus, I snapped at myself.

Considering I had a prior engagement and didn't really feel like spending time with this lying bastard, I had to find a way to get rid of him. I made up my mind. He was a no-good con artist, so it hurt being in his presence, even though I tried to pretend otherwise.

I had a newfound appreciation for undercover cops. They had a difficult, tricky job to perform.

I continued to muse about my options. What could I say to make him leave? He already knew I didn't have a job, so a work emergency was out of the question. He knew I was estranged from my family, so I couldn't use them either.

So what's left?

Luckily, I had time to try to come up with something since Samuel was too busy cooking to engage me in deeper conversation. But then the meal was done, and we sat down to eat. And I still had nothing.

Can I simply tell him to leave because I want to be alone? I banished that thought immediately. Then he would definitely know something was up, and my working with Interpol would be pointless.

"Isn't this nice?" he asked rhetorically as he sipped on his wine.

I simply nodded in return and took a sip of my drink as well.

"Is everything all right, my darling? You look kind of distracted."

At times, it was a pain in the ass how observant he was.

"Everything's fine," I was quick to reassure him.

"Are you worried about Nora?" he pressed.

Surprisingly, no. As it turns out, I have other worries on my mind at the moment. Like how to put you in jail. I half-shrugged. "How can I not be?"

"I'm handling it. Besides, haven't you noticed how quiet it got in the last week or so?"

Should I be happy about that? "What did you do?"

"Nothing you need to concern yourself with."

I almost rolled my eyes. I hated when he did that shit, gave me no answers, but now I knew why. Of course he couldn't tell me the truth since our relationship was built on lies.

"Good," I replied eventually, forcing a small smile.

I was running out of freaking time.

"Why are you checking your clock every so often? Are you expecting someone or are you just bored of me?" He tried to joke, except I could tell he was genuinely curious.

"You could never bore me," I replied, making a guilty face. "However, I do have an appointment with my therapist at four. If I knew you were coming . . ." I left the sentence hanging.

I also didn't want to give him the impression that I was prepared to reschedule for him.

Samuel looked surprised at hearing me say that. "I thought you fired your counselor."

I cursed inwardly. I should have known he would remember that.

"I found a new one."

"You said you weren't going to therapy anymore. What changed?" he challenged.

"What's with all the questions?" I countered.

"I'm just surprised, that's all."

"Yes, well, I thought about it, and I realized that with everything that is going on with Nora," I stressed, "I needed someone to speak with so I can retain my peace of mind."

"You can always speak to me, my love."

"I know. But it's not like we see eye to eye regarding this."

"What do you mean?" he asked with a slight frown.

I shrugged, giving my head a shake. "If it were up to me, I would have called the cops on her ages ago."

It took him a moment to reply, as though he was assessing. I hoped I didn't go overboard with this. The last thing I wanted was to plant the notion in his head that I would call the cops behind his back, which was exactly what I had done. But at the moment, that was beside the point.

"I see," he said eventually. "Well, I suppose you're right. If it helps you, then you should go, indeed."

I nodded. "Do we have some dessert?" I asked simply to change the subject. I was relieved this had gone well, but all the same, I still had a role to play.

"I'm afraid not, but we can go for that Italian ice cream you like so much, or we can finally try the carrot cake at that downtown bakery everyone is crazy about these days. After your therapy session, of course," he offered.

"That sounds great. Will you be heading back to work?"

He shook his head. "I was thinking I would busy myself down here while you have your online session."

I made a face. I couldn't help it. Yet in this case, it worked in my favor. "I'm not doing it online this time," I explained.

"Need a ride?"

I pretended to think about it. How would that look, letting Samuel take me to my meeting with Agent Aubrey?

"No, I don't want to bother you. Besides, it'll be nice to drive for a change." I tried to make a joke.

"All right, we can simply meet wherever you like afterward."

"Sounds like a good plan," I said with a smile.

He leaned in for a kiss, which I gave him despite wishing I could bite him instead.

"I'd better go and change since I cooked in these clothes," I said, getting up.

"And you did that marvelously so," he replied without moving.

He really planned on staying here while I was out and about. *Damn it.*

The man barely let me be alone. *Is he suspecting something is wrong?* My paranoia kicked in. No, he simply wanted to stay in the house, which did not make me feel any better.

I had no idea whether my bedroom safe would pose a challenge for such a skilled thief. *I guess I will find out,* I thought glumly.

It felt weird leaving him all alone in my house as I drove away. He looked so relaxed, so at home while lounging on my couch, reading some emails on his phone. Yet I knew that was all an act. *It had to be, right?*

Part of me was certain he would clean my house out of anything valuable by the time I returned from my meeting. More than just a part.

I was meeting Agent Aubrey in Rockefeller Park near the medical center. I came a little early, not wanting him to wait on me.

I sat on the bench, twirling my fingers. I had no idea what this guy looked like, only what his voice sounded like, so I watched intently any man who was approaching me and passing by me. I must have looked like a nervous lunatic, but I didn't care.

And then someone stopped in front of me. "Charlene Bell?" he inquired.

That voice was something else. "Yes," I stammered in return, standing up, my eyes taking him in.

He was actually here. *Agent Aubrey.* He looked like a man in his early forties, medium height, with wavy dark hair and green eyes. He was attractive, not distractingly so, but I would never in a million years peg him as an Interpol agent. He looked normal, not too muscular, not too handsome.

Maybe that's the point.

"Blake Aubrey," he introduced, and we shook hands.

Another shiver sliced through me as our hands connected, and my eyes flicked to his. I smiled awkwardly.

We both sat back down on the bench. And then nothing happened. I waited for him to say something since I was clueless about how all of this was supposed to be done.

"There's no need for you to be nervous, *chérie*," he tried to reassure me.

"Easy for you to say."

"You're doing the right thing."

"I know, it's just hard," I explained, hoping he would understand.

"If it's any consolation, Samuel has never been a violent man. I do not believe he will try to harm you in any way."

Which didn't mean he couldn't become one, especially after discovering how I betrayed him. That wasn't what I said, though. I nodded and decided once again that I was doing this. "What do you need from me?"

"First, I have to make sure we're actually speaking about the same man."

I nodded. That made sense. Wouldn't it be funny if I went

to all this trouble and tormented myself with all those thoughts, only to discover he was chasing after some other Samuel?

"I have some pictures of him," I provided as I took my phone out and started scrolling through my gallery.

Samuel was a bit skittish regarding taking pictures, which I now understood perfectly, but I'd still managed to snap a couple of photos of him while he wasn't looking.

I pulled up one with him while he was petting a horse since I believed that was the best one I had. Most of his face was in the shot, and he wasn't wearing sunglasses.

"It looks like this could be the same man I am after, but I will need a physical confirmation as well."

"If it helps, he's at my house right now."

"*Je vois.*" He held up a finger and then took out his phone to make a call. He spoke with someone briefly in French, I assumed with another agent, and asked me for my address. I recited it to him.

Will he send someone over there right now? I had to wonder.

He ended the call. "*Merci.* An agent is going to check it out."

"And if it is him?" I asked, although I really didn't want to hear the answer.

"Well, I will be frank with you. Even if we manage to find Samuel, there's not much we can do."

I frowned. "What do you mean?"

"Unfortunately, we don't have enough to make an arrest. Everything we have is circumstantial at best, and the witnesses we've managed to find aren't willing to go on the stand. He is very good at, shall we say, covering his tracks?"

"So you're missing the smoking gun," I added.

"Smoking gun? Ah, *oui*," he said with a half-smile. "Exactly."

"Is there a plan?" I asked next.

"We could set a trap for him. Perhaps he will take the bait."

I realized I liked this agent. He was very honest with me, admitting his shortcomings from the start, which was a refreshing thing. It made me respect the man even more.

"We?" I inquired, not failing to notice the pronoun.

"*Oui*, I would need your help to catch him."

"What would I need to do?" I asked without missing a beat.

"Nothing dangerous. I would give you a valuable item that you would place inside your home," he replied.

"And that's it?" I asked incredulously. That didn't sound too hard.

"*Oui*. The item will have a tracking device inside, and then all we have to do is wait for him to take it."

"I see."

It really sounded pretty simple.

If Samuel failed to react to the valuable item, then I would know he wasn't Agent Aubrey's guy or that he'd turned the other cheek and wanted to become legitimate for me.

Don't forget the necklace he's already stolen from you. I sighed. He had already stolen from me. How he thought I wouldn't notice was beyond me. It wasn't like I had a group of people trampling through my house on a daily basis. We were the only two there. Of course I was going to notice! I shook my head slightly and returned to the idea Agent Aubrey was presenting. The valuable item with the tracker.

If he steals the damn thing, then he'll carry the tracker with him, and Interpol will catch him and arrest him.

I liked it.

"Okay, I'll do it."

"*Merveilleux*." Agent Aubrey looked relieved. He pulled out his phone and sent a text; then with a nod, he looked back at me. "*Oui*, your Samuel is the man we are after."

"Oh, so your agent has already gone to see?"

"*Oui*, he just confirmed."

I think my heart broke even more in that moment. I'd been holding out the tiniest shred of hope that he wasn't, but of course, there was no doubt he was an international thief. I had to blink back a few tears. I wasn't going to cry in front of this agent. I closed my eyes and took a steadying breath. *Come on, Charlene, you can do this. You can be strong and go after the asshole, make him pay for what he's done to you and all the others.* I mentally psyched myself up. When I opened my eyes, it was with determination to go through with this and see it through to the end.

"If you would come to the office with me, we can settle everything *immédiatement*."

"Now?" I asked in surprise.

He smiled. "*Oui*. In my line of work, it is better not to waste time."

"Right." Because the criminals didn't sit around either.

Without wasting time, we headed to his office. I had no idea Interpol offices were just around the corner from where we were. When I suggested this place, I did so at random, but no wonder he so eagerly accepted. *Talk about fate.*

I had been inside a US police station before, but this was something else entirely. It looked more bureaucratic than I would have guessed. We ended up in a smallish office. Agent Aubrey excused himself and returned a couple of minutes later holding a small case.

Inside was a Fabergé egg, and I recoiled.

"I can't take this." The worth of that thing must be insane. I would worry something might happen to it.

"*Oui, vous pouvez*. It is the perfect bait for Samuel."

Yeah, as I came to know, the man loved his eggs. He'd snatched a couple during his criminal career, from what Alice had said.

"And it has to be authentic," Agent Audrey continued, unaware of my musings, "or he won't take the bait."

I knew he was right. I had no doubt that Samuel had skills. He would never fall for a fake.

Hell, what am I to do?

What if Samuel was trying to be better despite that necklace? Would I ruin everything returning home with this to taunt him? I had a moment of doubt. *Then again, if he takes this egg, then he deserves what happens to him, plain and simple.*

"Are you sure he won't be able to tell there is a tracker?"

"*Absolument.* Our tech people are skilled," he reassured me.

I wasn't. I took a deep breath. *Am I really going to do this?* It was all fine in theory, and here I was now, past that line.

If I took this home, then there was a chance Samuel would end up in jail. Despite everything, did I want that?

"I know this must be hard for you." The agent started to speak, clearly seeing how upset I had become all of a sudden. "But look at it this way. This valuable can't trap anyone if no one steals it," he said sympathetically.

I nodded since I had been thinking the same thing mere seconds ago.

"Right. You're right, Agent. So, how am I going to take this home?" I asked.

"It will be delivered to you this evening. You just have to come up with a plausible reason for buying it."

Piece of cake, I grumbled.

"All right. I can do that," I said with confidence, although I felt anything but.

We worked on some more details before it was time for me to return home.

"I will be in touch, Miss Bell. *Au revoir,*" Agent Aubrey assured me with a smile.

"Goodbye," I murmured.

As I walked out of the building, for some reason, the theme song from the movie *Mission Impossible* kept playing inside my head.

36

I tried not to think about the fact that there might have been an agent lurking somewhere around my house, trying to spot Samuel inside. *If he is still inside,* I corrected. There was a big chance he'd robbed me blind and run away.

At the same time, this was Interpol, the international police, not the NYPD. So maybe they needed more time to set everything up before actually coming here. Either way, I wasn't trying to spot anyone as I parked my car. And then I sat there for a few moments. I had no idea how I was going to explain the Fabergé egg being delivered to my house later today.

It wasn't like I could say, *hey, honey, guess what I found at the market.* They did not grow on trees. I needed a plausible lie or he would see right through me.

There was one thing I could use in this case, but I would hate myself for it later. *Desperate times require desperate measures.*

I saw movement inside my house and sighed with relief. *He stayed.* Naturally, my reaction irked me to no end. *You have to turn your heart to stone, Charlene, or you'll never be able to pull this off,* I reminded myself.

Taking a few deep breaths, I exited the car and walked the short distance toward my house. The front door opened, and there was Samuel, looking at me as though a starved man would gaze upon a buffet. "Darling, you've finally returned. I have to say, being here without you, I got extremely bored."

Despite myself, I had to smile. "I'm sorry for being late."

I also forgot to call him so we could meet in the city to go and have some dessert. I just remembered that. What could I say? My mind was preoccupied with other things.

"No need for you to apologize. Just get me out of this ghastly house and treat me with something sweet," he said in an overly dramatic manner.

Usually, this would be a place where I would say something teasing in return like *I thought I was your sweet thing,* but not today. I simply couldn't force myself to say that no matter what.

"Of course," I said, forcing a smile. "Just give me one minute," I added, reaching for the stairs.

"Take two," he called after me.

Forcing myself not to run, I reached my destination before I started to hyperventilate. I locked myself in the bathroom. *I can't do this. I can't do this.* Being in his presence was tearing me apart. No matter what I knew, I still wanted to be with him, and that was maddening.

Get a grip on yourself, Charlene, I snapped at myself. *What if he figures everything out? I am no undercover cop.* I didn't know how to do this. I started to spiral.

Everything will be all right if you only keep it cool. Besides, it wasn't like I had to do anything. The egg would be delivered to me, and then it was up to Samuel. I remembered what Agent Aubrey had told me as well, and that managed to calm me down.

After splashing some water on my face, I left my hiding place. However, I didn't immediately return downstairs. I checked my jewelry box. All was there.

I couldn't check the safe, but I believed it would be pretty accurate to assume all was inside it as well.

He stayed put, in this house, all alone, and didn't take anything.

What does it matter? part of me challenged. *A thief is a thief.*

At the same time, it did make me wonder what his deal was. I couldn't make sense of his behavior. This was the perfect opportunity for him to take everything and disappear without a trace. Why didn't he?

"Charlene?" he called out to me, snapping me from my thoughts.

"Coming," I yelled in return and returned downstairs.

He grinned at me, looking at the earrings I'd put on, the earrings he'd bought for me.

"I decided to glam up for this excursion a bit," I said.

"And that you did, my darling."

Without wasting any more time, we left the house. *Are there any agents around?* I thought.

"Oh, dear Lord, this is pure perfection," Samuel declared while eating his ice cream. "This is my favorite flavor," he continued in the same manner.

"It's that good, huh?" I smiled. I already knew it was. He always got that flavor when we went to the store.

"Would you like a taste?" he offered.

I shook my head. It was a salty caramel, which was not my thing.

"So how was therapy?" he asked conversationally.

I really didn't know what to say to that. Especially since I didn't go. I decided to stick to the basics. "The usual."

You get caught in a lie when you try to provide too many details.

"Do you like your new counselor?"

"He's all right."

I probably said he because of Agent Aubrey, I realized. Luckily, Samuel saw nothing wrong in the fact that I chose a male therapist this time around.

So many lies . . .

"Charlene, why are you so sad?" he asked with concern. "Is something wrong?"

Yes, everything is wrong.

Now that I knew everything was a lie, that he was simply playing a part, I couldn't shake this deep sadness I was feeling. No matter what, I felt the loss of what we had.

It wasn't as bad as when Christopher died. Nothing could come close to that feeling, yet this was pretty earth-shattering as well.

And I only got relief from feeling like that in those moments I felt something different, like undiluted anger for his trying to con me.

That wasn't what I said, though. "Everything's fine." I tried to brush it off. It didn't work.

"Then why do you look like that? You're not even enjoying your ice cream, and we both know dark chocolate and mango are your favorites."

I hated that he knew that. "It's nothing serious."

He gave me a look. "Why do you look like the fate of the world is resting on your shoulders?"

Not the world's. Yours.

I took a deep breath and exhaled slowly. "All right, there is something that's on my mind, and I've been meaning to talk to you about it."

"What is it? You know you can tell me anything."

Hah. Can I really?

"You know how I told you my father left me some

money?" I stated, and by his reaction, I saw I'd completely taken him by surprise. *Good.*

"Yes," he replied slowly.

"Well, that's not all he left me. I also inherited a Fabergé egg, and well, it's being sent to me by courier later today."

"A Fabergé egg?"

"Yes."

"So why is that a cause for such sadness?"

I shrugged in return. "I don't know. It made me think of him, the fact that we never had a relationship. I actually never met the guy," I shared.

He hugged me. "I'm sorry you didn't have the parents you deserve," he surprised me by saying. "But he did try to make amends at the end. He obviously gave you his most prized possession."

"I guess," I muttered in return.

"How come it's arriving today? I thought your father died two years ago," he questioned.

"He loaned the egg to a museum, and when he died, I decided to honor that agreement. The contract ran out, so they are returning it to me. It's arriving sometime this evening, they said." I lied like a pro. I was very much proud of myself and the lies I'd managed to say as though they were true. I hoped I wouldn't mess up in some way.

"From which period is the Fabergé egg? Did the master himself make it?" Samuel asked.

He truly loves his eggs, I thought with exasperation.

I shrugged. "I don't know much about it, honestly." That part was true, and I wouldn't even attempt to lie about it. If he was such an expert, he would know.

"I have to admit, I am something of an aficionado, and I am a bit embarrassed to ask, but would you allow me to examine it?"

"Of course you can," I replied instantly, offering a smile.

And he smiled in return before kissing me. "Thank you."

If my heart wasn't already broken, it would be now. I was sure he would try to steal it. *A thief is a thief.*

Since I'd given him a plausible explanation, I didn't have to hide my bad mood anymore. On the other hand, Samuel was skipping with joy, probably wondering how he would spend millions from stealing a Fabergé egg. *Bastard.*

We were at the house eating some dinner, although I couldn't eat anything, too nervous and too heartbroken, when the courier finally arrived.

"Why did they come so late?" Samuel wondered out loud.

"It's probably a security thing," I offered.

He shrugged it off.

I was sure the courier was an undercover agent, one of Agent Aubrey's colleagues.

Luckily, Samuel joined me by the door, so I hoped Interpol had their confirmation. I signed something before accepting the case with the egg.

"May I?" Samuel asked, and I handed it to him.

He took the case into the living room before opening it up.

He gasped when he saw the contents inside. "This is marvelous," he announced, and after putting some latex gloves on—I had no idea where those came from—he took the egg and started to examine it.

Although I had seen it already inside Agent Aubrey's office, it still took my breath away. I was completely in accord with Samuel on this. The level of skill and mastery were mind-blowing. It was a piece of art in all its glory.

It was on the small side, burgundy, and adorned with pearls and gems highlighted in gold. And when you opened it, you got a jewelry box.

Samuel couldn't stop looking at it, marveling, explaining

all the details to me. He knew the meaning of each piece and why it was placed in a certain way, at a certain place.

All that I knew was that Peter Fabergé was a Russian jeweler who made a bunch of these for the czar family. But Samuel knew everything. He was extremely knowledgeable. It was kind of impressive hearing him speak with such admiration, respect, and reverence.

All the same, while he did all that, I prayed like hell that he wouldn't be able to spot the tracker because that would mean all of this was in vain. I really hoped Agent Aubrey's tech guys were as good as he believed because we only had one shot at bringing Samuel to justice.

"This is an exquisite piece of art, and I am not saying that lightly. A beautiful model from the Fabergé jewelry house."

"Thank you," I said simply to say something.

"Your father had a good eye."

I really wouldn't know.

Samuel started to put it back in its casing.

"No," I said, probably a little louder than I should have, and he stopped in his tracks. "I want to place it somewhere," I added in a much calmer manner.

"Where would you like to put it?" he inquired, looking about.

I took the egg from him without breathing, since I knew that thing probably cost more than I had in my bank account, and placed it on the mantel. "How's that?"

"Excellent choice. It really is beautiful," he said, coming behind me to wrap his arms around my waist. By habit, I leaned into him.

"The most beautiful thing in my living room," I tried to make a joke, simply to distract myself from his closeness.

Samuel chuckled. "Almost," he replied, kissing my temple.

"Do you still think my living room is dull?" I continued to tease.

"I would never say such a thing." He pretended to be outraged.

I was about to reply when my phone started ringing.

I half expected it was Agent Aubrey calling me. In reality, Alice Adams was trying to reach me, which was equally troubling.

I excused myself so I could take the call in the other room. "Yes?" I answered in a hushed voice.

"Sorry for calling so late, but I have some new information regarding Nora Drake that I believe cannot wait until tomorrow," she said without preamble.

"What did you find?"

"I just spoke with Detective Eckles, who was assigned to Zachary Drake's case."

"His case?" I asked in confusion. "I thought he died of a heart attack."

"Yes, that is stated in the official report, but the detective was convinced that Nora killed him by tampering with his medications. He just couldn't prove it," she explained.

I was shocked, to say the least. "Thank you for calling." She was right. I really needed to know that.

"Be careful. That woman is dangerous, and if she has a grudge against you, then there's no telling what she would do," she warned.

I nodded, although she couldn't see me.

Nora killed her husband. She is a killer. She is dangerous. And she had been stalking Samuel for years. And now, since we'd both provoked her, there was no telling what she would do next. Miss Adams was right about that. *We are both in danger,* I thought with dread. My heart started to beat like crazy. *Nora is far more dangerous than I believed.* We should have alerted the police from the start. *Is it too late to do that now? Perhaps not.*

Either way, I had to warn Samuel. After getting off the phone, I rushed back to the living room. Samuel was still admiring the egg. He had his phone out and was taking a picture of it. However, hearing me come back into the room, he quickly put his phone away and instantly became concerned upon seeing the state of me. I must have looked whiter than a sheet of paper.

"What happened?" he demanded, rushing to my side.

It was time for me to face some things. There was no other way around it.

"Samuel, I think you need to sit down because I have something to tell you."

He didn't listen. "You're frightening me, Charlene."

I was frightened too.

"A while back, I . . ." A loud crash stopped my narrative. It sounded like glass was breaking, and it was definitely coming from my kitchen.

I guess I've run out of time.

37

It all happened so fast I acted purely on instinct. We heard the crash, and Samuel pushed me. "Hide. Hide now," he hissed at me as he ran toward the kitchen.

I turned to comply, to maybe jump behind the couch, when I stopped. *Screw that,* I thought as I started running toward my bedroom.

Getting into my closet, I fell on my knees to reach a metal box that sat all the way in the back. Opening it up, I pulled out my gun. I'd bought it after Christopher died. I'd hated how powerless I'd felt and needed to protect myself from feeling like that ever again.

However, I never got a chance to use it. I didn't even know how to handle one since it wasn't like I'd gone to the shooting range during my solitary years. All the same, I hoped I could bluff my way out of this and defeat whoever had dared to break into my house simply by flashing it around.

I made sure it was fully loaded before proceeding. It was. Without wasting any more time, I rushed back downstairs to help Samuel out. As I ran down the stairs, I could hear a scuffle and shouting, and I pressed forward.

Samuel was definitely shouting at someone, and that someone was screaming in return. A female someone.

Reaching the kitchen with my gun raised high, I could see that, just as I'd suspected, Nora was the one who had broken into my house. She'd broken the glass on the back door to get inside. *That crazy bitch.*

And this time, she was not dressed in high couture. She was dressed to kill. She wore all black and was brandishing a knife. I was horrified at seeing she was armed. She came here to hurt us. *She is dangerous,* Alice had warned me, and she was right.

"Look who decided to join the party," she said in a strange voice. "Finally."

She had obviously lost her mind. Something had pushed her over the edge, and she came here to do some serious harm.

Was it me? Not that it mattered at the moment. The damage was done.

"Leave her be," Samuel growled in return.

She started laughing. "Don't try to tell me you actually care for this woman. She's not even pretty."

"Nora, stop this madness."

"I'll stop when you're dead," she hissed in return.

Nora looked utterly deranged. "And then I'll kill her too."

Her words scared me, but I refused to back down. This was my home, and I would defend it until the end. I would defend Samuel till the end.

And then she attacked him.

Nora and Samuel were locked in a deadly fight. Samuel was without a doubt bigger and stronger, but the crazy bitch had a huge knife. It reminded me of the mugger in Cairo, and I froze for a moment, terrified that Samuel was about to die. I might have been willing to see him go to jail, see him pay for his crimes, but I didn't want to see him dead. I still had feelings for him, no matter what he'd done.

"I will finally end you, you bastard." She laughed as she swung her arm down toward Samuel's chest.

I gasped, but Samuel blocked the blow and grabbed her arm.

"Nora, listen to yourself! This behavior isn't normal," Samuel insisted in return.

Was he really trying to reason with her? *I can't believe those two dated* also passed through my head.

"You deserve to suffer!" she screamed as she wrangled her arm free and attempted to stab him again.

Seeing no other way, I took a stance and pointed my gun at Nora. Or at least I tried to do that. It wasn't easy with her constantly moving around, slashing with her blade, trying to stab Samuel.

I can do this. Yet my hands shook for some reason. *Get a grip of yourself.*

"Stop, Nora!" I yelled. "And drop that knife, or I'll shoot you," I warned. At that moment, I really meant it.

"You're pointing that thing at the wrong person. It's him you need to kill," she argued in return without slowing down or doing as told.

She still looked pretty determined to hurt Samuel, and he was doing everything in his power to prevent that.

"I'm serious, Nora! I will shoot you!"

"So am I. This motherfucker ruined my life, and he will do the same to you," she screamed, attacking anew. This time, her hit landed on the side of Samuel's thigh.

Samuel grunted, but it didn't look like the knife had done too much damage, thankfully. Despite being injured, Samuel managed to grab my metal service tray in his effort to protect himself, but hyped on adrenaline, Nora was faster. She nicked his fingers, and he yelled. Thankfully, that didn't make him lose his shield.

I groaned inwardly. They were both ignoring me, as though I weren't even there holding a firearm. Nora cleverly figured that I was bluffing with the whole shooting-her thing.

Damn it. What was I to do now? I couldn't simply stand around and do nothing, impersonate a house decoration while she tried her best to harm him, *kill him*, I corrected.

She had clearly figured out that we were hiding inside this house from her, lost her patience, and decided to attack. *Lucky us.* Where were the police when you truly needed them? I wondered. And then I realized I hadn't called them yet. Should I?

Crap, crap, crap. I didn't have my phone with me. I had obviously dropped it someplace during those first moments, and I didn't want to leave to find it. I didn't want to leave Samuel with this psycho. Not that I was contributing much to this fight. I felt completely useless.

As I stressed about what to do, locked in place, petrified, Nora grabbed a toaster and flung it at Samuel, then used his moment of distraction as he was trying to avoid being hit in the head to smack the tray out of his hands.

I had to do something now.

Samuel yelled as she slashed his arm. Blood started soaking his shirt immediately. As he retreated from her, she started yelling, more like emitting battle cries, and attacked again, stabbing him in the left side and then his chest.

Samuel staggered backward, gasping.

"Samuel," I yelled. *She's killing him,* I thought with dread.

This is happening in front of my eyes, again, and I am unable to stop it. Another man is fated to die in my arms.

Acting on impulse, I raised the gun and pulled the trigger. My aim would have been better if I didn't close my eyes in the process. Unfortunately, I missed my target completely. Nora looked unscathed, but as I did this, I definitely became the center of her focus. And apparently, she was pissed that I'd tried to shoot her.

"Bitch," she yelled, coming at me.

I panicked, going backward as she slashed her knife at me. She nicked me in the arm with which I was holding the gun, and I dropped it. "No," I yelled. I needed that.

That didn't stop her from advancing, but then she reconsidered and turned as though to pick up the gun. I couldn't allow that.

She almost got it, but I pushed her out of the way. As a result, Nora fell on her ass, but she didn't stay down for long. Using the moment of her distraction and picking herself up, I tried to reach the gun myself when I felt something pulling at my hair. It was Nora, and her grip was tight.

"Let go of me!" I yelled at her.

"You're as bad as he is," she seethed in return. "I'll take care of you. I'll take care of both of you."

I tried to loosen her grip, but it was hard struggling while I constantly had to check my balance as she pulled me backward.

"Let go of me, you lunatic!" I continued to struggle. Antagonizing a deranged person with a weapon definitely wasn't the best approach, but I was panicking, trying to save my life.

"I'll slit your throat, you bitch," she threatened.

And I was pretty sure she would make good on her threat. *What am I going to do?* I panicked. *Please, God, help me. I don't want to die.*

"Charlene . . ." Samuel gasped. "Move . . . darling," Samuel cried out, his voice filled with pain.

I twisted as I struggled against Nora to see Samuel on the floor, his chest bleeding profusely as he unsteadily held the gun pointed at Nora. My eyes went wide, and I jerked hard from Nora's grasp. I turned just in time to see him pull the trigger. The sound was loud, and my hands immediately went to my ears as if to protect them.

Something warm hit my face, and I realized I'd closed my eyes in that moment. There was a thump, and when I opened my eyes, I glanced down to see Nora's body lying on the floor beside me. She was dead. Her glassy eyes stared right at me.

I started to scream, moving away from her as I stared in horror at her body.

"Charlene . . ." Samuel's voice was barely a whisper.

"She's dead, she's dead," I repeated over and over, barely hearing him.

"Over now. Can't hurt you anymore," he panted.

My eyes went to him then. "You killed her," I said, confused. I couldn't wrap my head around any of this.

"No choice . . . couldn't . . . let her . . . hurt . . . you." His voice was barely audible now, as if he were fading. Blood was pooling on the floor around him.

My mind wasn't working as it should, I was aware of that, so it took me a minute to realize that he was dying. I moved toward him. "Oh, my God, oh, my God . . . Samuel, what can I do?" My eyes scanned him. I pulled my shirt off and started pressing it to his chest. "Samuel, talk to me!"

"Sorry . . . darling . . ." Again, his words were barely audible. "I do . . . love . . . you." He gripped my fingers for a moment, and then his grip went slack.

"Samuel! No! No! This can't be happening! No!" I cried as I pulled him close to me. "No! You can't die like this! You can't!"

He couldn't die. He just couldn't. Not after what he did. *He saved my life.*

I heard sirens heading toward the house. One of the neighbors must have heard the gunshots. I didn't move. I couldn't leave him. He'd saved me, and I couldn't just leave him there on the floor. I continued to press my shirt to his chest, praying. Praying that he wasn't dead, merely unconscious.

"Please, please don't die; don't leave me like this." Tears poured down my face as I bent over him.

People came into the house, but I didn't move. Not until someone pulled me away. I cried and screamed for them to let me stay with him, but as another officer bent down to press her fingers to Samuel's neck, she looked grim and shook her head.

"No!" I wailed. "No! You have to save him!" I cried.

Someone held me tight, wrapped in their arms. I didn't know who. I was too far out of my head to recognize anyone at that point. They stroked my hair and lifted me up, carrying me out of my house as I sobbed uncontrollably on their shoulder. "He can't be gone, not like Christopher! He can't!" I shuddered.

"I'll stay with her," the voice said as I was settled on some sort of bed.

There was something about the voice that I recognized, but I was too out of it to put a name to the voice.

"We'll need to sedate her," another voice said, but I wasn't paying too much attention.

I felt a prick in my arm, and then my world faded.

38

I woke up groggy in a hospital bed with an IV in my arm. I rolled my head on my pillow as my eyelids fluttered. A man sat in the chair next to the bed, but the room was slightly darkened. "Samuel?" I asked.

"No, I'm sorry, Miss Bell. He didn't make it."

"Agent Aubrey?" I blinked at him. My heart hurt that Samuel had died. He was a criminal, one who had stolen from me, but he did, in the end, save my life.

"*Oui.*"

"He saved my life," I murmured.

"Can you talk about what happened?" he asked gently, and his exotic voice soothed my nerves. "As soon as the call came in, I recognized your address, and we came along with the NYPD, but obviously, not in time to save anyone." He sounded sad about that.

I yawned, still feeling lethargic. My left arm was bandaged and very sore. My right held the IV, but I used it to push me up in the bed.

"Allow me," Agent Aubrey said, hopping up from his

chair. He gently lifted me and adjusted the pillow so I could sit comfortably. "Better?"

I nodded. My mind shifted to the events of the evening . . . was it even still evening? How long had I been out? "What time is it?"

"About three in the morning," he answered.

"Oh." I nodded again, as if it made a difference. Samuel was gone, just like Christopher. Stabbed right in front of me. At least his killer didn't live. I took a moment to process the fact that he was gone. Was I upset? Yes. Was I as upset about his leaving me as I was when Christopher died? It took me a moment, and I had to wonder if I was just numb, but no. His death wasn't hitting me as hard as Christopher's had. Maybe that had to do with the fact that I never quite gave Samuel my whole heart.

"I am sorry all of this happened to you," Agent Aubrey said quietly.

"Thank you."

"Do you feel able to talk about it?" he asked.

I took a breath and nodded. "Yes. I'm . . . I'm not sure where to start."

"How about after Agent Swenson delivered the case to you?" he suggested.

I thought back to that moment. "Okay. Samuel was with me when I opened the door. I showed him the egg and told him I wanted to put it on the mantel. We had just done that when Alice Adams called. She's my PI."

"*Oui*, I remember," he replied with a nod.

"She had information about Nora, so I stepped out of the room to take her call. Alice said she was being investigated for her husband's death. I went back to tell Samuel. I was nervous because he didn't know I'd hired a PI. He was taking a picture of the egg when I returned. I started telling him about the call, but then there was a crash. Nora had broken in. I ran upstairs and got my gun, and when I came back, she was attacking Samuel."

"Did she say why?"

I shook my head. "I know from the papers that she claimed he stole stuff from her, and I believe he did after hearing everything he's done. She wasn't saying anything about the thefts, though, only that he'd ruined her life. She was acting insane. I . . . I shot at her, but I missed. She knocked the gun out of my hand and sliced up my arm. By that time, she'd already stabbed Samuel a few times."

"How did she die, Charlene?" he asked gently.

"Samuel. I was struggling with her. She was pulling my hair, and he . . . he told me to move. That's when he shot her."

"Did he say anything before he died?"

Tears welled in my eyes as I nodded. "He . . . he said he couldn't let her hurt me. And that he was sorry. And . . ." I gasped as the tears poured down my cheeks. "And he said he loved me." I swiped at the tears, wishing them to go away.

"Perhaps he actually did," Agent Aubrey said, his voice soft. "Perhaps he had changed."

I shook my head and gave him a watery smile. "I'm not so sure about that. I saw the look in his eyes when I opened that case, Agent Aubrey." I sniffled and took the tissue he offered me. "I would almost call it lust."

He nodded. "I guess we'll never know."

"What happens now?"

"Samuel had associates that he worked with. We'll see if we can round them up."

"Do you think they will try to come after my jewels and the egg?" I asked, suddenly worried.

His brows rose. "*Je ne sais pas.*" He shrugged. "That is a possibility. Would you mind if we left the egg with you to see if that is the case?"

I didn't know how to feel about that. Was it possible that

Samuel's cohorts would make a move? And did I want to be a part of stopping them? I glanced at Agent Aubrey. The man had been nothing but kind to me. I wanted to help him. It was why I'd contacted him in the first place. I wanted to see justice done. Finally, I nodded slowly. "Okay," I agreed.

"*Bien*. I will drive you home once the hospital releases you." He smiled. "And do not worry about the . . ." He stopped for a moment and met my eyes. "I've sent a crew to clean up your kitchen and repair your door. I know it won't erase what happened, but you won't have to deal with cleaning."

I was grateful that he'd taken care of that. I wasn't sure that was the responsibility of Interpol, but I was glad all the same. "Thank you."

Five and a half hours later, after Agent Aubrey had brought us breakfast to share—he had declared the hospital food inedible and had insisted—the doctor finally came in, and after a brief look at me and my chart, he released me.

Agent Aubrey drove me home and waited until I'd gone inside before driving away. I walked through the house, feeling as though it was no longer my home. Not anymore. It had been violated, first by Samuel and his deceit, even if he did decide to change his mind, not that I was sure about that. Maybe if Nora hadn't killed him, he really would have stopped stealing and settled into a life with me, but I would never know for sure. In the end, I was grateful he'd saved my life, and I could at least think of him with fondness, even if he had stolen a necklace from me.

I paused at the edge of the kitchen, looking at the floor where Samuel had died. I didn't think I would ever be able to go in there without seeing him or Nora. Maybe I should have it remodeled. I didn't want to be reminded of his and Nora's deaths every time I went to make coffee. I turned away, heading into the living room. The Fabergé egg sat on the mantel exactly where I'd left it before Nora had broken in.

I sank down onto the couch and stared at it. Feeling restless, I decided I needed to get out of the house, but first, I needed a shower and a change of clothes. An hour later, as I was about to walk out the door, my phone rang. Frowning, I answered it.

"Hello?"

"Charlene, it's Dr. Neal."

I scowled. "What do you want?"

"I . . ." She sniffled, and her voice sounded a little off. "I wanted to say . . . I heard what happened and . . ." She stopped speaking, her words trailing off into nothing.

"Why are you calling me?" I couldn't understand why she was so upset. I was the one who lost someone, again, not her. I was the one with my life threatened.

"I . . . I know we ended your therapy on a bad note. I just wanted to offer my condolences and offer for you to come back . . ."

"Come back?" I asked in surprise. I probably did need to return to therapy, I just didn't know if I wanted to return to her. She'd been wrong, and I just couldn't trust her again. "I don't think so. Even if I do decide to return to therapy, it won't be with you, Dr. Neal."

"I . . . I understand," she replied, but her words turned to sobs as she hung up the phone.

Everything about that call had seemed bizarre to me. I didn't know quite what to make of it. However, returning to therapy really was a good idea. I didn't want to become a hermit locked away in my house again. I didn't want to go back to the way I was before Samuel. If there was one thing I learned from him, it was that life was too short to live it without joy. I was going to find my joy. With that thought in mind, I headed out to the park, locking the door behind me.

As I walked, I called Selina. I hadn't talked to her in a while, and I needed to share everything that had happened.

"Hey, where have you been?" Selina asked. "You haven't been answering any of my calls."

"I know, I'm sorry. It's been . . . things have . . . Samuel's dead."

"What!"

I sighed. "It's a long story. You sure you have time to listen?"

"Spill it."

So I did. I told her about Alice Adams, the PI, and what she'd found out. Then I told her I fired Dr. Neal and about the bizarre phone call. And then I told her about Agent Aubrey and how everything had played out with Nora. "So I was in the hospital overnight, basically."

"Damn. Your life is like a soap opera! I can't believe she went so crazy. She must have been mentally unstable to break in like that."

"I know." I nodded my head, agreeing.

"So what happens now?"

"With what?" I asked, frowning as I walked.

"With the investigation? Is it over? I mean, he's dead. It would have to be, right?"

"Oh. Well, no. Agent Aubrey said Samuel's crew might still try to steal the egg. He's working to find them as quickly as possible, though. My bet is that without any evidence, they won't be able to hold them."

"So you still aren't exactly safe?" Selina sounded worried.

"I'll be fine, I'm sure." My thoughts turned to Agent Aubrey. I hoped that he would be watching my house just in case one of those people did decide to break in.

"Even so, you be careful, okay?"

I smiled. "I will. So, what's up with you? How's Patrick?" I asked, turning the conversation to her.

"Amazing. We went to Tahoe over the weekend. I tried to call you beforehand, but you didn't answer."

"I know. I'm sorry. I didn't want you talking me out of hiring the PI," I replied, feeling ashamed.

"I get it. But just so you know, I wouldn't have. With all the suspicious things going on, I would have backed you up."

"Thank you." I smiled, taking a seat on one of the park benches by a pond. "So Tahoe was fun?"

"It was great. We had a really good time. I hope you can meet him sometime."

I laughed. "Wouldn't it be good for us to meet in person first?"

Selina laughed too. "You know, I forgot that we hadn't! I swear I feel like I've known you forever."

"Me too. I'm glad we met."

"Me too."

We chatted for a little while longer and then hung up. I was feeling much better by the time I headed home. I spent the rest of the afternoon cleaning the house and then headed out to the store to purchase groceries. As I stood in front of the ice cream, I automatically reached for Samuel's favorite. With the carton in my hand, I started crying. Silently, I put it back. I swiped my hand over my cheeks and moved on, not buying any ice cream at all.

After putting the groceries away, I couldn't bring myself to cook anything. I couldn't be in that kitchen without remembering everything that had happened. I picked up the phone and called for takeout.

A little while later, when the doorbell rang, I assumed it was the delivery driver with my dinner, so I didn't bother to check the peephole and just opened the door.

"Dr. Neal? What are you doing here?" I asked, startled.

"Hello, Charlene," she said. "May I come in?"

Without my saying anything, she pushed past me and into the house. "Hey! Why are you here? What do you want?"

That was when she pulled out a gun.

I took a step away from her. "What?"

"Shut the door, Charlene." She pointed the weapon at me, the look on her face determined.

"I don't understand. What . . . what are you doing? Why are you pointing a gun at me?"

She snarled. "It's your fault he's dead! If you had just been like those other bitches and flaunted your wealth, he wouldn't have had to stick around for so damn long that Nora caught on to him!" she ranted.

"Wait . . . what? I don't . . . how did you know Samuel?" I asked in shock.

She glared at me. "His name is Jonathon! He's my brother! And you took him from me, you fucking bitch!"

"Jonathon?" I blinked. I'd heard that name before. Then I recalled, Jonathon Samuel Clarkson, the name Alice had said he'd had before he changed it ten years ago. But Dr. Neal was his sister? Was that how he found out about me? My heart began to race. Had she betrayed me by telling him about me? "It was you!" I gasped.

She laughed cynically. "Finally figured that out, did you? Yes, I was the one who told him all about you. The poor emotionally damaged woman who'd been living her life like a recluse. So desperately in need of getting laid . . . and with all that money just sitting there. You didn't deserve it! And then the damn fool had to go and fucking fall in love with you! He tried to ghost you, did you know that? He was going to stop the scam after all the work I'd done! We even fought about it. Took me three days to convince him he still had to go through with it, the idiot. Then he pulled that shit with Danny, having him beat him up so he could play on your sympathy. I should have known he'd go off script again."

I couldn't believe what I was hearing. My jaw ticked. I'd poured my heart out to this woman. I'd told her everything, and she'd betrayed me. For money! "Are you even a licensed therapist?"

She grinned. "Yes, actually. You women make it so damn easy to scam you." She shook her head. "Enough. Where's the jewels Jonathon got you to buy?"

"I'm not telling you." I crossed my arms over my chest, defiant.

She cocked the gun. "I suggest you do. I'm going to take what's owed to me. What should have been my brother's. Both the jewels and the Fabergé egg." She smirked.

I sighed, but my heart sped up at her mention of the egg. "How do you even know about that?"

"Jonathon sent me a picture of it before—" She stopped talking, and her lips tightened in a thin line.

The picture he took . . . that was what he was doing! I was so naïve. I shook my head. Of course he'd been sending the picture to his cohorts. He was a thief. He might have fallen in love with me, but it wasn't going to stop him from acting on his greed. Had he lived, he would have stolen it and my jewels and ended up in prison for it. The bastard. Now his sister was going to do the same. Well, fine. I'd let her, and I'd call Agent Aubrey the moment she left with that damn egg. I wanted to see her behind bars, and I'd be pressing charges against her for more than the theft as well.

"Fine." I spun on my heel and marched upstairs to my bedroom. I went to the closet and opened the safe. "There."

Dr. Neal grabbed the jewels and the jewelry box. "Now the egg."

"It's downstairs, on the mantel. Get it yourself, then leave."

"What, so you can call the cops on me the minute I leave you alone? I don't think so." She waved the gun for me to go first out of the room.

I rolled my eyes and headed down the stairs to the living room. "There." I pointed at the egg.

"Where's the case?" she asked.

"Next to the couch."

"Put it in the case."

Sighing, I gently lifted the egg and returned it to the case.

"Now give me your phone."

I widened my eyes. "Why?"

"Give me the phone, or I'll shoot you."

I handed it over.

She opened the back door and threw it as if she were a star pitcher in the major leagues. It went over the fence and into the neighbor's yard.

"Any other phones? Landline?"

I nodded and pointed at the phone with the answering machine.

She went to the wall and ripped the cord out of it and from the phone, pocketing it. "That it?"

"Yes."

"Goodbye, Charlene. With all of this, I'll be out of the States before you can find me."

"Fuck off, you snake," I muttered, glaring at her.

She laughed as she headed backward toward the door, the gun still in her hand and pointed at me. "Be seeing you." She turned the knob and left my house.

As soon as she climbed into her car, I headed for the back door and ran outside. I had to get to my phone. Using one of the patio chairs, I climbed over the fence into my neighbor's yard. I found my phone in their rose garden. I headed for the gate as I dialed Agent Aubrey.

"Agent Aubrey, it's Charlene. I just wanted to let you know that your egg is on the move," I said as though it were no big deal, but my heart was racing.

"*Merde*. Who took it?" he asked.

"My therapist." I ignored how it pained me to say that. "Apparently, she was Samuel's sister and the reason he targeted me."

"Dr. Neal?" he questioned, sounding surprised. "I had not considered her as being part of his crew. It makes much more sense now how he came to know the women he targeted."

"She also took my jewelry."

"We will get it back for you, *chérie*."

"Thank you, Agent Aubrey." I hung up. I wished I could see the look on her face when Interpol caught her. Instead, I would have to wait until we went to court. And I was so looking forward to that.

39

Later that night, I went to my room, but as I started to get ready to go to sleep, I couldn't make myself climb into the bed. Too many memories. The entire house held too many memories of Samuel. There were a few rooms that reminded me of Christopher, but this room, my room, no longer did. I grabbed my pillow and went downstairs to the living room to sleep on the couch. In the morning, I would call a contractor to start the process of remodeling the house. All of it, not just the kitchen. Maybe I'd stay in a hotel while they worked. Or maybe I'd go traveling. Who knew? All I knew was I no longer wanted to live the way I had been living.

The next morning, after a very restless sleep on the couch, I woke up and made some coffee. I moved the coffee maker into the dining room to brew since I still couldn't stand to be in the kitchen. Once I'd had coffee, I got my laptop out and began looking for remodeling contractors. I found one that had a good reputation and called their office.

"Doran Contracting, Janet speaking. How may I help you?"

"Hi, I would like to schedule a consultation."

"Of course. What kind of remodel are you considering? One room or several?"

"Several, possibly the entire house," I answered.

"I see. We have an opening at three. Does that work for you?"

I had nothing planned for the day, so I replied, "That's perfect." I gave her my name and address.

"Wonderful. Lauren will see you at three."

With that done, I started thinking about what I wanted. I had the money to do whatever I wanted, so I might as well consider my needs and wants. I spent the next hour writing up a list of things. Only three rooms were going to stay the same. First, the den, which had been Christopher's, and everything in there remained the same since the day we'd gone to Cairo. Second was the dining room. It was fine as it was. And lastly, the laundry room, which functioned fine. Everything else I planned to have remodeled.

As I was closing my laptop, my phone rang. I smiled seeing Agent Aubrey's name come up.

"Hello?"

"Ah, Miss Bell, it's Blake Aubrey," he said. He sounded happy, as if he had good news.

"Good afternoon, Agent Aubrey. Do you have news for me?"

"I do indeed, *chérie*. We've caught Dr. Neal and two of Samuel's cohorts with her as they were attempting to catch a plane to Costa Rica."

"Two of his cohorts?" I asked. "Who?"

"*Oui*. I don't have any details to share as of yet, but as soon as I have them, I will share those as well."

"But you caught her?" I wanted to be sure.

"*Oui*," he replied.

Karma is a bitch, Dr. Neal. I smirked. With her being

arrested, it didn't mean all the drama revolving around this ended. If anything, it had only just begun because now there would be a trial.

"Were all my valuables recovered?" I asked, needing to make sure because I would have to involve the insurance company if they weren't.

"*Oui*, I believe so, but if you provide me with a list, I will double-check everything."

"Thank you. I'll text it to you."

"My pleasure, *chérie*. I'm glad we were able to capture them all."

"Me too. When will I be able to get everything back?"

I didn't particularly care about the jewels or the money. I just didn't want Dr. Neal to have it. Or my mother, for that matter. I was worried she would try to use this entire event as proof I was incapable of taking care of myself. However, I knew I wouldn't let her. I would prove that I was fully capable and that, in being fully capable, I'd stopped a criminal scam ring.

Agent Aubrey pulled me from my thoughts. "There's a procedure revolving around everything confiscated from Dr. Neal and the others. Right now, everything is perceived as evidence."

I had been afraid of that. "And let me guess, I'll get everything back after the trial." I chuckled.

"*Oui*, I am afraid so, *chérie*."

Despite what we saw on TV and in movies, trials were scheduled months in advance. So, in other words, I could get my possessions back in a couple of months or even in a year. It all depended on when the trial would be held.

"Thank you for letting me know," I replied.

"Would you like to see her?" he surprised me by asking.

"No," I replied without missing a beat. "I have nothing to

say to that woman." As far as I was concerned, she could rot in jail feeling miserable for herself.

"I understand," he replied.

"I do have a question, though. Will I have to testify?"

"I'm not sure. That is up to the district attorney, but I believe so."

I couldn't say if I was disappointed or relieved by his answer.

Part of me wished to take the stand so she could see I was the nail in her coffin, but the rest simply wanted to move on with my life as soon as possible and forget any of this had happened. That part never wanted to see her stupid face ever again.

In the months that came, I learned a great deal about Samuel and Dr. Neal, the con artists who had come into my life.

While she was in jail waiting for the trial to begin, Interpol continued to work on the case, and they'd managed to dig up a lot.

It turned out that one of Samuel's associates, Jimmy Grant, was the true owner of the apartment Samuel had taken me to and lied about it being his.

Jimmy, it seemed, had turned on Dr. Neal and spilled his guts to Agent Aubrey for a lighter sentence.

They'd also arrested a guy name Danny Neal. He was the one who had been following me. He was married to Dr. Neal and had been paid by Samuel to frighten me. He had also been the one to beat Samuel up and slash his tires, all so Samuel could play on my sympathy and use that to move in with me.

It was frightening how the events were all connected. However, they all denied being involved with setting the fire in my backyard. I guessed I would never know who did that. It could have been Nora, or it could have been that these criminals were lying. In the end, that particular event wasn't worth pursuing.

I also learned that Samuel had been a failed actor who'd discovered somewhere along the line that he could use his limited talents and great looks in slightly different endeavors. Naturally, he started small but, pretty quickly, his appetites grew bigger, and his expenses too, so from cash he switched to jewels.

Why bus tables and be a starving actor when he could put on a suit, play with fake accents, and seduce rich women so he could rob them? All it took was a little help from his sister to get him all the intel on his victims.

When the word got out that I would be testifying against Dr. Neal, a couple of other women came forward as well. That was when I realized they had targeted married and widowed women for a reason. They were more likely to keep quiet about the robberies since they didn't want to jeopardize their marriages, or with widows like me, they were already emotionally a mess and didn't want the world to know they'd fallen for a scam artist.

But as it turned out, Samuel had overplayed his hand and made a mistake with me by actually falling in love with me. Dr. Neal had been angry about that, ranting about him in her initial interview, blaming him for how everything had happened. She ranted that her being involved was his fault and she was only taking what was owed to her. She was clearly as delusional as she'd tried to make me believe I was. She'd even brought up how she'd attempted to get me to break things off with him by telling me I was codependent. She even went so far as to suggest that he'd still be alive if I had dumped him and that the police should arrest me for his death.

I was aware that Samuel and his crew had conned far more women than the few of us ready to testify, but even four of us would be able to ensure a guilty conviction for Dr. Neal and the others from the jury. I was sure of that.

By accident, I heard one of the women admit she was still in love with him and that she was extremely saddened that he was gone. Perhaps that was a case with some others as well who had hoped he would return to them despite the deceit. Like Nora. Although she definitely took that to the next level. I felt sorry for them. On some level, I felt sorry for all of us. We'd entered into therapy with Dr. Neal and then something pure-hearted with Samuel, and they had used that against us to get what they wanted. *That's all over now.*

Just like Nora made her choices, which got her killed, and they made theirs, which got Dr. Neal and the others locked up, it was now my turn to stand behind my choices, testify, and learn how to live with them.

I would do what was right no matter the cost.

I knew I was stronger than I'd been just months ago and that I would be able to continue with my life and put all of this behind me. Somehow.

When the trial started three months later, I didn't go to watch it, but I patiently waited for my day in court.

I didn't want to hear the other women's testimonies. I didn't want to be forced to compare how similar our stories were. I didn't want that knowledge in my head. Instead, when I was summoned, I went with my head held high, and I refused to acknowledge Dr. Neal in any way as I answered the prosecutor's questions.

All the same, in the corner of my eye, I saw her staring at me, sulking while I spoke. Apparently, she didn't like hearing all those things about her brother or herself. Not that I cared. She looked surprised to learn that I'd hired a private investigator and at the fact that I'd cooperated with Interpol. It brought me some joy that I'd managed to con the cons at the end. In the end, I won.

I was pretty confident I knew how all of this would play out, and I was right.

Dr. Neal, her husband, and Jimmy were each found guilty.

I stayed in court to listen to the sentencing. Dr. Neal received forty years with a chance at parole in ten. However, she still had to face a trial for fraud, which was a separate case, and I was looking forward to testifying in that case as well.

Her husband, Daniel Neal, was sentenced to twenty years with a chance at parole in five years for his part in the scam. Jimmy got off with the lightest sentence of ten years and a chance of parole in two.

Eventually, after all the circus ended and they were sent to prison, I got my jewelry and jewelry box back, minus the one necklace, the gaudy necklace that Samuel had stolen from me. He'd used that to pay Jimmy and Daniel for their work. But I wasn't too saddened about it. It was a piece that I hadn't really cared for to begin with, and my insurance covered the loss.

I thought long and hard about what to do with all those valuables. Truth be told, I was never that attached to them to begin with. Although they were all fine pieces of art or valuable collectibles, I'd only bought them because of Samuel.

At one point, I really wanted to get rid of it all since I didn't want anything reminding me of him. Samuel had been conning me during our entire relationship, if one could even call it that considering everything, and I didn't want to have things reminding me of him.

Eventually, I ended up deciding to keep it all. No matter how I'd ended up buying all those things, Samuel was right about one thing. They were a fine investment, and despite the fact that he'd been conning me, he had redeemed himself a bit by saving my life.

Nevertheless, based on my experience, I knew I had to make some changes. I had a state-of-the-art home security system installed once the remodel of the house was complete, which paid off in the first week since I caught my mother on camera while she was trying to break inside. It depressed me to call the cops on my mother. However, not so much that I cut her a break. The cops were there within minutes.

Her reign of terror was about to end for good. Although I'd made attempts in the past to cut ties with her, my stepdad, and my sister, I hadn't been strong enough. This time, though, I was going through with it. I no longer considered them my family.

They were all bad, broken people, and I didn't want to have anything to do with them for the rest of my life.

I ended up having the contractor build a gazebo in place of the burned-down shed, and she had her landscape designer deal with my garden and turn it into something beautiful, something I could use and enjoy using.

Unfortunately, none of that made me feel any better, not in the long run, anyway.

Two strikes in love meant I was out of the game, didn't they? And that was beyond depressing.

I just couldn't see a romance in my future. Too much had happened to make me distrustful, and I wasn't sure that was going to change, but I was working on it.

40

"I don't want to feel like this anymore," I stressed. "I don't want to be lonely."

Once the trial had ended, I'd decided it was time for me to return to therapy. Only this time, I called Alice Adams and had her vet the therapist I chose. Which was a smart move, as there were some really shady ones out there, apparently. In the end, I'd chosen another female therapist.

I didn't feel like barricading myself into the house again, despite how gorgeous it was now after the remodel. No, this time, I went to an office in downtown Manhattan. This whole experience had shown me that no matter what I did, there was no place safe for me to hide like I had after losing Christopher. I'd locked myself away as a means to keep myself safe, but that hadn't worked. Besides, I had enjoyed going out and doing things again, and I didn't want to give that up. The main reason I'd decided I needed to return to therapy was that I needed to learn to deal with all the hardships of life the proper way.

It wasn't easy.

It was especially brutal listening to Dr. Chesney tell me

about codependent relationships. And after a lot of soul-searching and a great deal more crying, I had to admit that she was right.

"You're too hard on yourself, Charlene," Dr. Chesney countered. "You need to give yourself time to properly heal."

"I know, but . . ."

"There are no shortcuts in taking care of your mental health."

I wanted to argue, but I couldn't. She was right.

"Besides, from what you've told me, you are doing better this time around," she pointed out.

I shrugged. "I know. But I think that is because I didn't fully trust Samuel."

"Of course, and it is a good thing your instincts told you not to. You have to learn to listen to those."

"Maybe. But in the end, he did save my life, so were my instincts right about him? Was he really a bad person? And if he was, what does that say about me?"

"It says that you are a kind person who sees the good in everyone and that even people who are bad are capable of doing good things occasionally. That doesn't make them good relationship partners, though, you understand?" Dr. Chesney smiled at me. "Look, seeing the good in people is not a bad trait to have, although it might seem like it at the moment."

"So what should I do?" I asked. "I want to stop entering those codependent kind of relationships."

"You work on yourself. You work on being independent, and most of all, you work on learning to love yourself."

Hearing her say that truly shook me. Did I love myself? I thought I did, but I also always sought validation from others. Growing up without a father, with a mother who had never loved me, had fucked me up more than I was capable of admitting at the moment.

So it was no wonder that I'd clung to the people who said

they loved me. They were the most precious things to me in the world. And with Dr. Chesney's help, I'd realized that even though Christopher had loved me, he, too, had taken advantage of my need to be loved without probably realizing it. He'd taken control of my life, but in a protective way. He'd wanted to be my protector, my defender. He'd needed to be a hero, which might have been the reason he'd died. Not because I had begged to go to that restaurant, but because he hadn't wanted me to see him as weak. Of course, in the end, it was the mugger's fault he had actually died, but Dr. Chesney made me realize not only my motivations, but also Christopher's, and it helped me to understand how our relationship had been codependent.

Dr. Chesney was right, though. I needed to learn to love myself. Only then would I be capable of truly living my life and enjoying it fully.

"And eventually, you will be ready to get back in the game and meet someone deserving of your love," she concluded.

I looked at her incredulously. "I don't know. Are you sure the universe hasn't spoken loud and clear about such a matter? I'm pretty sure I'm not cut out for dating." I shook my head.

"You shouldn't say things like that."

"Why not?" I challenged.

"Because it's not true. Look how well you handled this whole situation with Samuel."

I must have heard that wrong. "Yeah, I was great. I fell for a con artist who got murdered because of me."

Dr. Chesney frowned. "That isn't what I mean, and you are aware of that, I think. You like to deflect compliments. Don't think I haven't noticed." She gave me a wry look. "What I meant was look how you proved how strong you are. You hired a private investigator, you secretly met with Interpol to lay a trap, and sure, things didn't go as planned, but in the end, you stood up, you helped take down his crew, and then you testified in court. You showed your strength to the world," she pointed out.

I guess that's one way of looking at things.

"After all that, after dealing with a master manipulator, a true con artist, mere dating will be a piece of cake."

Did she just make a joke? And compliment me again? Either way, I could see her point. She'd definitely given me something to think about.

"We'll see," I eventually allowed. "However, at the moment, I can't even imagine dating someone new. I have too many trust issues," I pointed out.

Dr. Chesney nodded. "That's understandable, but things will change as we work on this together. You'll see." She remained adamant.

And she was right.

After our session, I decided to go for a walk in the park near her office. It was the same park I'd met Agent Aubrey in months ago. As I sat down on a park bench, I got a text from Selina.

Guess what!

I laughed. *What?* I sent back to her.

I've got a plane ticket to New York for next week!

I had to admit, that got me pretty excited, and instead of texting, I called her. "That is amazing! I am so excited to see you!" I said when she answered.

We'd been the best of friends for a long time. It was long overdue for us to finally meet each other in person.

"Me too! I'll be there on Tuesday. Do I need to get a hotel, or . . .?"

I laughed. "You're staying with me. I've got plenty of room, and it's all been fully remodeled, so it's the perfect time for me to have guests!"

"How is the new therapist?" she asked as we chatted.

"Pretty good. We're working on things." I started telling her about what we'd talked about because I didn't want to keep secrets from her anymore. I knew she had my back, just like I had hers.

"Hey, Dr. Chesney is right. You'll get back out there eventually. You know there will be plenty of guys who will break your heart in the future." She laughed.

I knew she meant that as a joke, but I couldn't really see it as such. To me, that was a reality and something I wanted to avoid.

"Yeah, I really hope not," I replied, but then I heard someone calling my name.

"Charlene!"

I turned to see Agent Blake Aubrey jogging toward me. "Hey, Selina, I need to go. I'll call you later."

"Okay, bye!"

As I watched him draw closer, I thought, *He really is cute*. I was surprised to see him. Honestly, after the trial, I believed I would never see him again, as he'd probably returned to France.

"Hello, Miss Bell."

"It's actually Mrs., but call me Charlene, Agent Aubrey," I corrected with a smile. "What are you doing out and about? Chasing another international criminal mastermind?" I only half-joked.

He chuckled. "*Non*, I am on my lunch break," he explained, grinning.

"Oh." I felt silly for not realizing that although he was this international secret agent, he, too, could do mundane things.

"You?" he asked in return.

I shrugged. "Just needed some fresh air after my therapy appointment."

"It's a nice day for it, *chérie*," he commented.

And then we simply looked at one another with goofy

smiles on our faces. Clearly, neither one of us knew what to say next.

"I've been thinking about you." He broke the silence first.

"Did something happen?" I asked in surprise. Not that I hadn't thought about him upon occasion as well, but somehow, I figured his reason wasn't the same as mine.

He understood my meaning. "They are all still in prison, as far as I know. But that's not why I have been thinking of you."

"Oh?" My heart began to beat a little faster. I had to wonder if maybe he'd thought about me the same way I'd thought about him . . . not that I would admit that to anyone. I didn't even want to admit that to myself! I didn't think I was ready to date anyone, but then . . . well, I hadn't considered that Agent Aubrey might be a real option either.

"I have been wondering how long I needed to wait before calling to ask you on a date," he said. His eyes sparkled, and his grin was infectious.

I could only gape at him. *He has been thinking of me in the same way. He wants to ask me on a date!*

He chuckled. "I know, *chérie*, this is perhaps unexpected, but I would really like the chance to get to know you."

"Why?" I heard myself say. I sounded breathless and wistful, almost enchanted.

He laughed, and the sound of it did something to my heart.

"*Je ne sais pas*. I cannot explain in words how taken I am with you. I will say you impressed me with how you handled yourself from the moment we met and throughout the trial."

"You mean when I discovered my boyfriend was an international criminal and decided to turn him in?" I joked.

"*Oui*." His eyes sparkled. "You have a true strength that is rare. I admire that."

His words made me feel good. It was nice to be seen as

strong and admirable, especially when I was so hard on myself. I worried that would somehow lead me to become dependent upon him to make me feel good, but then I remembered that Dr. Chesney and I would be working on that. I could take the compliment and not depend on him to bolster me up. I could do that for myself. So where did that leave me? Did I want to go out with this handsome and exotic man? I did. I really did want to go out with him. "Okay," I replied.

"Okay?" He looked slightly confused.

"Yes." I grinned back at him. "I'll go out with you when you ask me on a proper date."

He chuckled. "*Bien*. Would you care to join me for lunch?"

I nodded. "I could eat."

"Great, I know an exquisite spot around the corner from here."

We started walking toward it.

"*Juste pour que nous soyons clairs*, this will not be considered our first date. I want to take you out somewhere special for our date, *chérie*."

"Noted," I said with a smile. "Let's call this a preliminary interview, then."

He laughed once more. "*Oui*, I like that."

I knew he would.

"Oh, and so we're clear," I said, giggling as I used his words from a moment ago, but in English, "I'll be ordering a full background check on you before our official date." I looked at him and grinned.

"*Oui*, that is only fair, *chérie*, considering I've already done one on you," he replied with a straight face, but he couldn't keep it for long and broke out in another grin. "And please call me Blake."

"Blake." I tested the word. I liked it.

. . .

Well, I'll be damned, I thought a few months later. Dr. Chesney was right. Compared to everything I'd gone through, dating was a piece of cake. Especially dating Blake, because he was the sweetest, kindest, and most loving man on the planet, and I was head over heels in love with him. No matter what you thought of love, no matter how you felt about it or tried to avoid it, love could find you, and the only thing you could do in those moments is surrender to the feeling because when you do, something magical might occur.

Something like true love.

I looked over at Blake as we walked in the park where we first met. We'd taken things slowly, but I couldn't deny that this man was everything I could ever hope for in a partner. A true partner, not a codependent one.

And he was worth waiting for.

THANK YOU FOR READING

Did you enjoy reading *The Perfect Suitor*? Please consider leaving a review on Amazon. Your review will help other readers to discover the novel.

ABOUT THE AUTHOR

Cole Baxter loves writing psychological suspense thrillers. It's all about that last reveal that he loves shocking readers with.

He grew up in New York, where there crime was all around. He decided to turn that into something positive with his fiction.

His stories will have you reading through the night—they are very addictive!

ALSO BY COLE BAXTER

Inkubator Books Titles

The Perfect Suitor

Other Titles

Prime Suspect

What She Witnessed

Deadly Truth

Finding The Other Woman

Trust A Stranger

Follow You

Did He Do It

What Happened Last Night

Perfect Obsession

Going Insane

She's Missing

The Perfect Nanny

What She Forgot

Stolen Son

Before She's Gone

Made in the USA
Columbia, SC
08 April 2022

58715175R00248